Sky Road Walker

Your Very Own Adventure - #1

By
S.M. Carrière

First published 2016 by S.M. Carrière. Copyright © 2016 by S.M. Carrière

All rights reserved. Published in Canada by S.M. Carrière and distributed by Createspace.com.

Cover art by S.M. Carrière Cover Art Copyright © 2015 by S.M. Carrière.

Cover and Interior design by Éric Desmarais: http://www.EricDesmarais.ca

ISBN-13: 978-0-9938509-4-3

ISBN: 0-9938509-4-4

Foreword

This book was an experiment. I had wanted for a long time to try this kind of project, and I'm very pleased that it actually worked! Hah!

For that, I have my readers to thank. Their participation during the two years it took to finish this project of mine ensured that the book was written. Without them, you wouldn't be reading this fearfully dull foreword. There wouldn't be a book at all.

What is this project? Well, for a while now, I've been wanting to give back. I really had no spare funds or any discernible talent for helping others. What I did have was the ability to write books. I decided, therefore, that I would create a book with the express purpose of raising funds towards local charity.

For the charity, I chose a group local to where I live (or lived at the time. Who knows when you're reading this foreword and what has happened since then). *The Ottawa Caring and Sharing Exchange* is a charity devoted to ensuring underprivileged families have all they need for a joyous Christmas season and their children have the supplies and food they need to attend and excel in school. They do wonderful work.

Desiring to involve my readership, I decided to create a book democratically. How does one write a book democratically? Well, I don't know how one does. I only know how I did. Who names their kid 'one' anyway? I digress.

The set-up was incredibly simple. I started off with the beginning of the book (this should surprise no one) as a blog post. I then offered the readers three actions that the character could perform. Readers voted on which option they liked the most. The option with the most votes was the course of action that would begin the next section of story.

I did this once a week for over two years until, at long last, the story was complete.

In truth, I had expected the story would take no more than a year to finish. I was expecting nothing more than an amusing novella. As it turns out, even with the involvement of a fair few other people, I am incapable of writing anything but a novel-length piece.

Oh well. No one is perfect.

There are a good many people I have to thank in making this book a reality. Not least of all are my readers, who made it work by voting every week. Honestly, I have the best readers a writer could hope for. It was fun interacting with them, and I adored how some of them listed their reasoning for their votes. It made me smile so very much!

Also in need of an incredible thank you is the interior and cover designer, Éric of *JenEric Designs*. Not only did he do a marvellous job with the interior formatting and the cover design, but did it for free for charity. Such a generous act cannot go uncelebrated. Thank you, Éric. I'm so honoured and proud to call you a friend.

You are wonderful!

And that leaves but one more thank you to make. This is to you, the reader, for picking up this book. With this purchase, you are helping underprivileged families acquire what they need to live and thrive. It means the world to me that you're willing to do so.

Thank you all so very much.

I do hope that you enjoy this story created with love by many hands.

Thank you again.

For Bill, who was the last man standing,

and,

For Anne, whose constant encouragement never fails to make me blush.

Chapter One

I awoke feeling groggy on a broad plain, surrounded by tall, golden grasses. All I could see was the grass, stretching up to a clear blue sky, the pointed leaves waving in a slight breeze. I could hear the buzz of insects as they sang to one another in the hazy afternoon heat. I felt drained; the kind of tired that makes your limbs feel like lead, and the muscles ache when you try to move. My mouth was dry; chalky, as though I hadn't had a drink of water in over a year.

Gazing up at the sun, I tried to recall how I came to be here and realised with a sinking feeling that I had no memory of my life before this moment. Lost memories loomed like trees in the mist; obscured and obfuscated, never becoming clear. The mist in my mind grew thicker and the trees were lost forever. I tried to recall them, panic gripping my chest, labouring my breath as I fought to remember something. Anything.

I struggled to sit up. My head spun as I rose from the ground. Now instead of merely exhausted, I was also nauseated. The strong sun beat on my head. It was hot. Too hot. I needed to find shade. Struggling against the weight of my own limbs, I staggered to my feet and looked around. Waist-high grass stretched as far as the eye could see. It danced in my swimming vision. Raising my hand to my head in an effort to relieve the pounding, I touched something wet. I pulled my hand away and stared down at it.

Blood.

How did that happen? The whisper of a memory echoed in my head, then was lost to the mist with the rest of them. I was somewhere in the middle of a vast savannah, bleeding from my head, and I could not remember why or how.

Turning around I spied a lone tree. Its stunted limbs had few leaves. The shade it provided was, if I was being generous, minimal. Still, where a tree grows, there must be water. Funny how the mind works. I remembered that trees required water, but I could not remember my own name.

Lurching forward, I made my unsteady way to the tree and collapsed.

It was late afternoon when I woke again, if the position of the sun was any indicator. Long shadows made the area cooler, if only a little. Placing my hand against the smooth, white bark of the tree, I hauled myself upright. Other than the angle of the sun, not much had changed. It was still hot, the insects still buzzed, and I felt like I had just come out of the wrong side in a fight with a raging bull.

I noticed a small patch of green in the otherwise golden expanse of grass near the base of the tree. Green flowering tufts of long grass sprouted around a rock roughly the size of my own head – if my head had been flattened some. Curious and desperate, I lifted the rock slightly. It proved a horrific effort and my stomach clenched in protest.

Brown water glistened as dark insects scurried from underneath the disturbed rock. Shuddering against the sight of the crawling critters, and heartened by the mere scent of water, I tossed the rock aside and knelt. Brushing the thin layer of film away from the top of the water, I cupped the life-saving liquid in my hands. Desperate for water, I drank.

It tasted like dirt.

As I drank, the pounding in my head eased slightly and my stomach settled a little. My mouth still felt chalky, but at least I was salivating again. It seemed to me that preserving my water supply was important, so I replaced the rock to save the water from the brutal sun. I turned to climb the tree. Perhaps I would be fortunate, and catch sight of a village, or another tree; somewhere that might lead to something other than a slow death in this abhorrent heat.

I never got to climb that tree. Upon turning, I stopped dead in my tracks. There, out in the grass, stood a dark-skinned woman leaning on a spear.

She wore almost nothing. Why would she, in this heat? The only thing she wore that might be considered clothing was a belt made from some kind of spotted pelt. It sat lightly on her slender waist. I could not help but stare. By any account, she was an incredibly beautiful woman, her heart-shaped face featuring a high, proud brow matched only by equally high and proud cheekbones. Her full lips were pursed, as if threatening a smile. Most striking of all were her eyes. Large and almond-shaped, they tilted up slightly at the end and were a shocking shade of pale green.

For a time we both simply stood and observed one another, me awkwardly by the tree and her leaning on her spear. We stood that way under lengthening shadows before I decided that if she had meant to kill me, she would have long before now. I ventured a greeting.

The woman tilted her head slightly and returned my cautious 'hello' with silence. I tried again, louder this time. Her smooth ebony brow creased in a scowl. She straightened and beckoned me over with a slow hand motion.

Barely hesitating, I walked over to her.

"It is rude to shout," she said softly once I was in earshot.

I apologised profusely. She raised her brows at me as if impatient for me to stop talking. I clamped my mouth shut. She cocked her head again, again regarding me in silence. She asked me for my name.

I had no answer to give her. What was my name? I did not know. I could not remember. The trees in the mist had faded so completely that even the mist seemed to vanish, leaving behind nothing at all. I did the only thing I could. I shrugged. The woman scowled and I explained everything; I had just woken up with blood all over my head. I had lost all of my memories. I did not know who I was, or where I was, or why or how I came to be here at all. When I finished my admittedly very short tale, she looked me over with an appraising eye.

Seemingly satisfied that I was telling the truth she said, "My village is not far from here. Come. It is not safe in the grass after dark."

What else could I do? Stay in a strange place with no means to defend myself all alone at night? I nodded, smiling in gratitude, and she turned, loping gracefully through the grass.

I was nowhere near as graceful. I stomped along behind her sounding like a herd of angry bovines. I heard her laugh and I grimaced. Unable to do aught else, I continued to crash through the grass behind the graceful woman, keeping my eyes firmly on the ground, watchful for anything that might trip me.

My lungs burned and my legs felt like jelly by the time we cleared the grass. We found ourselves on red dirt. Looking up, I spied a village entirely surrounded by wooden walls. Four towers broke the monotony of the palisades around the village. Two guards stood atop each tower.

"Come," the woman said and she ran inside the village through the open gate. With no other option, I followed.

The sky was streaked in the brilliant plumage of the final phase of sunset on the horizon directly before me. Behind me, sapphire night had taken hold. Inside the village, young children chased each other around the circular houses, shrieking and laughing. A man walked confidently forward with a flaming torch, lighting the torches delineating the dusty streets.

The woman I followed was evidently a woman of import. People respectfully moved out of her path as she strode forward. She did not acknowledge them. I followed meekly behind. Despite the obvious naked, but proud people and my own clothed, dishevelled self, no one paid me any mind. Only the children stopped their play to peer at me curiously.

I followed the woman to the largest of the circular buildings. The door, little more than a hide covered opening in the hut, was flanked on either side by tall, muscle-bound spearmen. They were also naked, save for red twin belts that hung loosely on their hips. The woman disappeared inside. Thinking that I was supposed to follow her still, I moved to enter the hut, but the firm hand of one of the spearmen stopped me.

The guard glared, and I stepped back, unsure of what to do.

In the end, I stood in awkward silence, waving away the flies that sought purchase on my face and enjoying the cooling breeze that occasionally moved through the village. After what felt like an age, the woman returned and beckoned me to follow. I did.

It was dark inside the large round building. The light from a large central fire did nothing to help me see until my eyes adjusted to the smoke and shadows. Before me sat a large, muscular man on a woven wattle throne. He held an especially long spear and peered at me with curiosity.

From her position behind him, a grey-haired woman gasped. She shuddered and opened her mouth. Her entire body convulsed. Then she spoke these words through dry, wrinkled lips:

"The seeker's son has taken one.

The seeker's son has two.

The seeker's son takes another one.

The seeker's son seeks you."

To say that her actions and proclamation were disturbing does great disservice to the chills that crawled up my spine and along my arms, puckering my skin and making my hair stand on end. I stared as the woman convulsed again and sagged as if she had just finished a great labour. Her eyes opened and she raised her weary head to look at me. There was no hostility in her gaze, only a deep, reserved thoughtfulness. Swallowing back my discomfort, I fidgeted with the hem of my tunic. Where did I get this tunic? I had no idea. Silence enveloped the room.

"You," the man said in an impossibly deep voice. "Have no memory, yes?"

I nodded.

"You have no name?"

I shook my head. The man on the throne grunted and leant back, eyeing me suspiciously. I hazarded a glance at the woman who brought me here. She sat on a chair to the side, looking relaxed.

"Where you going?" the man on the throne asked.

I shrugged again.

"You must come from somewhere. Therefore, you must be going to somewhere."

"I don't know," I replied. "I don't remember anything. I don't even know how I came to the grassland."

"Humph." The man considered. "We house you a night. Maybe two. Then you go. Yes?"

"Go where?"

The man shrugged.

"Fine," I mumbled. As if I had a choice.

"Good. I give my guest a gift. Here. Choose."

The old woman reached behind her, grabbed something and scurried forward with a package wrapped in cloth. She laid it on the ground at my feet and, kneeling, arranged the objects on the cloth. She rose and stepped back. I looked down and paused. There were three objects, a small flint knife, large chips marring the blade, an ancient-looking wooden mask, and two gold coins.

"Just one," the man said.

I stared down at the objects spread on the blanket. I considered carefully. For all I knew, this was some kind of test. What were they testing? What could my choice mean? Was this some strange ceremony by which they decided to kill me or not? It was a long, unnerving moment I spent, staring down at these things. With no answers available to me, I tried my hand at logic. What could two gold coins get me in this place? Probably no more than a hot meal and a flea-ridden bed. The wooden mask looked intriguing, but what purpose could it possibly serve? Was it magic? If so, was the magic a blessing or a curse?

The knife. The knife seemed the best option. It might have been broken and small, but I could probably still kill something with it. I bent down and picked it up. The flint blade gleamed strangely in the firelight. I thought I saw a streak of blue flash down the blade. I stared at it, wondering if my mind had played a trick on me. I could understand a flash or orange or yellow; a reflection of the flickering firelight. But blue? The shining black blade now reflected only the fire. I convinced myself that the blue flicker had been nothing but my imagination, strained as it was in this strange place with these strange people and no memory to guide my thoughts or actions.

"Interesting," the man upon the throne said.

"Yes," the woman who brought me here noted, the sarcasm in her voice so thick I needed that knife to cut through it.

"Daughter," the man said to her. "Find a place for our guest tonight. Ensure the stranger is fed and rested."

The slender, elegant woman stood. She bowed slightly to her father and left the room, disappearing into an opening that stood directly behind the woven throne. All eyes fell on me. I just stood there, uncomprehending. The woman returned.

"Are you coming?" she asked haughtily.

Moved into action, I scurried across the room and followed the woman out. I entered a dark, tunnel that sloped steadily downwards. It was carved from the dense red earth upon which the village rested.

A large door stood at the far end, flanked on either side by flaming torches. The woman took them both, and handed one to me.

In strained silence, we walked through the door and down some earthen stairs.

Either these people were really odd and slept underground, or I was being taken to a dungeon. I wanted to ask the woman leading me where we were headed, but I had the distinct impression any talk would be extremely unwelcome.

After more walking in increasingly unpleasant silence, the woman stopped and opened a small door. "Here," she said. That was all she said.

I peered inside. I couldn't see anything in the dark. The woman rolled her eyes at me and walked into the room. The light from her torch revealed a small, but comfortably furnished room, complete with a small fireplace. It looked nothing like a prison.

Relieved, I walked forward, smiling. I mounted my torch and, thanking the woman, collapsed on the pile of woven mats that served as a bed.

I awoke the following morning to the tantalising smell of barley stew. A hearty breakfast had been laid out on a blanket on the floor of the room. The green-eyed woman stood silently at the door, leaning on her spear and watching me.

"Creepy," I noted, then winced. That was not supposed to be spoken out loud.

The woman smiled slightly. "You must eat well this morning. It is a long walk to the nearest city, and there is little food in the grass."

I suddenly realised that I was very hungry. It stood to reason. When was the last time I ate anything? Who knows? I certainly didn't. I slid from the bed and sat on the floor to eat. The woman joined me. I ate as much as was able and still half the food remained. It was a very large breakfast. The woman smiled, covered the pot with a lid and tied it down and wrapped it all up in the blanket.

"You will take with you," she said.

I thanked her profusely, and accepted the wrapped food. For all that was there, it packed very neatly into a small cube. I tied it to my belt.

"Water waits for you at the gate. Follow."

I did.

At the gate of the village sat a small table with three water skins.

"Take them," the woman said. After a brief hesitation I obeyed, slinging them around my torso.

"You must head that way," the woman said, pointing north. "Keep the sun on this side of you. You will find tall brown grass. Do not go in. It is the hungry grass and it will eat you. There is a path through the hungry grass. Do not stray. In the night, you will see grass dogs. They are hungry. They will eat you. But they are stupid and easily fooled, and they cannot climb. If you are clever, you will be able to escape them. It will take three weeks to walk to the city. Good luck."

With that, she left, returning to the centre of the village. I stared out over the red dirt for a while, my eyes falling to the horizon where the tall grass grew. "Do not go in the brown grass?" I muttered to myself. "Everything here is brown grass!"

Sighing, and feeling the gazes of the villagers at my back, I walked forward. For three days and nights I walked. In the night, I got very little sleep. Yips and barks, though far off, kept me awake, fretting about an encounter with a hungry grass dog. Whatever a grass dog was.

On the fourth morning, I came across a vast stretch of dark brown grass and paused. This brown was not the dry golden brown of the other grass. It was a dark, sickly mud colour and the leaves shone with a thick layer of wax. I wrinkled my nose as the stench of stagnant water and rot assaulted it.

I scanned the grass. If the woman had spoken true, there should have been a path. After a brief search, I spied it... and a grass dog at the same time.

As it turned out, grass dogs are, in fact, lizards. Roughly the size of a small pony, and with legs shaped much like that of a hound, I could be reasonably sure these giant lizards were faster than I. I froze as the lizard flicked its bright purple tongue into the air, tasting it.

The massive grey and gold head swung towards me. The lizard snarled, revealing two rows of sharp teeth, the back row longer than the front. Before I had time to wonder at an animal with two rows of razor sharp teeth, two more dogs appeared, flanking the first in a movement that was uncannily just like a pack of dogs; giant, cold-blooded, hungry dogs.

My eyes flickered to the path and my mind launched into a frantic spiral of thoughts. Could I make it? Would it do any good? I slowly pulled the flint knife from my belt.

Time seemed to slow, as if the world paused after a deep breath.

The lizards leapt forward.

So did I.

Sprinting for the path, I noted that one of the grass dogs had run into the hungry grass. It would have been clever, having one lizard cut me off further up the path. Only the beast was too stupid or too famished to realise that this was hungry grass.

Terrible sharp yelps filled the air.

The other grass dogs stopped abruptly, turning their attention towards the sound of their hunting partner being attacked by the grass. One of them hissed.

I didn't stop. I ran for all I was worth, even long after the grass dogs vanished from sight as I flew headlong down the path through the hungry grass. I kept running until my legs felt like mush and my lungs burned.

As the terror waned and I slowed, I noticed something the woman did not warn me about; a three-tined fork in the road.

Worried that the giant lizards in the grass were still hunting me, I paused only briefly before sprinting down the middle path. The ground below my feet was hard-packed and dry, but I could smell water rot emanating from the greasy brown grass all around me. Their tall blades loomed in towards me as I ran; the plant equivalent of a predatory leer. One or two blades sliced my face, drawing blood.

Adrenalin kept me running long after my legs abandoned all feeling. It took me some time to notice that I was no longer running on hard-packed earth, but on an archaic and rotting path of wooden slats. I slowed down, noticing a worrying wobble to the now wooden path.

It rose slowly from the ground, slanting upwards into the air in a shallow slope. There were no support structures that I could see. It was as if each wooden slat merely hovered in the air, held there by magic, or the wind, or perhaps invisible hands. There were no guard-rails either. Nothing connected one slat to another, and yet they rose up into the sky as if part of the same structure. I glanced around.

Everywhere else, save the path stretching back behind me was a sea of hungry grass. I didn't particularly fancy wading into that, and going back to face the grass dogs on my trail seemed equally as appealing. There was nowhere for me to go but forward. And up. Moving cautiously now, I walked forward. The slats creaked and groaned, swaying slightly in the air as I began the slow climb into the sky.

Up and up and up I went until a chance glance down revealed that I was miles in the air. It was then that I discovered that I detested heights. My legs seized in fear as I stared down at the patchwork of brown and golden grass in the expansive plains below. A sparkle caught my eye. Looking over to my right, I noticed a lake shimmering in the hazy sunlight. A small town sat on the far side of the lake.

Surely if such a town were occupied the woman would have told me? Perhaps it was a ghost town, a fishing village abandoned for some reason? Thinking about the village and imagining all kinds of scenarios regarding its fate eased the muscle-seizing fear that had gripped me. Keeping my mind on that tiny village and not on the great height at which I now stood on floating stairs helped me take a step, and another, and another.

The wood was dry here, but that only meant it suffered from dry rot. Despite my caution, a plank snapped beneath my feet and I stumbled backwards, almost falling off the path altogether. My arms wheeled in the air in a comical impersonation of a windmill as I struggled to regain my balance. Those moments hovering at the edge of life and death seemed to last for an eternity, though it was in all likelihood not more than a few seconds. Once I had my balance back, my legs again seized, refusing to move. I closed my eyes and thought of the little abandoned fishing village. It helped. Shaking, I stepped over the new gap in the path and walked forward at a crawling pace.

Before the day was out, the path began to slope downwards again. I looked left and saw the vague shape of a ruined tower looming through the heat haze. Wondering briefly at it, I continued my cautious march down.

Another slat broke. This time I was more prepared and I leapt forward to avoid having my foot plunge down into nothingness.

I tripped.

Unable to stop screaming, I tumbled down the path. As land and sky summersaulted in my vision, I heard a sing-song voice chant:

> *The seeker's son has taken one.*
> *The seeker's son has two.*
> *The seeker's son takes another one.*
> *The seeker's son seeks you.*

My uncontrolled fall threw me off the path. Screaming, I plummeted through the air.

Chapter Two

I hit the ground hard, knocking the wind from my lungs. My lungs spasmed, and I could not draw breath. I closed my eyes and concentrated, reigning in my rising panic. After a while, my battered lungs found their rhythm again. I blinked stupidly as I realised that I was not dead, just bruised.

Looking around me, I found that I had landed in a busy marketplace. People in brightly coloured silks with strange hats and various other head pieces stared at me in astonishment.

One young boy in rags squinted up at the sky in confusion.

"My friend," someone said as they placed their hand on my shoulder. "Are you all right?"

Unable to yet form words, I groaned and looked over. A slender man in crimson silk and a yellow turban knelt on the ground beside me.

"Are you all right, my friend?" he asked again.

I nodded and, with his help, struggled to my feet. Two more men rushed forward. One wore golden silks and had a feathered blue hat. The other wore black silk from head to toe, revealing nothing but his eyes. "You must come with me," the man in gold said. "I will take good care of you."

"No, no," the man in crimson argued. "Come home with me. My wife is a healer. She can help you."

The man in black said nothing. Instead, he took my wrist in a gloved hand and tugged my arm twice.

An argument broke out between the men in coloured silks. They yelled at one another until the man in crimson turned to me and said, "You must choose. This will not be settled any other way."

I looked at the three men. They looked at me. I looked at them.

"You must come," the man in crimson said. "You must let my wife look at you."

The man in black shook his head vigorously. He pulled twice at my sleeve, dark eyes imploring.

"You cannot go with either of them," the man in gold said. "You cannot trust a man who will not show his face, and any man who calls a stranger 'friend' is anything but. Come with me. I will help you."

Again the man in black shook his head and tugged at my arm.

"Let them go," the man in crimson demanded of the man in black.

The man in black ignored him, staring at me, his eyes pleading.

"I said," the man in crimson growled. He withdrew a curved blade from under his silken robe. "Let them go."

The man in black slowly released me and drew out his own, similarly curved, blade. The man in gold stumbled backwards as a crowd formed around me and the two armed men. Hands pulled me back out of the way, hauling me to my feet. I stood numbly on the edge of the circle of spectators that had formed a make-shift arena.

A wind blew, and the robes of the two men fluttered in response to it. The murmur of silk in the breeze was the only sound that could be heard in the silent, anticipating market place.

The men coiled. Then, like two desert snakes, they struck.

I watched in awe as the two men battled before me. Their movements were so graceful it was easy to forget that I was watching a fight and not a dance. It was easy to forget also that the curved blades of these men could easily separate heads from necks in a single, graceful slash.

The silken fabrics of the two combatants whispered and snapped, moving as if alive; organic forms undulating in a counter-dance to the men who wore them.

Blades flashed, casting ribbons of reflected sunlight over the crowd. They sang as they collided, humming in distinct keys. Wind whistled over the blades in a high-pitched shriek as they cut through the air.

The beauty of the fight quickly faded, however. A clever spinning step and the man in crimson brought his blade down to slash the man in black's thigh. Maroon blood sprayed across the pale paving stones of the market place.

Excited, the crowd cheered. My stomach clenched. There was a lot of blood.

Unable to do aught else, I watched on as the man in crimson danced around the man in black, who struggled to keep his feet. The swords flew faster now, and the man in black stumbled, leaving a trail of bloody footprints.

"You have interfered for the last time, mute!" the man in crimson snarled.

The man in black closed his eyes briefly and straightened. Pulling himself upright, his dark eyes bore into the man in crimson. It was not hatred that lit the dark fire in those eyes, but cold, unfeeling indifference.

Grinning, the man in crimson danced forward, certain now that the wound in his opponent's leg would render him immobile. He was only half right.

The man in black did not take a single step. Instead he writhed and twisted, duck and spun. His hands moved with a speed unmatchable and the man in crimson could not breach such a defence, though not for trying. The frustration began to wear on the man in crimson. His grin turned into a grimace. His grimace turned into a scowl.

Then, just like that, it ended.

The crowd gasped when the sword pushed through the belly of the man in crimson. How it had gotten there was anyone's guess. I was certain no one even saw the man in black move. Yet he gripped the hilt of the curved blade that now was slick with the blood of the crimson man.

A sharp whistle brought everyone out of their shock. As one, the crowd turned to spy the city guard running to them. They dispersed. In the confusion, my hand was grabbed. I looked up to find the earnest dark eyes of the man in black. Looking around, I noticed that the man in gold had disappeared with the rest of the crowd.

With nowhere else to go, and not particularly wanting to end up in gaol, I let the man in black lead me away at a sprint. I looked down at the man's leg. He was limping, but that didn't seem to slow his pace any. I had a difficult time keeping up with him.

The bright sun of the spacious marketplace vanished as we bolted headlong into the city. A warren of twisting alleys greeted me.

Everything here seemed grey. On and on we sprinted into this maze, turning around more corners than I could possibly keep track of until finally, we reached a small courtyard. In the centre stood a tall statue of a woman in armour. A black silk scarf adorned the statue, covering her face and leaving only her eyes.

Beside that statue, the man in black collapsed.

I rushed to his aid, only to find myself suddenly surrounded by men in black silks. They moved silently, gently taking me aside so they could treat my wounded companion. Wordlessly, I was guided through a door hidden behind the statue by five of those silent men. I chanced a glance back at my companion before stepping through. It seemed, though the black silk covering his face made it difficult to tell, he was smiling at me.

The secret door opened onto a long drop. I stared down into the blackness in shock and surprise, a barrier of woven wood was the only thing that had stopped me from walking off the edge and plummeting into that darkness. I found myself in a large basket of woven wood, along with the five men who had guided me here. There was a jolt that almost made me scream, and the basket began its descent, lowered carefully down by one of the men in the basket, who controlled the ropes. No one spoke, and any attempt I made to begin a conversation was quickly shut down with a scowl. It was an uncomfortable ride down.

When the basket alighted gently on the ground, I found myself in a large underground room, carved almost entirely out of the grey rock which must lay beneath much of the city. Before me stood a beautifully crafted stone table. Three women in armour, wearing black silk over their faces which revealed only their eyes stared down at a map on that table. One woman looked up, grey eyes crinkling into a smile.

The men delivered me to her and slipped away down the various tunnels that led from the room.

"Ah!" the grey eyed woman said. "The mysterious traveller! It has been many an age since anyone has traversed the Sky Road. Welcome."

"You talk," I noted in surprise, wincing at the stupidly obvious remark.

The woman's eyes crinkled again and I heard a soft chuckle.

"I am Saschana," she said in answer to my stupidity. "Leader of the

Black Blades."

"Black Blades?"

"We were once the empress' guard. But there have not been any empresses for a very long time. Now, it seems, we must work from the shadows to protect the bloodline we have served since the dawn of time."

Not sure I followed, I simply nodded. Was this something that I was supposed to know? Was it something I would know if I had not lost my memories out on the grassy plain?

"But that is a discussion for another time. You are tired and injured. Let my healers look at you, and we will discuss our history more over some much-needed food, yes?"

Not trusting myself to speak with any level of intelligence, I nodded dumbly.

"Good." The woman motioned and three men in black materialised from the shadows. Had they been there all this time? I had not noticed them at all. "You may choose which healer you wish to treat you." Saschana indicated the three new arrivals. I turned to them.

"What's the difference?" I asked.

Saschana smiled, but declined to comment.

"Am I being tested?"

Again, the woman smiled and said nothing.

I stared at the three men.

One man had a scar that marred his left eye. The eye was clouded, indicating he could no longer see from it.

"That is Jaquin," Saschana said, noticing my gaze. "He was wounded trying to rescue an infant girl from a mage."

I turned to the second man. He seemed perfectly fine. A closer look, however, revealed that he was missing a foot.

"That is Gammen," Saschana informed me. "He was attacked by a grass dog on his return journey from the village of Himhimbah. It took his foot."

I turned to the third man. His exposed hands were pink and crinkled.

"That is Machi. His hands were burnt in a hearth fire when he pulled a child of twelve out from the flames."

I turned back to the grey-eyed woman. "Who healed these men?"

"Ah. Well asked, Stranger. Machi healed Gammen. Gammen healed Jaquin. Jaquin healed Machi. Who will heal you?"

I folded my arms and pondered. Surely this was some kind of trial. I observed the men and tried to puzzle out this test.

Jaquin, wounded eye. Healed Machi. Machi, wounded hands. Healed Gammen. Gammen, missing foot. Healed Jaquin.

Getting dizzy thinking about a puzzle I knew I could not solve, I made a snap decision.

"Gammen."

Saschana nodded. She indicated with her hand, and the man named Gammen bowed. Producing a crutch from behind his back he started to hobble away.

"Well?" Saschana asked expectantly. When I stared at her, uncomprehending me, she scowled and said, "Follow."

I moved immediately, feeling not a little foolish, and followed Gammen down one of the long, dark tunnels that stretched away from the main room. It was not difficult to catch up with him. He moved slowly.

"Where are we going?" I asked as we passed by door after door in the earthen walls.

Gammen said nothing.

"What is this place?" I tried again.

This time, Gammen stopped his hobbling and turned to me. His dark eyes flashed dangerously, and I swallowed back the question I wanted to ask next.

In silence, I followed the healer until he opened a door and ushered me in. The opened door revealed a clean stone room with a bed and a fireplace and little else. Steered inside, I seated myself on the bed and watched as Gammen lit a fire, then pulled a chord that hung from the ceiling near the fireplace. Before he could turn back to me, three young men in grey – their faces uncovered – entered, carrying a large cauldron of water and a tray of implements between them. In silence, they walked into the room, set the water on the hook above the fire, lay the tray on the bed beside me and exited. Not a word was spoken either to each other or Gammen, and certainly not to me.

Gammen moved over to me and gently removed my shirt.

I stiffened as Gammen examined me. His hands were cool, and I was tense. I was not sure what to expect. To my surprise, Gammen proved a gentle healer. Though the instruments he used to test me looked more like torture devices than medical implements, I barely felt any pain; until he began his examination. Ebbing adrenalin revealed pain in my ribs, my right knee, and my right arm. Suspecting my ribs broken, I observed as Gammen felt around my knee. He took my ankle in a strong hand and pressed on my thigh with his other. In one quick motion, he twisted my leg. I heard a small popping sound and pain shot through my leg.

I yelped in surprise, then blinked. The ache in my knee had vanished. Gammen quickly pressed a small Hessian bag filled with a sweet-smelling poultice against my knee and wrapped that firmly on with strips of clean linen. He turned his attention to my arm, testing and moving and wiggling. Seemingly satisfied, he moved to my ribs. He was much gentler examining my ribs than he had been with my arm, noting every wince and sharp intake of breath as he worked. Nodding to himself, he wrapped one arm around my shoulders and pressed the butt of his palm against my ribs. He waited until I breathed out before simultaneously pushing on my ribs and twisting my shoulders around. Sharp pain knocked whatever breath remained in my lungs out. The room spun momentarily.

It took me some time to realise that Gammen had applied a bag of poultice and was wrapping it in place. To his credit, my chest no longer hurt as much as it once did, though the site of what must have been a break throbbed violently.

Finishing his work, Gammen stepped back, handed me my shirt, and left. I dressed slowly, worried that I would undo the resetting of my ribs.

"An interesting choice. Why Gammen?" Saschana asked from the door. I jumped. I had not heard her approach at all. Were all these people so light-footed? I turned, to face her. She still wore her black silk veil. All I could see were her eyes.

I shrugged. "Because."

Saschana raised her brows and her eyes crinkled at the corners. "Dinner is prepared. Here." She handed me a cane. "You will need this." I gratefully accepted the cane and, leaning heavily whenever I stepped on my injured knee, I shuffled after the woman named Saschana.

She led me through winding tunnels, through doors that opened into more tunnels, down stairs and upstairs. I was certain I had walked the same tunnel twice, though it was impossible to tell. They all looked the same.

Eventually, I stepped out into a large room with two fireplaces and an enormous table between them. Women, now without their headdress, sat at the table, sipping politely at wine in terracotta cups. They all stood to attention when Saschana arrived, forgetting their meal and their conversations.

Saschana stepped into the room and I followed. As soon as the door closed behind us, Saschana removed her headdress. I was suddenly faced with a woman in her late forties, long grey hair held back in a tight braid. She smiled at me.

"Please, a place has been made for you. Sit."

I hobbled over to the spare seat near the head of the table and awkwardly sat myself down. Immediately a young girl dressed in grey walked forward and filled the terracotta cup at my place setting with garnet-coloured wine.

"Thank you," I murmured. The girl smiled at me, and resumed her position at the wall.

Saschana took her place at the head of the table and everyone sat. Conversation slowly returned, though it was subdued now, almost distracted as many pairs of eyes stared curiously at me. I could bear it no longer.

"Who are you? What is this place? How did you come to be here? Why don't the men talk? What is going on?!" The questions gushed out with such speed I was not entirely sure that I even managed to make any sense. Saschana answered with a small smile.

"I told you. We are the empress' guard. Or we were. Now, it seems, we have been reduced to criminals, working in secret to find and keep safe the bloodline that will one day, we hope, reclaim its rightful position on the throne. This place is our hideout, dug in secret beneath the statue of our founder during the Time of Strife, when a powerful advisor sought to take the throne from the last empress."

"The Time of Strife?"

"Yes, a long, bloody civil war that began with the play for power, and ended with both the empress and the advisor dead. The then Steward, a good man, eventually brought the war to a close. But he was angry at the loss of his empress and at the war. He punished the empress' guard for their failure by disbanding them, and later outlawing them. Many of our sisters fled. Many more were captured and killed. It has taken many generations to raise our numbers to match those of the days of the empress. It is the Steward's family who has reigned for these intervening generations. The Steward's rage has lasted. His goodness has not. They are now small and corrupt, and the people are suffering. We dedicate ourselves to finding and restoring the empress' blood to the throne."

"I see," I said, not entirely sure I did. "So... why don't the men talk?"

"Their silence is penance. It was Farim's betrayal of his own fighters that lead to the murder of the empress."

"Farim?"

"He was a commander of the empress' guard. He murdered his co-commander, Assa, and handed the traitor the sword used to behead the empress. Until an empress rules again, the men are forbidden to speak."

"A bit extreme, don't you think?"

"It was a self-imposed penance."

"Oh."

"And you? It has been long since anyone has come to this city via the Sky Road."

"I don't know what to tell you. I was chased by grass dogs, and just ran. And then I fell."

"I envy you. Very few can see the road," Saschana said quietly. "Fewer still dare to walk it."

"Well, it's crumbling. I almost fell more than once. What do you mean few can see it?"

"That road is sometimes called the Wizard's Way. People have taken to believing that only those in possession of magic could possibly see it, let alone traverse it. That is not entirely true, but it does take someone special to climb into the heavens."

"Special how?"

Saschana shrugged. "I do not know. Tell me of yourself. Where do you come from, traveller? What was it like there?"

I sighed and related my story to Saschana, who listened eagerly. When I spoke of the gift from the chieftain of the village I had travelled from, Saschana's eyes sparkled.

"May I see it?"

"Uh..." Not wanting to upset my host, I withdrew the blade from my boot and handed it gingerly over. Saschana examined it carefully.

"Interesting," she said handing it back to me.

"How?" I asked. "It's just a broken old knife."

"Old is the key word."

The food arrived and for a moment conversation stopped as the hungry diners tucked in.

"So," Saschana asked after a while. "Where shall you go next?"

I shrugged. "I have no idea."

"May I ask a favour, in that case?"

I looked up in surprise. What on earth could a woman like that ask of an idiot like me?

"The Imperial Sceptre has been missing for nearly three hundred years. We think we know now where it is located. Will you retrieve it for us?"

"Uh...."

"We shall make it worth your while."

I did not take long to ponder the request. "Sure," I said. Why not? What else was I going to do? Wander around lost and purposeless for the rest of my life?

"Good." Saschana raised her hand and two young women dressed in armour walked in. "You need not go alone. This is Basadia and Grumissa. They are noviates. They must go on a quest and return successful if they hope to be accepted into the ranks of the Black Blades. Will you let one of them accompany you?"

I looked the girls over. Basadia had short red hair and a swirling tattoo on her pale cheek. Her sharp grey eyes looked boldly back at me. She possessed a slight build and carried with her a bow, two quivers of arrows and two short blades strapped to her back.

Grumissa was broader by far, with thick brown hair tied into a plait and wound around her head. She carried a long pole-axe and a thick broadsword on her back, covered by a massive round shield.

I scowled. The two women looked back at me expectantly. How on earth could I choose? I did not remember anything about myself, but I was fairly certain that I would know nothing of adventuring even if I had all of my memories. I tried to think logically again.

Grumissa was clearly a very strong woman, and strength was most certainly an asset. What if a boulder fell on me? Or if I had to carry an obscene amount of weight? Or if I ended up fighting some bizarre group of strongmen?

Then again, a great deal could be said for speed and ranged weapons. I turned my attention to Basadia. She looked like she could move quickly if it came to a close quarter fight. Speed is important. She also carried a bow...

"Basadia," I said.

Saschana nodded. She addressed the girls. "You are dismissed." Turning back to me, Saschana indicated the food on the table. "Please, eat. You will rest until you are well enough. I will show you where the sceptre can be found."

Taking Saschana's advice to heart, I ate well. I spent the better part of the next three weeks relaxing as my bones knit back together.

Chapter Three

While I waited for my body to heal, I took to wandering around the labyrinthine tunnels of the secret underground home of the Black Blades. The place was enormous, with construction and more tunnelling happening in certain sections. By my estimate, the secret hideout must cover at least half the city. That was, of course, entirely speculation. I had no real idea of how large the city was. Or wasn't.

Or anything.

At the end of three weeks, Saschana summoned me to the library - a massive seemingly natural cavern space filled with bookshelves several stories high. The grey-haired woman stood at a table covered in books and maps. She smiled when I walked in and beckoned me over. Basadia, I noticed, was by her side.

"There are a lot of books here," I noted. It was an understatement.

"Yes. We rescued as many from the Imperial Library as we could. Knowledge, you understand, is power. In his bid the kill the empress, the traitor had burnt nearly half the library. He assumed the rest of the books were scattered or destroyed by other means."

"Oh."

"The loss was unimaginable. Thousands of years of collected knowledge and wisdom, long forgotten songs and records of ancient traditions... It is said the Imperial Librarian wept solidly for three days before throwing herself from the tallest tower in the Citadel. That loss is one of the main reasons why it has taken us so long to find the location of the sceptre. Even so, the location we have is little more than an educated guess; formed mostly from rumours and gossip." Saschana sighed. "But we need that sceptre. Without it, we will never be able to crown the empress, and the Stewards shall rule in tyranny forever."

"Right."

Saschana turned her attention back to the map immediately before her. She pointed to a tower-shaped blob near a river delta. "You are here, in the city of Bashan. It was made powerful and prosperous because of its advantageous situation. Trade must come through here. But that is a story for a different day, I think. You came in from the grasslands, where live the tribal Tsui people." Saschana pointed. "The sceptre, we think, was sent away by the then Steward for safe-keeping after the empress was murdered. But the ship was attacked by pirates. Where the sceptre went, no one knows. However, rumours of it began popping up in the kingdom of Frut. It was lost and resurfaced several times over the years. The latest we've heard is that the sceptre has returned to her home kingdom, but is kept by outlaws in the caves up here."

I looked at the map. Saschana pointed to a large mountain range that sat on the border between three kingdoms; this one, the Kingdom of Gitrel, and the Kingdom of Norb.

"All right," I said guardedly.

Saschana smiled. "You are right to be cautious. This area is not populated, and therefore not policed. More worrisome still, trolls and worse live here, as if the outlaws aren't enough of a problem."

"Oh... great."

"Yes. I cannot promise you the quest will be easy. We can help you some on that score. I can part with the map, and get you a proper weapon. Unfortunately, we have but one smith, and so can offer you only one weapon."

Saschana signalled, and three young girls scurried in from a side door, each holding something wrapped in blankets. They laid their parcels on the table and scurried away again. Saschana threw back the blankets to reveal three weapons.

First there was a staff that was folded in three. Linked by short, heavy chains, the staff could be wielded in sections or each section could be screwed together to form a single pole.

The second weapon was a long, elegant sabre, its blade curved like those typical of the Black Blades' swords, though narrower.

The third looked like a crescent-shaped shield, but, I noticed that the curved outer edge of the shield had been ground down into a sharp blade.

I stared down at the weapons dumbly. What did I know about weapons? If I had known anything, it had been forgotten with the rest. I couldn't even remember my own name! I looked up at the women watching me with expectant expressions.

"Which would you choose?" I asked.

Saschana smiled. "Would that matter? I am not you. I cannot walk your path. You must decide for yourself."

Cursing under my breath, I stared back down at the weapons.

"Perhaps," Basadia said. "It would help to see how each is used?"

I nodded vigorously.

"Very well," Saschana replied. "Follow me."

I nodded again and helped the women wrap the weapons back up in their fabric bundles. Basadia lifted the weapons and tied the bundle to her back somehow. Despite watching carefully, I could not see how she managed it.

Following the women, I found myself in a massive underground arena. Large stone benches rose around the sandy oval in elaborate tiers. It must have taken a very long time to carve out.

Basadia walked down the stairs with the bundle of weapons. From the massive arched entrance to the arena on the ground floor, three young women in black with hidden faces ran onto the sandy oval. They accepted the bundle from Basadia, chose their weapons and stood at the ready.

One by one, they stepped forward. The young woman holding the three-sectional staff started first. I watched as she performed a series of fluid movements with the staff connected so it looked like little more than your average walking stick. With a skilled flick of her wrist, the staff separated, the two ends shooting out in a spiral. Only their chains kept them from hitting the ground. The woman whirled and danced, the two loose ends of the staff whipping out with devastating speed. She finished her display with a deep bow.

Impressed, I clapped.

The young girl with the sabre stepped forward. She bowed to me and began her display. The movements, at first, appeared basic. Slashes and stabs and a few blocks dominated her performance. The tempo increased and a series of extremely complex manoeuvres unfolded before my eyes. Strikes became blocks and blocks became strikes. I realised that every movement was simultaneously defensive and offensive. Though not nearly as long as the staff, the sabre would be an effective weapon at a comfortable range. The sabre, wielded in this fashion, was both sword and shield. The girl finished and bowed, stepping back.

Again impressed, I clapped.

Saschana nodded at the final girl and she stepped forward, carrying the crescent bladed shield. The curious object was strapped to her arm and she gripped the handle tightly in a strong hand. Eager after the first two displays, I watched as she began her performance. At first, she moved deliberately, making motions similar to that of the girl with the sabre, adjusted slightly for the shape of the bladed edge of the shield. Then she truly began. I noticed her torque her body downward, twisting her arm at the shoulder and plunging one of the pointed ends of the shield into the ground. I guessed that the move was intended to deflect and disarm. In other instances, the woman lunged forward, the shield raised. A savage backhand followed, a move intended to strike an opponent with the flat of the shield. Slashes arced this way and that and I realised that this weapon would be fantastic during a close-range fight. The girl stopped, bowed to me and stepped back.

I clapped again, so impressed with all of them I was no better off than when I first started. I looked helplessly at Saschana, hoping for guidance. She merely smiled at me. She motioned with her hand.

The three girls bowed in unison, spread out and faced one another. Saschana clapped and the three girls prepared to engage in battle. They fanned out and faced one another. Slowly, they took their ready positions. One girl cried out and all three clashed in fierce fighting.

I tried to keep up as the girls whirled and spun, danced and ducked - each one fighting two opponents at once. I watched in awe as their feet stepped, slid, skipped and switched. I observed their faces; each one had their expression set in extreme concentration. I watched their weapons as they flashed with light, colliding against one another with an awful din.

The fight was so rapid, I could barely absorb everything I was seeing. I did notice, however, that the weight of the crescent shield had begun to take its toll. The longer the fight lasted, the more the weight of the weapon mattered. Though at first, the wielder of the shield was able to block and deflect every strike that came her way and counter attack with surprising speed, she was now able to only block or deflect.

Sensing her distress, a temporary alliance formed between the wielder of the staff and the wielder of the sabre. From a safe distance, the girl wielding the staff struck the shield-wielder's knee as a flurry of close range strikes from the sabre-wielding girl rained down on the shield. On the ground, she was easily disarmed and mock-beheaded by the sabre-wielding girl.

Wasting no time whatsoever, the two remaining combatants continued the fight. The sabre flashed viscously, catching the orange light of the torches in the room and reflecting it back gold. She seemed to have the advantage as the staff-wielding girl stepped backwards, wheeling her staff to block the flurry of sabre strikes with both ends of her weapon.

The beleaguered girl ducked and spun around, twisting the staff in the specific way that loosened both ends. The forward-facing end shot out, striking the sabre-wielding girl in the chest. The sabre-wielding girl was mid-motion at the time and the strike was so forceful and unexpected that she stumbled.

Now the staff-wielding girl had the advantage. She spun and twisted, contorting her body in strange ways to achieve unexpected and difficult angles of attack. My awe only increased as I watched the girl wielding the staff as she cleverly manoeuvred her opponent around the arena. The sabre-wielding girl lashed out in a desperate bid to close the distance created by the staff. She over-extended her reach.

Beside me, Basadia breathed in sharply through her teeth. "Rookie mistake," she mumbled.

I did not take my eyes off the fight. I could not help but appreciate just how sophisticated a weapon the three-sectional staff could be as the girl wielding it managed to get the chain of one end wrapped around the sabre. A twist and a yank disarmed the sabre-wielding girl. Without waiting, the girl with the staff spun around again and managed to wrap the chain on the other end of the staff around the sabre-wielding girl's neck. The staff-wielder spun back around, but not all the way. She turned just enough to give the chain a slight tug with the understanding that if she went full force, she would snap the neck of her opponent.

The fight was over. I clapped enthusiastically as the girls retrieved their weapons and bowed to me.

"I really like that staff," I told Saschana. The woman smiled and nodded. "But," I added. "I doubt very much I will be able to use it half as well."

"I can teach you some," Saschana replied. "And Basadia can continue your instruction on the road. Come, we will eat, then we will work. You can head off tomorrow morning."

Thinking that sounded like a very good plan, I nodded and followed Saschana and Basadia out of the arena. After my meal, I returned to the arena with Saschana and trained until I could no longer move. I gratefully sank into the warm bath provided for me after dinner before sliding into bed and falling asleep immediately.

I was awoken the following morning by a young boy dressed in grey. He silently served me breakfast before leaving. It was a simple meal, savoury porridge with eggs. As I finished my meal another man walked into the room. He beckoned me to follow and, of course, I did. The tunnels I found myself walking down looked and felt unused. The further I walked the fewer and farther in-between the wall sconces holding lit torches were until there were none at all. Only the flickering orange light of my guide's torch showed the way. At length, I saw a dim light ahead.

We walked on to a grate. Large and heavy, it looked designed to provide a secure exit for the copious amounts of water caused by severe storms. I wondered briefly if the city laboured under such storms often. The man that served as my guide placed his torch in a sconce and pushed the grate open. I stepped out to find Basadia and Saschana in full armour, their faces covered over save for their eyes standing on the ledge that the grate opened upon. It sat high on a steep slope that descended to a small plain bordered by forest. Behind me loomed the tall thick walls of the city. It was first light, and the barest signs of the waking sun had started their slow spread on the distant horizon.

"Good morning," Saschana said. I could tell by the crinkling at the corners of her eyes that she smiled.

"Today we begin our journey," Basadia said. I noted she was carrying a large pack as well as her bow and several quivers bristling with arrows. "There are three ways to the rogues' hideout. There is a western road that passes beneath it. That is the fastest way, but there are bandits there and the rogues will be able to see us coming. We can come up from the south, but we will have to travel through woods. Wolves and worse live there. We could attempt to come down from the north, but we will have to travel over the mountains to get there. Which route do you propose?"

I stared out at the lightening world, not sure which direction to take. I glanced at Basadia, hoping that she might be able to prompt me, but she remained annoyingly impassive.

"Uh... the woods, I guess."

Basadia nodded once in affirmation. She turned to Saschana and the women clasped one another's forearms.

"Good luck, Basadia," Saschana said. "Stand proud, fight hard, and return alive."

"I will," Basadia replied. She stepped back from Saschana and fell in behind me. Saschana turned her attention to me and offered her hand. I took it.

"And you, Stranger," she said. "Be safe, and thank you for your aid."

Suddenly nervous, I smiled shakily. "Thank you," I mumbled. With little else to say and my heart pounding in my ears at the thought of the vast unknown before me, I started walking down the steep slope.

"Go left," Basadia whispered.

I swung around and started walking westward. When I looked back, Saschana had vanished, and so too had the underground entrance to the hideout. I paused briefly to stare up at the grey stone walls of the city, imposing despite their decay. With a sigh, I turned and trudged away.

After an hour or so, I engaged my companion in conversation.

"You know, you can lead if you want to," I said.

Basadia cocked her head at me, but did not answer.

"Because, you know where we're going and how to get there. And you can fight. I'm sure you've been trained to lead. I, on the other hand, am completely useless. I don't know how to fight. I don't know how to lead. I don't even know who I am!"

"So, how do you know?" Basadia replied.

"Pardon?"

"How do you know you cannot lead? Perhaps you were a general or something similar before you lost your memory? Perhaps you've been leading all your life and it is as natural to you as breathing."

"I'd have to be the worst general in the world to wake up without an army."

Basadia laughed. "Even the best generals can suffer misfortune."

"Well leading doesn't feel very natural to me."

Basadia stopped walking and looked at me, her expression serious. "You and I may not know who you are yet. But I do know that you came to us by the Wizard's Way - the Sky Road. That makes you special. I am pleased you came to us."

"Which reminds me, I never did ask who those two men were."

"Which two men?"

"At the market. There was a man dressed in gold silk and a man dressed in red silk, as well as the brother who brought me to you."

"Ah. Those men." There was a note of distaste in Basadia's voice. Evidently she thought very little of 'those men.' "The man dressed in gold was Aba Bun-Sibid. He is a very wealthy merchant who trades in human lives. He is a slaver. And a coward. I'm sure you noticed. The man dressed in red was Ulah Mansiri. He is the current Steward's man; married to the Steward's own physician, I believe. He would have taken you to the Steward. What would have happened to you, I cannot tell."

I fell silent, wondering what my fate might have been if anyone save the Black Blade had won the fight that day.

It took a week of constant walking before we reached the edge of the forest. In that time, Basadia spent every evening teaching me how to use the staff. Most of the time, I used it for a walking stick. Under Basadia's patient, though strict, tutelage, I had become fairly proficient. Not spectacular, mind, but good enough to defend myself for a time.

I sincerely hoped it was enough as I stood at the edge of the dense woods that marked the final stage of our journey. The trees were ancient, tangled things, their boughs heavy with stringy moss and mostly devoid of foliage, save for the very tops. Sunlight did not reach the forest floor.

I swallowed.

"We will camp here for the evening," Basadia said quietly, eyeing the setting sun. "And enter the forest on the morrow."

"Yes," I agreed. "That sounds like a great idea."

Chapter Four

The forest did not look any more appealing in the morning light. Basadia and I stared at the woods for a moment after the camp had been packed away and we were ready to march again.

I noticed the only path into the woods forked into three paths not ten feet past the line of trees. I took a deep breath in to calm my rising panic. It proved ineffective. Nonetheless, I walked boldly into the woods with Basadia half a step behind. I stopped at the splitting of the path.

The path on the left looked damp and boggy. I could hear the buzzing of a cloud of tiny blackflies, and I guessed they were the reason why the darkness down that path appeared to undulate. The path in the centre looked clear. The ground, though damp, was not boggy, and the trees arched nicely into a tunnel. Nevertheless, it felt just as sinister as the buzzing darkness to the left. The path on the right looked ill-used. Barely visible through the hanging moss, this path was darker than both of the others; more closed in. It looked terrifying, but it travelled directly north – at least as far as I could see.

I looked at Basadia. "Have you been in these woods before?"

Basadia shook her head. "No."

"Wonderful."

Turning back to the paths again, I stared at each in turn, trying to decide where to go.

The left path was barely an option. It headed south from the look of it, and we were looking to go north. Of the two remaining options, the centre path looked the best. There were no flies, it was relatively free of mud and muck and nowhere near as closed in as the other two paths. Perhaps I had already been through too much and had become cynical, but the clear path made my skin inexplicably crawl.

Any traveller simply trying to get from one place to another quickly and easily would have likely taken this path. It stood to reason, therefore, that it would be swarming with predators, be they bandits or wolves, looking for some easy prey. It would also likely be closely watched, and taking that road would have likely led to being detected by the rogues we were trying to surprise.

I turned and looked down the right path. The dark tunnel through the twisted trees, obscured by the hair-like fibres of the hanging moss, made me shudder. Still, it was going in the right direction and looked relatively unused. Stealth was our aim and this road was unlikely to be watched. The darkness, though terrifying, might serve as cover if things went awry.

Sighing, I started walking up the right path. Basadia grabbed my arm.

"Are you sure?" she asked in a whisper.

I turned to look at her. She stared out at the dark tunnel on the right with wide, frightened eyes. For a moment, I was struck dumb by the sudden realisation of just how young Basadia was. I patted her hand affectionately.

"No," I admitted. "But it's going in the right direction, and probably won't be watched. I mean, who in their right mind would choose such a path, right?"

Basadia slowly lowered her hand. "It's dark."

"We can use that as cover."

"So can they," she noted.

I paused. I had not thought of that.

"That's true," I noted sourly. "Still, it evens out the odds a little more."

Basadia nodded, still looking terrified. I smiled at her and started walking. After a brief pause, Basadia followed.

The darkness swallowed us.

The woods were unusually silent. I could hear only the occasional buzz of insect wings and, in the distance, the gravelly call of a raven or two. The melancholy howl of a lone wolf made me stop, heart pounding in my chest like an overzealous drummer. It took a moment for me to recover my courage.

I had difficulty seeing in the murk so my other senses heightened. Every soft, damp breath of the forest prickled on my skin, giving me goose flesh. Noises, though quiet, rang in my ears as if they were happening right beside me. I had trouble locating the origins of those sounds. They were directionless, distorted by the closeness of the trees and moss.

But the howl... The howl was close.

"There," Basadia whispered. She pointed.

I saw him too; a large grey wolf slinking through the trees. He paused and looked back at us. His eyes, picking up what little light there was, glowed pale yellow.

"He is only one, and we are two, and both of us larger. He will not attack."

I hoped against hope that Basadia was correct. Still, I clutched my staff tightly and shifted my weight, preparing for a fight. The wolf growled, turned and loped off into the trees.

Breathing a slow sigh of relief, I smiled at Basadia and resumed walking.

We walked and walked and walked. At times, I was not even sure if we were still following a path. It vanished beneath my feet only to reappear later. We made our way around trees and moss-covered boulders. Several times I found I had strayed from the path entirely, seeing it a few steps to our right.

"I am so lost," I grumbled to myself. I heard Basadia stifle a giggle behind me

We continued walking until it became impossible to see anything at all.

"Um..." I said.

"It cannot be night already," Basadia replied with a scowl.

"Dusk, maybe? And the trees just make it look like night down here."

"You are probably right. Here, let's climb. With wolves and goodness knows what else, I do not think it wise to sleep on the ground."

"Truer words were never spoken."

Basadia leapt up and hauled herself into the nearest tree. She paused to help me up as well. Together we climbed the tree until we breeched the forest canopy. I stopped in awe. The sky was a brilliant pink, laced with orange and green. Golden light spilled over the canopy, turning the dark leaves into bouquets of glowing flowers. In the distance, I could see the brown and white of the snowy mountain-tops. Where the light touched, the snow gleamed golden and bright, and the shadows were deep, misty purple.

"Beautiful," Basadia murmured. She sank down onto the thick branch on which we both stood.

I followed suit and together in comfortable silence, we watched the sunset.

Dawn saw us reluctantly descending into darkness again.

"I hate everything," I grumbled as we made our way down. During the climb, I missed my footing and slipped, sliding down the massive trunk to the ground, where I promptly fell over. I was certain that I had felt the tree shudder, as if it was trying to displace me deliberately.

"Are you all right?" Basadia asked as she leapt down from the tree and helped me to my feet.

"Fine," I said, offering a sheepish smile.

With nothing else to say, we walked on.

And walked.

And walked.

And walked.

For two more weeks, we walked.

Always the quiet forest tested my nerves. By the time I saw light at the end of the tunnel of trees, I was so tense I trembled and even the smallest flutter of sound made me jump.

When I spied the orange light of the warm afternoon sun through the trees, I was so relieved that tears welled. Relief flooded through me, relaxing my limbs. I could breathe again. Grinning, I turned to Basadia, who did not seem so relieved. She slunk forward in a crouch, ducking behind trees as she did so.

I attempted to do the same, and ended up tripping over a root. Twice.

At length, I caught up to Basadia, who crouched behind the massive exposed root of a tree.

"There, you see?" she asked, pointing.

I did not see. I could see a wide road cut deep into the side of the rising land, which looked warm and inviting, basked in sunlight as it was. I scowled and shook my head.

"There." Basadia pointed again. This time I did see, but only because the man she indicated moved. He shifted his weight from one foot to the other, his eyes fixed on the road.

"Their den is behind that cluster of rocks," Basadia said. "I can just make out the opening. How do you want to do this?"

"I have no clue," I replied. "I've never done this kind of thing before... I think. What should we do?"

"This is your quest. You must decide."

I groaned. Why? Why must I decide? "You realise that you're in as much trouble as I am if I choose poorly, right?"

Basadia simply smiled. I rolled my eyes.

I scowled at the man. He appeared oddly well armed and armoured, for a rogue.

"Are you sure he's a rogue?" I asked my companion.

"Who else would hide in a cave?" Basadia asked in return.

I shrugged. "Good point."

I shifted my weight. Storming the place was completely out of the question. There may have been only one guard, but who knew how many rogues were inside their hideout? We were only two.

Skulking was definitely our best option. Uneasy with the thought of fighting and killing, I considered the issues with sneaking into the hideout, stealing the sceptre and sneaking out again. If we were successful, there would be no need for death. Of course, with the way things were going for me, I'd likely trip over something, make a ruckus and get myself caught.

"Can you get a shot off from here?" I asked.

Basadia frowned and shook her head. "I can from there though." She pointed. I saw a tall, white boulder that had been cut to make room for the road, creating a short, artificial bluff to the west. It looked exposed to me, but the guard was looking east, down the road. He likely would not see us.

I nodded. Carefully, Basadia and I rose slightly and started creeping westward. A root caught my ankle at the same time a low branch caught my opposite shoulder. I spun, feeling like I was floating for a brief moment, before I crashed onto the ground.

The sound of snapping twigs beneath me made me cringe.

"Don't move!" Basadia hissed as she pressed herself against the trunk to the enormous tree we were hiding behind.

Over the sound of my frantic heartbeat, I heard two male voices.

"Anything?" one man asked.

"Not that I can see," another replied. "But I definitely *heard* something."

The first man grunted and, for a while, there was a deep silence. I started to move, but Basadia stopped me. I slumped back, still crumpled in the position I had fallen in. My shoulder started throbbing wildly, sending shooting pains through my chest and down my back. I blinked back tears.

"Perhaps I should stay here while you check it out?" the first man said.

"You check it out."

"I'm not going in there."

"Giant baby."

I heard the loud crunch of booted feet hitting the loose gravel of the road.

Beside me, Basadia whispered a long string of unpleasant words. She looked around, then up. She pointed upwards. I understood immediately. The tree we were using as cover was of the massive, gnarled kind that dominated the forest. That meant it was high, and its branches were sturdy. It was a place to hide. The only place to hide.

As quickly and quietly as I could, I followed Basadia up the tree. I managed to climb a fair number of branches before the man came into view, stopping at the base of the tree and looking around.

"Anything?" the first man called from the rocks by the road.

"Not yet," the man answered. He crouched down to observe the me-shaped disturbance in the litter of the forest floor. He scowled as he traced the outline with his finger.

Still crouching, he looked around, then up. He saw the arrow that struck him right between the eyes, but had no time to make an expression of surprise. He toppled backwards.

I looked across at Basadia, but she had already moved around the tree. I heard the soft snaps of a bowstring, followed shortly by two thuds in rapid succession - the second louder than the first.

"Good enough," Basadia said. "Let's go."

I nodded mutely and clambered down the tree. Once at the base, I stood and stared mutely at the dead man in front of me. His open eyes stared upwards at nothing.

"The first death is always the hardest," Basadia said, placing a comforting hand on my shoulder. "Come, we should move."

Not trusting my voice, I nodded and followed Basadia, mimicking her crouching walk as best I could. We both darted across the road and peered around the rocks to the entrance of the cave. No one was there.

Crouched and quiet, we entered.

Chapter Five

It took a moment for my eyes to adjust to the dark. When they did, I found myself in a tunnel, standing on a soft, dry dirt floor - perfect for muffling footfalls. Certain the entire world could hear my heartbeat, I moved slowly forward.

As I walked, I noticed a warm, orange light flickering around the edges of an opening to our left. A fire. Where there is fire, there are people. We approached with caution. At the entrance, I could see three men crouching around an open fire pit. Above the dancing flames, a creature that looked suspiciously like a large rat sizzled on a spit.

The men looked miserable. They also looked as well armed and armoured as the two men that had guarded the entrance, for all the good that did them. The armour was suspiciously well regulated.

Should it come to a fight, the odds were fairly good. Three on two. We would be making the first strike or, rather, Basadia would be making the first strike, evening out the odds completely. I motioned with my hand. Basadia moved forward slightly, nocked the arrow, drew and aimed. She breathed out slowly, steadying her arm, and loosed her arrow. It struck her target clean in the side of his head. He toppled over wordlessly.

"What the...?" one man yelped as he leapt backwards and onto his feet.

He said no more as an arrow hit his left eye, sinking into his brain.

Things appeared to be going well. Until the third man cried for help. Basadia could not hit him fast enough. His voice found air before he, too, toppled backwards.

I saw light from three openings into the small cavern. Voices and the sound of running feet followed the light. I looked around in a panic, before spying a small ledge above the central opening.

With no time to explain, I grabbed Basadia's hand and bolted forward. We both made it onto the ledge just as the rogues poured into the cavern. They stopped their charge when faced with an empty cavern with three dead bodies in it.

I held my breath as another rogue entered. He was tall and broad, and clearly in charge.

"They must have bolted when Mark cried for help," one man spat.

"No they didn't," I heard a voice to my right say. I turned my head. There, at the other side of the short ledge, stood a man, right in front of the opening I somehow did not see. The man grinned at me, before grabbing me by my hair and throwing me to the ground. I instinctively tucked my knees to my chest and curved my back as my shoulder struck the ground, managing to roll to my feet unharmed.

The rogues immediately set upon me. I fought back, instinct taking over. I saw two of Basadia's arrows hit two bandits, giving me some room to manoeuvre. She continued to support me until return fire forced her to the ground to enter into close combat.

I lost sight of my companion as I fought. I could not focus beyond my immediate danger, and had to trust that she could hold her own. I was not managing badly, myself.

"Stop!" a deep voice roared.

The rogues immediately ceased their attack, moving out of range of my staff but keeping their weapons drawn. Panting, I moved to a ready position, until I saw Basadia held fast by the tall man, a knife pressed against her throat.

"Throw down your weapon," the man growled.

I tensed, glaring at him.

"Put it down."

Knowing I did not really have an option, I straightened and tossed my staff to the ground. The man released Basadia and stormed away, down the right opening. Basadia and I were shoved forward and we stumbled after him.

"I'm sorry," Basadia whispered as she fell in beside me.

"It's not your fault," I replied.

The slight turn of the head of the man ahead of us indicated that the leader of the bandits heard me. He said nothing.

We marched through a tunnel until we entered another cavern, this one smaller, with prison cells built into it. Basadia and I were tossed unceremoniously into separate cells. The bandits left - except for their leader. He addressed Basadia first.

"Take off your headscarf, traitor."

Traitor? I looked across at Basadia. She glared balefully at him and folded her arms across her chest. The man reached over to a pillar and pulled the lever there. A clinking thunk above Basadia's head drew both our gazes. I gasped.

A cruel spiked trap hovered above Basadia's head. She looked in alarm at me, and I nodded slowly. Shaking, Basadia removed her headscarf. The man frowned.

"A little young to be gallivanting out in the wilderness, aren't you?" he asked.

Basadia's eyes narrowed, her stance becoming aggressive. The man grunted and turned to me.

"And who are you?" he asked.

"Funny you should ask," I replied.

The man raised one eyebrow, looking unimpressed.

"I don't know," I said.

"You don't know," he repeated.

"I don't know."

The man moved forward, his dark eyes glinting in the dim light. "How can you not know?"

"I woke up one day with no memory," I said, sick to death of having to repeat the same story over and over.

The man grunted, looking me over. He turned back to Basadia and looked between us.

"I expect Saschana has sent you here looking for the sceptre," he said. "The treacherous bitch will be disappointed."

"Mind how you speak of her!" Basadia snapped.

The man looked her over before turning to me. "And what wild story have they concocted to acquire your help? I'm sure it contained enough half-truths to be convincing."

"Half-truths? Like what?"

"Tell me what they told you, and I will tell you the truth."

I glanced at Basadia, then started telling the tale of the last empress and how she was betrayed. At the end of my story the man shook his head.

"It is true," he said. "The empress was betrayed, but it was by the female Black Blade commander."

"That's a lie!" Basadia said hotly.

"She was going to disband them. They had grown powerful and, as it is with things power touches, corrupt. When the fearless leader of the Black Blades discovered this, she murdered her empress and blamed her co-commander. That is what started the war that brought on the Time of Strife."

The man looked at me with curiosity. "How did you get dragged into all of this?"

I stood silently a moment, trying to process the information. "Uh..." I said, unable to think.

"Are you the one that came by the Sky Road? The city was buzzing about it for days."

"Yes," I said slowly.

"It's a pity you met the traitors first. The sceptre you seek for them, incidentally, is not here. Not all of it, at least."

"Sorry?"

"It was destroyed during the Time of Strife; split into three. We guard the head, but even that is incomplete. The crystal it once held is gone. We know not where. We've been keeping it here in safety while we search."

The man cocked his head as he regarded me.

"I have a proposition for you," he said.

"Oh?"

"You've proven yourself a competent fighter, and an able tactician."

I looked around at the prison cell I was currently locked in. "Clearly," I noted dryly.

The man rumbled a laugh. "You are not to blame. The odds of your success were never spectacular. You handled yourself well, however. In any case, the proposition is thus: Help us find the missing pieces of the sceptre. Help us restore this symbol of the empire."

"Why? What's so important about this sceptre?"

"There are rumours that an heir to the throne exists. These rumours crop up every so often. The only way we will know is if we have the sceptre. The crystal is said to glow when held by a royal hand, but only if it is fitted in the sceptre. We need it to verify this new pretender and restore the order and glory of the empire."

"You are a mindless fool," Basadia spat. "And I feel sorry for you."

"I am not the one who has been indoctrinated in a lie," the man answered her evenly, not bothering to look at the girl. Still looking at me, he said, "The choice is yours, Stranger."

"I need time to think," I replied.

"Of course. Don't take too long," he said. He turned and marched from the room, taking with him the only source of light - a torch that sputtered a feeble flame near the entrance.

"You cannot seriously be considering this," Basadia hissed. "He is lying!"

"Shh," I said. "I need to think."

If the man was correct, it would be best to relent and help him find the rest of the sceptre. If he was lying to try and get me on side, the best thing I could do was try and escape with Basadia and steal the sceptre piece while I was at it. But... Which was it? Was he telling the truth, or was he lying through his unusually straight and clean teeth?

For a long time I sat and thought. Basadia respectfully remained silent, though I could hear her shift her weight as she shuffled around her tiny cell.

The steady growth of a flickering orange light approaching through the tunnel drew my attention. I could smell food and my stomach rumbled in eager anticipation.

"What was that?" Basadia asked in alarm.

"Just my stomach," I replied. "Relax."

The man who was clearly leader of the 'bandits' re-entered the prison, bringing with him a younger bandit and a large platter of food. The young man carried two torches. He placed one in the sconce at the entrance and moved forward. He stood, holding the other. He did not so much as look at Basadia or myself, or utter a sound.

"I expect you're hungry," the leader of the bandits said. He placed the platter on a barrel near my cage and lifted the wooden, bowl-like covering that sat upon it. My mouth watered as the small cavern filled with the scent of roasted duck.

Basadia groaned quietly.

I narrowed my eyes at the man as he took up a carving knife and began to slice off pieces of duck. He looked up and smiled slightly as both Basadia and I stared at the food with wide, hungry eyes.

"My name is Martel, incidentally. It occurred to me that I had not yet properly introduced myself."

I did not reply.

"If you promise not to do anything foolish, I'll let you out to eat with me like a civilized person." Martel looked directly at me. I turned to Basadia.

"Not her," Martel said firmly. "I don't trust a Black Blade as far as I could throw one."

I eyed Basadia's petite frame, then turned back and look at Martel's very broad frame. I had a sneaking suspicion that Martel could throw Basadia a fair distance. I decided not to mention it.

"All right," I said slowly.

Basadia hissed in anger and I turned back to her. *Stay calm*, I mouthed to her. She raised her brows and crossed her arms.

The jingling of keys turned my attention to the cell door as the young, torch bearer expertly flipped through the keys with one hand. In a few moments, my cell door opened and I wandered out.

"We'll have to sit on the ground," Martel said apologetically. "So... not as civilized as I would like."

I shrugged and sat. Martel walked over with the platter of carved duck and placed it in front of me before sitting so that he faced me.

"Don't eat it," Basadia cautioned. "It's poisoned. Or drugged."

Martel smirked. He picked up a piece of steaming duck and put it in his mouth.

"Ah," he said, his mouth still full. He pulled a face and opened his mouth, fanning it rapidly. "Don't eat it. It's hot." He did his best to chew the steaming meat and swallowed it down. "Burnt my tongue."

I stared at him. He shrugged. "You're not the only one who hasn't eaten all day."

Shaking my head, I picked up a large piece of duck breast. I took it over to Basadia's cell and handed her the meat through the bars.

"Thank you!" Basadia said, taking the meat as gently as her hunger would allow. She blew on it to try and cool it down.

Martel scowled at me, but did not interfere.

"Civilized people don't let other people starve," I said haughtily.

Martel smiled a little and shrugged. I returned to my position on the floor, picking at the duck and eating slowly in an effort to allow the meat to cool.

"I have questions," I said.

"I expected as much."

"There were three men trying to help me at the market. One was dressed in gold, one in crimson and one in black. Who were they?"

"You already know that the man in black was a Black Blade. Poor bastard. I do not know the man in gold, and couldn't tell you who he was. Perhaps simply a well-meaning merchant. But the man in crimson, it is a good thing he did not win the fight. He is the Steward's man. I would rather see you taken to the Black Blades than fall in with the Steward. "

"How kind," I replied dryly.

Martel laughed softly. "That was a test, wasn't it? You were trying to see if I would lie to you."

I narrowed my eyes at him and chewed on a leg bone. "Who are you, really?" I asked.

Martel raised his brows at me.

"Oh come on," I said. "You can't expect me to believe that you're just a group of people hunting for the missing pieces of the sceptre. Who are you and what is your purpose? Who are you working for?"

Sighing, Martel put down his food and leant back.

"My name is Martel. That you know. Clearly our uniforms gave us away as something more than just a rabble of men hunting for a treasure. In this, of course, you are right. We are all that remains of the rangers, agents of the empire whose sole purpose was to vanish into the wilds to live and from there defend the empire's boarders. There used to be twenty sizeable groups stationed all over the empire. Now there is only us.

"As to our purpose, I've already told you that. We intend to find all the pieces of the sceptre, so that we may restore the royal bloodline to the throne. We work for no one but ourselves. Unlike the Black Blades, the Steward does not even know we exist, so we are free to move around without challenge. Thus far, at least."

"If you are so free, why do you care who sits on the throne?"

Running his fingers through his dark hair, Martel took a moment before answering. "Ordinarily, we would not. Except that it was the current Steward who disbanded us. We are the first line of defence against an attack. With us gone, the first people to feel the enemy's blade will be the peasants. We were supposed to be the wall that defended them at least long enough for them to flee to safety. Most of us have family in that class. Most of us take our vows to protect them very seriously. The Steward, however, views his obligations to those he taxes with disdain. I cannot abide that. An empress must be restored."

"You can't be sure that an empress will do any better," I pointed out.

"No," Martel replied. "But the Steward is enough of a tyrant to force my hand. We must at least try."

"So what you're telling me is that the rangers and the Black Blades have the same goal."

"No!" Martel said sharply. "Saschana is a manipulative woman."

"Oh?"

"She wants herself on the throne, and no one else."

"You liar!" Basadia cried from her cell. "Saschana's intentions are honourable!"

"That woman wouldn't know honour if it beat her about the head with a broomstick!"

Basadia's eyes grew wide. "I know who you are!" she said. "Saschana told me about you. You're her former lover - the Steward's brother!"

"Half-brother," Martel replied. "And probably the reason he tried to disband the rangers. And yes, Saschana and I had once been... intimate. That is how I know her for what she is."

"You are nothing more than a spurned lover, seeking petty revenge," Basadia spat.

Martel scoffed and shook his head. "If it was revenge I wanted, I would find far more imaginative things to do than go sceptre hunting."

"So you think that Saschana wants the sceptre for herself because she wants to be the next empress," I said slowly. I could scarce believe it. I had met her, and though she seemed hardened by life, I would not have thought her malicious.

"Yes."

"And you don't want to be the next ruler?"

"Not for all the gold in the world."

"Why not?"

"If I trusted you more, I might take you outside so you can watch the sun set over the ranges. The snow glows golden on one side, the shadows turn it purple on the other. If we had the time, I might take you up the slopes to spy on the Rocs going fishing for shark. Or perhaps we might head into the woods to the grove of singing trees." Martel shook his head. "Palaces and politics have no interest for me. It is the wilds that have my heart."

"What heart?" Basadia growled.

Ignoring her, Martel stood. I followed suit.

"Please," Martel said, indicating the open cell. I sighed and walked in. The door closed behind me, locking with a depressing click.

"I have answered your questions, Stranger. And I offer you the same proposition as last time we spoke. Join me. Or not."

Martel turned and left, kicking the tray of left-over duck to Basadia's cell before doing so. He took the torch from the sconce and, with the young key-bearer in tow, left me once again in the dark to think.

I could hear my own brain buzz in the oppressive darkness of my prison cell as I tried to puzzle my way through my options. In truth, I really only had one. If I did not join the rangers, I would be sitting in this cell for the rest of my life - a life that could be greatly shortened by my current captors.

"Basadia?"

"Yes?"

"Do you trust me?"

A long silence followed.

"I assume you are asking because you are about to do something of which I disapprove?"

Smiling, I answered, "Yes."

I heard Basadia sigh. "You're joining the rangers, aren't you?"

"Yes," I answered. "But I have conditions."

"Oh?"

"You will not be harmed and, when this is all over, you'll be returned safely to the Black Blades."

"You have forgotten," Basadia said sadly. "I cannot return to the Black Blades having failed my test. I will never be inducted because I did not return with the sceptre."

"Oh." I had forgotten. Falling silent, I thought a little more.

There was still no other way around my current predicament, as far as I could tell. Scowling out into the darkness, I said, "I'm sorry."

Basadia did not reply. I heard the clink of her armour and the harsh whisper of movement against the floor as she shifted in her cell. I imagined she had turned her back on me. Feeling miserable, I lay on the floor and curled into myself.

Chapter Six

The gradual invasion of light through my closed eyes gently woke me from my slumber. I did not recall falling asleep and so was surprised when I awoke. Struggling against the fog of a mind not quite aware, I hauled myself to my feet.

Martel stood in the prison cavern, smiling at me and holding a tray with two bowls of steaming oatmeal. "Breakfast," he announced. A young ranger scurried forward with the keys and unlocked my cell. I stepped out and again sat on the floor to share my food with Martel.

Basadia lay curled into a corner of her cell, her back to me. Martel noticed.

"Did you have an argument?" he asked.

I shook my head. Breakfast was the last thing I wanted, despite my nagging stomach. I took my bowl and placed it by Basadia's cell. "Eat," I told her. "You'll need your strength."

Basadia did not respond. I sighed and turned to Martel.

"If you want my help, I'll give it. But there are a few demands that must be met first."

"Speak them, and I will see what can be done."

"First, and most importantly, no harm will come to my companion."

Martel hesitated. "All right. In this we can compromise."

"Wait. You were going to harm her?"

"She murdered my men, Stranger. That cannot go unpunished."

"There is punishment enough in failure," I replied. "My second demand is this: when the quest is over, and you have all the pieces of the staff, you will let her go."

Martel straightened at this. "No."

"Those are the terms," I said, crossing my arms and scowling at the broad-shouldered man.

"She is a criminal."

"You and your men were disbanded. Technically, so are you, outlaw."

Martel blinked, and slowly smiled. "Yes," he admitted. "I suppose I am." He sighed and walked over to Basadia's cell. She had turned her head when the conversation began and was now staring at Martel, her face betraying the depth of her distrust.

"Where will you go?" Martel asked her. "Saschana will not allow you to return to the Black Blades without the sceptre."

"What do you care?" Basadia hissed angrily.

"I don't," Martel responded with a shrug. He looked Basadia over. "Except that you fight exceedingly well. We could use you."

"Find someone else to *use*," Basadia replied before once again turning her back.

Martel shook his head. "Loyalty," he murmured. "It is a frustrating trait, but admirable. Saschana is lucky to have yours. I just wish you knew her for what she really is."

Turning to me, he said, "Fine. I will let your companion free, unharmed, when the sceptre is restored. Though where she will go is a problem."

"Anywhere is better than a prison cell," I replied.

"Perhaps. Perhaps not. At least in prison you know where your next meal is coming from. Still, I agree to your terms."

"Then I will help you."

Martel looked me over carefully, as if anticipating... something.

"What?" I demanded.

"You have asked nothing for yourself," he noted.

I shrugged. "I assume you will feed me and house me if you intend for me to aid you. I don't really require anything else right now."

"You are an uncommon kind, Stranger," Martel murmured thoughtfully. "Now come. We need to get your armour fitted."

I followed Martel from the prison, stopping once at the entrance to look back. Basadia remained on the ground of her cell, her back to me and her food untouched. I shook my head sadly and left her behind as the darkness swallowed the prison.

Having my armour fitted took most of the day. By the end of it,

however, I had beautiful new steel and leather armour, and a full set of
weapons, none of which I knew how to use.

I wore my new armour to dinner that evening and did not look out
of place. The rangers all wore their armour as they sat at the long tables
in the massive cavern that served as a dining hall. I noticed that as
commander, Martel did not bother to sit apart from the rest of the
men. Though the men showed him some respect, the deference I
expected to be afforded to a commander simply was not present.

A young ranger ran into the room and bowed before Martel. A brief
exchange followed before Martel stood abruptly. He looked over at me
and beckoned. Sighing, I stood, leaving the rest of my dinner uneaten,
and followed Martel from the hall.

I found myself in a slightly smaller cavern, with a large table in the
centre. There were no chairs, only maps painted on vellum that lined
the walls and sat in haphazard piles on the table. Three very tired-
looking rangers stood to attention as we entered the room.

"At ease," Martel said. "News?"

"Yes," one ranger replied. "I've just come from the north. There are
rumours that a chieftain there has a piece of the sceptre."

"Did you see if for yourself?"

"No. I did speak to a clansman, who mentioned a southern treasure
that the chieftain guards jealously. If it is the sceptre, we will not have
an easy time getting it back."

"If," Martel replied. "I'm not keen on taking on a northern tribe if
the treasure is not a piece of the sceptre." He turned to another ranger.
"News?"

"I come from the east," the ranger replied. "And have seen part of
the sceptre."

"But?"

"But it is guarded by a very large pack of grass dogs. The lizards have
clearly been trained. They do not normally travel in such large groups,
and they certainly do not patrol. My guess is that whoever has that
piece knows someone is after it. Any manner of other traps and snares
will be set in place to prevent us taking it."

"Less appetizing even than going north," Martel said. He turned to
the final man. "And what news from you?"

"I come from the South," the ranger replied. "I heard no rumours of a piece of the sceptre save for this." The ranger pulled out a fragment of cloth and handed it to Martel. Martel stared down at the section of map he was just given.

"I am assuming the mark on the coast means something?"

"I took this map from a dying man, who fought me even until his last breath," the ranger said. "According to him, it is the location of a piece of the sceptre. There is a cave on the coast, frequented by pirates. The cave was once the hideout for the Red Band."

Martel looked sharply at the man.

"The Red Band?" I asked.

"Pirates for hire. They were the ones who attacked and sank the ship which was transporting the sceptre to a safe place," Martel replied. "The ship was wrecked and the sceptre shattered. It was the rangers who sailed to intervene. We were too late. The Red Band disappeared and we managed only to wrest the head of the sceptre from them."

Martel walked over to the map on the table and placed a marker to match the one on the fabric scrap the third ranger had given him. He did the same for the approximate locations in the east and in the north. "Where to?" he muttered. He looked up at me.

"Well, Stranger," he said. "Where would you like to go?"

I stared down at the map. I looked up at Martel. He stood behind the table, his arms folded, staring expectantly at me.

"How am I supposed to know?" I asked.

Martel shrugged. "You came by the Sky Road," he said. "You must be important, even if you cannot remember who you are."

"I was chased onto that road by three grass dogs," I replied. "I hardly think that makes me important."

"Very few can even see the Sky Road," Martel answered. "Let alone walk it."

I shook my head and turned back to the map. Which way? What would help me learn the most about myself and where I came from; what happened and why? I considered going east. At least the piece of sceptre there had been sighted. And perhaps the person or persons guarding it would be able to help me remember. Or they might just kill me.

Going north might not be a bad idea. The chieftain may prove to be a reasonable man. And perhaps he might know more about me? Or he might just kill me.

The thoughts whirled in my mind as I tried to choose what was best. I looked up at the ranger who came in from the south. "Is the hideout still in use?" I asked.

The ranger shrugged. "I did not go to see. It was another month's ride, and the risk of losing the piece of map was too great."

"Pirates exist," Martel interjected. "They always have. It is likely that hideout is in use. If it is the Red Band you are enquiring after, I cannot tell you. They have been neither seen nor heard since the night they stole the sceptre away."

"Comforting," I noted. "Look, this isn't an awful lot of information to go on."

"Welcome to the life of a ranger," Martel replied, smirking.

"Fun." I pondered for a moment longer. "South."

Martel raised his eyebrows. "Why?" he asked.

I did not have a good response so I simply shrugged. "No idea."

Laughing, Martel said, "Well, you're honest at least. South it is."

Martel dismissed the rangers. "We will leave tomorrow," he told me. "I must make preparations. Take some time to rest. I will summon you when we are ready to leave."

I nodded and turned to do as I was bid. I stopped. "May I visit Basadia?" I asked.

Martel first raised his brows in surprise, then lowered them in a deep scowl.

"Please. She has been a good friend, and surely I do not know anything that is secret?"

After a thoughtful pause, Martel nodded. "You may. But be cautious, Stranger. The Black Blades are duplicitous by nature. She is not who you think she is."

I turned and made my way through the labyrinthine tunnels to the prison cavern, stopping to collect food.

Basadia, I noted, had not moved from her position curled on the floor.

"Hi," I said tentatively.

Basadia turned her head and scowled at me. "What do you want?"

she demanded.

"I came to make sure you were all right. Are you?"

Standing, Basadia turned to face me. She shrugged. Her expression of distrust did not fade when she replied. "I have no cause for complaint, other than captivity. And you?"

I shrugged. "I'm all right. I guess. I mean, they've been pretty good to me so far. Here. I brought you food."

"Thank you," Basadia said hesitantly. She took the plate I offered and stared down at the freshly made black bread and strips of pork.

"I stopped by the kitchens on the way here," I explained.

Basadia nodded and began to eat.

"We're heading south," I said. "A ranger returned with a scrap of map showing the location of an old pirate hideout. Apparently there is probably a piece of the sceptre there."

Basadia stopped eating and stared at me. "Pirates," she said slowly.

"Yes."

"You mean the Red Band."

"Oh. You've heard of them."

"Everyone has heard of them."

I gave Basadia a pointed look and she smiled slightly. "Sorry," she said. "But you must listen to me. You cannot go south. You cannot take on the Red Band."

"Nobody has heard from them in years and years," I replied. "They probably don't even exist anymore."

"They exist, just as surely as the Black Blades or the rangers. They exist, and they will kill you. Don't go south."

I frowned. "But—"

"No!" Basadia snapped. "There is no 'but'. You don't understand. They are devils. *Devils.*" Basadia's voice shook when she said, "Please, don't go south. You will never return."

Unsure what to say, I simply smiled. Martel appeared at the entrance to the cavern. "Still here," he noted. "The smith wanted to see you. He thinks you need a few cursory lessons on how to use a blade." Martel glanced briefly at Basadia, whose gaze did not leave my face, before vanishing from the cavern.

"I should probably go. I'll see you when we get back."

Basadia said nothing. She watched me leave, looking miserable.

My training that day did not go well. The smith dismissed me at dinner time with disgust and I trudged, weary and troubled, to a table in the massive dining hall. I ate without tasting as I mulled over Basadia's warning.

"The smith thinks you're a moron," Martel said as he sat down heavily opposite me. I blinked and looked up.

"I'm fairly certain you're not, though you do seem distracted. Any thoughts you'd like to share?"

"Basadia told me the Red Band are still around. And that they're devils."

Martel grunted. "Time has a habit of stretching truths," he noted. "They were vicious and cruel men, there can be no doubt. But supernatural? No, I do not think so; despite what the myths may say."

"So you knew about them being devils."

"I know the myths, yes. It has been my experience, however, that mortal men are capable of far more terrifying acts than any beast of Hell. The Red Band were nothing more than men. And people who could not rationalise another of their kind being so brutal turned them into supernatural beings to make themselves feel better. That is all."

I decided not to press the issue further. Instead, I sat and ate and listened to the men who gathered around Martel trade stories. If they were afraid of the devils that made up the Red Band, they did not show it.

The morning found me after a long, sleepless night. I roused myself and dressed in my new armour, strapping on the sword I acquired yesterday. I joined the group of twenty men for breakfast before heading to the stables.

"Have you ridden before?" Martel asked as he measured a stirrup strap against my arm.

"I don't think so."

Martel grunted. "This is Fas," he said, patting the horse he was dressing. "The steadiest horse we have."

"Not saying much," a ranger noted as he strode past with a saddle in his arms.

"Ignore him," Martel said. "Fas is a good horse. She is a bit on the bossy side, however, so you will need to act as if you know what you're doing, or before long she will be riding you."

I smiled and patted Fas gently on her neck. Martel handed me the reigns and left to dress his own horse. Before long, I was following a train of men and horses as they walked from the cavern that was the stable into the fresh air. It was not yet first light when I stepped out into the lightening grey gloom.

"Mount," Martel said quietly.

As one, the men lifted themselves into their saddles. I, on the other hand, struggled to throw my leg over Fas' back. She snorted and skipped sideways as I bounced hard on the ground with one leg in the stirrup like a crow suffering a stroke. The rangers started laughing. My face burning red from the embarrassment, I managed to clamber onto my horse.

Martel grinned across at me from his thick-necked stallion.

"Shut up," I mumbled as I straightened in my saddle.

Martel shook his head silently, but did not stop grinning. He lifted his hand high and the horses bolted forward, thundering at a gallop from the rangers' hideout.

Fas did not move.

She sat and watched the group ride away, chewing on her bit as I fruitlessly kicked her flanks. "Come on, you bastard!" I hissed as I kicked.

"Martel!" someone from the group called out. Martel looked behind him at my shrinking image.

"Continue," he commanded as he turned his horse around. He galloped back to me, going past me and around Fas' flank. He slapped Fas' haunch hard, crying, "Go on!" Snorting, Fas bolted forward.

Only sheer luck kept me in the saddle as my mount leapt from standing into a run. Martel joined me soon after. Together we galloped on and joined the rest of the rangers.

The gallop lasted until the hideout was long out of sight. The group slowed to a walk and remained so until the sun began to set. They moved away from the road to a small grove of trees and there set up camp.

Not much was said that night. The group sat around the fire, each member lost to their own thoughts. Martel did not join his men immediately. He stood with his stallion and watched the golden moon climb into the sky. I, exhausted from the brutal exertion that is a full day's ride, leant against a tree and closed my eyes, feeling myself start to fall asleep.

A small tug at the top of my boot where I kept my broken flint knife snapped my eyes open again. In a swift move, I twisted my arm around and my hand closed on whatever was trying to get my knife.

It proved to be something small and furry. The small furry thing shrieked as I pulled it around my body to get a look at it. I stared dumbly at the creature in my hand. It looked like a tiny, potbellied child, with a snub nose, enormous dish-like ears and large, bright green eyes. Its wide, thin lipped mouth was slightly open as it struggled in my grip, revealing two rows of sharply pointed teeth.

It screeched and squealed as it tried to push itself out of my hand, straining just as I might if I had been caught in the grip of a giant.

"What the hell is that?" a ranger demanded of me as the creature uttered a pitiful howl, its thin, furry tail thrashing from side to side.

"I have no idea," I replied, not taking my eyes off the creature. "It tried to steal my knife."

The rangers gathered around me, trying to get a better look at the thing in my hand.

"What the hell is all this noise?" Martel demanded from behind the group. Everyone immediately straightened and stood aside, letting him through. He strode forward and knelt by my side, staring at the creature.

For a moment, it stared back, forgetting its struggles. It blinked twice before starting to struggle again.

"It tried to steal my knife," I said.

"It's actually kind of adorable," a ranger noted.

The creature stopped struggling and turned its head around to face him, much like an owl. Its large eyes stared out into the gloom at the ranger.

"And now creepy."

The creature turned back to me. Apparently realising it would not manage to break free of my grip, it threw the tiniest, most adorable temper-tantrum I had ever seen. It balled its tiny, long fingered hands into fists and pounded on my hand while kicking its long-toed, tiny feet pointlessly in the air and wailing at the top of its tiny lungs.

I could not help myself. I laughed. "What do I do with it?" I asked Martel.

"That's up to you."

"Thieves have their hands cut off in the city," a ranger noted.

The creature stopped its tantrum and turned to him, its large eyes growing larger. It did nothing but stare at the ranger for a long time before turning back to me and whimpering. It stared at me with eyes like saucers.

I sighed.

"All right," I told it. "I'm going to let you go. And you're going to go back to wherever you came from and leave my knife alone. Got it?"

The creature blinked at me, its tail swishing back and forth.

Slowly, hesitantly, I lowered the tiny thing in my hand until its feet touched the ground. I let it go. It stood upright for a moment, shocked to be free of my grasp. It looked up at me and narrowed its oversized eyes to slits.

"You're free to go," I said.

The creature exploded into animated, angry chatter. It paced back and forth in front of me, chirping, clicking and babbling and throwing its hands in the air in a tiny show of utter exasperation. It even shook one tiny fist up at me. The incomprehensible tirade took a surprisingly long time before the creature ran out of steam.

It stared up at me in silence a moment, its tiny hands balled into fists. "Humph!" it said before turning around and stalking over to the nearest tree.

My mouth hung agape as I watched it clamber up the trunk. It stopped on the first branch and scampered over like a squirrel. The tirade began again. It scampered back and forth on all fours spewing its unintelligible abuse at me.

The cry of an owl on the hunt stopped the creature in its tracks. It uttered a small scream and bounded away on all fours, vanishing into the trees in silence.

"That was... weird," Martel noted. He looked at me, as if I might have some explanation for it all. I shrugged helplessly at him. He shrugged back and everyone returned to their original positions.

Before long, I drifted off to sleep.

Chapter Seven

Dawn arrived far too soon for my liking. I grumbled as I forced my aching body into motion. My grumbling increased when I saw that most of the rangers had been awake since first light. The fire was blazing cheerily, with a rabbit roasting on a spit above it. Most of the bedding was packed away and several horses had already been saddled.

Sighing, I rose and packed everything away. A cursory check revealed that my knife had not been stolen as I slept. The little creature that attempted the theft must have surely left. Unused to having a bedroll, it took me several moments to figure out how to fold and roll it so it would fit on my saddle correctly. It took me longer to remember how to saddle the horse.

Martel watched me, ready to step in and help if I needed it. I pointedly shooed him away when he tried. He responded with an approving nod.

"You'll get there," he noted when I had finally saddled Fas. The horse snorted and flicked one ear. I could not help but feel as if she was being derisive.

"Shut up, you," I murmured at her. She shifted her weight and I joined the others for breakfast.

Before long everyone was back in their saddles and heading south. For three weeks I rode with the rangers. In that time, I managed to get far more comfortable in my saddle. My legs and knees did not ache nearly as much at the end of the day. In the evenings when we had made camp, Martel also patiently continued to teach me how to use a sword. Feeling like I had probably never held one in my life, I struggled through the lessons. Though Martel insisted I was improving, I still felt completely incompetent.

I continued practising with my staff as well, and found that I felt far more comfortable with it than a blade. It would have been helpful to have Basadia on hand to show me more, but I made do with what I remembered of her lessons.

The time passed swiftly. As busy as I was, I could not shake the feeling that unfriendly eyes were watching us. I kept glancing at Martel, who often rode at my side. Perhaps he feared that I would lose control of my horse. I did not notice any sign that he felt he was being watched. It was difficult to tell, however. Martel, like the other rangers, always appeared to be on alert.

On the third day of the third week, we came across a river.

Martel scowled.

"What?" I asked.

"There is no river on our maps."

"That's because there shouldn't be a river," a ranger - the same who had delivered the scrap of map indicating the pirate hideout - said. He rode forward. "I did not cross a river either to or from the town."

"Did we go the wrong way?" someone else asked.

Martel checked his shadow. "No," he answered. "We're headed south."

"I don't understand," the first ranger said. "There was no river."

"Clearly there was," Martel said.

"No," the ranger replied. "There wasn't."

"Rivers don't just appear out of nowhere," Martel countered.

I spied a dark hooded figure on the far side.

"Uh," I said.

Martel and the ranger ignored me, choosing instead to continue their argument.

"Gentlemen," I tried again, staring at the dark hooded figure across the rushing water.

Again I was ignored.

"Hey!" I shouted.

"What?" Martel snapped back. I nodded my head to indicate the figure standing across the water.

A chilled silence fell over the group.

"It cannot be," a ranger whispered.

"What?" I asked.

"A Seeker's Son," Martel answered quietly.

My jaw dropped as I recalled the rhyme spoken to me in the tiny mud hut village I first encountered after waking with a blank mind. I whispered it.

"The Seeker's Son has taken one, The Seeker's Son has two. The Seeker's Son takes another one, The Seeker's Son seeks you."

Martel turned to me. "How do you know that?"

"A witch doctor recited it to me in the village I went to when I first woke up," I answered. "What's a Seeker's Son?"

"I'll explain later," Martel replied. "For now, run!"

As a group, the rangers turned their horses east and fled at a dead run. Behind us, I could hear the horrid scream of the Seeker's Son. It froze my blood.

"It's chasing us!" one ranger yelled.

"Go! Go! Go!" Martel cried.

I could hear the hooded creature behind us wail as it gave chase. I kicked Fas' flanks to keep her going. Steady she may have been, but she was not the fastest horse in the group. I watched as a ranger in front of me took up his bow and, dropping his reigns, notched an arrow. He turned in his saddle and loosed the projectile. I turned around to see the arrow glide smoothly through the creature's forehead as if there was nothing there. The creature exploded into dark mist. The mist hovered a moment before drawing itself back together, reforming into the hooded creature known as the Seeker's Son.

"Um..." I managed to say.

"Keep going!" Martel screamed.

I turned back around and urged Fas to fly. She tried, but we were rapidly falling behind. "No, no, no, no, no, no..." I muttered as the last horse passed me.

Fas thundered on, her neck now flecked with the foam of sweat and saliva. Ahead, I saw the looming grey of a forest. Not sure how that would help, I nevertheless understood that the rangers were trying desperately to get to the trees.

An arrow flashed past my head as another ranger loosed it. I knew that they knew it was futile, save to buy some time as the wisp-ish thing reconstituted itself. The group drifted further and further away from me until they disappeared into the trees. Feeling stranded and terrified I swallowed back bile and kept my eyes firmly on the line of trees that may or may not prove to be my salvation.

Another arrow whizzed by my head. The rangers had not abandoned me entirely.

I plunged past the first line of trees, and pulled Fas to a hard stop. The horse neighed in complaint as she planted her feet and slid to a halt. I blinked in the suddenly dim light. The rangers sat and silent on their horses, surrounded by strangely dressed men and women, each aiming arrows at them.

Something moved behind me and I saw three more of these people drop smoothly from the trees. They ran forward and stopped suddenly, each throwing their hands forward. The air between the trees shimmered. The smoky Seeker's Son smashed into the wall of shimmering air and dissipated completely. The three strangers straightened and slowly lowered their arms. The shimmering air between the trees vanished. They turned back to me.

For a long moment I stared at the three strangely dressed people. I noticed that they were not quite normal. Large, sharply pointed ears that stretched to the tops of their heads were not the strangest thing about them. What was stranger were their large, sharply angular eyes that dominated their faces. Their eyes were almost uniformly blue, though a few of them had green or pale brown eyes.

"Uh... Thanks," I said.

I heard Martel hiss behind me and swallowed. Had I just uttered an insult?

The people simply stared at me.

"Who are you?" demanded a woman, standing on a slender limb above my head. "To bring a Seeker's Son here?"

I looked up at the woman. Her shimmering honey-coloured hair hung long and loose as she stared down at me with her oversized eyes.

"It wasn't a deliberate choice," I replied. "We were being pursued."

The woman smiled slightly. "It is always a deliberate choice to enter these woods," she said. She leapt to the ground moving more like a cat than a person. "And we do not suffer trespassers."

"Um... Oh," I responded. "To be fair, though, I had no idea these woods were taken. So... Sorry for the trouble. We'll just be on our way."

"I'm afraid not," the woman replied.

"Look," I said pointedly.

"Don't," Martel warned me quietly. I turned to look at him and noticed that he had turned a shocking pale shade. His right arm hung uselessly by his side.

"A paralytic arrow," the woman before me explained. "If it remains untreated, his heart will stop beating. It is a powerful poison."

I swung back and blinked at the woman. "Why would you...?"

"You are trespassing," the woman replied.

"Can you... Can you treat it?"

"Yes."

"Could you. Please?"

The woman cocked her head in a bird-like manner. "Why should I? You entered my woods uninvited. You brought a Seeker's Son to us. Tell me why I shouldn't kill you all where you stand!"

I opened my mouth to argue, and quickly shut it once more.

"I really am sorry that we have trespassed," I said quickly. "But we are on an important mission, one that may just decide the fate of the world. Please. Martel is our leader. We need him."

The cat-like woman in front of me arched an eyebrow. "The fate of the world? What is this important mission?"

I glanced back at Martel. His face twisted in agony and a sheen of cold sweat covered his head and chest, catching the meagre light filtering down from the canopy. He nodded once to me.

"We're on a mission to recover the pieces of the empress' sceptre."

"And how does this impact us?" the woman demanded. "Your empire is not ours. We have never bent our knees and we never shall. This mission has no bearing on the fate of the world at all. Only yours. Only your small, narrow little world. Such typical human self-aggrandisement."

The words of the last sentence were spat out with extreme distaste. The forest filled with hissing, and I realised, for the first time, that there were hundreds of these people. Most of them were in the trees, hidden until they decided to show themselves and hiss angrily down at us.

Martel issued a small groan. I looked back again. His lips had turned blue and I could see that he was struggling to breathe, let alone remain conscious. Thinking quickly, I said, "And why is that? Is it because the empress decided not to invade? You have your forest, your own pocket of safety in the middle of an Empire. You are surrounded. Why is it you were never attacked? And can you be certain that the villain who sits on the throne will not come for you?"

"I'd like to see him try," the woman replied archly, but I had her thinking.

"You just might," I retorted. "But if you help us find the sceptre and restore the throne, I swear that no one will ever touch your woods as long as the empire shall last."

The woman cocked her head at me, her large eyes narrowing. "And your price for this is that man's life?" She points at Martel.

"Yes," I said, trying to keep the desperation from my voice.

Behind me, I heard Martel's tortured breath stop abruptly. I turned to find him collapsed against his horse's neck. The rangers looked to me with wide eyes. I faced the woman.

"Please!"

After another pause, which felt like an age, the woman looked past me at one of her people and nodded. One of the archers un-nocked his arrow and ran forward. He pulled Martel onto his back and stabbed a pointed glass needle into Martel's neck. I winced, watching as the contents of the needle were pushed into the leader of the rangers' bloodstream.

For a torturous moment, nothing happened. I watched him closely, my body tense. Martel convulsed and began to breathe again. I sighed in relief.

A sharp pain on the back of my head and a blinding flash knocked me into unconsciousness.

I woke up several hours later with a pounding headache. Perhaps because of the state of my head, it took me quite a while to realise that I was no longer on my horse, but on a bed. In a tree. I stared up at the leafy canopy, clearly visible through the finely woven cloth that surrounded me. The bed rocked ever so gently as the wind pushed its way through the trees.

It was when I tried to sit up that I noticed the terrible, throbbing pain on the back of my head. I squeezed my eyes shut as the pain sent my vision spinning.

"Don't move too quickly," a gentle masculine voice said.

Opening my eyes, I turned to spy one of the strange people of the woods, his large blue eyes fixed upon me. The man smiled slightly. "Hessa hit you harder than necessary," he said apologetically. "Your head is probably still swimming."

"Was it necessary to hit me at all?" I demanded in a slurred voice. Deciding that sitting up simply was not worth the agony, I let myself relax on the bed.

"You are lucky you are not dead, trespasser," the man said. He moved to the bedside and, from the bedside table I had not even noticed was there, lifted up a glass of amber-coloured fluid. "The accord was for Martel's life, not yours."

"Martel," I said, suddenly remembering that the leader of the rangers had been half dead the last I saw him.

"Recovering. The poison is very effective, and a great deal of damage was done. It will be a while before he is fit to ride again. But he is a ranger, and of a strong constitution. No doubt he will recover well. Now, drink this. It will help with the pain."

I stared at the glass, then up at the man. His small smile broadened at my open look of suspicion.

"It is a drug, but not a poison. You will fall to sleep and be relieved of your pain and that is all."

I struggled to sit up again. This time, the tall, slender man of the woods helped me. He was surprisingly strong given his delicate-looking frame.

"The other rangers?" I asked as the man brought the glass up to my lips. I drank as the man answered. The liquid was sweet and sharp at once.

"Probably in the same state you're in. Though I dare say their captors showed more restraint. Hessa has a temper."

I nodded. It was the last thing I did before slipping into the land of dreams.

When I next awoke, it was first light. A gentle breeze rocked my bed soothingly. The wind was cold, but I had been covered in furs and felt cosy warm. I turned around and met a pair of large blue eyes. The owner of those eyes froze in his crouched position and gasped. Pulling my gaze back, I found that the eyes belonged to a child of the tree people, and that child knew that he definitely should not have been near my bed.

"Good morning," I said amicably.

The child slowly straightened. He offered a meek smile. "You sleep a lot," he said.

I grinned. "I was in a lot of pain."

"Mother says your nothing but a filthy human trespasser."

I raised my brows.

"But you don't smell all that bad, and you look clean enough."

"Thank you," I replied. "I try to bathe often."

The boy giggled. "Father thinks you're special. He says he can smell it on you."

"Smell what?"

"I don't know. I've been trying to find out. You don't smell all that different from the other humans. Except your leader. He smells like poison. Still."

"Martel. Is he all right?"

"He sleeps like you," the boy said. "But he is getting stronger. Mother has him in isolation at the edge of the city. That way he can get rest and be ill and not assault everyone with his smell."

"I would like to see him."

"I can take you," the boy said, brightening. "I know the way. I help father treat him, after all."

"You," the man who drugged me last time said from the edge of the cloth room that held my bed in the tree. "Should not be awake, young man."

"But father," the boy said plaintively. "It's first light already. I'm allowed to be up. You agreed."

The man sighed. "We agreed that you could get up when the Dawn Greeter begins her song. She has not yet sung."

"It's not my fault she's late."

"She is not late. You are early."

Just as the man finished speaking, a low hum followed by a high note sounded through the grey air. More notes followed, creating a joyous melody that proved so enchanting I could not help but lie back and listen. The rhythm of a hand drum joined the song and, after what I thought were two verses, more voices joined in the song.

The boy folded his arms across his chest and smirked at his father. The man rolled his eyes. "Go on, then," he said. "Your mother will be up and making breakfast."

"Yes, Father," the boy replied. He smiled at me and left the cloth room. I watched him through the gossamer cloth as he moved lithely over the branches, like a well-practiced cat, perhaps one that has only ever led an arboreal life.

"I apologise if my son woke you. The curiosity of the very young seems to have been granted in ample supply to him."

"I was awake already," I replied. I sat up, finding it much easier this time around. Only the dullest of aches throbbed in my head.

"You are looking better," the man noted. He entered the room, pulling the cloth aside and gliding in. He carried a tray with food, which he handed to me. I looked down. Two hard boiled eggs and a large platter of fruit - an appetising breakfast.

"Thank you," I said as I accepted the plate. "I feel better."

"You should. You slept for two straight days."

"Oh."

"You are probably anxious to speak to your leader."

"Yes."

"I shall leave you to your meal, then, and return when he has awoken."

"Thank you."

The man nodded and slipped away, moving through the canopy as lithely as his son before him. I happily ate as the Sun Greeting song drifted through the air. Birds had joined their voices, trilling and chirping as the first of the gold rays burst over the horizon, spreading warm golden light across the trees, and my bed.

The song ended, though the birds carried on. For the first time in a long time, I felt contented. The mood of the place where I was, for all intents and purposes, held captive proved to be both joyous and soothing. A strange, anxiety-free captivity.

Sitting up now, I could see that my bed was actually constructed from the branch upon which it sat. Smaller branches were coaxed over time to fold into one another in a decorative lattice, resulting in a rectangular outcropping with a flat top. The same was done for the bedside table.

I placed my empty platter on the table and cast the blankets aside. Standing, I took the time to stretch, pleased to be moving again.

"Hello again," a young voice greeted.

I turned to find the boy from earlier this morning standing just inside the cloth that delineated my room. "Father said I can fetch you. Your leader is awake now. Do you wish to speak with him?"

"I do indeed. Lead on."

The boy smiled. He turned and scurried away, leaping and swinging between branches. I managed to get to the edge of my branch before stopping. There seemed nowhere for me to go. The nearest branch was a very far leap away. I looked around for a rope or something to help me. There was nothing.

I noticed in my search that the houses of these tree people were nothing like houses at all. They were trees; trees with parts that had been carefully, painstakingly sculpted over time to serve uses. Beds appeared in random places along branches. Some of the thicker branches lower down had tables and chairs. The concept of personal housing seemed foreign to these people. They used whichever table set was nearest to eat a meal together. Most did not even bother, sitting happily on branches and eating their meals. I watched them with curiosity, momentarily forgetting my immediate problem.

I surmised that these people only ever walked on the ground when absolutely necessary. Their whole lives were spent in the trees.

The boy reappeared. "Are you not coming?"

"It's adorable how you think I could possibly follow you," I said.

The boy blinked and grinned. "I do apologise. I forget how clumsy and ungainly humans are, despite the stories I hear. Come, we will go the long way."

"The long way?"

The boy pointed down. I looked down and swallowed hard. The ground could not be seen from here. How on earth was I supposed to get down?

With careful patience, the boy climbed down, showing me how to place my hands and let myself more or less fall onto the branches below. I have never felt clumsier before or since. It took an hour for me to descend.

I was a trembling wreck by the time my feet touched the ground. I wanted to fall to my knees and kiss the soft, steady earth. I refrained, choosing instead to follow the boy as he skipped along a path only he could possibly see. As far as I was concerned, the ground beneath these trees had never before been trodden upon.

After another hour of scrambling over rocks and being tripped by roots and fallen branches hidden in the mulch, we came to a smaller tree growing in the space left by a larger, now toppled goliath of a tree. Sitting on a newly formed bed on a lower branch, Martel rested his back against the trunk, wrapped in furs. He did not look well.

"I'll come back with lunch," the boy whispered. He offered a sad smile and scurried away.

I clambered up the tree in my boorish fashion. Martel's eyes opened as I hauled myself onto his branch. He offered a shaky smile.

"You look awful," I said. It was not a lie. Dark circles under his eyes told me that though he had spent much of his time sleeping, he had not really rested. His lips were still slightly blue, and his face ashen. His breath, I noted, came in wheezing gasps and was painful to draw, if his wincing was anything to go by.

"I guarantee you I feel worse," he croaked back.

I smiled slightly. "Did you know?"

"That we'd be attacked by the tuatha?" Martel nodded and closed his eyes. "Yes. I also knew that they were the only ones who could properly banish a Seeker's Son. It was a risk I had no choice but to take." He opened one eye to peer at me. "I owe you much. You think fast in a pinch."

"Not fast enough," I replied. "You'd be in better shape if I was more convincing."

Martel shrugged, wincing. "Short of begging, there wasn't anything else that you could have done."

"I should have begged, then," I muttered.

"You did well," Martel insisted.

I fell silent, not knowing what to say.

"I think after your display at the edge of the forest, the men will look to you to lead. The gods know I'm in no state to."

I looked up sharply.

"As the new leader, you have a decision to make."

"About?"

"Me."

"You?"

Martel nodded. "You will be released as soon as you and the rest of the rangers are fully recovered from the elders'... hospitality. I will not be ready to ride by then, and so you must decide what to do with me."

I opened my mouth to protest and shut it again. I had severe doubts as to how well we could achieve our goals without Martel at the helm.

"I'm not deciding anything right now," I said. I moved to Martel's side and sat down next to him. Closer now, I noted that despite the warming sun and the thick furs, Martel was shivering uncontrollably.

"You were going to tell me about the Seeker's Son," I said, hoping to take his mind off the pain.

Martel closed his eyes a moment and smiled. "I was, wasn't I?" He shifted his weight and sighed, wincing as he did so.

"There are twelve in total," he said.

"Twelve what? Seeker's Sons?"

Martel nodded. "They were once the same man."

I frowned, not understanding.

"A very long time ago, long before the empire, there was a king of a powerful kingdom. The man was a natural mage; born with powers beyond imagining. He knew his powers were superior to anyone else's, and he liked it. He used them to conquer the lands surrounding his kingdom, and he was not kind about it. No one was safe from his cruelty. We call this time the Dark Days.

"During the march of his army, he came upon resistance from the tuatha. They had seen his coming, and they despised it. He tore down forests, burnt grasslands and made living things be dead stone. He had never before heard of the tuatha. He did not know what they were capable of.

"In the battle with them, he found they were talented mages themselves. He could not use his magic against them without them countering with their own. So, on the third night of battle, he summoned the Seeker."

Martel paused to catch his breath.

"The Seeker?" I asked.

Nodding, Martel closed his eyes again. After a long pause, he renewed his tale. "The Seeker is an Underworld creature. One of the most powerful demons in existence. Some claim he is a god, cast down from the Overworld for some unknown terrible crime. He rules the Underworld, they say, having conquered it long ago. It was foolish arrogance that convinced the king that he could control such a spirit.

"For a time, he managed. The Seeker wreaked hell upon the tuatha. They died in the thousands. That was when Moua, the warrior queen of Masina, rallied her brave warriors and convinced all kingdoms to rise up against the evil king. As head of an army created from the entire continent, she marched to the aid of the tuatha and the Silver Blade Alliance was born.

"The battle was terrible. But Moua had a stout heart, and her courage made others brave. Despite the slaughter, she stood before the demon lord and called him by name. She challenged him to combat. The hearts of the alliance broke, for they knew that Moua could never defeat the Seeker. No one could.

"Still, she faced her foe with weapons drawn and they fought. Moua was not just brave, but cunning as well. She used the fight to speak to the Seeker; to strike a deal. She would release him from his bondage if he promised to destroy the evil king. Angry at his capture and slavery, the Seeker agreed to Moua's terms and she, carrying a magical flint blade given to her by the king of the shadow realm, cut the invisible bonds that tied the Seeker to the king.

"True to his word, the Seeker turned on his former master. He destroyed the armies and broke the magic of the king. His wrath was so fierce, that it levelled all the king's lands, and turned his supporters into pillars of dust where they stood, wherever in the land they stood. But he did not kill the king.

"Instead, the Seeker split the king in twelve, casting each of the newly made shades into the Underworld, there to await a summoning; there to await enslavement by any mage keen enough to test their might against him. He was banished to slavery, twelve times over and for all eternity. None dare speak that king's name, for fear it will summon a part of him, so we all simply call the shades Seeker's Sons."

I sat in silence when Martel finished his story. "So that... spirit. That powerful spirit that cannot be killed, that was only one twelfth of a man?"

"One twelfth," Martel confirmed. "And in possession of such power. Can you imagine what a monster he must have been when he was all twelve twelfths of himself?"

"Is that what he's doing, then? Seeking parts of himself?"

Martel's eyes snapped open. "Gods above and below, I hope not!" His already pale face paled more. "I just assumed that the shade was summoned against us by someone. That someone was working against restoring the throne. But if it was indeed a Seeker's Son acting on its own, then..."

Martel looked queasy now. I placed a steadying hand on his shoulder. He looked up at me.

"It means that at least one shade has broken the bonds of the Seeker. If it reunites all twelve parts of itself then... Then the king returns, and we are all doomed." Martel trembled harder than ever, and I was certain it was not the poison that caused it.

"What do we do?"

"We must move quickly," Martel answered. "The empire is the legacy of Queen Moua. It was always her blood, her strength that sat upon the throne. If the king of old is trying to return, only Moua's blood can help us. We need to restore the throne. Do you hear?"

I nodded. Martel slumped back against the tree, his breath now so ragged I feared it would stop altogether.

"You know so much," I said.

Martel smiled slightly. "I read," his voice rasping now from overuse. "Few rangers do any more. It is considered... unnecessary."

"Why do you?"

"The legacy of being a high-born," Martel replied sardonically. "An unimportant high-born, but that is a tale for another day."

I bit my lip against the flood of sudden questions and nodded. "You're like a walking library," I said with a smile.

"Knowledge is power," Martel murmured, fading quickly.

I opened my mouth to reply, but Martel, exhausted, had fallen asleep. So I closed my mouth again and pondered.

The problem of Martel remained. I needed to decide, and soon. Time was of the essence.

Chapter Eight

I sat in silence as Martel snored fitfully. He had fallen asleep, still sitting up with his chin resting on his muscular chest. Despite his snoring, it was peaceful. The sun filtered through the leaves of the prison tree, casting contrasting speckles of golden light and purple shadow. The meadow nearby hosted tall grasses with large white clusters of flowers that looked like snowflakes. Small spotted deer grazed amongst them, almost hidden entirely in the grass.

This place was certainly beautiful, but there was something beyond the beauty. There was something powerful here. I could feel it tingle across my skin if I concentrated hard enough; a small jittery zap that danced across the small hairs on my arms and neck. It was odd, but not uncomfortable. I closed my eyes and enjoyed the sensation of the soft breeze whispering through the leaves.

Forcing myself away from sleep that threatened in this calm place, I turned my mind to the situation at hand. I was painfully aware that I did not have a grasp on the full extent of what was going on in this world. How could I have? I could not even remember my own name. Whether or not a Seeker's Son has gotten free of its restraints in the Underworld, or whether or not it was summoned by someone to do us harm was completely irrelevant. What I did know was that we must find the pieces of the sceptre, and find them quickly. Whatever the reason, time was not our ally.

The sad fact was that Martel would only slow us down, and the delay caused by the tuatha was already too long. I opened my eyes and looked across at Martel. His face was a terrible grey pallor. It would be many weeks before he was well enough to ride again, and he'd be next to useless in a fight.

His expertise notwithstanding, I realised with a heavy heart that we could not take him with us. I sighed and close my eyes again.

I did not keep time as I sat next to Martel, listening to him snore. It was long before a subtle shift in the sensation of the power surrounding me alerted me to the presence of another person. I opened my eyes and looked up to see our host and his son standing on Martel's platform.

The young tuatha held a platter of food. His father held a jug and a clay cup.

"Good afternoon," he greeted.

"Hi," I answered.

"How is he?"

"In a bad way. He's been sleeping all morning."

"Of course he has. He is healing. It takes a great deal of energy for the body to heal itself. All other functions are reduced to a minimum. I'm afraid we're going to have to wake him, however. He needs his medicine and food."

I nodded and turned to Martel. I gently shook him. He stirred slightly and shifted his weight. I shook him again, harder.

"Go away," Martel mumbled.

The tuatha man laughed. "Not yet, ranger. Awaken. We have your medicine."

Martel's eyes opened and he looked at the man. "How do I know you're not poisoning me more?" he demanded.

The man laughed again. "If that were the case, ranger, you would already be dead. And so would your friends."

Martel grunted. He struggled to sit up properly, pushing me away when I tried to help. Our tuatha host poured the contents of his jug into the clay cup and handed it to Martel.

"Drink all of it," he instructed.

Martel sighed and did so, pulling a face.

Three times the tuatha man poured the medicine, and three times Martel swallowed it down. The boy brought the food over. He tried very hard not to wrinkle his nose as he placed the platter at Martel's feet. He failed.

"Thank you," the tuatha man said to his son. "Now run along. Your mother is awaiting you in the training yard."

The tuatha boy nodded and scampered off, running up into the trees and away from sight.

The man sat down and began dividing the food between the three of us.

"Thank you," Martel mumbled as he accepted a plate of food from him. "Who are you, anyway?"

The man blinked and smiled. "Have I not introduced myself before now? Please forgive me. That was rude. My name is Zach. I am husband to the elder, Hessa, whom you've already met and spoken with."

"You poor bastard," Martel muttered.

Halfway through a sip of water, I choked and started coughing. Zach smiled slightly. "There is more to Hessa than her temper," he said. "Besides, you are a trespasser, and so are not deserving of consideration."

Martel grunted. I watched him, heartened as he ate hungrily. Having an appetite could only be a good sign.

"So," Zach asked as he ate. "What are your plans now?"

Martel shrugged. "It's not up to me anymore."

Zach turned his large eyes to me.

"Um..." I said. "I haven't thought enough about it. Except that Martel is too ill to ride with us."

"Yes," Zach said. "He is at that. For now."

"It's a bit of a problem. We need the pieces of the sceptre, and we need them soon."

"You've decided to continue on without me, I take it," Martel said, sounding slightly disappointed.

I nodded sadly and Martel sighed. "It's probably for the best. I cannot ride, I'll not be able to fight. I would be more of a hindrance than any kind of help."

"The rangers will leave soon, then?" Zach asked.

I nodded. Already feeling stronger and less concussed, I imagined that the rest of the rangers would be far more fit to ride and fight than I. I looked across at Martel again, who had stopped eating. He stared sadly down at his plate.

"Are you able to take care of him until he is fit again?" I asked.

"Yes," Zach replied. "To not do so would be to renege on our half of the accord. What happens to him after he is well and has left our woods, however... It is dangerous to be alone."

"I'll manage," Martel said.

Not doubting his abilities, I nodded. "Shall we meet you back at your hideout?"

"It seems to be the best course of action." Martel resumed eating, though the difficulty he had in swallowing told me that he was forcing himself.

"It's not a mark on your honour," I said to him.

"I know," Martel replied, offering me a wan smile. "But I do not like being useless. Lying around doing nothing while I wait for your return does not sit well with me."

I knew exactly what Martel was talking about. Prior to the fateful fight which threw me into the care of the Black Blades, I was lost and floundering. Now I had something to work towards. Danger or no, I would never want to return to being so without purpose.

"You could stay until Martel is well and take him with you," Zach offered.

I shook my head. "Time is against us, I'm afraid."

Zach frowned at me.

Martel spoke. "There is a concern that the Seeker's Son that chased us is acting of its own volition; that it has broken free of the Seeker's bonds and is trying to reclaim the other eleven shades. Should the Mage King return..." He shook his head.

The tuatha man stopped chewing altogether and stared at Martel. "You cannot be serious?"

"We need to restore the throne. Only Moua's bloodline can save us."

"There is no evidence," I added. "But it is a possibility. It might also be that someone has summoned the Seeker's Son to stop us from reclaiming the sceptre and restoring the throne. Either way, the sooner we solve the mystery and get the sceptre the sooner we can avoid disaster - whatever form that might take."

"So, you do not know the end game?" Zach asked.

Martel and I shook our heads.

"Then why are you playing?"

Martel smiled slightly. "The rangers are sworn protectors of the realm," he said. "We took a vow to defend the empire and the empress. Restoring the throne honours that vow. Thus, I am honour bound to see it through to whatever end."

Zach looked at me. I shrugged. "I've got nothing better to do."

Martel snorted a laugh and immediately regretted it. He placed the butt of his palm against his head and groaned. Not knowing what else to do, I placed a comforting hand on his shoulder.

Sighing, Zach took up the jug and emptied it into Martel's cup. He handed it to the leader of the rangers. "Last one," he said. "Now that you've eaten, you must drink. Then you must sleep."

Martel did not protest. He downed the medicine in one gulp and settled himself, closing his eyes.

"I'll be back," I told him.

He grunted, then started to snore.

I helped Zach tidy up the meal and followed him from Martel's tree.

"He ate a lot," Zach noted. "More than last time. This is a good sign."

I smiled a little, before returning to my thoughts.

"The Council should hear of this development, trespasser," Zach said. "Follow me to the plaza."

The plaza, I discovered, was actually a grove of tall, slender trees that surrounded an ancient stone circle. As to the location of the plaza within the tuatha village, I could not tell. All I could see were trees. Zach entered the circle and told me to stay before vanishing with the tray of food. After a moment, the plaza began to fill with tuatha, and Zach returned to my side.

"A Council has been called. You will tell them what you told me, and speak only when asked," he said.

I nodded. Zach clapped me on the shoulder and took his place amongst the spectators. The crowd fell silent as four tuatha in elegant robes walked into the stone circle. One of them, I noted, was Hessa. I swallowed hard.

I followed Zach's instructions, speaking only when spoken to. When asked, I told the tuatha council everything. When I mentioned the possibility that a Seeker's Son may have freed itself from the Seeker, I was met with gasps of surprise and snorts of derision from the crowd, and narrowed eyes from the elders.

"Impossible," Hessa snapped dismissively.

"There is no evidence to suggest it is actually the case," I reasoned. "But it is a possibility."

"I agree," another of the four elegantly dressed tuatha said. "And if it is so, we cannot take the risk of inaction. Wait here, trespasser. We must discuss."

I nodded, frowning. The tuatha went nowhere. They simply bowed their heads and closed their eyes. The entire forest seemed to silence itself in aid of their concentration.

At length, they opened their eyes and affixed unnerving gazes upon me.

"The possibility, however unlikely, remains," one of the Council members said. "Therefore, in this endeavour, you have been favoured by the tuatha with aid. You may choose one of three gifts; an orb, which glows upon command, a soul trap able to contain one soul, or a tuatha warrior."

I blinked. "Who will be the tuatha warrior?"

Hessa smiled. "Me."

I stared for a moment at Hessa. "You?"

"Yes," Hessa replied. I could not help but feel she made the suggestion just to irk me. I frowned and thought over my options.

The orb, while useful, may well be as much a hindrance in dark places. A glowing light may just alert any unfriendly creatures in the darkness of our exact whereabouts. Not to mention the possibility of causing night blindness if looked at directly.

Proving much more interesting and useful was the soul trap. I could imagine that being able to capture and hold a soul would be extremely useful. For what, exactly, I could not quite figure out, but the thought of it was very appealing. That aside, and more to the point, I had no clue as to how to actually use the thing.

Hessa would. I imagined that Hessa knew a great deal. As one of the tuatha, I knew that she knew how to deal with a Seeker's Son, should one appear again. I also suspected that she knew a great deal of lore that would prove useful. In this way, she could replace the brutal loss of knowledge that we would be leaving behind in Martel. The fact that I did not much like her was now, unfortunately, irrelevant. I sighed.

"Thank you," I told the Council. I looked Hessa straight in the eye and spoke with a perfectly straight face. "We would be honoured to have you accompany us."

This was one of my finer moments, and clearly not the response Hessa was expecting. She blinked, then smiled broadly. "It will be an honour to be included," she said with an equally straight face. I was not entirely sure she was being sincere.

"We call this Council to an end," one of the other four dignitaries intoned. Somewhere in the forest, a gong sounded and the mood of the place shifted. Birds begin their chirping once more as the gathered crowd slowly drifted away. I stood awkwardly, unsure of what to do until Zach returned to my side. He clapped my shoulder in greeting.

"Well," he said. "You proved surprisingly eloquent, trespasser."

"Thank you. I think."

Zach laughed softly. "There is a small track behind you. The deer use it often. It will take you straight to the clearing where your rangers' horses are kept. Your rangers will meet you there."

Murmuring another small thank you, I turned around and started on the path broken by rocks and roots Zach had indicated. I turned back briefly to find Zach and Hessa embracing each other closely. I shook my head and continued on.

True to Zach's description, the difficult little path led me straight into a bright clearing where the ranger's horses grazed happily. They had been carefully groomed and look extremely well rested and contented.

Fas raised her head and saw me standing at the edge of the meadow. She snorted in greeting and trotted over to me. I smiled and greeted her with a scratch.

"She likes you," a ranger noted as he pushed past me, dressed in his uniform and carrying his horse's tack. "God knows why. You can't even ride properly."

"I'd trust a horse's taste in people. Fas knows her stuff," said another ranger, offering me a small smile as he, too, brushed past me.

I stepped forward into the meadow to escape the steady stream of rangers now trudging in with their tack to collect and saddle their horses. Standing beside Fas, I watched on until a small tug on my shirt drew my attention downward.

I blinked as I stared down at Fas' tack, below which protruded a small body.

"Father said to give you this," a familiar young voice said from beneath the saddle. I grinned and crouched down so I could see the wide-eyed face of my host's son smiling out at me.

"Thank you," I said, giving the boy a wide grin. I stood up again, took the bundle from the boy and began to dress Fas.

"Where is Martel?" a ranger asked suddenly, once everyone save myself had mounted.

"Martel is not well enough to ride," I said as I tugged at the saddle's girdle. Fas snorted in irritation. "Sorry, girl," I murmured to her.

"What?" the ranger asked. "Where is he?"

"Recovering in a tree on the outskirts of the ..." I paused. What on earth would one call the cluster of trees that served as a dwelling for the tuatha? "City." Close enough. "He'll remain there until he is well again, and will meet us back at your hideout."

"I'm not leaving Martel with these... things," the ranger spat.

Done saddling, I hauled myself onto Fas' back. "Then stay," I said with a shrug. "But you should know that there is a distinct possibility that the Seeker's Son is free and acting of its own accord. Martel himself admits that restoring the throne is imperative if we're going to stop the evil Mage King from returning. That means we collect all the pieces of the sceptre, and restore Empress Moua's bloodline to the throne. And we need to do it quickly."

"No one knows the world like Martel," the ranger replied stubbornly. "There's no way we can do any of this without him."

"Luckily, we have help," I said.

"Oh? Who?"

"Me." Hessa entered the meadow, sitting astride the back of an enormous red and black striped stag. She wore strangely designed armour that looked as beautiful as it did functional. The hilts of two short blades protrude from her back like the folded wings of a gargoyle.

The ranger looked her over. He turned to me. "You cannot be serious."

I could tell from the expression of his companions that no one in the company rangers was pleased by this development.

"I am," I said.

"No," the ranger replied. "I'm not riding with *that*."

"You will," Martel said from the edge of the clearing. Everyone turned to face him. He leant heavily on Zach, a blanket wrapped firmly around his shoulders. He still looked like death to my eyes, and the effort of his words had caused him to start wheezing.

"Martel!" the ranger said in surprise.

"You will ride," Martel managed to wheeze. "And you will obey. That is an order."

The ranger fell silent, cowed by Martel; as ill as he was.

"Do you understand?" Martel demanded.

"Yes, sir," the ranger replied sullenly, casting only the barest of evil glances at Hessa.

"Good." Martel turned his head to me and beckoned me closer. I nudged Fas forward until was close enough for Martel to lean on her. Zach helped him find his balance before moving away to speak with his wife.

"Listen well," Martel said. "The tuatha are as dangerous as they come. They are not to be trifled with. But they are, at least, honest. Once given, their word is like granite ‐ damned near impossible to break. Consult with her. Listen to her. But do not let her overrule you. You are the leader now. Don't forget that."

Still unsure, I nodded. Martel nodded in return. He indicated with his head, and I turned to look. Hessa remained on her mount, but was leaning down to embrace her husband and son, who sat in his father's arms fighting back tears.

"They are not so unlike us," Martel remarked. "And we were friends once. Lead well, Stranger, and we may well be again."

I offered Martel a small smile before Zach returned to help Martel step away from myself and Fas. I turned my horse and met Hessa's eye.

"These woods are your home," I said to her. "I defer to your knowledge in getting us safely through."

"Where do you wish to go?" Hessa asked.

"South," I replied.

Nodding, Hessa lightly touched her mount's neck and the massive stag turned. It stepped delicately through the long grass of the meadow before disappearing into the forest once more. I understood the purpose of its stripes. I could barely see the beast as it moved through the trees. I nudged Fas and she moved to follow. One by one, the rangers fell in behind.

Chapter Nine

The rangers, while accepting the final order of their commander, were not shy about hiding their dislike of our new companion. Hessa seemed unfazed. She looked content to take her nightly meals in the company of the stag alone and speak to no one during the day. For a week, we rode in uncomfortable silence.

At last, I could not stand the separation, and, at the night's camp on the southernmost edge of the forest, made a point of sitting with her. The stag watched us both as it grazed. At one point, Hessa started laughing though I was certain I had said and done nothing particularly humorous.

"My apologies," Hessa said when she saw me look at her oddly. "Yumani thinks you... odd."

"Yumani?" I asked. The great stag lifted his noble head and looked directly at me.

"Oh." I frowned. "What do you mean, odd?"

"Something in you is missing. It's difficult to explain, but the manner in which he spoke of it was very amusing."

"Oh." Wonderful. I was being mocked by a stag.

"Do not feel badly," Hessa said. "Your horse has a great deal of affection for you."

I looked at Fas, who was off grazing with the rest of the horses. "Is that so?"

"Yes. She has trained many rangers, she tells me, and thinks that, with a little patience, you will make a fine ranger one day."

I turned back to Hessa with a frown. "Are you playing with me?" I demanded.

Hessa only smiled.

"We should come to a fork in the road tomorrow," a ranger said. He walked so quietly to our position, I did not hear him. I looked up at him in surprise. His expression did not alter as he drew out a map from his boot and squatted down beside me. He looked up at me.

"What?" he demanded.

"Nothing," I murmured. "Go on."

"There is a three pronged fork in the road. They all head south, more or less. Two of them pass through a bog." He indicated on the map. "The third one skirts it on the east side and turns east, away from our target. Which would you like to take?"

Finally I recognised him. He was the man who had told Martel of the sceptre piece location. I tried to focus on the issue at hand, but found myself too tired to think.

"Which did you take last time?"

The ranger smiled slightly. "The eastern road. I left the road once I was a day past the bog and headed south west across country until I met up with another southern road. It cost me several days, but I considered that a fair trade."

"Why?"

The ranger's smile turned into a grin. "There are things that live in bogs, Stranger. Things that would lead us astray until we become hopelessly lost and suffer a slow death of starvation and thirst, and things that would rip us all to shreds and gorge on our innards."

"Lovely," I said. I looked down at the map.

The westernmost road followed the line of the coast, more or less, and was the most direct route. It did, however, cut right into the heart of the bog. There would be at least four days journey through. The central road skirted the bog fairly often, cutting through only when absolutely necessary. The eastern road gave the bog a wide berth, but took any traveller hoping to go south well out of their way. I sighed.

"What do you think, Hessa?" I asked.

Hessa raised an eyebrow and observed me with her overly large eyes. She said nothing.

"Are you afraid of the monsters of the bog?" I asked.

"There are monsters everywhere," Hessa replied.

"I'm beginning to notice," I remarked wryly. I rubbed the side of my face as I stared down at the map and thought.

Time was of the essence, immediately ruling out the easternmost road, however appealing it might seem. The Western road would take us to the cave faster than the central road, but it cut deep into the bog. The warning of terrible creatures in that bog chilled me. They called giant, ravenous reptiles in this land 'grass dogs.' Goodness knows what actually qualified for the moniker of monster. What if they were too terrible to overcome? I, and the rangers I now commanded, would all be killed, and the quest would come to nothing.

"The central road," I said after a long, ponderous silence. "We'll take the centre road. It's the only way to manage our risks and not lose too much time."

"Prudent," Hessa noted. I could not tell from her tone whether or not she spoke in approval.

"Thanks," I answered, trying to keep my tone equally as neutral.

"I will tell the others," the ranger said. He folded his map and returned to the rangers. I watched him a moment before turning back to watching Fas graze until it became dark. That night was spent in uneasy half-sleep at the edge of the forest. My imagination concocted truly terrifying bog beasts, all of whom laughed at my incompetence before devouring me.

We had not travelled three days before the smell of wet rot assaulted our noses. I wrinkled mine as we approached the thin grey line that indicated the first section of bog.

"Ignore the flames," Hessa told me. "Ignore the mists."

"All right," I answered with a shrug.

The road, I noted, devolved into wooden planks laid across the wet ground. The planks were in poor condition, wet rot making them splinter in places. Still, it worked well enough for keeping the horses' hooves out of the bog. So long as there were planks, the horses were not likely to get stuck.

As we moved further along, swarms of tiny black flies rose up from the water and surrounded us. I lifted my tunic up and covered my mouth and nose in an effort to keep the hateful things from my lungs. They buzzed as they swarmed, biting me and my horse in what felt like a black cloud of angry needles. Looking behind, I could see the rangers were just as miserable as I, but not one uttered a complaint.

We travelled along the boards until Fas stepped onto solid ground.

The swarm did not let up, even though the terrain had improved. Everything still smelled of rot. The smell did not abate as the bog slipped slowly from sight, returning on the horizon again some hours later. Once again we found ourselves guiding our horse carefully along rotten planks. New swarms of flies joined the first, stinging our skins with their nasty bites until every exposed part was one enormous red welt.

For several more hours we walked along the planks until the fen receded from sight once more.

"The shadows are getting long," Hessa noted.

No one had spoken all day. Her voice distracted me from my misery for a moment. "Yes," I agreed. "I suppose we ought to set up camp soon."

"I would agree," Hessa said. "Preferably on solid ground."

"And as far away from those bloody insects as possible!" a ranger added.

I grinned. "Here?" I asked.

"Here is as good as anywhere," Hessa answered with a shrug. I called the rangers to a halt, and they gratefully slid out of their saddles and began to set up camp.

"I'm one giant welt," I muttered. "Damned bog."

"Fortunate, then, that the bog provides a cure for the ills of its inhabitants," Hessa said with a smile. I turned to her.

"Sorry?"

"Mallow," Hessa replied. "There is plenty of it, as they favour wet, marshy places. Tell everyone not to scratch and I'll have a salve for you soon."

I blinked stupidly as Hessa turned and walked through the tall grasses, stopping to harvest the leaves, stems and the large, white, fluffy-looking flowers of a plant I could only assume was mallow. When she had gathered a considerable amount, she returned to the camp and dumped it all into one of the pots.

"I was going to use that," a ranger complained. Hessa merely rolled her eyes at him, poured a little water into the pot and started pounding the plant parts to pulp. She worked diligently as the rangers prepared a fire and the evening meal.

Before long, the pot filled with goo. "Come," she commanded me. Curious, I did as she bid and she dipped her hand in the goo. It looked revolting; a mush of green snot. Still I permitted her to rub it on my arm. The effect was instantaneous. The burning itch of my bites immediately dulled.

I blinked stupidly again. "Wow!" I said, eagerly turning so she could smother my other arm in the sticky salve.

"I told you," Hessa said.

She finished with my arm and began to apply it to herself. I helped myself to more of the salve and covered my stinging face.

"What are you doing?" a ranger asked.

"Mallow," I replied. "Apparently."

"Oh!" another ranger said, brightening. "My grandmother taught me about that! I'm an idiot for forgetting. Can I have some?"

"I've made enough for everyone," Hessa replied.

The ranger rose from the fire and ran to the pot of salve, attracting the attention of others. Before long, everyone was covered in sticky goo, sitting by the fire, happily munching on marsh hens.

For twelve more days we travelled without incident, clearing the bog on the evening of the twelfth day. We rode on until we were well clear before setting up camp.

"We are about two weeks from the cave," a ranger informed me that evening. "We must give some thought on our approach."

I nodded.

"The way I see it," the ranger said slowly. "We have three options, we could storm the place. Pirates typically have the majority of their force out at sea. It's the right season for it. Perhaps we can surprise them out of a fight. Or, we could sneak in. There are a fair number of us, and sneaking is going to be difficult with so many. And there is no guarantee that we won't be detected. Our third option is to draw them out of the cave - create a diversion, and have just one or two people go in and steal the sceptre piece. Of course the problem with that is not knowing the layout of the cave. The chance of getting lost, or captured, or killed are high. What do you want to do?"

I scowled in thought a moment. "A diversion, I think," I said. I looked up to find both the ranger and Hessa nodding sagely. Everyone agreed, it seemed.

"I am quiet," Hessa said. "And have a knack for picking locks. I will go into the cave."

"Not without one of us you're not," the ranger growled darkly.

"Calm down," I murmured. "I'll go as well."

The ranger frowned at me.

"I can't send you, you'll start a damned argument and get caught," I said. Hessa laughed softly at this and the ranger, fighting a smile, shrugged.

"Fine," he said. "But I'll be saying 'I told you so' before this mission is over."

I shrugged.

The discussion over for the night, everyone turned their attention to finding a place to sleep. Sleeping out of doors was getting easier for me. In fact, I had begun to think that it was preferable. Tonight, despite the ever-present fear of the Seeker's Son haunting us, I could not help but feel content to lie on the soft grass and stare up at the stars blinking in the dark blue sky.

The following morning, and every morning for sixteen days after, I rolled onto my feet, saddled my horse and commenced the long trek to the cave. On the way, we passed the grass-covered foundations of what used to be a small village. One sturdy stone door frame remained standing, though the lintel has long ago cracked in half and tumbled down.

"This was once a farming village," a ranger whispered sadly. "In the days before the empire. The Mage King destroyed it in his quest for domination. They weren't soldiers, just farmers; simple folk. They'd have kept on farming no matter who wore the crown. I wonder what they were like."

I stared at the stone door frame and, for a brief moment, I fancied I spied a round stone house with a roof of grass upon which grazed contented goats. Inside, a red-headed woman stirred a pot over the central hearth while a dark haired man dressed himself beside the large bed. The image faded as quickly as it came and I was left infected by the same wistful melancholy as the ranger who spoke.

"We'll never know, I suppose," I said. Sighing, I turned my head back to the road. I noticed Hessa staring at me from atop her stag and so offered her a small smile. She frowned.

On the thirteenth day, I smelled the briny breath of the ocean. Looking west, I could occasionally see the first shimmering glints of salt water.

"I've always loved the sea," Hessa said almost to herself.

On the fifteenth day, the ranger who was serving as our guide pointed to a grey smudge that sprawled like a demented spider on the side of the white limestone cliffs and across a good stretch of beach. "That is the fisher's village," he said. "I'm sure the Red Band have ears and eyes there, so it's best if we avoid it altogether. The cave is a day southeast of here."

"Brilliant," I replied. "In that case, why don't we get off the road and head west for a time. We'll start south again in the morning."

With no one objecting, I led the group away from the road and we rode until dusk. Camp that night was quiet, with everyone munching on leftover cold meats and dried fruits. This close to the village, and to the cave, we were not keen to invite trouble by starting a fire.

In the morning, I decided that Hessa and I would split from the group and head southwest until we hit the coast. We would follow it south until we hit the cave. The rangers, in the meantime would head directly south, and call a challenge to the Red Band.

The plan set, I saddled Fas and mounted. I extended my hand to help Hessa, but she declined the aid and simply leapt onto Fas' back as if she weighed nothing more than a feather. I turned the horse and, with my heart in my mouth, we made our way south.

Not a word was spoken during the uneventful ride. Fas, feeling my nerves, kept her pace smart, and we reached the coast a little after midday. North east of us, we could see the smoke rising from the chimneys of the smoking houses in the fishing village. I turned Fas south and searched for a way down from the top of the cliffs to the sandy beach below.

"There," Hessa said suddenly, pointing. I saw the large slope of grass to the bay first, then the entrance to the cave second. It faced out to sea and was only visible because waves and winds had worn the bottom of the jutting cliff away, making it look a little like a large, yawing mouth trying to swallow the incoming tide. A lone sentry sat on a stool outside of the cave, a fishing rod in his hands. I backed Fas up slowly until the bay was no longer in sight and dismounted. Hessa jumped down from her seat.

"Fas," I said. "I need you to stay here."

"She'll stay," Hessa said quietly.

I nodded and crouching down, I ran up to the edge of the cliff and lay flat, peering across the beach.

"We'll be seen if we try and go around," I said. "We'll be seen if we go across the beach. Ideas?"

"We could swim," Hessa replied. "If there are no sharks in the water."

I looked at her. "Are there sharks in the water?"

Hessa shrugged. "The rangers will not make their move until nightfall. We'll have darkness to cover us. I say we go across the beach when the pirates have been drawn out. It's the fastest."

"All right."

We both lay on our stomachs and watched carefully as night fell. The sentry did not bother to light a fire as the sun slipped behind the horizon. When the sky was dark save for the last of the flame-coloured vestiges of the vanished sun, the sound of a ranger's horn shattered the peace.

"On behalf of the empress," a ranger bellowed into the dark. "We are come to visit justice upon you. Stand, you foul thieves, and face the law!"

"Oh, that's rich," I murmured.

I eagerly watched as the sentry on the stool dropped his fishing rod and stood. He turned and walked stiffly along the side of the cliff and up the slope. There he stopped, reached for his own horn, and sounded it twice.

At first nothing happened. I realised I had been holding my breath so I exhaled slowly. I drew in a sharp gasp as the cave began to empty. In the gloom, I could not make out the individual features of the pirates as they moved. All I could see were figures scurrying out of the cave. The Red Band moved quickly, if a little jerkily. Some climbed the cliff like so many ants, others ran up the side of the cliff to join the sentry. All told, some fifty pirates now stood atop the cliff, facing the rangers.

"Let's go," I whispered.

I followed Hessa a little way along the cliff towards the slope and jumped down once the height proved safe enough for even my clumsy landing. We sprinted across the fine sand - no small feat - passed the sentry's stool and into the cave.

The cave was accessed by a long tunnel. Once the white, chalky limestone gave way, Hessa and I found ourselves walking on grey stones, each stone perfectly hexagonal and fitted together as if by some design other than nature. Once my eyes adjusted to the dim light, I marvelled at it.

The tunnel eventually opened into a massive cavern, filled mostly with sea water save for a few large islands upon which sat mounds of chests, coins, silks and other treasures. The piece of sceptre was recognisable immediately. It sat upon the ornately carved throne on the island at the very back of the cavern; the seat of the pirate king. The elaborately carved wood was pale, almost grey, and affixed to the unbroken end was a beautiful rose gold hand, the fingers of which were clenched into a fist, as if that hand was preparing to pound down on some hapless victim.

I touched Hessa's shoulder, and she nodded. She had seen it too. I walked forward, careful to keep quiet. The islands were all connected by little bridges, some natural and some artificial, each connection leading closer to the throne. At the first island, I stopped dead. A pirate in rags was sitting unmoving against a chest, his chin on his chest. He did not appear to be breathing. I poked him. My finger slid through dry, crumbling skin to touch bone. Startled, I leapt back, staring at the finger-sized hole now in the man's arm.

"Dead," I whispered to Hessa. "Dead a while, too."

"There's more," Hessa noted, pointing to another island where three more bodies lay propped up against their hoarded treasure.

"I don't like this," I muttered. "You go right, I'll go straight up the middle. First one to the sceptre wins a prize."

Hessa grinned at me, turned and scurried to the farthest island on the right. I straightened and walked boldly forward, crossing bridges in the most direct path to the sceptre. A whispering hiss greeted my ears as I stepped onto the central island. I heard Hessa swear and turned my head to see her duck out of sight. I turned back the other way.

All the dead pirates were now standing, their empty eye sockets trained on me. I turned. They were behind me as well. I looked towards the sceptre, then around at the cavern. There were three tunnels leading deeper into the cave in the western wall, but the only exit, now behind me, was blocked by the standing skeletons with paper skins. I looked back at Hessa, whom I could only see because I knew where to look. The tuatha elder, apparently, was quite good at being unseen. I realised suddenly that the undead pirates had not yet spotted her.

Very slowly in the hopes that it would not elicit a response from the undead before me, I removed my staff from my back. I'd had this weapon longer than my sword, and thanks to the sharp tongue of the rangers' blacksmith, I did not think a sword would be much use to me now.

What are you doing? Hessa demanded. At least, I was fairly certain that the voice inside my head was Hessa.

We've got to get that sceptre piece. I thought the words with as much ferocity as I could muster.

Are you insane? We're completely outnumbered!

Would you rather return without it?

The voice in my head fell silent a moment. *Damn it!* she hissed. *Fine. Let's do this, then.*

I nodded once, very slowly. Trusting that Hessa would not let me fall without aid, I leapt into action. Charging forward, I swung my staff with surprising expertise. Fear and purpose drove my movements, making them faster and more accurate than I thought possible.

We were facing a cave full of undead pirates, however. There were at least thirty of them, and only two of us. Behind me, I could hear Hessa fighting. She was far more agile than I could ever be, and was faring better in her fight. I chanced a glance in her direction to find that I could not see her in the press of desiccated bodies.

The pirates fought in eerie silence. The only sounds I could hear were the clash of weapons, my own breathing and Hessa's grunts as she fought. I hollered at the top of my lungs just to create some sort of sound.

Over the top of my shout, I heard the faint sound of a horn. Two blasts. The rangers had called a retreat.

"They're leaving!" Hessa shouted.

Swearing under my breath, I pushed harder, managing to knock several pirates off my island into the water. This cleared a path across the bridge to the next island, where yet more pirates awaited. With nothing else available to me, I charged forward and clashed with the new set of mummified pirates.

Thankful for such a long range weapon, I twirled my staff, keeping the walking corpses and their swords well away from striking distance. Even so, they simply could not be killed. Even the ones I had decapitated stumbled blindly around, swinging their weapons wildly. In a desperate lunge, I held my staff across my chest and bolted forward, knocking down another line of pirates. In the space now cleared, I saw the sceptre piece, sitting placidly on the throne. It was just one more island away.

Throwing caution to the wind, I tucked my staff beneath one arm and, ducking the incoming blows, sprinted for the bridge. Somehow I made it. I could hardly believe my luck as I darted across the bridge to the island at the far back of the cavern. I stretched out my hand eagerly and clasped the smooth carved white wood of the sceptre piece.

"I have it!" I shouted triumphantly, holding the piece above my head and grinning as I turned. The grin slid from my face in an instant.

Chapter Ten

The cave was full of corpses, some dripping wet having crawled back up from the water, the rest dry and papery. Many no longer had heads, but they stood facing me nonetheless. They were no longer fighting. They were simply standing, staring at me with eyeless gazes. I could see no sign of Hessa.

"You're going to want to put that down, Stranger," a harsh, masculine voice said from somewhere near the mouth of the cave.

I slowly lowered my arm as I scanned the back of the cave. An arrow whistled through the air and landed with thunk in the tall back of the throne before which I stood.

"I said, put that back," the voice commanded.

"Who are you?" I demanded in return. "Show yourself."

The corpses moved, making a dry hissing noise as they did so. A path cleared and I spied a small group of men and women dressed in matching red leather armour. One man, tall and extremely muscular, stood at the fore of the group. Half a step behind him stood a woman, shorter, but almost as muscular. She held a bow, the arrow knocked and aimed directly for me.

The man grinned at me. His teeth had, the smile revealed, been filed into sharp points. "Hello," he said in a friendly manner. It made my skin crawl.

"Where's Hessa?" I demanded. Though I was terrified, my voice sounded strong and bold. It surprised me.

The man waved his hand vaguely, and the undead pirates moved again. This time, they exposed Hessa's body. She lay on the ground, a small pool of blood forming beneath her. My eyes widened.

"She's alive," the man said. "For now. Now, put down my sparkly. And your weapon."

I tore my eyes away from Hessa and narrowed them at the man.

"Or else?" I asked.

"Or else my puppets here will rend you limb from limb. You and your pretty companion, there." The man pointed at Hessa's still form. "I'm going to gut you, clean you out, stitch you back together, and make me another couple of puppets."

My eyes widened again. "You did this? You're a necromancer?"

The man folded his thick arms in front of his chest and laughed a hearty laugh. "Obviously," he said. "What's the matter?" he asked as I stared at him in disbelief. "You were expecting dark robes and pale skin, no doubt? Greasy black hair, perhaps?"

"Yes, actually," I admitted.

The Necromancer laughed again. It was the sort of laugh I might have expected coming from a jolly inn keeper, or perhaps a baker. But a necromancer and pirate?

"Maybe I'll let you keep your brain," he said after his booming laugh. "A puppet with a brain. The thought amuses me. Now, put down my treasure, lay down your weapon, and I might just spare you and your pretty friend with the big eyes."

"Maybe we should talk about this," I said hopefully.

The pirate necromancer blinked. He roared another hearty laugh, laughing so hard his face turned pink. The woman holding the bow glanced at him briefly.

"What on earth could you possibly say to change my mind?"

I shrugged, scanning my brain furiously in search of something, anything I could say that might make this pirate sympathetic to our cause.

"You have more treasure here than you can possibly spend in one lifetime," I said. "What do you care about a broken piece of ancient wood?"

The necromancer grinned. "I think the question is, what do *you* care?"

"Pardon?"

"Look around, Stranger," the pirate said, extending his arms. "This cave is full of precious things, many of which would let you retire with a hundred slaves and more. All you had to do was stretch your hand into the cave, grab the nearest sparkly and run away. But no. You aren't just some very daring thieves. You were after that piece of ancient wood specifically. So, I ask again, why do you care?"

I took a deep breath in. "We need this piece of sceptre so we can save the world," I said hurriedly, squishing all the words together so they came out in one long, unbroken string of sound.

The pirate necromancer cocked his head, grinning. "Too bad, so sad. Put it back."

"Oh, come on!" I said, more irritated now than afraid. "The world will end! There'll be nothing left for you to plunder, if you're not all killed."

"Here's the thing, Stranger," the pirate said, not losing his vicious grin. "Being a necromancer and all, I'm not afraid of death. Everything dies. Everything ends. I'm not afraid of that fate. And, frankly, I'm pretty sure we can make it through whatever imminent disaster is waiting on the horizon. We've done it before."

"You can't sell it," I said. "It's just going to sit here, collecting dust."

"Yeah, but I like looking at it."

"A deal, then. I'll get you something of equal value."

"You just said that this piece of sparkly would save the world. There is nothing of equal value."

I realised with a sinking heart that there was nothing I could possibly say that would make this pirate necromancer give a damn about the impending collapse of the world. What would a pirate care of the return of a wicked king? He was wicked himself. For all I knew, they may just end up best friends and sit down to lunch every other Thursday.

"Please," I tried at last.

The necromancer pretended to think about it. "No."

Sighing, I turned and placed the piece of sceptre back on the throne.

"Wise," the necromancer said. The woman holding the bow lowered it, unknocking the arrow and sliding it back into the quiver at her side. Others of the Red Band moved forward. They took me roughly by the shoulders and marched me to the central island, where no treasure mound sat. The papery undead shuffled back to their original positions and sat back down, leaning against the various mounts of precious objects and falling still.

I was forced to sit down on the sandy island. Some of the Red Band dragged Hessa over and tossed her unceremoniously at my side. She groaned.

"Are you all right?" I whispered to her as her eyes fluttered open.

"Stabbed," she whispered in return. "But not lethal. Unless I bleed to death."

"Oh." I sat in silence a moment, then said, "I'm sorry."

Hessa smiled. "You should be."

I watched as the pirates set up a small fire. Using a golden cauldron from one of the piles of treasure, they started to boil sea water. As it began to steam, they threw in chunks of freshly cut meat. All the while, the necromancer rested on the ground and watched me with an unnerving gaze.

"Why don't you care?" I asked him at last.

"Why should I?" he asked in return.

I shrugged and sullenly turned to watch the dinner preparations. The necromancer simply watched me.

"He's trying to decide if he wants to make you into a puppet," the muscular woman informed me, grinning her sharp-toothed grin. "Do you know how he does it?"

I shook my head.

"Of course you don't. No one does. But I do know some things." She turned to me and withdrew a small dagger from her belt. She placed the dagger at my navel. "First," she said. "He cuts you open and spills your innards. If he's feeling nice, you'll be dead first." The woman licked her lips. "That's my favourite part. Watching guts empty. We catch it all in a bowl and make a stew. Delicious."

My stomached turned at the thought of eating human entrail stew, but the woman was not finished.

"He cuts out your heart. And he eats it. Right there and then. The last time, the poor bastard was still alive. He watched his heart get eaten." The woman frowned. "I wish I could eat a heart. But no one else is allowed to. It's part of the magic."

"Please shut up," I moaned.

The woman laughed, but moved away to help with the rest of the dinner preparations. I glanced at the necromancer. He grinned wildly, still watching me. Shuddering, I turned away and stared instead at the sceptre piece. In the deepening dark of the cave, it seemed to me that the sceptre glowed slightly. I scowled.

"We have to get that sceptre," Hessa whispered from the ground.

"How, exactly?" I asked. "We've lost the rangers. You are completely incapacitated. And we're surrounded by walking, fighting mummified corpses and their really creepy creator."

Hessa did not answer. I looked down to find her unconscious.

"Great," I muttered. I stared at the sceptre piece and mulled over my options.

Sitting in sullen silence, my eyes flickered between the sceptre on the throne, the pirate necromancer and Hessa's unconscious form. There was no way out of this mess I had gotten myself into, as far as I could tell. All I could do was sit and wait. Perhaps the rangers were regrouping. Perhaps they were on their way to attempt a rescue.

Or perhaps not. I had no way of knowing.

I sighed and closed my eyes.

The sound of rushing water woke me. I sat up and looked around with wide eyes as I tried to get my bearings. I silently chastised myself for falling asleep in such company. Who knows what these people could have done to me while I slept?

I looked down at my chest, slapping my hand against it and feeling around just to ensure a hole had not been carved there. With relief, I found no hole. I still had my heart; a heart which was, as of right now, racing.

The sound of rushing water grew louder, waking up the necromancer. He sat up and looked around himself with a frown. Our eyes met.

"Are you making that noise?" the pirate demanded.

"Seeker's Son," Hessa murmured from the ground. She spoke so quietly that only I could hear her. I looked down. She returned my terrified gaze with a small smile.

A chance, she said in my head. *A chance for the sceptre.*

You cannot be serious! I thought back furiously. *It's a Seeker's Son!*

A diversion. Not ideal, but a diversion.

I swallowed and nodded. Turning back to the necromancer pirate, I said, "That is the sound of an approaching Seeker's Son."

The necromancer raised his brows and laughed. "I like your humour, Stranger!"

The rushing water grew louder, and in the hiss and gurgle of the noise, a shrill shriek could be heard. I smiled, though I was terrified.

"Sure," I said. "Humour. Except that my ranger friends and I ran into one on our way here. Hessa and her people managed to vanquish it, but it's not a permanent fix. The spectre is back."

Again, the necromancer laughed. His laugh was cut short by a shriek at the entrance of the cave. I turned my gaze to find the Seeker's Son hovering at the entrance, slipping sideways, back and forth, nothing more than a tattered black hooded cloak hiding the sickly piece of soul which gave it shape.

"Death's giant steel balls," the necromancer breathed.

The soft dry whisper of a thousand animated corpses alerted me to the fact that the Red Band's undead army had awoken, ready to defend their disgusting creator.

"Told you," I said in a soft sing-song.

The necromancer said nothing. He stared incredulously at the Seeker's Son as it hovered at the entrance to the cave, the strange spectral river it carried with it rushing in a loop around the edges of the cloak. With a chilling shriek, the Seeker's Son rushed forward, drawing a translucent grey-blue blade. The undead rushed forward to meet it in a silent wave. The Red Band joined the fight, loosing their arrows. But mortal weapons had no effect on the shade. The arrows passed through with nothing more than a puff of spectral smoke to show for it.

A small blue glow drew my eyes to Hessa. She lay on the ground, encircled by a blue orb - protection against the Seeker's Son. Looking around, I saw that the Red Band was now fully engaged with the fraction of the evil king's soul, so I started slowly moving backwards towards the throne, my eyes fixed on the fight.

The blade of the Seeker's Son did what my own weapon could not. Every strike of the blade wounded the undead pirates as if they were very much alive and it was a real blade. Decapitated mummies collapsed, their dry, brittle bodies becoming dust as they hit the ground. Any limbs that were hewed off remained still without even so much as a twitch. The Seeker's Son proved horrifically efficient at dispatching the undead. It carved a steady path; right for me. Realising that I had no time for stealth, I turned and sprinted for the back island. I stretched out my eager hand and grabbed the sceptre piece.

Someone grabbed my elbow and spun me around.

"Keep your thieving fingers off my sparkly!" the necromancer hissed, raising his blade to strike me.

I could see behind him the Seeker's Son break through the line and rush right towards me, completely ignoring Hessa as it moved past. I did the only thing I could. I swung out with my free hand, striking the necromancer on the cheek with the metal end of the sceptre. The necromancer grunted, releasing me. Seizing the opportunity, I kicked the man full in the chest, sending him reeling backwards, right into the Seeker's Son.

The Seeker's Son stopped its rush, the wispy folds of cloak wrapping tightly around the necromancer. He screamed. I could smell burning flesh as the Seeker's Son started to burn away the body to get at the soul.

Moved out of my shock by the only woman in the Red Band screaming for her commander, I dove into the shallow pool of seawater and swam to the central island. In the rush to free their leader, the Red Band ignored me completely as I dragged myself out of the water and ran to Hessa.

"Come on," I said, helping her to her feet. The faint blue glow that protected Hessa enlarged, encompassing both of us.

Helping Hessa, I ran as fast as I could from the cave and onto the beach. Blinking in surprise, I found Fas and Hessa's stag waiting for us. I helped Hessa onto the stag and jumped on Fas. I need not have directed my horse. She knew what I wanted. She turned and bolted, fleeing from the cave, where the necromancer still screamed, as fast as possible. A few minutes into our run, we came across the rangers.

"What the...?" a ranger asked, pulling his horse to a stop. "We were on our way to get you."

"Appreciated," I said. "Hessa's hurt. The Seeker's Son is back."

The ranger paled.

"I have the sceptre piece."

The ranger blinked as I lifted the surprisingly heavy treasure. "How did you manage...? Never mind. We need to get that back to our headquarters."

"We need to get Hessa some help," I countered.

In the brief, tense silence that followed, I could hear the distant sounds of rushing water. I swore. "The Seeker's Son is coming," I said. "We're going to the forest. Now."

Not waiting for the ranger to respond, I turned Fas and kicked her flanks. She bolted forward again, Hessa's stag following immediately. I heard a ranger swear, but the thunder of hooves told me that they were following. I smiled grimly.

Fas, sturdy and sure though she was, was not the fastest horse of the herd. I was soon overtaken, first by Hessa's stag, then by the other rangers. Fas snorted in irritation and tried to run faster.

"It's all right, girl," I told her. "Just keep going."

Fas snorted again, flicking an ear back.

The rushing water that heralded the Seeker's Son continued to sound in my ears, growing neither louder nor softer. Around me, the rangers checked their horses, keen not to lose me, and the sceptre piece, to the spectre chasing us.

It took a little over a week of hard riding to get to the bog. We were all tired, the horses were tired, and Hessa's condition had not improved. The riding wreaked havoc on her wounds.

"Are you certain about this?" a ranger yelled at me as the slick, sulphurous waters of the bog came into view.

"No choice," I yelled back. "We need to get to safety. This is the fastest road."

"There are monsters in there!"

"Maybe there are and maybe there aren't," I shouted. "But there is definitely one behind us."

"Well," the ranger replied with a crazed, crooked grin. "Here goes!"

The group funnelled onto the narrow path that marked the only way through the marsh. There was only enough room on the path for two horses abreast, and, in some places, only one at a time. I chaffed at the slower pace, but it could not be helped. To stray from the path would be to trap the horses, and probably ourselves, not to mention wake whatever sleeping beasts used the water for cover. Besides, Fas was tiring. I could feel it in her stride, though she tried hard to keep her pace.

"Whoa," I said gently. "Whoa." I slowed Fas down to a trot. She snorted.

The rangers followed suit knowing full well that running a horse to death would not do them any good. I noted, with a start, that the rushing water of the Seeker's Son seemed to have quietened some. I glanced behind and saw nothing.

Facing forward, I watched Hessa with concern as she sat on her stag, doubled over in pain. Swarms of black flies buzzed around me, biting down on me and my mount with frenzied bloodlust. I was far too tired to do much about it.

"If we continue to push, we should be through the bog in a week," a ranger told me.

"That is good," I replied, yawning. "Please tell me we're going to make camp soon?"

"Make camp? Where do you suggest we do that? There isn't any space large enough for a camp. Just this trail through the bog. You'll have to sleep in your saddle."

"What about the horses?"

The ranger smiled grimly. "We'll take turns to nap. They'll plod on. It'll save us some time, too."

"They will drop dead of exhaustion."

"Not our horses, Stranger," the ranger said proudly. "They're a special breed."

"That I don't doubt, but they aren't magical. Nothing can run on no sleep for an entire week."

The ranger grinned. "They know a good long rest and plenty of apples await them after this. They'll be fine."

I barely heard the ranger. I was so tired from the frenzied flight away from the Seeker's Son that I started nodding off in my saddle, jerking awake every time I felt myself start to list one way or another in my seat. Fas plodded on, somehow able to walk and doze at the same time.

The horses ate as they walked, grabbing at the long grasses and stunted shrubs that have made the bog their home. Every so often, the horses pushed into a gallop, but each time the run grew shorter and shorter, and longer and longer breaks were required in between.

I was so tired, it took me three days to realise that I no longer heard the Seeker's Son. Perhaps the smell of rot that enveloped the marsh had somehow hidden our scent. Perhaps the spectre feared the bog as much as the rangers did. Perhaps it guessed our plan and skirted the bog altogether, to await us on the other side. I had no idea where the soul-eater went or why.

What I could hear, however, was the squelch and squish of something moving through the foul water, occasionally accompanied by a low growl. Whatever it was, I was sure it was tracking us. I swivelled my head around, searching for any sign of the kind of creature it might be.

"You hear it too, huh?" a ranger asked in a low voice.

"Yes," I whispered back. Now fully alert, I noticed that the rangers had their weapons drawn.

"It's been tracking us for three days now. It sounds big. If we're lucky, it won't attack."

"There it is," another ranger said in a harsh whisper. I looked at him, then where he pointed. Hidden in the marsh grass was a creature that looked something like a grass dog, only with a longer snout and three very large tusks on either side of the jaw. Its long, thick tail ended with five barbed spikes.

"What the hell is that?" I demanded.

"We call them water hogs," the ranger replied. "She's big."

"She?"

"Only the females have tusks."

"Oh."

The rangers watched the water hog warily as they moved along the track. Their arrows were trained on the beast, and it knew it. I was certain that the only reason it had not attacked yet was because it understood that its prey was fully armed. Its yellow eyes moved often to Hessa, who struggled to stay on her mount.

"Don't even think about it," I told the beast quietly.

The beast must have heard me, because its baleful gaze shifted to me. I stared at it, unflinching as Fas nervously walked on.

That was the first and only brush with the bog monsters we had on our journey through the marsh. The water hog never attacked, dissuaded perhaps by the bristling arrows of the rangers. More likely, it was the approaching tuatha that ensured it slunk away instead of charging forward. They met our group on the sixth day.

Hessa, upon seeing her kin, permitted herself to fall at long last. Her husband caught her before she tipped off her stag entirely. He dragged her onto his mount. In silence, our number bolstered, the entire group made its way back to the forest of the tuatha.

We stayed a week in the care of the strange, slender people of the woods. Martel, I was informed, returned to the headquarters a week ago. He made it safely, I was assured, as he was accompanied by a guard of tuatha, who were determined to see their word was honoured.

Fas and the rest of the rangers' horses were returned to the clearing where they were kept last time. Many of them sank to their sides and spent the first day like that, moving only to eat. It was a rest all of us, man and horse, desperately needed. I passed the week sleeping and relaying our adventures to the tuatha. Hessa, I learnt after some inquiry, was slowly recovering. The flight from the Seeker's Son through the marsh had given her an infection, and it had poisoned her blood. But with rest and the care of her husband, she would recover.

I never had the chance to thank her before we left. She was rarely awake.

Chapter Eleven

The journey back to the rangers' hideout was taken at a leisurely pace. None of us were in a hurry to return to previous levels of exhaustion. The journey, fortunately, passed without incident. Martel greeted us at the entrance. He still looked pale, and had lost much of his mass during his long illness, but appeared otherwise strong and in good spirits.

"I was beginning to think I'd never see you again," he said, taking my hand.

I grinned and drew out the sceptre piece. "To be honest," I said, handing it over. "I wasn't sure we'd make it, either."

Martel hesitantly took the sceptre piece. He examined it in the late afternoon light. "I can't believe it," he said. "It's in amazing condition."

"The Red Band seemed particularly attached to it."

"Come inside. Dinner has been prepared."

We entered the cave. Upon stepping into the large dining hall, I found myself ploughed into and embraced roughly. It took me a moment to realise who had tackled me.

"Basadia!"

"I thought you were dead," Basadia whispered.

I laughed and hugged her closely. "I did not expect to see you out here."

Basadia released me and smiled shyly. "I promised the ranger that I would behave myself if he would let me make sure you were safe."

"It was a compromise," Martel said. "She wanted to go after you."

I smiled at Basadia. "I appreciate the thought. Come on, let's eat!"

We dined that evening with Martel.

"I know you have just returned," Martel said over the steaming bowl of stew. I was certain I had never tasted such magnificent food as this. Travelling food can be quite tasteless. "But we must turn our minds to what to do next."

I raised an eyebrow. "What do you mean?"

Well," Martel replied. "You have helped us immensely by acquiring the sceptre piece. I understand it very nearly cost you your life. I have no wish to involve you any further if you are not willing to die for the cause. You may take your companion and leave, if you wish. Or you can help us acquire the other pieces of the sceptre."

"You know where both remaining pieces are?"

"Not for certain. That said, it's looking more likely that the chieftain in the north we mentioned earlier does have a piece of the sceptre. And, of course, there is that piece guarded by the grass dogs in the east."

I grunted, mulling it over.

"I'm not very keen on another fight," I admitted. "We should go north, I suppose. Perhaps the chieftain can be reasoned with. Grass dogs are not very good with the whole negotiation thing."

Martel's mouth quirked and he nodded. "Very well," he said. "I'll come with you."

"Are you sure? You still look pale."

"I can manage," Martel replied with a grunt. "I'm almost back to normal."

I nodded, feeling that to enquire again would bruise the ranger's ego.

"Martel may have the blood of a nobleman, but he fights like a rogue," Basadia said with a small smile. Martel grinned and returned to his food. I looked questioningly at Basadia.

"We've trained a little together," she explained. "I was anxious and restless. It was good to keep my mind off you."

Martel grunted. "She might have tried to escape otherwise."

"I was crawling from my own skin," Basadia added.

I looked between the two a moment. "Does that mean you've decided to help the rangers?" I asked Basadia.

Basadia pondered for a while. "I... I do not know," she said at length. "I cannot return to the Black Blades a failure... I... I need to think on it more."

I nodded. "It's all right. I understand."

"North, then," Martel said, changing the subject. "We'll rest a week before heading out."

That is precisely what we did. It surprised me just how much sleep I still needed, despite my leisurely return from the woods of the tuatha. I spent the majority of my days asleep, returning to my bed whenever I was not eating or training. Basadia, having been released from her cell, shared my room. While I slept, she spent her time with Martel or the other rangers, training and talking.

I had, on one occasion petitioned Martel to let Basadia come with us, but Martel very firmly refused. He was concerned that she might be planning something untoward and that, though he would not lock her in a cell again, while we were away north, she would be locked in our room. She would be comfortable, but still a prisoner.

Knowing that Martel was about as stubborn as they came, I decided not to bring it up again... this mission.

The week flew by, and before I cared to be, I found myself in my saddle, walking Fas beside Martel and his mount in the grey pre-dawn light.

"The northern clans are brash, stubborn and extremely proud," Martel told me. "Most of the southern lords find them uncouth and unpleasant, but, to tell you the truth, I find it refreshing. There are no false airs and graces with the people of the north."

I nodded.

"That said, they have tempers and are unpredictable. If they feel they have been insulted, they will not hesitate to lop off your head. There is a tale of one chieftain who felt the ocean had insulted him by wetting his toes during a storm. He ran into the water with his sword drawn and slashed at the waves for three days before he was drowned."

I looked at Martel sceptically. He grinned. "Of course," he admitted. "That might not be a true story, but it is one that has made the rounds more than once in the empire."

"How far north is this chieftain?" I asked on the third evening.

"It'll be another few weeks yet," Martel replied. "His is the kingdom closest to the borders of the empire. The northern part of the empire is sparsely populated, which means it is a great place for brigands and outlaws to hide." Martel smiled. "These were our wilds once. The rangers were kings here, when we were in our prime."

"Martel, sir?" a young ranger asked as he dumped an armful of wood near the fire.

"Yes?"

"Rama says his maps are entirely out of date."

Martel raised an eyebrow and turned his head. "Rama!" he barked.

A ranger with a thick scar that ran the length of his left jaw, and grey hair stood and marched smartly over. "Sir?"

"What's this I hear you complaining about?"

Rama grinned. He sat down and pulled out a map painted on oil-softened leather. Martel leant in, as did I, to get a better look.

"The information on this map dates back to the third era of the empire. See here? The hamlet of Fruu? That hamlet hasn't existed in a very long time. It was destroyed by fire during the Ground Revolt a hundred and fifty years ago. It must be a copy of an ancient map. It seems no one has bothered to update our knowledge on the northerners in a very long time. This here says that we're headed straight for Letini territory, but I remember hearing that the Dunkir clan from the Parin kingdom obliterated the entire Letini people some two hundred years ago."

"What?"

"Some dispute over who had the best cattle, apparently."

I looked up at Rama. "Sorry?"

"I only heard it in passing, but some bard at an inn I stayed at en route to becoming a ranger mentioned the tale in one of his songs. He claimed Letini heritage, you see. Anyway, the story goes that the chieftain of the Letini insulted the property of the chieftain of the Parin. The chieftain's mother's family, the Dunkir clan, took exception to that, since most of the wealth was theirs, and they attacked the Letini people in the spring. By the summer, the Letini had been thoroughly defeated. Only a few escaped the slaughter. The Dunkir clan turned around and returned home, hauling the wealth of the entire Letini people with them, leaving the survivors destitute."

I stared down at the map. The Letini territory marked there looked very large. I could not imagine one clan destroying such a vast territory in one or two seasons.

"So which kingdom is the sceptre with?" Martel asked.

"Well, if the scout who reported seeing it is to be believed, that would be the Nadube." Rama pointed at a marked section of the map. It was an extremely small territory wedged between two very large clan territories bordering the Letini territory.

"An unimpressive clan," Martel noted.

"It used to be," Rama agreed.

"Used to be?" I asked.

Rama shrugged. "This map is a little over two hundred years out of date. Who knows how things have changed up there? Besides, we don't even know if it is the Nadube, or just some chieftain that killed them all and assumed their colours."

"Fantastic," I muttered.

Martel looked at me. "What are you thinking?" he asked. I opened my mouth to speak and promptly shut it. I actually had nothing to say. The silence stretched on.

"Um..." I managed after Martel raised his brows at me. "Well..."

"Have you suddenly gone daft?" the ranger holding the map asked, looking at me strangely.

I scowled at him. Meanwhile, my mind raced.

What's the matter with you, you idiot! I thought madly to myself. *How hard can it possibly be to form sentences?*

Crap. I don't know what to do.

Well figure something out, you buffoon! For divinity's sake! Say something!

What am I supposed to say? 'I don't know?' That's not helpful.

Look, moron, just say something to buy some time while I think of something at least a little clever.

I ceased my antagonistic internal dialogue and looked at Martel. "Let's look at this logically," I said slowly. "Clearly, going home isn't an option, we need that sceptre piece or everything will be for naught."

"Yes," Martel replied. The word was spoken deliberately and measured, the tone suggesting that what Martel was actually saying was, 'This is painfully obvious. Why are you even saying it?' I cleared my throat.

"I think we all dislike the idea of walking in blind. If we can get into the territory unnoticed and spy on these northerners for a bit, we'll have a better idea of where the sceptre is, who, exactly has it, and how to approach them."

"All right," Rama agreed.

"But, if we're caught spying, it could be a diplomatic disaster," I countered.

"Not could," Martel corrected. "Would. They're proud bastards."

I nodded. "Right. And spying takes time, and we don't have a lot of it. And risking a diplomatic disaster is... uh... risky..."

The corners of Martel's mouth quirked again, threatening a smile, as he looked at me bemusedly. He and Rama exchanged a glance.

"So we could just head in bold as brass and speak our purpose to the first Chieftain we come across. If we head in the direction of the last known location of the sceptre piece, it is likelier we'll end up speaking to the chieftain who currently has it in his possession."

"That is sound reasoning," Martel agreed.

"Having no knowledge of the clan, however, or their customs and expectations, chances of an unintentional dangerous diplomatic blunder are high." I scowled. "We're damned if we do and damned if we don't, it seems."

"Which is why I asked you," Martel said. "I was hoping for some insight."

"Right."

Idiot! My mind hissed at me. *Make a decision!*

Another uncomfortable silence followed. Martel's already high eyebrows rose higher.

"So," he asked. "What is your recommendation?"

"Well," I said slowly. I paused, still trying to gather my frayed thoughts. "The risk of a diplomatic disaster happening just seems too great. And we're pressed for time. I say we head straight in the way we are going and hope for the best."

"I'm inclined to agree," Martel said. "However, I'm a little concerned about the state of your mind, so I'll take this recommendation with a grain of salt. No offence."

I shrugged, feeling not a little chastised.

"I'll need to think about it," Martel continued. "In the meantime, why don't we all eat and get some rest? You especially."

I nodded. Martel nodded in reply and everyone settled in for the evening. I found it difficult to sleep, worried that something might have actually happened to my mind. Eventually, exhaustion from travel won over my vexation, and I fell soundly to sleep.

The morning dawned brightly. I was kicked awake, forcibly roused despite the warm rays of sun burning my cheek. Ordinarily, and especially on the road, I would wake with the sun. Not this time.

"Are you all right?" Martel asked, frowning down at me, his leg raised for another kick.

"Fine," I mumbled, still half asleep. I struggled out of my bed roll and stood up, feeling groggy.

Martel nodded at me, but looked concerned.

"I'm fine," I insisted. "I couldn't get to sleep last night, is all."

"As you say," Martel responded. I got the feeling he did not believe me.

I frowned at him, but said nothing as I dressed my horse. Fas snorted and sniffed my elbow in greeting. It made me feel a little better to know that at least one member of this group of rangers did not think I had gone mad.

"We go in. No overt spying," Martel said to the group once they had finished packing away the camp. "But that doesn't mean let your guard down. Let's ride."

Fas trotted along happily during the rest of the day's ride. I, however, was less happy. Slumped in my saddle, I stared blankly ahead feeling tired, sore and sour.

"Cheer up," a ranger said brightly as he trotted past me on his mount. "S'not all that bad."

"Yeah," another ranger chimed in. "We all have bad days."

They rode off together, laughing. My mood did not improve.

"Right," Martel said quietly as the group moved past an ancient-looking standing stone. "We're now officially in tribal territory. Ride tall, and whatever you do, keep your weapons sheathed."

I straightened. The very act seemed to fortify me somewhat, and my sour mood lifted a little. The terrain here was mostly rocky. Green-grey outcrops of rock formed ancient valleys filled with green grasses. Small rivers and brooks snaked their way across the landscape in these wide valleys, glinting in the sun as we crested hill after hill. The resulting vista was stark and hauntingly savage. It took my breath away.

"We're being watched," a ranger murmured.

"Aye," Martel answered. "I know. Hand off your hilt, ranger. We're here on a diplomatic mission. Don't tell them otherwise."

"There!" another ranger said, pointing. I looked.

Standing at the top of one of the rocky crags, a man wearing only trousers and a bear pelt over one shoulder, his exposed skin tattooed in swirled designs, watched our group. He held a small, stout and undoubtedly powerful recurve bow in one hand, a quiver of arrows at his hip. Long blond hair flowed freely in the slight breeze. The man, knowing he was sighted, raised his free hand, his palm facing our group.

Martel signalled the group to a halt, moved his horse forward and returned the gesture. They both lowered their hands at the same time. For a while, nothing happened. The blond man turned, raised his fingers to his lips and issued a sharp whistle.

I watched in awe as a matched pair of ponies pulling a small chariot bolted forward, galloping unheeding over the sharp edge of the crag. I held my breath as I watched the horses freefall a brief moment, the chariot and charioteer behind. It looked as though the chariot would topple right over the top of the ponies until the blond man leapt in, bringing the back end of the chariot down. The horses galloped downhill, the chariot never once tipping or sliding.

"By all that is light and dark," a ranger whispered, clearly as in awe of the charioteer's skills as I.

The ponies slowed and stopped a few feet from Martel.

"Who are you?" the blond man demanded from the back of the chariot. I noted that his fingers hovered over his quiver. "And what are you doing here?"

"I am Martel, leader of the rangers of the empire. Please forgive our intrusion, but we come on a matter of dire urgency."

The blond man scowled. "And what are you doing here?" he demanded again.

"We are looking for something," Martel said. "An ancient artefact of the empire. A piece of the Imperial Sceptre. We would speak to your chieftain."

The man grinned viciously, his fingers still brushing the fletching of his arrows. "I am the chieftain," he declared.

"Shit," I heard Martel mutter.

"Is there one amongst your number who has trodden the Sky Road?" the chieftain demanded.

The rangers did very well not to look at me, though I could positively feel their desire to.

"Why do you want to know?" Martel countered.

"Curiosity," the chieftain replied. I could tell by his tone that there was more to it than that.

I chewed my lip.

There was a moment of uncomfortable silence as Martel watched the chieftain. I knew Martel was considering whether or not to reveal who I was to this chieftain, and also trying to understand why the chieftain would want to know.

Deciding I would save Martel the trouble, I hesitantly, haltingly raised one hand and waved it slightly.

"That would be me," I said. My voice sounded bizarrely clear to my own ears, considering just how frightened of the intimidatingly broad, muscular man in the back of the chariot I was.

The chieftain looked at me, his grin broadening. Martel turned in his saddle and glared. I shrugged at him apologetically.

"I thought it might be you," the chieftain said with an affirming nod. "You do not look like a ranger."

I looked down at myself. I was wearing the ranger uniform.

"You are not very good in your saddle."

Never having fallen off my horse, all I could do was frown at the chieftain in confusion.

"And you do not look accustomed to hard travel."

My frown vanished. That much must have been true. No doubt my troubled sleep and my sour mood had done nothing for my appearance.

"And you do not wear your sword correctly."

"Can we stop picking out my faults, now?" I snapped. I immediately clamped my mouth shut as Martel again turned in his saddle to glare at me. It was rude, and I knew it.

The chieftain, however, found the whole thing exceptionally funny. He laughed hard, his shoulders shaking. I stared at him bemusedly, wondering what could possibly have caught his humour so.

"I like you," the chieftain said as soon as he was able to control his mirth. "I do not like your empire."

"It's not my empire," I replied. "In my defence."

"No? Then why are you fighting for it?"

I opened my mouth to reply and shut it again. Why was I fighting for a land that I truly knew nothing about?

"They asked for help," I answered; a rather lame response.

"I see," the chieftain said, his expression becoming serious, though the twinkle in his grey eyes and his smirk never left. "And so you are helping them merely because they asked? Do you know the history of the people you are aiding, Sky Road Walker?"

"Bits and pieces," I replied.

"Well, perhaps you should come with me, and I will explain more."

Martel shook his head. "We do not have time for history lessons," he said. "Please, the sceptre piece is important. Evil things are happening and we need it to stop them."

"The empire is evil," the chieftain replied, losing all humour in an instant. His grey eyes flashed like steel. "And you, you claim to be rangers, and you wear their garb, but I know the rangers have been disbanded. So who are you truly and what is it you truly seek?"

Martel sighed and rubbed his cheek. "We are the rangers of the empire," he answered. "Or what's left of them. Of the twenty watches, only one remains, and only because we were and are too far into the wilds for the powers to care about. What is one watch to their armies, in any case? As it happens, the empire is currently unaware of our activities."

The chieftain narrowed his eyes at Martel, cocking his head to the side as he thought. "You are seeking an artefact for the empire against the empire's wishes," he said slowly. "This is what you wish me to believe?"

"Only because it is the truth."

"And what great evil do you wish to save your empire from?"

Martel smiled grimly. "Have you ever heard of the Mage King?"

The chieftain raised his blond brows. "The one your first empress fought against and destroyed, yes?"

Martel nodded. "We fear he may have found a way to return. Only the empress' bloodline could possibly stop him."

"That bloodline is ended."

"Perhaps. Perhaps not. The woman is rumoured to have had many lovers. We need the sceptre to find our champion, or the empire will not be the only thing to fall when the Mage King returns."

"Many lovers indeed," the chieftain said with a snort. "Her demon included, they say."

"Rumours intended to discredit her," Martel replied dismissively.

"Perhaps," the chieftain said. He raised his hand and made a beckoning motion. The craggy valley came to life, with northern warriors appearing all over the valley from behind rocks. Some appeared to simply materialise where they stood. They were dressed much like their chieftain, some wearing scrappy-looking chainmaille and most of them blond and tattooed. Almost half their number were tall, muscular women.

"Come," the chieftain said. "We will share meat and talk. I am interested in this returning Mage King."

Martel dismounted as the chieftain leapt easily from his chariot.

"You too, loudmouth," Martel said to me.

Sighing, I slid off Fas and followed Martel and the chieftain. They walked only a few feet before coming to a blanket that the warriors had laid out. Before long, the three of us were sitting on the blanket, being served cold salted pork cut straight off the bone and thick chunks of dense, sour dark bread.

I sat in silence as Martel told the chieftain everything he knew and suspected. Despite the distrust I knew Martel felt for the northerners, he left nothing out and was as honest and frank as he had always been.

A silence fell when Martel finished his explanation. The chieftain sat a while with the information, saying nothing as he slowly chewed his pork.

"We fought for your empress, did you know that?" he asked Martel.

Martel shook his head. "I've never heard that mentioned."

"Aye, well you wouldn't. We allied ourselves with her because we knew the Mage King would one day come for us. Your empress was gracious, and she honoured the pact we made. She never invaded the north, nor tried to capture our people. But others in her bloodline were not so honourable. They invaded. Thrice. The pact was broken and the north has been an enemy of the empire ever since. The mutual attacks have been ongoing.

"They told us that all memory of our friendship had been erased. The children of the empire would never know the stories of our glorious dead; our heroes would never be mentioned in your tales. We of the north remember them. Our traditional songs and poems, stories and dances can be traced back to the war against the Mage King. We clung fiercely to those stories to spite your empire. You may not remember, but we do and will forever."

The chieftain sighed and looked up at the sky. "I often envied those heroes," he said. "The world they lived in was full of adventure; perilous, yes of course. But only in peril can a man choose."

"Choose what?" I asked.

"What he will do, what he will be. Peace has its benefits. Life is easier, there is more time for leisure, there are fewer tears. But a farmer will always be a farmer in times of peace. With strife, that farmer may pick up a sword and become a champion."

"Or he may flee and be a coward," I noted.

"Yes," the chieftain replied. "He may. But that is his to choose." He sighed. "We have kept that sceptre piece out of spite," he told Martel. "When the bloodline was broken, we celebrated. The first empress notwithstanding, that bloodline did nothing but evil. We travelled south and took that sceptre piece as a trophy; and as a reminder. The blood of the north outlasted the blood of our enemy. It is a treasure worth more to us than its weight in any precious stone. Giving it up is a price few are willing to pay. Our pride means something to us."

The company fell into contemplative silence. It surprised me just how comfortable that silence felt. The chieftain sighed again as he looked out over the valley.

"Perhaps it is time to mend what was broken," I said. "In returning the sceptre piece, you could restore the friendship between the warriors of the north and the empire. Surely the sceptre piece is worth that?"

The chieftain turned to look at me, cocking his head as he silently mulled over my words. He turned his gaze back to the valley. He said nothing.

"Your lands are beautiful," Martel noted.

"Aye," the chieftain agreed. "They are indeed. The soil is too shallow for tilling, however."

Martel smiled and the silence settled over the group again.

"And what would that make me to my own people, hmm?" the chieftain asked after a time, not bothering to look at me.

It took me a moment to realise that he was answering my request for the sceptre piece. "The proud noble warrior-chief, who yielded the treasure of the north to our enemy without even so much as a fight."

"It would make you wise," I replied. "That you set aside your pride to save your people and ensure that the north stays free. Warriors slain in battle are brave and have songs sung of them. Do not wise kings also have their songs?"

The chieftain turned to me and regarded me with his steel-coloured eyes. He stared at me for so long I shifted beneath the discomforting weight of that gaze.

"Can you?" he asked. "Have you the authority to promise that the north will stay forever free?"

I glanced at Martel. He looked uncomfortable, but would not speak. He was not addressed. To speak now would be insulting.

"No," I answered honestly. "I am just some ragged traveller who cannot remember their own name. I haven't the authority to promise you that the empire will leave the north alone. Neither does Martel. He's just the leader of a band of outlaws trying to honour their vows and do the right thing."

The chieftain grimaced and looked away.

"But I can promise to do everything in my power to make it so," I continued. "Martel, too. Though he's only a ranger now, surely the new empress will reward the man responsible for restoring the throne, and listen to his counsel carefully."

"And if the new empress proves as evil as the Mage King?" The chieftain turned to me again, his brows raised in query.

I grinned, shrugged my shoulders and said, "Oops."

The chieftain burst out laughing. He laughed long and loud. "I like you, Sky Road Walker," he said, wiping the tears of laughter from his eyes. "Oops!" The word set him laughing again.

I could not help but throw a bemused look at Martel. He was struggling to reign in a broad grin himself.

Eventually, the word 'oops' ceased to be quite so amusing and the chieftain's laughter died down. "Come. I will take you to my village and welcome you to my lands properly. The journey will give me time to think it over."

"That sounds like a fine idea," Martel replied.

Following the chieftain's lead, we stood up and returned to our mounts. The chieftain abandoned the chariot in favour of a short, but powerfully built horse that was brought forward by one of his warriors. I watched in fascination as the northern warriors mounted similar horses; horses that had, until now, been hidden from sight.

"It's like they just materialise from thin air," a ranger grumbled.

"Small horses are good for hiding," the chieftain said, turning to face the ranger. He grinned. "Hiding is good for killing." With that, the chieftain moved his horse into an easy canter.

"You know, I rather like him," another ranger said. He kicked his horse's flanks and the group thundered off after the chieftain.

Chapter Twelve

It took four days of hard riding to reach the chieftain's village, which was, in fact, a walled city situated atop an artificial hill in the middle of a valley surrounded on all sides by tall, snow-capped mountains. The tall wooden palisades enclosed the largest of the houses. Along the twisting road up to the oppidum, smaller round wattle-and-daub houses scattered over the uneven hillside. Cattle, short, stocky and long haired, grazed all over the valley floor, watched over by their owners. Goats and chickens dominated the slopes of the artificial hill, herded by enormous, shaggy dogs as hungry eagles circled overhead.

The men and women going about their chores stopped their labour at the sight of the northern warriors returning with a group of southerners in tow. They smiled and bowed low as their chieftain passed, rising again to stare at the strangers.

The warriors peeled off before the gates at the wall opened wide. Only the chieftain and the rangers entered the walled portion of the city. The difference was striking. The roads were clear and uncluttered, lined with flagstones and gutters on either side. The men and women here dressed much the same as those living beyond the wall, but bright flashes every so often belied the presence of jewels and other finery.

Men and women alike wore deep blue tattoos proudly. I could not help but trace the swirling patterns of ink on their exposed skin with my eyes. I wondered at their meaning, but suspected I would never have the chance to find out.

"My Lord!" a young woman greeted from the door of the chieftain's enormous round house. She wore boiled leather armour and chainmaille of bright steel. Around her neck she wore a torc of rose gold and her cheek bore a three-pronged tattooed swirl, marred now by the presence of a pinkish scar.

"My Lady!" the chieftain replied. He dismounted before the horse had stopped and ran up the stairs, greeting the woman with a deep, passionate kiss.

"Sky Road Walker, ranger Martel," the chieftain said, turning to face us and wrapping one enormous arm around her armoured waist. "This is the Lady Eilir, my wife."

"Lucky bastard," I heard Martel mutter as he dismounted. Concealing a grin, I also dismounted. The woman walked down the stairs to greet us. Her gaze was bright and direct, blue eyes shining from her pale face. She extended her hand and grasped myself and Martel both at the forearm in turn as she welcomed us.

"Welcome to our home," Lady Eilir said, offering a warm smile. Her cheek dimpled prettily. "I half expected my husband to bring me your heads."

"Might still happen," the chieftain said from the top of the stairs.

"I am very glad he did not," Martel told Eilir, ignoring the comment from the chieftain. Eilir's smile broadened.

"Come, then. There is a meal awaiting you." Lady Eilir turned and walked back up the stairs. She pecked her husband's cheek before walking inside. I followed Martel up the stairs and inside the house, noting that the chieftain was grinning like a madman.

Once my eyes adjusted to the dimmer light, I noticed that the chieftain's residence, though large, was merely a residence. A low circular table stood in the centre of the space, with a fire burning in a large hearth located on the floor in the centre of the round table. A wooden ladder on one side of the space led up to where the bed sat, exposed to anyone who bothered to peek in the door.

I frowned. "Where do you hold court?" I asked the chieftain.

"In the plaza," the chieftain replied, as if I was an idiot for asking.

"Oh," I said. "Of course."

Eilir laughed quietly as she took her place at the table. Martel, the chieftain and I joined her and the rangers found a place to sit down. Servants walked in, carrying trays of food and a large cauldron, which was placed over the central fire. Before long we were all eating heartily, munching down on freshly caught boar, pheasant, rock hens and various kinds of cheese. During the course of the meal, which was entirely lacking in any formality - the guests served themselves, as did the hosts - the chieftain explained everything to his beautiful wife. She listened with a slight frown. At the end of the tale, she remained silent for a time.

"You truly believe the Mage King seeks to return?" she asked Martel.

"To be honest, my Lady, I do not know for certain, but it appears so."

"And you require the sceptre piece why?"

"The sceptre is said to be able to identify the rightful ruler, but it cannot do so broken as it is. I wish only to repair the sceptre and restore the throne so that we might be able to combat the threat of the Mage King."

"You do not seek the throne yourself?"

Martel pulled a face. "Heavens no! I am content with my post as Watch Commander. Give me the wilds any day."

"Well, my wife?" the chieftain asked. "As mother of my people, what would you do?"

"As a woman of the north, I would advise you to keep the sceptre piece, and let the southern dogs reap what they have sown." Eilir smiled at my shocked expression. "But as a mother, I would do whatever I could to keep my children safe. My Lord, the Mage King returning would devastate us all. We will need friends, my love."

The chieftain nodded. "I was thinking the same. But we cannot simply just hand the piece over to them and consider our part in this complete."

Eilir turned to her husband and cast a searching gaze over his face. "You mean to go with them?" she asked softly.

The chieftain nodded. "Myself and some men. If it is friendship we must offer the empire, I would do it properly. And my presence may help to mollify the other chieftains."

"Yes," Eilir said. "That much is true. But..." Eilir raised one hand and placed it gently on her husband's cheek. "I do not wish to be parted from you."

The chieftain covered her hand with his own. "Someone must rule here, my love," he said. "And there is no one who would rule better than you in my absence." He took her hand and brought it to his lips, kissing her palm.

"I would go with you," she insisted. "Fergus is well enough to rule, and your son is healthy and strong. Fergus will take good care of all your children; blood or not."

Martel and I exchanged a glance, both entirely unaccustomed to such open and uninhibited public displays of affection.

"We will talk on it more in the evening," the chieftain said. Eilir nodded in agreement, and both turned back to their meals.

After a time Eilir looked to me. I suddenly realised that I had been staring at them during a relatively private conversation.

"And what do you think?" Eilir asked me. "Should a husband leave his wife behind?"

I opened my mouth to speak and shut it without uttering a word. This probably required more delicacy than a quick answer. What on earth could I possibly say? Siding with Eilir would likely irk the chieftain. Siding with the chieftain would earn the ire of Lady Eilir.

"We should probably think of what is best for this mission," I said at length. "And to be honest, we could use all the fighters we can get. So far we have the rangers, and myself. And I'm not really that skilled a fighter."

"Or skilled at all," a ranger offered from the other side of the round table. I glared at him, making him grin.

Eilir smiled. It was not the polite smile she usually wore, but a genuine smile that softened her features. She turned to her husband and raised her brows.

"Well, my love?" she asked haughtily. "Am I skilled enough to go to battle?"

The chieftain scowled.

"That question would make more sense if you knew how she captured my son's heart," a gruff voice said from the door. I turned to look.

A tall, impossibly broad man stood just inside the threshold of the residence. He did not wear armour, rather the long fur-trimmed coat that, had it not been so splattered with mud at the bottom, would have looked regal. Despite the lack of armour, the man wore a profusion of weapons, the most notable of which was a lochaber strapped to his back, a broad-headed, double-bladed axe tucked into his elaborately embroidered belt, and twin short axes tucked into his boots. Long grey hair hung down his back, bound in two braids. His grey beard was short and neatly trimmed.

"Father!" the chieftain said, rising from his seat and vaulting over the table. He marched over to the enormous bear of a man and wrapped him in a warm embrace. "You're back early!"

"Aye, well, there was little trouble on the road. Has there been some here? Why is my son entertaining these southern dogs?"

Martel and I exchanged a glance. "I'm guessing he likes axes," Martel whispered to me. I stifled a laugh, but it escaped my throat in a strange snort despite my efforts.

"They carry with them some interesting news, much of it troubling."

"Of course they carry troubling news. These are dogs of the empire."

"Not anymore," Martel replied clearly. "Technically we have been disbanded. We're working outside the knowledge of the empire at the moment."

The chieftain's father looked Martel over with sharp grey eyes before marching forward to face him more squarely. Martel drew himself up to his full height to meet the chieftain's father evenly.

It was anything but even. Martel was tall and broad, but even he looked like a greyhound facing down a bear. Still, he stood his ground, shoulders square, his steady gaze never flinching from the frosted grey eyes of the man before him.

The staring contest lasted a long while. Eventually, Martel broke his gaze so deliberately I could not help but feel he did so in order to make it clear he need not have.

"I didn't come here to fight," Martel said. "And should you wish us gone, we will put down our plates and leave without fuss."

I heard a ranger's disappointed sigh and glanced over. The ranger who sighed stared down at the uneaten food on his plate with considerable longing.

"If you did not come to cause trouble, southern maggot, why did you come?" the chieftain's father growled.

"We fear the Mage King is seeking a way back into the world. Only imperial blood can face that monster with any chance of victory. We have come for the sceptre piece so that we might rediscover that bloodline and restore the throne."

"So you are working for the empire!" The chieftain's father turned abruptly and marched back to his son at the door. "You should have taken their heads."

"We are working for the Empress Moua, with whom the north established a friendship." Martel sounded bold, but the barely visible sheen on his skin told me that he was nervous. The chieftain's father turned on his heel and glared at Martel. The gaze was nothing but pure venom.

"A friendship her children denied!" he barked. "Honour is not hereditary, and her blood was poisoned the moment she left this world. I will not see her throne restored!" He turned to his son. "Take their heads."

"No," the chieftain replied, pulling his father up short. The enormous man blinked at his son in surprise, then scowled, reaching slowly for the axe at his side.

"I have invited them as guests and given them food under my roof. Even if they proved liars, I could not take their heads now."

"Then I will!"

"Fergus," Eilir said softly. The chieftain's father paused, the axe half drawn. "Will you not sit, and share our food? These outlaws have a tale to tell and you may want to hear what they say before collecting their heads for trophies." She spoke softly and gently, and her tone was one of great respect.

"I will not listen to liars and braggarts."

"There is a Sky Road Walker amongst their number," the chieftain said. Fergus turned to him with a raised brow and the chieftain nodded in my direction. I gave a half-hearted wave.

Fergus very slowly let go of his axe, letting it slide back into position as he looked me over. "I will sit," he said at last. "But I will not share food with these bastards. If I do not like what they say, I will have their heads and not give cause for the gods to hate me."

"That is fair." Eilir motioned to a servant, who bowed and vanished, returning moments later with an extra chair. It was placed at her side. She held her hands out for the chieftain, who walked over and took them briefly before they both sat.

"You are fortunate, Oisín, that your wife is so beautiful," Fergus noted. "And is not nearly as daft as you."

The chieftain smiled. "Aye. I am."

"Sky Road Walker," Fergus said gruffly. "Tell me what you know."

I glanced at Martel, who nodded solemnly at me, before launching into my tale. By the end, Fergus was sitting back in his chair deep in thought. He looked over at Eilir.

"And you believe them?"

"My husband does," Eilir replied. "And his heart is good at seeing other hearts. I trust him on this."

"Aye, my son's heart is good." Fergus sighed. "Pity about his mind," he grumbled to himself. "And what of your pride?" he demanded of his son.

"I have it still," Oisín replied. "But it is not stronger than the love I have for my son, my land or my people. I will see them free forever. If these outlaws are successful, and if we had some part in that success, I would have done all I could to see them live happily. That, to me, is worth more than anything."

Fergus leant forward, placing his elbows on the table and rested his chin against his clasped hands. He closed his eyes, his brow furrowed. At length, he opened his eyes and looked squarely at his son.

"Fine," he said. "I concede your point, though I think you a fool for trusting them."

"Aye," Oisín replied. "I still have doubts myself, but there is nothing for it now."

"You must go with them," Fergus said. "And keep them honest."

"I had planned to."

Fergus nodded. "And speak to the other chieftains. You will need their support, or they may decide you a traitor and annex your lands."

Oisín sat back. "Time is of the essence. A conclave may take weeks, even months. We must move now. Will you go in my stead?"

"And risk insulting them? You are the chieftain now. This is your duty."

"They respect you more, father. I am but a dreamer, young and untested."

"Perhaps I could go with the southerners?" Eilir asked. "And you go to the conclave, my love."

"Or you go to the conclave. Or we all go." Oisín rubbed the side of his face. He glanced at me.

"What do you think, Sky Road Walker? What would you do were you me?"

I blinked and sighed. "Though time truly is of the essence, I fear insulting the other chieftains will do nothing for our cause," I said. "We should all go to the conclave together. Perhaps if all the chieftains see us standing united, it may sway their vote in our favour."

"Aye," Fergus growled. "Or piss them off."

"We're mighty enough, Father," Oisín replied. "And they might see me as nothing more than a dreamer, but I was trained by Fergus Battle Bear. They will find themselves surprised if they seek recourse by single combat."

"I'd be happier if you set your wife upon them. She is not called Blade Breaker for nothing."

Oisín grinned, though it looked a little pained. Eilir smiled and placed a reassuring hand on her husband's forearm. "Were it not for that stone, my love," she murmured. Oisín grunted and Eilir laughed. "Fret not!" she said. "I would not have gone to your bed if you had proven unskilled in combat. I have standards."

I concealed a broad grin behind my cup of elderberry wine.

"It is decided," Oisín said, changing the subject. "We go together. I will send out riders immediately."

Seemingly satisfied, Fergus broke his fast with his son's guests and soon the large, round dwelling was full of talk and laughter again. The meal, taken at a leisurely pace, lasted several hours. I learnt that it would be the only meal of the day. The news was a little disappointing, but that was their custom and I could hardly protest without seeming rude.

The rangers and I slept in the chieftain's village that night. As a Sky Road Walker, I was invited to stay with the chieftain and his wife. Their uninhibited adoration of each other had me regretting accepting the invitation long before midnight struck. The rest of the rangers were quartered in the houses of various warriors. Martel was given a bed in Fergus' own house. I could tell he was uneasy about it. Still, he seemed rested and well when we met the following morning. Fergus, he told me, was a distrusting but very attentive host. Apparently, to be anything but would earn the ire of the gods, and Fergus believed in those gods with every ounce of his considerable being.

The journey to the conclave began before first light the following morning. My breath frosted as I struggle to saddle Fas with numb fingers. Fas waited patiently, occasionally turning her large head to look back at me with a quizzical expression.

"Cold hands," I muttered to her on the third glance. Fas snorted and turned back to the hay bale she was casually munching. Saddled at last, I led her out and mounted. Everyone else, I noted with chagrin, was mounted and waiting for me.

"He's definitely not a ranger, this one," Fergus said. He sat on a short, stocky chestnut mount, a young boy with a shock of red hair sitting in front of the saddle. "I will ride with you to the end of the plains."

I nodded and, with Oisín and his armoured wife in the lead, the considerable force of rangers and northern warriors rode out. It was mid-morning by the time we reached the beginning of the mountain pass. Here, Fergus stopped his horse and turned to Eilir.

"You take care now, Blade Breaker," he said with an impish smile.

Eilir grinned. "I swear it."

The red-headed boy reached up and Eilir plucked him easily out of the saddle, squeezing him tight. "Be good, Llei," she said. "And mind you heed what your grandfather tells you."

"Aye, Mama," the boy said. "I'll be good. And I'll have learnt the staff by the time you get back, I swear it!"

Eilir laughed. "Good!"

The boy reached out to his father, who pulled him from Eilir's grasp and hugged him close. "You'll be a good boy, won't you?" Oisín asked his son.

The boy nodded. "Aye, Papa."

"And you'll mind your lessons, won't you?"

"Aye, Papa."

"That's my boy," Oisín said. He pulled his son closer briefly before handing the boy back to Fergus. "All right, Llei. We'll be back. Mind you put your grandfather on his arse with your staff."

Fergus raised one shaggy, grey brow at his son.

Oisín grinned. "It'll be good for him."

Llei smiled broadly, looking like a miniature red-headed version of his mother. "Aye, Papa. I swear."

"Aye, then." Oisín ruffled the boy's hair and moved off. I followed the group into the mountains, looking back once to see the grizzled old man with the fire-touched boy sitting on their mount, watching the warriors leave with sad eyes.

The mountains swallowed us. The company we kept were skilled fighters all, but even they were cowed by the great, snow-peaked mountains. The path wound its way through craggy fissures with sharp spires of rock so tall and pointed they looked like spears of stone jutting from the ground. Somewhere ahead, I could hear water plummet down a cliff face into an enormous hole, vanishing into a vast underground lake. We skirted the edge of that hole during the ride and I tried hard not to look down.

"A dragon once lived there," Eilir said to me. The mountain pass was only wide enough to permit two of the small northern horses to pass abreast. Stuck on Fas, who was almost two ponies wide, I was the only one in my row. Eilir had to turn around in her saddle to speak with me.

"Well, a drake, but they are more or less the same."

"What is the difference?" I asked.

"Size, mostly. Drakes are but the size of a large bull or so. Dragons are larger still. I have never seen one myself, but I have heard tales of dragons so large they reach from the tallest peak all the way down to the valley floor from tip of their noses to the tips of their tails."

"To be fair, they have very long tails," Oisín added.

I shuddered.

"Don't fret. They have neither been seen nor heard from in a thousand years."

"Oh good," I murmured. Oisín laughed.

It took two days of careful travel before the group cleared the mountains. Past the ranges and down again, we entered a broad pasture, where grazed a multitude of wild cattle. These shaggy beasts were taller than my horse and had three sets of horns crowning their broad heads.

"Good grief!" I said.

"They're far south for this time of the year," Oisín noted with a frown.

"Perhaps the winter has started early in the north," Eilir answered. "It has been known to do so from time to time."

Oisín grunted. He led the group around the herd of horned beasts, keeping a careful eye on them. They stood, mooing to each other on occasion, each of them chewing their cud as they watched us with unblinking eyes. The calves, I saw, were far from harm, grazing in the middle of the herd. I spied one bull, a black and brown beast composed entirely of fur and muscle, so large I was certain he could easily chew up my skull if he felt like it.

"That is Magni," Eilir said. "He has been the bull of this herd since I was a small girl. No one dares try to take him down."

"I can't imagine why," I replied dryly. Eilir grinned.

"He is a wise leader. He will not attack unless he feels the calves are threatened, but he never ceases his watching. That is how a chieftain ought to rule. That is how Oisín rules. The other chieftains mock him for his want of peace. Yet because of it, our people are happier, they are stronger and healthier, and they love their chieftain well."

"And his beautiful wife," I answered. Eilir shrugged.

Once clear of the herd of thrice-horned cattle, we rode for a further day before coming to the open-air paved plaza where the conclave would be held. We were not the first group of warriors to arrive. Two chieftains and their contingent of warriors had set up camp around the open air plaza. One, almost as broad as Fergus, though a good deal older, rose slowly to his feet as Oisín and his wife approached.

"Angus Mac Angus," Oisín greeted. He dismounted and walked over to the grizzled old man with a broad smile. They clasped forearms.

"Well met, Oisín Mac Fergus," Angus Mac Angus said. His voice was throaty and harsh. "I am saddened to see your father is not here."

"As is he," Oisín replied. "But there is no one else I trust to care for my people and my son, I fear."

"Aye. I should have known you'd leave him in charge. I would bet he has not aged a day since last we met."

"He is a little greyer," Oisín answered. "But I fear I still cannot best him in combat."

"Aye, well, there is no shame in that. Few could ever defeat the Battle Bear." Angus Mac Angus looked over at Eilir. "My girl! How you have blossomed in your time in the south!"

"Uncle!" Eilir said as she slid out of her saddle. She rushed forward and they embraced. "How fares my mother?"

"She misses her child fiercely, and will not stop talking about the day you broke ten blades at practice. She shames the men who owned those blades several times a day."

Eilir rolled her eyes. "Sounds like her."

Angus laughed. "I am pleased to see you, but surprised. Would Fergus not have been better company for Oisín during the conclave?"

Eilir smirked. "I don't know, Uncle. Shall we cross blades to decide?"

Laughing again, Angus shook his head. "I would not dare, Blade Breaker! I value my steel!"

No sooner had Angus finished speaking than three more chieftains arrived, apparently having travelled together.

"That accounts for the north east," Oisín said. "Where is Dafyd?"

"Did you not hear?" Angus said. "Dafyd is dead."

Oisín's jaw dropped. "What? When? How?"

"Last month. He was old, and they say it was natural causes, but some are speaking ill of his wife. Sylpha is now the chieftain."

"I had not heard," Oisín admitted. "I shall send a gift when I return home."

"Sylpha does not want your gifts," Angus said. "She is a hard woman."

"I would be too," Eilir muttered with a grunt. "If I had Dafyd for a husband."

"Hush, Eilir," Oisín chided. "It does not do to speak ill of the dead."

Eilir rolled her eyes.

I was so busy paying attention to the exchange that I failed to notice that the northern warriors and rangers both had dismounted and set up their camps. In fact, it took Martel's hissed command to rouse me.

"Stop gawking you fool and undress your horse!"

I blinked, awkwardly shifted my weight and turned Fas around to join the rest of the rangers' horses.

Chapter Thirteen

Another day passed before all the chieftains arrived. Last was Sylpha. She entered the camp riding tall, despite her silver hair and advanced age. Her face was set into a permanently fierce expression, her dark eyes glittering with secret knowledge. Had this woman been an animal, she'd have been a crow; accustomed to carnage and extremely clever. I do not fear admitting that I was cowed by her stern appearance and calculating gaze.

The evening of Sylpha's arrival saw the beginning of the conclave. I was with the rangers, standing at the edge of the plaza as the chieftains introduced themselves to the gathering. From the expressions of the gathering, I could easily pick out the existing alliances. Oisín and Angus were on friendly terms, since they were now, thanks to Eilir, family. A chieftain named Gordon and Angus also had a familial tie, though it was more distant. Most of the other chieftains did not much care for Oisín, since he was so young and untested, but nor did they particularly care for one another. Only Sylpha remained unreadable. I suspected her only alliance was to herself.

Oisín stepped forward into the plaza once the introductions were complete. He thanked everyone for their attendance and explained why he had called the conclave. Silence fell over the chieftains and their warriors when Oisín acknowledged Martel's request for the sceptre piece.

"No," someone barked. "Absolutely not. Let these southern dogs deal with their own. We in the north owe them nothing!"

The conclave exploded in a riot of profanities and accusations. Old wounds never quite addressed were dredged up from the past, and soon the conclave forgot the matter they came to discuss, opting to fight over slights committed hundreds of years ago. Oisín stood in the plaza, his arms folded, in silence. Sighing, Eilir left her position and walked to her husband's side.

"Aye, well, I suppose I have to now," Angus Mac Angus grumbled. He too walked forward to stand beside Oisín. Gordon, who was halfway through a long string of profanities, clamped his mouth shut when he noticed and marched forward to stand at Angus' side.

With four of the nine chieftains standing in silence in the plaza, the shouting dwindled, then ceased altogether.

"Are you done flinging insults at each other like children?" Oisín demanded.

"Aye, says the child!" a chieftain shouted back.

"A child of the Battle Bear, Brandun," Angus shot.

"Who was defeated by a woman!" Brandun replied.

"Aye," Oisín snapped. "And I'd let her at you as well if I didn't value your steel."

Eilir did not conceal her smile. She caressed her husband's back briefly. Brandun clamped his mouth shut. A woman she might be, but Eilir Blade Breaker was not a foe to be underestimated.

"I would hear the Sky Road Walker speak," Sylpha said, cutting through the silence with a soft voice that was commanding all the same. She had remained silent, deep in thought, while the argument swirled around her. Her fierce features never softening, she turned her dark eyes to me.

With a push from Martel, I walked forward. Oisín and his supporters walked to the side, yielding the centre of the plaza to me. Standing there, under the stern, dark gaze of the most frightening woman I had ever seen, it took me a moment to find my voice.

"Hi," I said, flashing a nervous smile.

Someone coughed, but there was no other sound. I paused. What could I possibly say? Oisín had explained everything already. What was left?

Sylpha raised one grey brow as I took a long moment to think. I smiled apologetically at her.

"I honestly do not know what else there is to say," I proclaimed. "Oisín has already told you everything of import. But he hasn't told you about the Seeker's Son."

The silence that followed was oppressive. Sylpha straightened in her seat and stared at me for a long moment.

"What about the Seeker's Son?" she asked.

"When I first awoke, I was discovered and taken to a village where an old woman spoke this to me:

"'The Seeker's Son has taken one. The Seeker's Son has two. The Seeker's Son takes another one. The Seeker's Son seeks you.' I had no idea what it could possibly mean, until I met a Seeker's Son."

"Liar!" Brandun called. "No one encounters a Seeker's Son and lives!"

"I had the very good fortune of being in the company of rangers at the time, and at the edge of tuatha territory. We fled to the tuatha forest and there, the tuatha themselves chased the phantom away with a shield of light."

"Lying again! The tuatha are no friends of the empire!"

"No, they're not," I agreed. "It was a risk to be sure, one that Martel almost paid for with his life." I turned to Martel. He nodded at me. "The tuatha poisoned him and held the cure for ransom. But they are not entirely heartless and, upon learning our cause, even aided us to acquire a piece of the sceptre. We went south, seeking the Red Band."

"The Red Band," Sylpha repeated. "The name is familiar."

"They were pirates," I said. "I first learnt of them during this mission, and only from a story which identified them as the ones who attacked the ship bearing the sceptre to safety after the imperial line was broken."

"Seems we owe them a favour, then," another chieftain grunted.

"Well, you'd be hard-pressed giving it to them. Their leader was a necromancer. He died when the Seeker's Son attacked for a second time. It is likely that the Red Band no longer exists."

"So you mean to tell me," Brandun said slowly to Oisín. "That you brought all the chieftains together in the presence of one with a Seeker's Son on his heels?"

I turned to Oisín, who now looked pale. "The Seeker's Son has not been seen nor heard of since that last attack," he replied. "I would not put you all in danger."

"No," I agreed. "I haven't even heard its approach."

"Heard its approach?" Sylpha enquired.

"Well, yes. It's the sound of rushing water when there is no water around that gives it away."

A very small quirk of her mouth was all that Sylpha offered by way of a smile. "Well then," she said. "I now believe you to be a Sky Road Walker."

I raised my brows. "You didn't before?"

"Only a Sky Road Walker, or those who share some tuatha blood, can hear the Seeker's Son approach, stranger with no name. We believe honesty is a virtue. It is something the empire does not believe. I would not hold it beneath agents of the empire to lie to get their way."

"Oh." I stood in the centre of the plaza in silence for a moment fidgeting with the hem of my tunic. "So... uh... what now?"

Angus Mac Angus barked a laugh at me. I turned to him and shrugged my shoulders helplessly.

"Now we consider," Sylpha answered. She stared at me with her twinkling dark eyes and I shifted in discomfort. "Can I go sit down?" I asked her. She waved me away, her eyes growing distant.

Returning to my place beside Martel, I asked him, "What is she doing?"

"I think Sylpha is tuatha," he whispered to me. "She is turning her vision to the internal world."

"Her mother was," Angus supplied. "A long-lived woman most of us believed was a witch. She just *knew* things."

"What kinds of things?"

"Terrifying things."

I clamped my mouth shut.

Perhaps it was just because I had been talking about it and my mind was playing tricks on me, but for a brief moment I thought I could hear the distant gurgling of water. I turned my head towards the imagined sound, but it vanished as soon as I did. I turned back to find Sylpha staring at me

She stood. "You may vote as you choose," she said, her voice powerful enough to make brave young men shrink before her. "But this one has spoken the truth. The Seeker's Son is but one of twelve identical shades, splintered in the evil Mage King's defeat, and it is seeking to return. If the old woman of the village spoke true, it has already found three other shades and absorbed them. It needs but eight more to return to full strength. I fear it is closer even than that to returning to our world to wreak havoc on all life once more." She turned to Oisín. "You have been untested and thus disdained, chieftain. But your heart is good and has led you true. I will stand with you."

"Thank you, chieftain," Oisín replied, standing. He bowed slightly before Sylpha, who smiled. The change on her features was tremendous. She looked young suddenly, and crackled with vibrant light. The youthfulness faded quickly as the smile vanished.

"Make your call, chieftains," Sylpha demanded. She crossed the plaza to stand by Oisín's side. She was both taller and far more slender than the young blond chieftain.

Slowly, in silence, one by one the chieftains stood and crossed the plaza to stand by Oisín. Brandun was left by himself at his seat. He glared at the other chieftains.

"You are weak," he declared. "To bend even now to the will of the empire, and to the will of this witch." He waved a hand loosely at Sylpha. The woman drew herself up and glared balefully at Brandun.

"Draw your steel, Brandun," she said in a low voice. "And I shall show you what this witch can do."

Brandun stood and placed his hand on the hilt of his sword.

Unthinking, I ran forward. "Wait!" I demanded.

Everyone stared at me in surprise.

"Please!" I said desperately as Brandun started to unsheathe his weapon. "Now is not the time for fighting! The Seeker's Son is still on the loose, we have more pieces of the sceptre to acquire and for all we know, that phantom has all it needs to return to this world and destroy everything! Please! You will need to save your strength and keep your friends."

"That witch is no friend of mine!" Brandun snapped, but he released his hilt regardless. I was convinced that it was more because the other chieftains had reached for their weapons than anything I might have said.

Sylpha also sheathed her steel. She turned to me. "You are wiser than you look, Sky Road Walker."

"Um... thanks. I guess."

"And you spoke true. We will need to save our steel. Perhaps, if ever we are faced with the Seeker's Son, Brandun will be thankful to have this witch in his company."

"It is decided," Oisín declared, denying Brandun a chance to retort. "The sceptre piece will travel with me and my chosen warriors south to the rangers' lair."

I smirked at the word 'lair' and my eyes flickered to Martel, who also smirked at the word.

"Together we shall attempt to take the third sceptre piece and thus restore the imperial throne. Assuming, of course, that the empress' bloodline still exists."

"I will also accompany you," Sylpha said. "My daughter is now old enough to rule, and I have faith that my Steward will serve her as well as he has served me. You will need the tuatha on your side in this fight. In that, I may be able to aid you."

"Thank you, Chieftain," Martel said.

Sylpha turned to him and smiled slightly. "There is something about you, ranger," she said.

I waited for her to elaborate. Instead she turned to her waiting warriors and beckoned one over. The man, though almost as tall Sylpha and twice as broad, approached with a great deal of respect and not a small amount of fear.

"Misha," she said. "You may take your company and return home. I am trusting my lands to your strength. Should this company of outlaws fail, or should the new ruler of the empire prove less honourable than we'd hoped, I will need you to be prepared. One way or another, war is coming for us."

The man named Misha bowed low. "We will make you proud, chieftain," he said in a deep voice.

"Go, then. And tell my daughter I love her."

Misha bowed low again and turned. He made a signal with his hands and Sylpha's warriors left the plaza and decamped. The dull rumble of a company of horses shook the ground as the warriors rode away.

Oisín turned to the other chieftains. "Sylpha is right. One way or another, war is coming. I suggest that you return to your clans and prepare. This conclave has officially concluded."

I yawned and it blocked my ears momentarily. In the dull absence of sound, I heard the gurgling of water. I stopped yawning abruptly.

Martel raised an eyebrow at me. "You've gone pale," he noted. "What is it?"

"Well," I said. "I don't want to alarm anyone, but I thought I just heard the Seeker's Son."

Everyone turned to me.

"I heard nothing," Sylpha said slowly.

"It was probably nothing," I replied. "It's just... well... I only heard it when I yawned and my ears were blocked."

"If your ears were blocked, how could you have heard it?" Brandun demanded.

I shrugged. "Maybe I'm just getting paranoid," I muttered.

"Whatever the case, we should be on the move," Martel said.

Oisín nodded. "We should. With your permission, chieftain Sylpha, I would like to return to my village. It is on the way south and should not put us behind by any more than half a day,"

"I have no complaints," Sylpha replied.

"Very well. Let us retrieve the sceptre piece."

Sylpha nodded. She and Oisín returned to the centre of the plaza and started sweeping the stones with their feet.

"This one," Oisín said, stomping down. Then, "Nope."

Sylpha chuckled before stamping her heel into a stone. It depressed. Somewhere deep beneath the ground came a rumbling sound followed by a short, rapid succession of clicks. I stared incredulously as half the plaza lowered to create of itself a spiral staircase.

Oisín looked up to find both Martel and I staring at him. He grinned. "Want to come in?"

"Yes!" Martel said immediately, walking forward. I followed. Before long, Martel, Oisín and I were walking down the stairs into darkness, following Sylpha.

It was only a short walk, but the darkness became so complete it took me a long while to adjust to the dim light filtering in from above. I very nearly ploughed into Sylpha's back when she stopped abruptly.

"The plaza stands above the cairn of Thowar Angry Axe, the last High King of the north, from whom our own Oisín is directly descended, and his wife Brega Battle Worn," Sylpha said.

The sparse light in the room revealed an enormous statue of a proud, bearded man standing, holding an enormous axe in one hand. His other arm was wrapped tightly around the waist of the statue of an armoured woman bearing a broken shield. The statue's features could have been carved after Oisín's father they looked so alike.

"My God," I heard Martel breathe. He walked forward to stand at the statue's feet and stared up at them.

"Thowar and Brega were betrayed," Oisín said quietly. "By their Steward, who had been bought by the empire. It came to war, and the Steward slew Brega on the field, before Thowar's very eyes. The rage that followed is the stuff of legends. They say Thowar won the field single-handedly that day."

"He also lost his life that day," Sylpha added. "Wounded, he stumbled back to the body of his wife and pulled her close. He died holding her to him, so the legend goes."

Oisín nodded. "They had been in love since they were children. Thowar defied his father in marrying her, but he would take no one else. They had been married less than two years and had but one child, a daughter, when they died."

Sylpha walked to Martel's side. "Thowar and Brega were much loved. The people of the north built this massive cairn for them, with this statue to mark it forever. But the earth swallowed it whole, and so the plaza was built over top to preserve the cairn and keep their memories alive."

"Here," Oisín said, walking forward. He moved to the front of the statue and, finding a latch at the base of the carved stone, slid open a secret compartment. Reaching in, he drew out a piece of pale carved wood the length of his forearm.

"So we have the entire shaft of the sceptre," Martel said with a sigh.

"That means the grass dogs are guarding the crystal," I noted.

Martel nodded. "We should get going."

Oisín turned to Martel and offered the sceptre piece. Martel reached for it, then stopped. "You keep it," he said. "For now, at least. I would feel safer knowing it is guarded by someone for whom it is an invaluable treasure."

Oisín grinned briefly, a flash of white in the gloom and nodded. Altogether, we turned and marched back up the stairs. Before the sun began to set, we were back on our way to Oisín's village. As we travelled closer, a feeling of unease grew in the corners of my mind.

"Something isn't right," I said to Martel.

Martel looked me over. "What is bothering you?"

"I don't know. Just... something isn't right."

As we approached the base of the mountain path that opened to the valley in which Oisín's village was located, I heard the mad rush of water that signalled the Seeker's Son. I gasped, my eyes instinctively searching for Sylpha. She met my gaze with a grim expression, looking pale.

I had not been mistaken. "Seekers Son!" I barked, kicking Fas' flanks. The horse snorted and bolted forward. The thundering of hooves behind me informed me that the rest of the company were fast on my heels.

The company broke through into the valley. Now away from the shelter of the mountains, the sounds of an attack reached our ears. Screams and cries from the fortified village echoed through the crisp air.

"No!" Eilir yelled. She kicked her horse and bolted past me, Oisín not far behind. Sylpha followed and the rest jumped into action. We passed the small round houses of the shepherds as we rushed forward towards the village. I noticed with a start that one man lay across the threshold of his own home, now nothing more than a desiccated husk.

The company thundered through the shattered gate to find more husks, and people running in all directions, screaming. Through the panicked crowds, I spied the Seeker's Son. Impossibly tall and thin, it hovered above the ground, its tattered black cloak moving in a breeze only it could feel.

There, bravely standing in its way, was the young red-headed prince, holding his staff.

Time slowed. I could hear my own ragged breath as I watched the scene gradually unfold. The unearthly breeze that constantly moved the tattered robes of the floating phantom touched my own face, bringing with it the smell of death and decay. Unable to move, I watched on as the Seeker's Son slowly raised one hand, reaching for the child standing bravely before it, guarding his home.

Without thinking, I opened my mouth and screamed. The sound was piercing and shrill, loud enough to catch the attention of the Seeker's Son. The spectre turned its head.

Time restored itself, moving at pace. The sudden shift left me slightly disoriented and unable to react as everything seemed to be happening too fast now. I froze in terror as the Seeker's Son turned to me. It rushed forward with a shriek, coming at me so fast I barely had time to blink before its desiccated fingers were inches away from my face.

Fas reared in alarm, but was not given the chance to bolt as the Seeker's Son exploded into inky smoke before my eyes. I blinked sheepishly, noting that the air before my face shimmered slightly. I turned to spy Sylpha on her mount. She looked absolutely exhausted, her pale skin ashen and covered in a sheen of sweat. She offered me a wan smile, before her eyes rolled and she fell from her mount.

I dismounted and ran to her.

Chapter Fourteen

All around me chaos reigned. Oisín and Eilir rushed to their son. Martel and the rangers had taken it upon themselves to sweep the town and ensure that there were not any other unsavoury creatures lurking around, and to help with the dead and wounded. Somewhere at the far end of the town, a woman was screaming.

I was concerned only with Sylpha, who lay on the ground at my feet, her breathing tortured.

"Sylpha!" I said as I knelt next to her.

Her eyes fluttered open. They were hazed and unfocussed. "That took more than I thought it would," she whispered. She reached across to take my hand. "Where did you learn to do that, Sky Road Walker?"

I frowned down at her. "Do what?"

But Sylpha did not respond. Her body relaxed. I feared she had died, but the slow rise of her chest as she took a breath informed me that she had merely fallen unconscious. I looked around, seeking help. All I could see were people running in panic, fathers holding their dead children, or women pulling their recently found children to them.

"Help!" I screamed. "HELP!"

The sounds of someone approaching at a run turned my head. Martel sprinted towards me.

"What happened?" he demanded as he arrived.

"Where the hell were you?" I demanded.

"We split up to help the villagers. Now, what happened?"

"She stopped the Seeker's Son and collapsed. Something about it taking more than she was expecting."

"Right." Martel moved me aside, checked Sylpha over briefly before lifting her easily in his arms. He turned. "Oisín! Chieftain!"

Oisín appeared from behind one of the round houses, blood smeared across his shoulder and arm. He looked a little dazed. "Yes, ranger?" he asked.

"We need some help here. Sylpha overreached herself with her spell, it seems."

"Yes. Of course. Take her to my house. I'll send the healer over when he is free."

Martel nodded and strode away, Sylpha's limp frame in his arms.

"Can I help?" I asked Oisín. "There must be something I can do?"

"Do you know the healing arts, Stranger?"

I shook my head.

"Then go to the temple of death. The priest and his acolytes will need help preparing the bodies for burial."

I nodded and turned to make my way to the temple.

"Stranger," Oisín called to me softly.

"Yes?"

"I do not know how you managed to shriek in the voice of the Seeker's Son, and I don't want to know. You saved my son's life, and I thank you."

Unsure what, exactly, Oisín meant but with no time to enquire, I nodded and left.

My arrival at the temple of death was barely acknowledged. Acolytes in black robes ran through the small space, piling bodies or sorting bits of bodies. Others ran in and out of the temple to fetch ingredients for more embalming fluid. Other residents of the town had also come to help. They were the ones carrying the prepared bodies out of the temple to the burial grounds to make room for the steady flow of bodies that streamed in.

"You!" a man in armour called to me. "Come. We need an extra hand with these stretchers."

I was put to work, taking the prepared bodies out of the temple and down to the burial grounds beyond the walls of the city. It was hard work, and the sun set long before I was done. Complaining, however, would be in very poor taste; everyone had been working hard. The funerary pyres were lit one by one, burning long before the last of the dead were prepared for burial and brought to the burial grounds. As the last stretcher bearing a body was laid upon its pyre, the priest of death walked forward, uttered a quick blessing before lighting the pyre.

No sooner did the flames catch than the exhausted old man crumpled to the ground. The acolytes swarmed him and, between six of them, carried him reverently back to the temple.

"Stranger," Martel said, appearing out of the dark like a ghost. I jumped, prompting the leader of the rangers to smile. "Sorry," he said. Then, "You look exhausted."

"You too," I noted. Martel nodded.

"Any news on Sylpha?"

"Asleep," Martel said. "The healer has been by several times to check on her. He thinks she'll recover with some food and rest."

"That's good."

"It is. So, is there something you want to tell me?"

I blinked stupidly and frowned at Martel. "Sorry?"

"You and the Seeker's Son. What is your connection?"

"I don't—"

"You spoke with its voice!" Martel snapped. "Don't tell me there isn't a connection!"

"All I did was scream!" I protested. "I have no idea what you're talking about!"

Martel clamped his mouth shut and eyed me intently. At length, he nodded. "I believe you," he said at last.

"Now what?" I asked him.

"I was about to ask the same. Oisín and Eilir are with their son, watching over Fergus, who hovers dangerously close to death."

I looked up sharply.

Martel grimaced. "It was his body the boy was trying to protect from the Seeker's Son."

"Gods above and below!" I breathed.

"Brave boy."

"Yes." I thought a moment. "It appears we should split up," I said.

Martel raised his eyebrows at me and I smiled.

"We will need more intelligence on that last piece of the sceptre. I doubt very much that those grass dogs are guarding it just for fun. There has to be more to it. It would probably be a good idea to find out who controls those reptiles and what, precisely, they can do. If you send some of your rangers back, they can rest up while a fresh group can go on the reconnaissance mission. It'll save time for when you, myself, Oisín and Sylpha arrive."

"You mean to stay?"

"Oisín has generously allied himself with us, and for it his people suffered an attack by a Seeker's Son. The very least we can do is help them get back on their feet. Besides, I feel that Oisín will be very reluctant to travel with his father so ill."

Martel nodded. "Yes. That makes good sense." He looked at me and grinned. "You have a good head on your shoulders, Stranger."

I smiled.

"Sometimes," he added.

This time it was me who raised their eyebrows. Martel chuckled. "Come on," he said. "You need some food and rest. There's hard work to be done in the days ahead."

Nodding, I followed Martel to Oisín's residence. Inside, Sylpha lay on a makeshift bed near the hearth. Though she still looked very unwell, her colour had improved. Eilir tended to her, looking up briefly and smiling sadly.

"Fergus?" Martel asked.

Eilir silently nodded her head towards the loft, where Oisín sat on a stool by his father's bed. A tall bundle of furs covered the bed and, I realised, kept the unmoving bulk of Fergus warm. Martel excused himself and climbed the ladder leading to the loft. I watched as he greeted Oisín, who barely responded.

They spoke briefly before Martel took his place and Oisín trudged wearily down the stairs. Something slid off the bed and, moments later, that something trundled down the stairs, red hair gleaming in the firelight. The boy stopped in his tracks when he saw me, and moved closer to his father.

"It's all right, Llei," Oisín said. "This is the Sky Road Walker."

Llei did not move, staring at me with swollen red eyes. He had been crying. "He's going to die," Llei said softly. "Grandpappy."

"Perhaps not," I answered, trying to sound chipper.

Llei frowned at me and shook his head. "No. He will die. I've seen it."

"That's enough, now," Oisín said. Llei looked up at him and fresh tears struck his eyes.

"I'm sorry, Papa," he whispered.

Sighing, Oisín knelt and looked his son in the eye. "Your great grandmother was a seer, did you know that?"

Llei smiled slightly. "I know."

"Do you?"

"Yes. She told me."

Oisín blinked rapidly. "Llei, she died long before you were born."

"I know."

Oisín turned to look at Eilir, who still sat by Sylpha, only now she was watching her solemn son.

"She told me to tell you that she isn't angry," Llei continued.

"Angry?"

"Yes. She said that she had appeared to you as well, when you were a boy. But you were fearful, and shunned her. She told me to tell you that she isn't angry. In fact, she said she is very proud of you. She thinks you have made a fine chieftain."

"No one knows about that," Oisín whispered. He turned to me and said, "I've told no one about that dream except Eilir."

"Perhaps, then, your son is telling the truth."

Oisín turned back to his son. "Were you not afraid?"

"Yes," Llei replied, nodding. "At first. But I saw she wasn't doing anything bad, and we talked."

"Llei," Eilir called softly. "What of Sylpha?"

The fire-touched child walked forward, around the hearth and scrambled onto his mother's lap. Reaching across, he gently touched the aged chieftain's cheek. After a short silence, he smiled slightly and turned to his mother.

"Nothing is certain, but it seems likeliest that she will live," he said. "And she told me to tell you to stop fussing and get something to eat."

Eilir pulled her son close and kissed the top of his head. She looked up at her husband. Tears trickled silently down his cheeks.

"Llei?"

"Yes, mother?"

"Will you run to the inn and fetch something to eat for us? Craig owes us some food, and I'll wager he'll not be feeding too many this night."

"Yes, mother." Llei slid off his mother's lap and ran out the door of the chieftain's house. Eilir rose and went to her husband, wrapping her strong arms around him in a tight embrace.

Oisín buried his face in her neck and wept. She, too, began to cry.

I had to turn to prevent my own tears, so I took Eilir's place by Sylpha and stared glumly into the fire. After a long silence, in which the only sound was the stifled grief of the chieftain and his wife, Oisín took a shaky breath and stepped back from his beloved.

"I need to go make funerary arrangements," he murmured. He kissed his wife softly before turning and leaving the round house. Eilir stared after him long after he had vanished from sight. She turned to meet my gaze.

"I'm so sorry," I whispered.

Eilir mustered a smile. "Thank you. Fergus seemed invincible to us all. I fear that Oisín will take it very hard."

"Is there no way to... I don't know.... fix this?"

Shrugging, Eilir fetched more wood from the pile near the door to throw onto the hearth fire. "It is unlikely. I do not have the blood, and none in my family ever has, so I know little of the way seeing works. I gather that nothing is revealed until it is the only thing possible. Besides, I think Fergus would be rather pleased, actually. He used to grumble fiercely about friends long gone who died glorious deaths, while he was left to waste away, withered by time and age and uselessness. This way, his name may yet live on in poems and song."

I smiled. "Facing down a Seeker's Son is surely worthy of the greatest fireside tales."

Eilir giggled. "Yes, that would suit him very well."

A noise at the door drew my attention. Oisín had returned from his visit to the temple of death. "What are you giggling about?" he asked his wife.

"Your father," Eilir answered, giving a quick peck on his cheek.

"And how pleased he will be to be sung of in the years to come."

Oisín smiled sadly. "That is true enough."

Llei came racing back into the house, ploughing into his father's leg and wrapping his arms around it. He turned his large grey eyes towards his mother. "Craig said the food will be ready soon. He will send his daughters up with it."

"Thank you, Llei."

Llei smiled and looked up at his father, resting his little chin against his father's thigh. "Papa, what will you do with the sceptre piece now?"

Oisín looked down at his son briefly, then across at me.

"We can stay for as long as your people need aid," I said. "Martel will be sending the majority of the rangers back, but he and I and a few others will stay behind to help in any way we can."

"Thank you," Oisín said. He frowned, fading into deep thought. "I will have to stay on," he whispered. He turned to his wife. "You will take the sceptre piece and go back with the rangers when the work here is done. You must be my representative in this. I will have to stay. I cannot leave our people without a leader."

"I could lead them," Llei offered helpfully.

"You're too young yet, little man," Oisín said with a small smile.

"No, my love," Eilir said, shaking her head. "I know you wish to go, even if only to prove to yourself that you are as worthy as your father. I will stay behind. The people trust me and I can rule in your name until you return."

"I cannot leave my people," Oisín insisted.

"You've wanted your chance at adventure since I've known you, Oisín."

"The time for that is past. It cannot be helped now. You will go in my stead."

Eilir straightened and folded her arms. "No. I will stay."

"You will go."

"And who is going to make me?"

Oisín turned to me, looking at me expectantly. Eilir did the same, her arms still folded. I looked between them, helpless.

"You know, it wasn't too long ago that you were arguing over which of you would come with us," I said with a half-hearted smile. The chieftain and his wife continued to look at me in silence. I sighed.

I looked between the two. Eilir and Oisín continued to stare at me, expecting an answer.

"Well," I said. "Oisín, as chieftain it was your decision to hand over the sceptre, and you did promise the other chieftains that you would be around to ensure that we were honest, and stayed honest."

Oisín scowled at me. "I did," he said slowly. "That is true."

"If only one of you must come," I continued. "It should be you."

Eilir smiled slightly, giving a quick sidelong glance at her husband. Oisín's scowl changed to a frown of thought. After a long silence, he nodded. "Fine," he said. "I will go." He turned to his wife. "You win."

Eilir's smile broadened. "I always win."

Oisín grunted.

"My lord," a young woman said from the door. "Forgive the intrusion. Father said that you requested food?"

"Yes," Eilir said. "Please come in."

No less than seven girls walked into the chieftain's abode, carrying platters of steaming food and pitchers of freshly de-oaked mead. It was as if the chieftain was hosting a feast, so much food streamed in.

"Good grief!" Eilir said. "We are not an army!"

"Father said the food will spoil if he didn't cook it up now."

"Greta, would you be a dear and run some of these dishes up to the temple of Death? The acolytes worked very hard today and the priest is unwell. They could use a hearty meal."

"Yes, my Lady. Right away."

The young girl named Greta chose four plates and three pitchers, handing them off to her sisters before the gaggle of girls vanished back into the destroyed village. Eilir sighed.

"This is still too much food."

"You might be surprised," Oisín said. "In spite of everything, I'm famished."

Smiling, Eilir indicated for her husband to sit. He beckoned me over to join him and, before long, the four of us were having a quiet meal. Halfway through, Eilir stood and filled a now empty plate and an extra mead horn and took them upstairs to Martel. After a brief, muted conversation, Eilir returned and continued to eat.

The stress of the day settled into my bones, making them ache and my eyelids wearily drooped despite my best efforts.

"Come on," Eilir said. "Let's find you somewhere to sleep. You will be asleep in your chair, otherwise."

I smiled sheepishly at her, but did not argue. She was right. I would likely have fallen asleep in my seat, and face-planted right in my plate. I followed her to the two beds that had been made beneath the second floor. Gratefully, I chose a bed and collapsed on it, falling asleep before Eilir had even returned to her place at the table.

Sobbing woke me. It was not quite dawn yet, but a thin film of soft grey over everything informed me that dawn was not far away. The sobbing was coming from upstairs. My heart sank. I rolled over, noticing Martel asleep in the bed beside mine. The crying had not woken him. Even asleep, he looked so tired that I doubted anything could. Sighing to myself, I slid out of the bed and made my slow way up the stairs.

Oisín stood behind his wife, who sat on the stool beside the bed. She rested her head on Fergus' now still chest and wept. Little red-headed Llei stood beside her, tears streaming silently down his cheeks. One hand rested on his mother's arm, the other wrapped around one of his father's knees. He saw me first and nodded a solemn greeting. I nodded in return. Oisín noticed me and offered a small, sad smile.

Leaving his wife and son, Oisín approached.

"I am so sorry," I said softly.

Oisín nodded. Now that he was closer, I could see that he had been crying as well. Now, however, there were no tears. "We were expecting it," he said softly. His voice trembled a little.

"This Seeker's Son," he said after a short pause. "Can it be killed?"

I shrugged. "I've only ever seen it expelled. But it always comes back. If there is a way to kill it, I do not know it."

Oisín's expression hardened and, for a moment, I found myself staring into the steel eyes of Fergus. "Help me find a way. I want to watch that thing burn."

I nodded. "I swear it. We will find a way."

Nodding Oisín glanced back at his family. "I have to go inform the acolytes of Death."

"Stay with your family," I said. "I know the way to the temple. I'll go."

"Thank you."

I offered a smile before turning around and heading down the stairs and out into the dull grey of first light. I returned after running my errand to a quiet house. Eilir had stopped sobbing, and now simply sat on the stool, her back resting against her husband and her son in her lap. Martel was still asleep on his bed, and still looked incredibly exhausted. I crawled back into bed and fell asleep promptly.

When I next awoke, it was lunch hour. Martel's bed was empty. I sat up and stretched, looking around. Oisín greeted me with a smile from a seat by the hearth.

"Martel has gone to help the shepherds rebuild their houses. He has already sent the majority of the rangers back with instructions. The others are moving through the village helping distribute food and administering aid to the injured."

I nodded. "He looked like death this morning."

"He still does. The man works hard."

"Anything I can do?"

Oisín shrugged. "Not really. Not yet. When Martel comes in this afternoon, you can convince him to get back into bed. He'll be no good to us half-dead."

I grinned and, when Martel walked through the door seeking a small bite to eat, I managed to get him into bed without much fuss, promising to take over his chores for the rest of the day.

That evening, the entire village gathered for the funeral of Fergus. No one was spared grief at his passing. There were tears enough to put out the funeral pyre, had they landed on it. Though the ceremony was brief, the mourners stayed on long into the night, watching the fire dance.

The next morning, I awoke late again to find Martel had already left to help the villagers. Eilir stayed behind this time, warning me that Martel needed to rest. So, as it was the last time, I sent Martel to bed when he returned in the afternoon and headed out to take over for him.

It went on like this for the better part of a week. Martel worked in the morning and returned exhausted in the afternoon. I took over his duties and encouraged him to rest. Sylpha slowly gained strength during this time and before the week was out, she stepped from her bed for the first time. With Eilir's constant attention, the aged chieftain managed a small walk around the house before having to lie down again. She rose at dinner once more, noting everyone's surprised expressions as she shuffled forward to sit at the table.

She looked across at Martel. "You look awful," she croaked.

Martel grunted. "Says the raven to the coal."

Sylpha laughed. "Aye, true enough. Still, you look unwell."

"I'm just tired, is all."

"That is not all," Llei offered. "You're getting sick."

"I am not," Martel countered. "I haven't been sick since I was a boy, poison notwithstanding."

"Aye, well, you're getting sick now," Sylpha noted. "You need bed rest."

"My work is not done."

"And it will never get done if you collapse of exhaustion, either," Oisín said. "Stay in bed tomorrow. The Sky Road Walker and I can take care of what little there is left to do."

I nodded in agreement.

"I can do it!" Martel insisted.

Oisín narrowed his eyes at him, then smiled. "You are not responsible for what happened here."

Martel looked down at his plate. "Aren't I? I knew we were being chased by the Seeker's Son. Perhaps it would not have attacked if we had not passed through here."

"Perhaps. But how else would you acquire the sceptre, the thing you need that will ultimately defeat this spectre?"

Martel grunted. "A lot of people have died."

"And a lot more will," Sylpha said. "That is the nature of war, my unhappy friend. But yet more would die if you had not done what you did."

"Well I never," Oisín teased. "A ranger of the empire who is squeamish about death."

"Death does not disturb me," Martel snapped. He sighed. "Sorry. I did not mean to be harsh. And it is not entirely true. Unnecessary deaths... preventable deaths... these disturb me a great deal."

Sylpha smiled. "May it ever be so," she said. "For that makes you a good man."

Martel smiled at her.

"Now go to bed," she commanded.

Eilir choked back a sudden laugh. Martel, the anger gone from him now, laughed softly and nodded. "Yes, my Lady," he said, standing. He retired to bed and the sound of his soft snores accompanied the conversation over dinner that evening.

Chapter Fifteen

It took three days more of back-breaking work to restore the village and have it functioning again. Thoroughly exhausted, I relished the slower pace and ample sleep that followed. Sylpha regained her strength and was able to ride again after the second week. Martel, in that time, deteriorated rapidly. His exhaustion was compounded by difficulty breathing, a thick cough, and a body that ached so terribly every movement made him wince.

Not knowing what else to do, I hovered by his bed and nursed him as much as possible, despite the flat stares he gave me. By the end of the third week, Martel was bedridden.

"We cannot wait any longer," Martel managed to wheeze at me as I spoon fed him soup. "We have to get going."

"You are in no state to travel," I said bluntly.

"Our work here is done," Martel insisted. "We need to get that last sceptre piece."

"You can't even get out of bed, Martel."

"I can." Martel attempted it, but could barely move. "With help," he admitted at last.

Despite myself, I laughed.

"Have a wagon made," Martel said. "My horse can pull it. That way I can rest as we move."

"And you will die of exposure," I argued. "You aren't well enough to be outside at all hours of the night."

"Don't argue with me," Martel said. "We're out of time, and you know it. The Seeker's Son will return. We cannot endanger the village for a second time."

I scowled at him. The silence stretched on as I turned thoughts over in my mind. There had to be some way to keep Martel safe and acquire the final sceptre piece. I blinked rapidly, realising that I had not spoken for quite some time. Martel stared at me expectantly, one eyebrow raised.

"Sorry," I mumbled. "I was running through our options and had a strange daydream."

Martel grunted and relaxed back down against his pillows, wincing as his body protested. "What was it about?" he asked.

"Just... well... it was me trying to head out on my own in an effort to draw the Seeker's Son away from the village while you recovered."

Both of Martel's eyebrows rose.

"It didn't end well," I noted.

"Nor would it. It's a stupid idea."

Nodding in agreement, and noticing that Martel was rapidly losing a battle with sleep, I said, "All right. We will have a wagon made for you. Now get as much rest as possible. It's going to be a long journey home."

Martel smiled and closed his eyes. He was asleep almost instantly. Sighing, I gathered what remained of his meal and left him to rest. Outside, I found Sylpha sitting on the long bench by the door, her eyes closed as she soaked up the golden sunlight.

"So," she said without opening her eyes. "We will leave the north soon."

I nodded before realising that she had her eyes closed and could not see me. "Yes," I said. I walked over to the bench and sat beside her.

"You are concerned."

"Martel is too unwell to move."

"Aye," Sylpha said. "But he won't be the one moving."

"You know what I mean."

Sylpha chuckled. "Fear not for your brave captain, Sky Road Walker. He is made of surprisingly stern stuff. The illness he has, for example, would have killed anyone else by now."

"You know what ails him?"

"Aye. I treat him for it, too."

"So this thing... it's usually fatal?"

"Not always. Largely so, though."

"Well... fantastic."

Sylpha chuckled again.

"Well," I said. "I ought to go see the cartwright. We'll be off in a couple of days, I expect."

I was right. The cartwright, a man of impeccable skill, took only a day to build a sturdy, narrow wagon suitable for dragging Martel across the country. News of Martel's illness had the village in a frenzy. Families spent much of their time baking travelling breads and sweet pastries to keep Martel fed. A woodsman and his trapper wife came into the village bearing smoked meats, sausages, dried fish and a strange, fatty meat leather they called Pumpum. The also bore enough furs to smother an ox. The furs were used to line the wagon, making it nice and soft and very warm. A bear skin was set aside to use as a blanket.

Martel's fiery stallion was dressed and the wagon attached in front of Oisín's house. Moments later, Martel, leaning heavily on the young chieftain, walked slowly from the round house. I could tell that his stumbling steps were excruciatingly painful. His face twisted in a perpetual grimace as each tiny step brought him closer to the wagon.

He made it to the first stone step down from the threshold of the chieftain's house before his knees buckled. Martel shuddered and fell heavily, Oisín struggling to keep him on his feet. I ran to Martel's side and helped him up.

"I can walk," Martel growled.

I simply rolled my eyes and, with Oisín, half-helped half-dragged Martel to the wagon. The woodsman jumped into the wagon. "Here," the swarthy man said. "Hand him over."

I did so, moving to get into the wagon to help. The woodsman did not need help. Despite his lanky, wiry frame, he easily lifted Martel up and into the wagon.

"I carry elk," he explained as I stared incredulously at him.

Shrugging, I jumped into the wagon to help Martel get comfortable. When everything was settled, I covered Martel over with the bear fur. He did not even notice, having fallen unconscious the moment he was hauled up into the wagon. I looked down at his ashen face and shook my head before jumping down.

It took another few minutes before Oisín was ready to ride. He re-emerged from his house in leather and chainmail, a fur wrapped around his shoulders, lending greater bulk to an already impressive frame. A short sword was strapped to his side, two long daggers rested comfortably into his boots, and his father's battle-axe sat squarely between his shoulders, strapped to his back.

Eilir followed her husband outside, carrying Llei on her hip. Oisín turned to them and uttered a soft, tender goodbye before turning away and mounting his horse. The small breed of mountain horse must have been incredibly strong to carry someone Oisín's size in full armour. The horse itself barely seemed to register the presence of its rider, choosing instead to continue grazing on the small lawn before the round house.

Sylpha, already on her mount, beckoned me over to Fas, who had been dressed for me. The rotund beast flicked her ears as I approached.

"Good morning to you, too," I said before launching myself into the saddle.

With one last glance at his beautiful wife, Oisín led our small group through the village to the tall gates in the palisades. There, the group was joined by a select number of warriors of Oisín's choosing. They saluted their chieftain smartly before falling in line behind him.

During the journey, Sylpha remained beside Martel's wagon and at every stop, she jumped from her mount into the wagon to administer Martel's medicine. He awoke on the second day briefly at lunch. I took the opportunity to force some Pumpum into his mouth and ensure he swallowed it, along with a warm cup of tea.

Martel looked annoyed at my mothering, but I reminded him that he is too ill to do anything about it. My challenge to have him stop me remained unanswered. This did not please me as much as one might think.

The wagon slowed our travel considerably. There were no roads in the north to facilitate the vehicle, making navigation something of a trick. After four days, we found ourselves on the crest of a rocky hill over-looking a familiar valley. From this angle, I had no difficulty finding any number of hiding places for fighting men and their small mountain horses.

Carefully as possible, the group made their descent into the valley. One of the northmen was forced to dismount and latch onto the back of the wagon, acting as a brace and brake down the steep slope. His horse trailed behind him, making things difficult by playfully biting the northman's rump.

It took the better part of three hours to reach the valley floor, but it was managed without the wagon upturning once.

That night, I sat at the fire and stared into the dancing flames. As my mind drifted away, I heard the distant sounds of rushing water. I jumped to my feet in alarm, drawing everyone's attention.

"What is it?" Oisín demanded.

"I heard the water," I replied.

"Seeker's Son," Sylpha said softly. "I heard it too. The spectre is far away yet, but we should try and move faster come the morning."

"Agreed," Oisín said. He sighed as he finished his meal. "I will take the first watch."

The company moved out before dawn the following morning. Oisín pushed a little harder, worry for what it might to do Martel overshadowed by the imminent arrival of the Seeker's Son. The terrain slowly changed, the rocky grasslands giving way to the forested lands of the south.

At the edge of the woods that mark the territory of the empire were three paths. I did not recall there being three paths when we came north, but there were three paths there nonetheless.

Oisín turned to me. "Which way, Sky Road Walker?"

I swallowed. I could not remember which path we might have come up on, and each path looked more or less the same as the others; neither more sinister nor more pleasant. All of them headed south.

"Honestly," I said to Oisín. "I have no clue, but I think we came up the path on the right."

Oisín raised his brows at me and looked back at Martel. The man was still unconscious in the wagon and could offer no aid. Oisín turned back to me and shrugged.

"All right," he said. Without another word, he kicked his horse and the group moved down the path on the right. Martel's wagon sat between two groups of mounted northern warriors. Sylpha rode beside him, checking on him frequently. I did not like the look of her furrowed brow each time she checked on the ranger.

Every so often, Oisín sent scouts ahead of the party. They returned with little news to report the first day. The path remained clear and movement was much easier for Martel's wagon. There was little space on the side of the pathway to make camp and so we were forced to sleep on the road, amongst the horses. I, very wisely, decided that I would not get trampled in the night if I slept under the wagon.

Sylpha, who appointed herself Martel's personal physician, took up what little space was left in the wagon, her long, slender frame barely fitting. She placed her hand on Martel's chest, so that she could feel the steady rise and fall. Should that cease, it would wake her immediately.

Oisín preferred to sleep sitting upright. He settled against the roots of a massive tree and closed his eyes. Two of his warriors, twins by the look of them, stood the first watch. The woman and her brother took up their vigil at either end of the long train of travellers.

Weary from the road and the worry about Martel, I fell asleep the moment my head touched the ground.

🐚🐚🐚

"Well, now. Who are you?" the voice was deep and dark. It sent a chill through my entire being. I opened my eyes, but saw nothing. It was pitch black.

"Who's there?" I asked. Fear turned my voice into a timid squeak.

The voice paused before saying, "You seem familiar to me. Who are you?"

"I don't know what you're talking about. Where am I? What is going on?"

"You are seeking what I am seeking, no? You want the imperial sceptre and thus the imperial throne."

I clamped my mouth shut. "Who are you?" I demanded again, gathering my courage. "Show yourself!"

In the darkness that surrounded me echoed a quiet, sinister laugh.

"Be gone, foul fiend!" a sharp feminine voice snapped.

I turned towards the sound and saw the faintly glowing image of a woman. She was tall and muscular, her bronze skin and hazel eyes shining. Upon her head she wore a crown that evoked the tines of many stags carved in a strange, pale wood.

"You cannot stop me," the deep, dark voice hissed.

"I have before," the woman countered. "I will again."

The deep voice did not reply, and the oppressive dark began to wane. The woman became clearer to me. She stared at me, observing me with those wide, hazel eyes. She reminded me of an eagle; fierce and regal. Her gaze made me slightly uncomfortable and I shifted my weight.

"Interesting," the woman said at last.

"What is?"

The woman simply smiled at me. It was a small, knowing smile; smug rather than mirthful. "The Seeker's Son has taken one. The Seeker's Son has three. The Seeker's Son takes another one. The Seeker's son seeks you."

I blinked. "Wait. Three? Two. That poem states that the Seeker's Son has two."

The woman's irritatingly knowing smile broadened.

"Three doesn't even rhyme," I ended lamely.

The woman laughed.

"Ever do the Seeker's Sons seek each other. And when they find one another, they battle. And the victor of the fight takes the loser, and thus fortifies itself. On and on these battles are fought until there remains but one."

"The Mage King."

The woman nodded. "His strength gathers. Always he is plotting and planning. But he is not the only power that exists. Trust the light, Sky Road Walker. You are not alone in this fight."

"You said you had stopped him before. That was the Mage King, wasn't it? And you're Empress Moua. Aren't you?"

The woman smiled brightly, this time looking genuinely happy, but she said nothing.

"This light you speak of... what is it? Where is it? How will I know it if I see it?"

"If it is the light you seek, Sky Road Walker, look within. There resides the light that will guide you, and the dark that will destroy you. Now you must wake. Danger approaches. Wake."

❧ ❧ ❧

My eyes snapped open and I sat bolt upright... or tried to. I smacked my forehead on the bottom of the wagon.

"Ow," I moaned, clutching my head.

Sylpha's head appeared upside-down to my right. "Are you all right?"

"Fine," I managed, though my sight was swimming.

"That sounded like you cracked your skull."

"Felt like it too. How is Martel?"

"Breathing. Which is good."

"We have to get moving."

Sylpha raised her eyebrows at me. "Oh?"

"Danger is coming."

To her credit, Sylpha did not argue. Her face disappeared. I saw her feet as she jumped lithely from the wagon. She ran off, silently waking everyone. Meanwhile, I slid out from under the wagon and ran to Fas, who dozed on her feet. She snorted at me as I grabbed my weapons from her tack and strapped them on.

Oisín tapped me on the shoulder and I turned. His eyes grew wide. "You're bleeding!" he hissed.

I reached up and touched my forehead. My fingers came away slick with blood. I shrugged. "Long story," I whispered back. "We need to get moving."

Oisín nodded. He beckoned one of his warriors forward and pointed at my cut forehead. The warrior nodded, opened one of the many pouches strapped to his person, and pulled out a phial and a cloth. He very quickly cleaned my wound and dressed it before letting me mount Fas.

In minutes, we were on the move through the black of the night. Scouts were sent ahead some time ago, but had not yet reported back. I kept my ears open, searching for the sound of rushing water, but could not hear it. After several tense minutes, Oisín rode to my side.

"Are you certain there is trouble?" he whispered.

"I was given a warning," I whispered back.

"By whom?"

"Long story."

Oisín scowled, but remained silent.

"My Lord," a northman whispered harshly. Oisín looked back at him, then over to where the man pointed.

Lights danced and flickered deep in the woods west of us. They looked like lanterns, but they moved through the air at an impossible height. Lanterns carried by giants? Very, very silent giants... with very, very small lanterns.

The thunder of horses at a dead run turned my head south. Both scouts returned, looking pale.

"My Lord," one said in a harsh whisper. "There is a stone bridge ahead. Much of it is destroyed. We'd be able to pass at the fjord nearby, but we saw evidence of trolls."

"A lot of evidence," the second scout said. "It might be an entire family."

"We're not enough to fight that!" another rider whispered in alarm.

"Shhhh!" Oisín hissed.

I heard the sound of rushing water far off in the distance and turned my head north. "Damn it!"

"Seeker's Son," Sylpha noted, her eyes also watching the north.

I looked around. The woods on the east side of the road were far too dense to bring Martel's wagon through. To the south sat a family of trolls, and whatever they are, they terrified the northmen. To the west danced the mysterious lantern lights.

"Right," Oisín said. "We can go south and hope that we can either pass by the trolls unnoticed or we can defeat them. Or we head east."

"Martel's wagon won't fit through there," I answered. "Why can't we go west?"

"Towards the lanterns? Are you insane? Those are wood wights!"

"What now?"

"Spirits of the trees," Sylpha answered for Oisín. "Folk legend of the south says they lure travellers off paths in order to get them lost in the woods where the wights descend upon them and feed."

"Oh. But that's just lore, right? It's not actual fact."

"Before now, the Seeker's Son was just lore," Oisín noted dryly.

"Point taken. Speaking of the Seeker's Son, it is chasing us south. We can't go north."

"We cannot go south," one of the scouts whispered with a shudder.

"We cannot go east," Sylpha added. "Not without killing Martel."

"And if we head west, we'll be eaten alive by wood wights." Oisín growled. He swore and looked at me. "All right, Sky Road Walker. What do we do?"

"I'm not risking Martel's life," I said. "The wagon won't fit through the woods on the eastern side, and it's unlikely that a wagon would be able to outrun trolls as well. We're going west."

"To the wood wights," Oisín whispered harshly. "Are you mad?"

"Would you rather fight the trolls?" I snapped back.

Silence descended on the northmen as they pondered their options.

"Fine," Oisín grated. "Fine. West it is."

"All right," I said. "Let's go. Quickly!"

No one moved. I sighed and kicked Fas' flanks. She trotted forward without hesitation, flicking her ear at Oisín as she passed. Behind me, I heard Sylpha chuckle.

With me leading, the group moved through the broad-based trees into the wilderness. Despite there being no wind, the trees creaked and groaned. The group unconsciously slowed, looking up at the swaying canopy in the sky as the forest came to life. Before us, the bizarre lights danced and flickered, zipping away from us if we got too close. The cluster of lights was beautiful, and I found myself marvelling at them, often forgetting the trouble we were in.

The sound of rushing water followed us, sometimes growing stronger, sometimes fading away.

"Sky Road Walker," Oisín hissed at me. "Don't follow the lights!"

"I'm not!" I hissed back. "They're just always in front!"

Oisín grunted.

"I don't like this," another northman noted, hunching down in his saddle.

"No one likes this," Sylpha answered. I smiled slightly at her irritated matronly tone.

I turned back to smile at her as she rode beside the wagon. The smile dropped from my face quickly. A shadow stalked the group. I could see nothing but darkness; a hooded figure of black. At first I mistook it for the Seeker's Son, and my heart dropped to my stomach. I was no longer paying attention to where I was going and Fas stopped.

Sylpha saw my wide-eyed fear and turned to look behind her. The shadow vanished. She never saw it. She turned back to me with a scowl.

I blinked stupidly at her. "There was a shadow," I said.

"Yes," Sylpha replied slowly. "That is what happens when there is light before you."

"No, I mean a shadowy figure. Wearing a hood. And riding... well... some kind of beast."

"Some kind of beast?"

I opened my mouth to explain, but the sound of rushing water throbbed loud in my ears, freezing my blood.

"The Seeker's Son!" Sylpha barked. "It's found our trail!"

I shuddered, turning back and kicking Fas into action. The horse snorted and bolted forward. I glanced behind, noting Martel's wagon following at a good pace, but Martel was bounced around as the wagon wheels hit tree roots and rocks.

The lights in front of us continued their dance, always in front of us, never too close. The Seeker's Son shrieked, the chilling sound echoing in the night, and the lights vanished, scattering like a pack of startled cats.

I gritted my teeth and pushed Fas harder. A rustling sound to my left turned my head. The shadow was back, riding a stag that was altogether too large to be any kind of deer I had ever seen. The deer-thing matched pace with Fas. The shadow turned its hooded head, and I found myself peering into the softly glowing green eyes of the shade.

The shadow veered off, disappearing into the night. I grimaced and continued our desperate flight. One of the lanterns reappeared ahead of me, at my right. It bounced up and down in an excited motion, as if trying to get my attention. I scowled at it and it vanished, zipping quickly through the trees and over the shoulder of the shade, which sat on its mount, its glowing eyes fixed on me. It turned and bolted into the night, disappearing through the trees in the same direction the wight lantern had fled.

The rushing water drew closer.

I tried to ignore the shade, but it reappeared, a wight lantern whipping around it and bouncing up and down, near my right. Again, the shade turned its mount and bolted away. The wight lantern did not, choosing instead to bounce up and down and spin around and around.

Swearing under my breath, I turned Fas a hard right. Snorting in irritation, Fas moved as quickly as her rotund body allowed.

Without questioning, the group followed. Martel's wagon took more time to turn the corner than I liked. I turned to see the wispy robes of the Seeker's Son flicker in the dark, not far behind the wagon.

Turning back, I saw the shade upon the dark stag, this time on my left. Again it bolted. Again I turned Fas to follow. Thrice more I weaved through the trees, following our silent, shadowy guide. The sound of rushing water punctuated by the occasional chilling shriek ensured we did not slow in our flight.

Until we had no choice.

Two large trees in front of me uprooted themselves, the ground rumbling as they moved. Wood creaking, they wound their free roots together, they pulled themselves close, blocking our path. Fas reared with a shrill neigh. I turned left, but the trees there did the same. I turned around the other way to find that path already blocked by yet more trees.

The group bunched up.

"Back!" I barked. Too late, the trees behind us had entwined their roots and pulled themselves close. Through the gaps between the massive trunks, I could see yet more trees doing the same, until the forest could not be seen. All that remained was a massive circle of tree trunks; a giant impenetrable fortress of living wood.

"Into what devilish trap have you led us?" Oisín demanded.

"Shh!" Sylpha hissed.

Silence immediately fell over the group. Beyond the encircling trees the Seeker's Son shrieked. I heard it utter a shriek every so often from various directions.

"It has lost our scent," Sylpha whispered. She turned and looked at me. I shrugged at her. Having not devised this plan, or knowing what to do now, there was little else I could do.

In silence, the group waited, listening to the cries of the Seeker's Son as it darted through the forest around our wooden prison. It sounded confused and lost. That alone put a smile on my face.

The smile faded when the Seeker's Son uttered one last sound; a howl so savage it caused my blood to run cold and my stomach to clench.

The forest fell silent. The trees no longer creaked. The wind did not rustle the leaves. The insects that usually sang in the night had silenced their chorus. Everything was dead silent. I exchanged glances with Oisín and Sylpha.

Chapter Sixteen

For some time the woods remained silent. We remained stuck inside the tree prison, with nothing to do and nowhere to go. Sylpha had long since dismounted and gone to Martel's side to treat him for the various cuts and bruises he sustained during the flight from the Seeker's Son. Several of Oisín's men had fallen asleep in their saddles. One was snoring. Oisín himself had not closed his eyes, but I could not help but feel that perhaps he was sleeping as well. A pair of northmen had pulled out a collapsible board and dice and were playing at some game I could not comprehend while still astride their horses.

I turned my attention upwards. The trees were so tightly entwined I could not see the sky, only masses of leaves and branches twisted together. I sighed. A light zipped between branches and began to slowly float down towards me.

It floated gently down until it was at eye-level, hovering just inches away from my face. The golden light flickered, forming various shapes before me. Mesmerised, I watched it a while. I lifted my hand slowly towards it. When I was almost touching it, the light skittered away, zipping around me. I turned to watch and stopped in surprise.

On the southern end of the prison, the trees had parted. It was still night, though a dull greyness alerted me to the coming sun. Standing at the newly formed entrance, the shade sat atop his oversized stag mount.

I reached out and shook Oisín. The chieftain blinked himself awake and turned to me. He noted my silent stare and turned towards the shade. He yelped, startling the rest of his warriors, and drew his sword.

The shade merely cocked its head. Raising one hand, it performed a flicking motion. Roots rose from the ground and wrapped themselves around Oisín's wrist. He yelled and struggled against the plant. The more he struggled, the tighter the roots grew.

"Stop!" I barked at him.

Oisín stopped, staring blankly at me in surprised obedience. The roots slackened a little and he looked at them a while before turning to the shade, who sat unmoving this whole time.

"Everyone, take your hands away from your weapons," I said calmly.

"Are you insane?" a ranger hissed. "That is a wood wight!"

The glowing green eyes of the shade turned to the woman who spoke. They narrowed at her slightly. She fell into silence, cowed.

"That is not a wood wight," Sylpha whispered, drawing the attention of everyone, including the shade.

"What the hell is it?" Oisín demanded.

"The tuatha call him The Hunter."

Sylpha dismounted the wagon and walked cautiously forward. She stopped before the mounted shade and bowed low. I got the impression she did not bow to many. This shade must surely have been a powerful thing. She spoke with it softly in a language I did not recognise. It was not the language employed by the tuatha who held me captive so many months ago.

The shade answered in kind, its voice soft but deep.

Sylpha turned to me, her eyes wet with tears. "I cannot believe this is real," she whispered. "Come, Sky Road Walker. The Hunter will speak with you."

Swallowing, and ignoring the looks of the northmen, I dismounted and walked slowly forward on legs trembling so hard they almost buckled beneath me. I bowed deeply before The Hunter, just as Sylpha had done. The Hunter spoke again, and I turned to Sylpha, questions written all over my face.

"The Hunter wants to know why you strayed from the road."

"We had little choice," I replied, Sylpha translating. "We were fleeing the Seeker's Son and—"

The Hunter held up its hand, stopping me mid-sentence. It spoke again.

"The Hunter wants to know why you are being pursued by the

Seeker's Son."

I bit my lip. "Beyond the Mage King wanting to return and thus wishing to stop us from restoring the Imperial Throne, I do not know. I only know that I have seen what this spectre does, and I do not wish for that to happen to me, or my friends."

The Hunter fell silent after Sylpha finished translating, sinking into a meditative state.

"Sylpha," I whispered. "Who is the Hunter?"

"The tuatha claim to be the first in these lands, but that is not entirely true. There were beings here before, beings of incredible power. They taught the tuatha all they knew. When men came here and battled the tuatha, they withdrew from the conflict into the shadow that first gave them life. They are guardians of this earth, not arbiters of conflict between peoples. They will kill anyone who harms their lands. The Hunter was... is their king, ruler of their lands and a reaper of the souls of the worthy."

"Souls of the worthy?"

"He and his guard, hunters all, ride out at the death of the year to collect the souls of the brave and generous and give them a place in the cool and calm of the shadow world to rest until they are ready."

"Ready for what?"

"To live again."

"Oh."

I realised the glowing green eyes of The Hunter were watching me carefully. I turned back and offered a weak smile. The Hunter spoke again.

"Why do you wish to restore the throne?" Sylpha translated.

"To stop the Mage King's return," I answered. "To stop the poison of his evil which would infect all things."

"I recall the Mage King," the Hunter said through Sylpha. "And I recall his poison. What assurance have I that you are not his agent?"

I blinked. "Would the Seeker's Son be chasing me if I was?"

"Yes."

It took me a moment to recall what Sylpha had said - that each part of the shattered soul of the Mage King was seeking the other, that those shattered spectres would battle one another for dominance, despite being of the same essence. Perhaps it would chase an agent of the Mage King in the struggle for dominance.

"I cannot offer you any. I don't know myself what game it is we're playing. All I can say is that I was first warned of the Seeker's Son in a village where I was given this as a gift."

I pulled out my broken flint knife from my boot and wiggled it. The glowing green eyes of the Hunter fixed upon it. I blinked in surprise.

"Is this knife important?" I asked. I could not imagine how it could be. It was absolutely useless, frail and broken as it was.

The Hunter reached into a small leather pouch at his side. He extended a gloved hand to reveal fragments of glinting flint. They rose slowly into the air spinning and arranging themselves until it became clear what they were - the pointed end of the knife I held. I stepped forward and placed the knife above the floating pieces. The moment they were in proximity, they connected, glowing red hot as they fused. I released the handle of the knife. Floating before my eyes was a complete dagger.

"The dagger is yours?" I asked.

The Hunter nodded once and spoke.

"Lost on the battlefield, fighting beside the empress in her struggle against the Mage King. Evil cannot touch this blade." Sylpha spoke reverently.

"If it is yours, you must keep it," I said.

The Hunter cocked his head at me again, the glowing in his eyes never wavering. He reached out his hand and the knife floated gently towards it. The shade slid the blade into its boot cuff and straightened. He made a small sign with his hand and a swarm of flickering lights entered the tree prison. Behind me, the northmen sucked in apprehensive breaths. The swarm danced before my eyes a moment before parting.

The parting of the wight lanterns revealed three objects; a plain, unadorned hunting horn, a short, leaf-shaped sword of bronze, and a plain wooden cup with a red crystal embedded in the bottom.

Sylpha looked at them wide-eyed. The Hunter spoke.

"You must choose one," Sylpha whispered. "A gift, to aid your cause."

With no information as to what these objects could possibly mean, or what enchantment may lie upon them, I made a blind guess. Timidly, I reached out and grasped the hunting horn. I could feel it vibrating in my grip.

When my hand moved clear, the wight lanterns descended upon the remaining two objects, covering them completely. When the lights parted, the objects were gone. I looked up at the Hunter.

He spoke and Sylpha translated.

"And so it shall be. Sky Road Walker, in your most desperate hour, blow thrice upon this horn and I, and my hunters, shall come to your aid."

I blinked. "Thank you."

"Take heed, Sky Road Walker. This does not make me your servant. Call upon me unnecessarily, and it shall be your head I collect."

I swallowed back my nervousness at the sinister tone in that warning and nodded.

The Hunter nodded once in return. He spoke directly to Sylpha, a single, short word that I assumed was a farewell. He turned his enormous mount.

"My Lord!" Sylpha said suddenly. "May I impinge upon your favour once more?"

The shadowy figure atop the enormous stag must have been made entirely of emotion. I could feel the irritation radiating from him as truly as if it were heat and he was the sun. He turned back to Sylpha and the proud woman shrank back slightly.

"One of our company is deathly ill," she whispered. "The flight from the Seeker's Son has drained what little strength he had left. I fear he will not survive the rest of our journey."

The Hunter turned his mount once more and stared at Sylpha, his head cocked.

"I fear I have nothing to trade for this aid," Sylpha continued. "But I am begging. Even my knowledge of tuatha medicine could not save him now."

"It is not my place," the Hunter replied. "To so upset the order of things."

"Please."

"It takes a life to save a life, Sylpha of the Purged."

I looked at the tall woman. "Of the Purged?" I asked her. She barely even glanced at me.

"Take mine," she said.

"What?" Oisín barked, turning to her in shock.

"No!" I cried at the same time.

Sylpha put up her hand and everyone fell silent, staring at her in disbelief.

"When our task is done, when the Mage King has at last been defeated, I will ride eternally at your side. I swear it."

The group sat in perfect stillness as the Hunter retreated into contemplative silence.

"It is not an eternity I require," he said at last. "Merely a lifetime. Yours and his." The Hunter nodded at Martel in the wagon.

Smiling slightly, Sylpha nodded. "I swear it."

"So it shall be." The Hunter dismounted, jumping from the giant stag's back with all the grace of a cat. A big, very dangerous cat. "Come."

Sylpha followed the Hunter to Martel's wagon.

"Sylpha, don't," I said as she passed.

The tall, aged warrior merely smiled at me before continuing on. I turned to watch as the Hunter leapt into the wagon, Sylpha close behind. I could feel myself shake with grief screaming for release as the Hunter checked Martel over. He extended a hand to Sylpha, who was standing on the wagon. She took it.

The forest began its unnatural creaking once more. Trees danced in the absence of wind, moving in rhythmic time. One whisper from the Hunter's hidden lips and the space filled with wight lanterns. They danced, a synchronised display of aerial geometry, as they traced lines of light in the air above Martel. I was so enamoured by their grace that it almost skipped my notice that Sylpha's face contorted in pain. Her eyes were squeezed tightly shut, her brows knitted together. I abandoned the light display when I noticed. I felt my stomach turn when she cried out, and blood trickled in a thick drip from her nose.

Then it was over. The wight lanterns vanished suddenly. In the silence, Martel breathed in deeply. My eyes remained fixed on Sylpha. Though her face was no longer contorted, she had yet to open her eyes, and her nose was still bleeding. She swayed dangerously and collapsed.

Despite being too far away to help, I reached out as if to stop her fall.

It was the Hunter who caught her, pulling her close to him to steady her before lowering her gently onto the wagon floor. I ran to the wagon.

"What did you do?" I demanded of the Hunter. The shade's glowing green eyes turned to me and he spoke.

"What she asked."

I looked down at Sylpha's ashen face and swallowed.

"She is bound," the Hunter said. The shadow with glowing eyes reached out and tenderly cleaned the blood from Sylpha's face. "By her vow to me. She has been marked, and will carry that mark until I come for her. It is done."

The Hunter leapt from the wagon, making not a sound when his shadowy feet landed on the mulch of the forest floor. He walked from the ring of trees and back to his mount.

"You are lost," he said. "Follow the lanterns. They will lead you back to the rangers."

"You know where they are?" I asked.

I imagined that the Hunter smiled, though there was nothing about the shade that I could actually see to confirm or deny that smile.

"Follow the lanterns," the Hunter said again. He turned his mount and the giant stag took off. I stared incredulously as other shades, these on horses, their eyes as dark as the rest of them, melted from the shadows and galloped after their king. They flitted through the trees so fast that their forms were impressed upon me rather than seen.

I looked at Oisín who looked back at me, white with fear. We both turned our gazes to the two unconscious figures in the wagon. After a long pause, I rearranged the blankets so that Sylpha was covered and returned to Fas. I mounted.

"I guess we go," I said. I turned my horse and walked from the ring of trees, into a long, dark tunnel made entirely of living wood.

In shocked silence, the northmen followed, one of the twins leading Sylpha's riderless mount. It took a surprisingly long time to reach the forest through the thick tunnel of trees that led away from our holding cell. There was some orange on the horizon when we finally exited. Sunrise. We walked on. A rustling sound made me turn. Our wooden prison was gone, the trees having returned to their previous position.

"There," Oisín said, pointing.

I looked and a lone wight lantern hovered on our left. "That way we go," I sighed.

Though I knew the sun had risen, the trees here were so tall and their canopies so broad that much of the forest remained dark. For days we walked through the woods, guided by that lone wight lantern until it vanished completely. I blinked stupidly when it did. I looked past where it previously hovered. I saw a road that I recognised through the trees, and a familiar rocky outcropping beside that road.

Fas recognised it too, and her ears shot forward, eager for home. I kicked her flanks gently and she walked on. The break in the trees was most welcome, and I smiled as the sun hit me full in the face. I paused a moment to soak it in before returning my attention to our path.

The northmen breathed a sigh of relief as three figures appeared at the rocky outcropping, figures wearing the uniform of the rangers of the empire. They ran forward.

"Gods above and below!" one breathed. "You were gone so long we thought you dead!"

"Almost," I replied with a smile. "How go things here?"

"Good. We are ready to depart at any time. Is Martel not with you?"

I nodded back at the wagon. "Martel was laid low by illness, but we think he is recovering."

"Best get him inside," the ranger said. He turned and, with his friends in tow, led the northmen into the ranger headquarters. I entered last, pausing a moment to look behind me.

There, at the edge of the forest, stood an enormous stag so dark it was almost black. It watched me, its eyes glowing green. I shuddered, turned my back and entered the concealed headquarters.

Basadia nearly tackled me when I entered the dining hall. She hugged me so close I could barely breathe. Laughing, I hugged her back.

"Next time, you take me with you!" she demanded.

"That is up to Martel still," I replied. "How have you been?"

"Bored. Worried. You?"

I smiled. "Hungry for something other than hard bread and leather."

Basadia grinned and walked with me to a table where an inviting plate of hot food waited.

I remained with the rangers for several weeks while Martel and Sylpha gathered their strength. Home and warm, Martel took a surprisingly short time before he was up and about. It was much more difficult for Sylpha, who complained of an ache in her bones. The ache was powerful enough to keep her in bed for two weeks, though she was, thankfully, awake and alert.

It took a month before Martel felt everyone was well enough to travel again. To that end he called Oisín, Sylpha and I to his study. First to arrive, I found him pouring over a map.

"Grass dogs," he said by way of greeting. "Vicious lizards. I hate them."

I recalled my first encounter with grass dogs and nodded. "In this we can agree."

Oisín's arrival drew both our gazes. He carried the sceptre piece with him.

"Thank you," Martel said. He indicated a chest at the far wall of the room. Oisín went to it. He opened it to reveal the first sceptre piece.

"This is what you recovered from the Red Band?" he asked me.

I nodded.

"How did you know it was the right one?"

I shrugged. Oisín shrugged as well. He laid his sceptre piece down in the chest. I heard an almighty clack and Oisín jumped back with a yelp.

"Are you all right?" I demanded.

Oisín looked at me with wide eyes and nodded. He indicated the chest with his head. I went and looked in. Only one piece of the sceptre sat inside the chest, barely fitting now. Twice as long as before, the piece was seamless. I could not tell where the sceptre had been rent. I pulled the singular piece out and held it for Martel to see. Martel walked forward and picked it up, running his fingers over the worked wood in an effort to find the join.

He looked up at me and smiled. "For the first time, I feel like all this effort has achieved something."

"We're going to need to find a better hiding spot," I noted. "If that happens with the piece you are hiding, Martel, the sceptre is not going to fit in that chest."

"No indeed," Martel mused. He turned and placed the almost complete sceptre on his table beside the map. "But that is the least of our concern. Grass dogs. Three at last count, none collared, so we can guess that they're likely wild and held to guard the final sceptre piece by some thrall spell."

"Sorcerers," Oisín grunted. "I hate them."

"Sorcery has saved lives," Sylpha responded.

"Aye," Oisín agreed. "And taken more."

"Blame the wielder, not the tool."

Oisín grunted.

"There are two approaches I can see," Martel continued, shooting an irritated look at both Sylpha and Oisín. "We try and sneak up. Grass dogs need to sleep like any other beast and a careful approach may just be able to get past them and collect the crystal. Alternatively, our numbers are great enough now that we can ride out and meet this sorcerer in open, old-fashioned combat. We may even be able to intimidate him into acquiescence."

"Or," Sylpha added. "We can use our numbers to create a diversion while someone sneaks in and steals the crystal."

"Well, Stranger," Oisín asked me. "What do you think?"

"A diversion seems the best idea, yes?" I suggested. "I mean, we have the numbers to draw him out. All we need is one person to sneak in."

"Seems a little," Oisín cocked his head. "Easy. Anyone clever enough to manipulate sorcery would surely anticipate such a ruse."

"He has a point," Sylpha noted.

Martel shrugged. "Let us hope that arrogance leads to oversight."

"We'll know better when we get a closer look," I said, nodding in agreement.

"That's what we'll do." Martel sighed. "East it is. We leave on the morn. This place will be empty for the first time since the empire began."

"Wait... empty?" I asked.

"Yes. We need the numbers."

"Who will stay to protect this place?"

"That is not necessary," Sylpha said, her lips twisting up in a small, slightly condescending smile.

I scowled at her.

"Have you not noticed the glyphs carved into the entrance stones?"

My scowl deepened and Sylpha scoffed. "You are not especially observant."

Martel shook his head. "Let the stranger be, chieftain."

"They are the reason why this hideout of yours has never been attacked by bandits, and why the Seeker's Son has never approached. They are ancient things, carved to ward away evil and those with evil intentions." Sylpha shifted her gaze and looked directly at Oisín before saying, "Sorcery."

Oisín grunted, and turned his attention back to the maps on the table. "Can we copy one of these glyphs and take it with us? It might be useful for hiding us from the Seeker's Son as we move."

Martel's eyes lit up. The light vanished almost as quickly when Sylpha said, "No. The glyph alone is not enough. The symbol is a physical record of the spell that has been cast over these stones. And I am afraid that no one knows the right words to speak into the carvings."

"No one knows?" I asked.

"It is forgotten."

"A nice thought, though," Martel mused.

"So, we're moving as one army east," I said. "Will that not draw the attention of, oh I don't know, everyone? I mean, you did say that there are people, other than the Mage King, who do not want to see the imperial throne restored, right? And aren't the rangers supposed to be disbanded? A group of them, moving in force? Isn't that problematic?"

"There's nothing for it now," Oisín said.

"Agreed," Martel answered. "Besides, if this proves successful, we will have the complete Imperial Sceptre, and with it we will be able to find the lost heir and the throne will be restored. Whatever comes after will be dealt with when it happens."

"The Sky Road Walker does have a point, however," Sylpha noted. "A force our size marching east is going to attract more attention than we'd like. Do the Black Blades not have eyes everywhere?"

"How do you know about the Black Blades?" Martel asked.

"What are the Black Blades?" Oisín asked immediately after.

"Liars," Martel growled in answer to the chieftain.

Sylpha looked at Martel and her lips twisted up in that small, patronising smile again. "Bitterness, ranger?"

Martel clenched his jaw and refused to answer.

"I have it on some authority that Martel and the leader of the Black Blades once had a rather one-sided love affair," I told Sylpha.

"This conversation is over," Martel snapped.

"No it's not," Oisín said. "Who are the Black Blades and why would they be a threat?"

Martel sighed. He rubbed his cheek with his palm a moment before answering. "The Black Blades were the personal guard of the Imperial Throne. Led by Assa and Farim, they were charged with guarding the empress. But it was one of them, Assa, who betrayed the throne she was sworn to serve, killing the last of the Imperial bloodline and starting the Time of Strife. They were disbanded and outlawed, much like we were though, granted, a great deal earlier than the rangers."

"Saschana, the current leader of the Black Blades, claimed to desire the same thing we do," I informed Oisín. "To find the sceptre and restore the throne."

"She's lying," Martel said quietly. "It's what she does. She lied to me to get information - that is how she knew that we held the head of the sceptre."

"And what lie did she offer you?" Sylpha asked.

Martel shook his head. "Love," he said. He smiled ruefully. "It was not long after she acquired that information that the rangers were suddenly disbanded, by decree of the Imperial Steward. I was not yet leader. I was young and foolish."

Never having heard Martel speak in such detail about what had happened, I remained silent. Oisín stared at him.

"What did you do?"

Martel smiled. "I was angry and hurt. I did the only thing I knew how. I sent a message to all the ranger posts. It simply read 'No' and included the symbol for this camp. Those rangers willing to risk imprisonment, and worse, to protect the empire understood and came here. The rest gave up their weapons, their uniforms, and their honour." Martel spat the last word as if it was a bitter fruit that left a sour taste in his mouth. "That is how I became the latest leader of the rangers - the Commander-Elect. I have made it my mission to restore the Imperial Throne. It is my hope that in so doing, the empire may yet be saved from the corruption and cruelty that has a stranglehold on her heart."

"You romantic," Sylpha scoffed.

Chapter Seventeen

A soft knock at the door interrupted the mood created by Martel's story.

"Enter," Martel called.

A young ranger opened the door and walked in, carrying something large and vaguely round and covered in a cloth in his arms. He struggled forward, weighed down by the object. He placed it on the map table and hastily retreated, closing the door again behind him.

Martel stood and carefully unwrapped the bundle. It was the head of the sceptre, and not round at all. It was a solid pink gold phoenix, its wings spread wide and its head tilted up, beak open as if it was crying out. Its long talons were clenched, the clawed ends curved tightly to create small fists. There was no room for a crystal, I realised. Perhaps the crystal fit a different way? I stared at the sceptre, trying to figure out where the crystal would go.

A piece of jagged white wood jutted from the base of the phoenix and was covered in the same carved designs as the rest of the sceptre. Those carvings were meant to represent the long tail feathers of a phoenix. I looked up at Martel. He looked briefly around the room before twisting the sceptre piece around so that the jagged end faced the broken, top end of the other piece.

I could scarce believe my eyes. The sceptre pieces snapped together with a loud crack, drawn to each other by some strange force more powerful than magnetism. Where the two pieces met, no seam or break of any kind could be seen. But the magic had not yet finished its weaving.

The hand on the other end of the sceptre curled into itself, shrinking down inside as the pink gold flowed through the grooves in the wood, flowing upwards to connect with the phoenix. Now I could see the tail feathers clearly as the grooves filled with gold. When it was all finished, the almost-complete sceptre hummed briefly and fell silent.

Sylpha rose from her seat and touched the wood gently. "This is old magic," she whispered. "Blood magic."

Before anything else could be said, Martel took up the cloth that formerly hid the sceptre head and wrapped the entire sceptre in it.

"Take some time to rest," he said. "We travel tomorrow."

"About that," Oisín said, somewhat distantly. His eyes were still on the sceptre, though the cloth now covered it. "It might draw less attention if we break into smaller groups and take different routes."

"But are we not supposed to be intimidating this sorcerer who guards the final piece?" Sylpha asked. "Small groups will not achieve that."

Martel scowled. "And smaller groups are more susceptible to attacks by bandits and such."

"Still," Sylpha mused. "It will not do to be arrested before even reaching this sorcerer." She looked up at me.

"What say you, Sky Road Walker? What would you recommend?"

I sighed. "It might be wiser to head out in small groups and rendezvous closer to the place we intend to attack. Bandits are not likely to attack if our groups are large enough, and if the groups are small enough, we may look like nothing more than larger than usual groups of bandits, if you follow."

"I do," Martel said. "It's a fine balance, but I'm sure we can manage it. Groups of twelve or less should work."

"Sounds good to me," Oisín said.

"I would like to mix the groups," Martel told him. "Will your northern men submit to the command of a ranger?"

"Will your rangers submit to the command of a northman?" Oisín countered, smiling.

Martel grunted. "Point," he conceded. "They will if I tell them to."

"I hope so," Oisín said.

"Mixed command, then," Martel said. He turned back to the maps. "According to our intel, the sceptre crystal is right here." He tapped the map twice at the spot where the crystal had been spied. "It is guarded by grass dogs who are, we suspect, under thrall of a sorcerer. If we head out in groups, we shall each have to take a different routes. We will lose sight of each other. Risk of being waylaid is high." Martel sighed. "Assuming we all make it with barely a scratch, we should probably gather... here." The ranger pointed to a small clear space on the map. "There is a small hill that overlooks the plain where the sceptre piece is held. That should serve to conceal us until we're ready to attack."

"It sounds doable," Oisín said.

"It's a month of travel, if we go straight. Most of us will not be. I say we wait a further two weeks. Then we attack, full strength or no."

I chewed my lip, unsure if splitting up the force was the best way to proceed.

Oisín looked down at the map a moment and shrugged his shoulders. "Looks about right. I will assume, as Commander-Elect, that you will take the most direct route to arrive first?"

Martel shrugged. "It makes the most sense. Do you have an objection?"

"None," Oisín said. "I do request that I take the northern road."

Sylpha smirked. "It is not the actual north, chieftain. You will still be in the empire."

Without bothering to look at the tall woman, Oisín continued. "The terrain is closer to that of home. I will know how to better work in it, should something go awry."

"Aye," Martel said. "I see no problem with that."

"So I must go south?" Sylpha asked.

"It doesn't matter," Martel replied with a smile. "We will all be leaving at different times during the day tomorrow, and headed out in all directions. You may traverse the tree tops if it pleases you."

"I might just," Sylpha answered.

I chuckled to myself at Sylpha's impish tone.

"And what shall we do with you, Sky Road Walker?" she asked. "Shall you accompany one of us, or dare you command a group of your own?"

"Of more concern is what to do with our own Black Blade," Martel growled. "You can stop eavesdropping now, Basadia."

A muffled curse made it through the door and I turned to it in surprise.

"Come in, woman," Martel snapped.

The door creaked open and Basadia stepped into the room. Martel folded his arms across his chest, scowling.

"Next time you try and listen into a conversation in secret, be sure that the shadow of your feet cannot be seen under the door," he said.

"She is a Black Blade?" Oisín asked, looking her over critically. "Seems a little young."

"Young minds offer less resistance," Martel noted.

"Says an outlawed ranger," Basadia snapped back.

"The Black Blades are also outlaws," Martel retorted. "And villains besides, or had you forgotten their part in beginning the Time of Strife?"

"All right children!" Sylpha said, standing.

Basadia, whose mouth was open to utter a reply, pressed her lips together and glared hard at Martel before retorting. "The Black Blades only ever wanted to restore the throne," she said.

Martel scoffed, but said nothing.

"We do!" Basadia said hotly. "No matter what your childish bitterness tells you."

I had never seen Martel lose his temper, but the dark flash in his eyes at the moment told me that it might yet happen. Sylpha stepped forward, preventing Martel from lunging across the room at Basadia.

"It is possible," the tall chieftain said. "That you both seek the same end, though through different means."

"We do not," Martel said. "I want the throne restored. The Black Blades want their power restored."

"That is a lie!" Basadia cried.

"Nothing you say can convince me otherwise," Martel replied. His temper now under control, he spoke softly and kindly. "And you may believe it yourself. That would not surprise me. Your dedication to that cause is noble and I cannot resent it. But please believe me when I say that your leader is a master manipulator. She is using you."

"That is not true," Basadia answered. The heat had left her voice and I could tell that the accusation hurt her.

It was entirely possible that Saschana was plotting some mischief and moving her Black Blades around like pawn pieces to achieve it. Then again....

"The same could be said for you," I noted.

Martel raised his brows and turned to me. "Stranger?"

"Look, I'm not saying that mischief is your goal, but a man's motivations can remain secret from even his closest friends and advisors. We really don't have any guarantee that you aren't up to some malice yourself, and that Saschana is honestly trying to do what is right."

Blinking, Martel opened his mouth to counter my claim and, finding he could not, closed it again. There was an uncomfortable pause before he nodded.

"It is true," he said at length. "You have no real guarantee that my will is not bent towards less honourable intentions than I have claimed. I can only appeal to the testimony of those who know me best. I see your point, Stranger. Still, I mistrust Saschana and, by extension, her representative in our midst. I don't want to let her out of my sight."

"Would another watcher be less satisfactory?" Sylpha asked mildly.

"Yes," Martel replied, turning to her. "They may be beguiled by her words. Or her beauty. Or both. They may prove less proficient at arms and so she manages to escape. The Sky Road Walker may go wherever. This one," he pointed to Basadia, "stays with me."

Basadia looked at me. "My task was to see you safe from harm as you collected the pieces of the sceptre to bring to Saschana. In whomever you place your trust, please do not let me from your sight. I have failed at one task already. My heart would break should I fail another."

"The division of people should not be this complicated," Oisín growled.

"You will not let Basadia come with me?" I asked Martel.

"Not unless you accompany me. I am not letting that girl from my sight."

I frowned. "Fine," I said a little bitterly to Martel. "I will accompany you."

Martel raised his brows at me. "Do not trust me, Stranger? Even now?"

"I trust your motives, but I do not trust your temper. Besides, Basadia has been nothing but true to me to date. I will not abandon her now."

I glanced across at Basadia, who stared at me with large, tear-filled eyes. She smiled slightly at me and I smiled back.

Martel grunted. "As you like."

Sylpha nodded once as if in approval and Oisín said, "Defying advancement in favour of friendship is admiral, Sky Road Walker."

"Just 'ware the friends you choose," Martel growled.

"Indeed," Basadia said, glaring at Martel.

Despite himself, Martel grunted a short laugh. "So, Black Blade," he asked. "Can you ride?"

"Well enough," Basadia answered.

"Good. We leave today. The rest will follow in the coming days. By the end of the week, this place will be empty. I suggest you and the Sky Road Walker take some time to prepare."

I nodded and, smiling at Basadia, left the study with her at my side. Once the door closed behind us, Basadia turned suddenly and wrapped me in a tight hug.

"Thank you," she whispered.

I awkwardly patted Basadia on her back. "You're welcome," I said. "Now come on, let's spend the rest of today at rest. We'll be out in the woods for a few months."

Rest we did. I gathered my armour and weapons and found myself an empty bench to lie on. I spent the time alternately snoozing and staring up at the ceiling. Basadia settled on the floor beside me, apparently keen to be at my side.

After a few hours, Martel arrived. "It's getting on twilight," he said. "Time to move."

I sighed and sat up, stretching out cramped muscles. "Have you given thought as to what you will do when this is all over?" I asked Martel as I rose to my feet and helped Basadia up. "I mean, if everything turns out as you want it to - you find the heir and restore the throne, and the rangers are reformed."

Martel shrugged. "Return here, I suppose."

"Really? You wouldn't take a position in the Imperial Court?"

Martel snorted and turned, leading us to the stables where Fas patiently awaited me. "No," he said at length. "Not that I expect such an honour to be bestowed on me, but even if it were, I would lose my mind locked inside all day. The wilds have been my home for so long now that I can't imagine myself anywhere else."

"What if you were offered a ridiculously large salary?"

"Not even then. What good is money if its acquisition denies you fresh air and the peace of the wilderness?"

I shrugged. "You could buy things, I guess."

Again, Martel snorted. "Things. I have my weapons, my horse and my wits. I don't need 'things.'"

"I should like a house," I said as I groomed and dressed Fas. "A great big one, and a yard with a couple of fruit trees."

Martel laughed. "I dare say you will be entitled to one, Sky Road Walker, if all goes well."

"Well, then," Sylpha said from the stable entrance as I turned to lead Fas outside. "You are off?"

"We are," Martel said. "It is time."

"Travel safe and swift, ranger," she said. "We shall be along soon."

Martel nodded and he moved on. As I led Fas past, Sylpha reached out and grasped my forearm. "Follow your heart, Sky Road Walker," she said. "But bring your mind with you."

I nodded at her and she smiled, turned and left. I walked on. Once outside, where waited a small group of already mounted warriors, I mounted up.

At a silent signal from Martel, the group moved off. I did not miss the long look behind Martel gave his home. There was longing in his expression.

Martel's group was not the first to have left today, nor was it the last. I saw six other groups leave the headquarters, each taking a different path. I knew that groups of rangers and northmen would be leaving all through the night and into the week ahead.

"And we're off," Martel said, mostly to himself.

Chapter Eighteen

The first few days of travel were uneventful. Even so, the rangers and northmen in our group remained alert. They rode tall in their saddles, invigorated by a common purpose. They were close, now, so close to restoring the throne, reinstating the rangers and their becoming once again citizens of the empire; able to travel wheresoever they wished without fear of authority.

It struck me suddenly how crushing it must have been to be evicted from the society one had loved and served one's entire life. I looked at Martel, who sat in silent thought, eyes always checking his surrounds even as his mind travelled elsewhere.

Twice our group had to skirt around certain blocks; one troll cave - a new habitation, I was told, made possible only because there are too few rangers protecting the empire; and one known bandit camp. The bandits were less of a threat than the trolls, but Martel prudently refused to engage them.

Scouts rode out and returned periodically, speaking in low tones to their leader before falling back into the group. Martel sat on his horse and pondered.

"What are you thinking about?" I asked him at the first camp of the second week of travel.

"My mother, if you must know," Martel said with a smile. "Since becoming an outlaw, I have not dared return home to visit, or even to write and enquire after my family, lest it lead the Steward back to me and my men. I am looking forward to seeing her again. If she lives."

"Is there any reason she wouldn't?"

Martel shrugged. "She is a delicate woman, with a delicate constitution. I do not know how she handled the news that her son has gone rogue. I do not know what sicknesses have infested the southern reaches of the empire. There is too little news that touches my ears."

"I'm sure she is proud," I said.

"Perhaps. Father will not be."

I smiled. "A stickler for the rules?"

Martel grunted in affirmation. "And fond of the Steward. The man has never known a hard day in his life and has little compassion for those who have. I might have been the same, had I not felt the call of the wilds."

"I somehow doubt that," I said. "I recall you saying you were noble born, but not so noble to be of any import to anyone. That affords you a better vantage point than most. You probably would still be trying to restore the throne."

"You give me a little too much credit, Stranger."

"I believe a sense of justice is innate in people, and that injustice and entitlement are learned. You, I think, would have been too headstrong to unlearn that which you were born with."

Martel laughed a little. "That I might have been. Headstrong is a good description."

For much of the journey I remained with Basadia. Martel was seldom in the mood for conversation. The impending confrontation was, I had no doubt, occupying a considerable amount of his thoughts. Strategies considered and discarded or stored for future reference traced lightning flashes across his eyes.

They were interrupted by the arrival of a grim-faced scout. "The bridge is destroyed," he announced sourly.

Martel scowled. "Flood?"

"No, sir," the scout said. "Dismantled. I can see the axe marks in the struts clear as day. I'd say the work of bandits, or perhaps the sorcerer who long ago anticipated assault."

Growling, Martel halted the group and dismounted. Everyone did the same. Martel beckoned me over and pulled out a map. He spread it out over his knee. "This would never have happened if the rangers were still on patrol." He sighed.

"You see this canyon?" he said, indicating a large fissure drawn on the vellum resting on his knee. "This is the bridge we have used to cross since before I was born. The canyon is deep and narrow, with a swift river at its base. The walls of the canyon are sheer. There is no way down for a man without a rope, let alone a horse."

"Not to mention that even should we find a way down, the water is too swift to cross without drowning," the scout noted.

"Now," Martel said. "We can travel a week or so out of our way north and cross at the falls. It is dangerous. The current is very strong, the falls are very high, and the rocks are sharp and slick. Five days to the south, there is the township of Sech. It has a ferry. Going that way, however, exposes us to prying eyes and is therefore dangerous, not only to us, but the entire mission."

"How wide is the canyon? Could we not rebuild the bridge?" Basadia asked.

Martel blinked at her. "It is possible, I suppose," he admitted. "But it will take time and make noise." The leader of the rangers turned to me. "What do you think?"

I scowled down at the map, and let my mind work through the options.

The falls sounded horrific. I had to forcefully pull my mind back from the vision of me tumbling over the falls in the north, my lips blue from the freezing water. Blinking to clear my head of the images, I turned my mind towards the other two options. The northern path was right out now, even if the vision was nothing more than the imaginings of an over-taxed mind.

I was not taking any chances.

Rebuilding the bridge was not a bad idea, all things considered. It would keep us away from prying eyes and would allow others coming our way to cross without hindrance. We were pressed for time, however, and I felt that our group ought to be the first at the rendezvous point.

"South," I said. "We should take the ferry. It's the easiest crossing, and if we remove our armour and pretend to be mere travellers, we might escape any suspicion."

Martel nodded sharply. "That's true. But we'll keep our armour on until we reach the settlement. I have seen enough signs of bandits to keep me from sleeping at all."

"These woods have never been so thick with criminals," the scout that accompanied us noted.

I smirked at him. "No, indeed."

Martel chuckled softly. "Other criminals," he said, looking up at me. He turned back to the waiting rangers. "Come on," he told Basadia and I as he walked back to the group. "We'll let them know the plan."

"Right," Martel said when he arrived to stand with the rest of the warriors. "We're headed south." He mounted his stallion and led the group on.

It took another week and half of uneventful riding before Martel called the group to a halt. Though it was midday, the woods here were so thick it might as well have been twilight.

"The settlement is around the corner over the next rise," Martel said. "Remove your armour. We are now simple woodsmen looking for a place to set up where the competition isn't nearly as great."

"A bit flimsy," one northerner noted as she dismounted.

"And what would you rather?" Martel asked.

The woman grinned. "Troll hunter," she said. "There's good money in that."

Martel laughed. "Fine. You can be a troll hunter."

"Can I be a troll hunter, too?" asked a young ranger. "After all, any group of woodsmen who are travelling in search of a new location without a troll hunter guard will end up dead before long. And we want to seem an intelligent, prepared group do we not?"

"Me too?" another one asked. "I want to be a troll hunter."

Martel raised his brows, a smile threatening at the edges of his mouth. "All right, who here wants to be a troll hunter?"

There was not a single member of the group who did not raise their hand.

I burst out laughing and the smile that had been threatening Martel's mouth found its release. "Well, we can't all be troll hunters, can we? I will have a guard of no more than five troll hunters. The rest of you poor sods will have to be woodsmen. Sort it out yourselves."

There was a lot of grumbling as the mixed group of rangers and Northerners sorted themselves out into two groups. Before long, there was one group of five standing apart from the rest, grinning as if they had just located a hoard of gold. There were several in the other group who looked thoroughly disappointed.

"Good enough," Martel said, still smiling. "Now take off your armour. The troll hunters may keep their maille, but the identifying armour comes off."

Everyone set to work. I noted that the 'troll hunters' removed most of their armour, but kept on bits and pieces to make it appear as if they came across a cache of armour, or a dead ranger or two, and scavenged armour from them. They traded some of their pieces with similarly-sized companions and soon were wearing a mish-mash of northern and ranger armour, with pieces clearly missing.

Martel grinned at them. "Nice touch," he said as he stowed away his armour and remounted his stallion. He had stripped down entirely, and wore only his riding boots, trousers and undershirt. He kept his short sword strapped to his side.

I looked across at Basadia who was similarly dressed. Without her armour, she looked impossibly slight. She smiled at me and we both mounted. With a silent signal from Martel, the group moved forward.

As we crested the hill, we found ourselves looking down on a crude settlement of no more than five wattle-and-daub houses. The streets were unpaved, muddy paths between the houses, where three milch cows roamed free, chewing on whatever tufts of grass that grew in front of the houses. A small hut sat near the forest on the far side, and a lumber mill operated with a dull drone on the western edge. The focal point of the hamlet, however, was the two-story inn, which sat just above the flood line near the river and from which, I noted, the ferry operated. Everything looked dishevelled and filthy; a brown scar in an otherwise lush green world.

"People," I heard Martel mutter. "The filthiest of all the living creatures." He sighed, slumped in his saddle, expertly losing the military air he usually carried, and nudged his stallion forward. As if sensing the deception, the normally spirited animal dropped his head and trudged forward, looking haggard.

Fas snorted and followed suit, moving before I need kick her flanks. She laid her ears back, flicking them occasionally and dragged the tips of her hooves as she walked on.

"You are a fine actress," I murmured to her.

She snorted softly in response.

Our group arrived into the hamlet just as a soft drizzle began. I rolled my shoulders, not used to the feeling of cold water hitting my back. I noted the broken remains of several more houses before we reached the main road leading to the inn.

Most everyone, except the cowherd and his family, were at work in the woods or at the lumber mill. A few children played in the street, looking up in curiosity only momentarily before returning to their game of tag. The cowherd looked up in surprise and watched us as we made our weary way to the inn.

Once there, Martel dismounted and walked to the door. He turned. "Wait here," he said. "I'll go make arrangements." He disappeared inside the tavern. Everyone slumped mutely into their saddles and waited in the rain.

After a moment, Martel exited the inn with a tall, burly man in tow.

"You weren't lying," the man said gruffly. "I haven't room for all these horses, but there's a paddock we use to pen the cows in at night near the western edge of town. You ought to have passed it on your way in."

"Aye," Martel said. "We saw it."

"You can put the horses there. We won't charge you for the use of the stalls. Now, do you mind sharing rooms? There's only six upstairs, and two of them belong to me and mine."

"Most of us will be glad to not be sharing blankets for a night," Martel answered. "We'll take what you got, and not complain." I noticed that the usual crisp snap of his voice was gone. He did not appear to be a commander of any kind at all.

"Good. If you want, I'll get the children to lead your horses to the paddock. I imagine you'll want out of the rain as quick as possible."

"That we do," Martel replied.

In a moment it was all arranged. With a shout, the inn-keeper enlisted the help of the children playing tag, and his own eldest son. Once the horses were undressed, the children led them off. We carried our saddles and tack inside.

"Here," the inn-keeper said. "I'll let you get settled in before I start supper. Anything particular you want to eat?" He led the way up the stairs as he talked.

"Something other than dried meat and hard bread will do."

"And something sweet," one of the northern 'troll hunters' said. "I miss my honey rolls."

The inn-keeper turned to her a moment. "From the north are you? Didn't think you were the kind to show up in the south."

"This isn't so far south," the woman replied. "Besides, you won't find better troll hunters than us northerners. You southern boys are too soft for that kind of work."

"Sensible, you mean," the inn-keeper said, grunting.

The northern woman laughed. "Semantics," she said with an easy shrug.

I tried to conceal a smile. The northerners were all having a great deal of fun with this charade, and I could see it in their twinkling grey eyes and impish glances.

"I can take you across the river on the morrow," the inn-keeper said. "Haven't used the ferry in a long while now, and I'll have to give it some repairs to make it worthy again. Won't do to have you all sink before you've had a chance to stake a claim. In the meantime, I'll get me daughter to draw you a bath or two and I'll have supper ready downstairs near sundown."

"That sounds most agreeable," Martel said. "Gods, but a bed will be most welcome."

The inn-keeper grunted in agreement, sighing as he topped the stair case and began walking down the hall, opening up the rooms.

"Bit musty," he said apologetically. "Been a long time since anyone's come through here."

"Times are tough everywhere, my friend," Martel said. "That's why were headed out into the unknown."

The inn-keeper shrugged and, once finished opening everything up, trudged back downstairs wearily. I entered a room, threw my saddle and tack onto the trunk at the end of one of the two beds and sat down on a bed. I ran my hands over the thick woollen blanket that covered the bed, noting the multitude of moth holes, and smiled.

"It'll be nice not sleeping on the ground for a change," I mused aloud.

"Stranger?" Martel asked as he claimed the other bed.

"Yes?" I replied, still distracted by the wool beneath my hands.

"I need your opinion on something."

"All right."

"If you were to woo a woman, what would you do?"

I blinked. "Pardon?"

"If you met a woman, and wanted to woo her, what would you do?"

I stared at Martel incredulously before a slow smile spread across my face. "Who has caught your eye?" I demanded.

"No one," Martel snapped a little too quickly. "I was just wondering, that's all." He looked at me expectantly.

Trying hard not to laugh at him, a slow smile nevertheless spread across my face. "So," I asked casually. "Who is it?"

"Never you mind," Martel answered gruffly. After a brief pause, he looked back at me. "Assume she knows how to handle a weapon."

"This really is impossible to answer unless I know who it is. It's different for every woman, I would imagine. That said, the best advice I can offer is to be yourself and treat her with the same respect you would the rest of your peers. Giant showy proclamations of affection would probably make her uncomfortable."

"But all the stories..."

"They're just stories, Martel. If she knows her way around a sword, let her do what she does, compliment her when she does it well, and, if she's interested, the rest will follow."

Martel grunted, swung his legs onto the bed and laid down. "You know what I think, Stranger?"

"I have a feeling I'm going to find out."

"I think you haven't a clue either."

I laughed. "You might be right."

After a long silence, I looked across at Martel who did nothing but stare up at the ceiling. "You never struck me as the lovelorn type," I said.

"You should have seen me when I met Saschana," Martel replied with a smile. "It was pathetic."

I laughed and Basadia walked into the room. She frowned at Martel and went to my bed to sit beside me. The silence in the room lent itself to rest, and before long, all three of us were asleep; Basadia and I sharing a bed, Martel in the next bed over. It was dark when a northerner stomped into the room and shook us all awake.

"Baths are ready," he said gruffly. "Down the hall. There's two. Innkeeper says food will be on the table soon. There's a nice fire downstairs. Most of us are there."

Grunting, Martel rose groggily to his feet. "Thank you," he muttered before making his unsteady way out of the room. He must have been exhausted. He had taken first and last watch almost every night out in the wilds, and spent much of his mental energy chewing through possible tactics while being on constant alert.

"Works too hard," the northerner said to no one in particular before exiting the room.

I looked across at Basadia. "You first?" I offered.

"Wait for the ranger," Basadia answered. I shrugged.

Not long after, Martel walked back into the room, wearing a fresh pair of trousers and nothing else, his muscular arms and torso covered in various scars. He blinked in surprise when he saw Basadia and I still there.

"Thought you'd be downstairs," he said by way of apology for his state of undress.

"Not without a bath," I replied, sliding off the bed.

Wordlessly Basadia followed and before long we were both sinking gratefully into a hot bath. I scrubbed myself clean as best I could before joining the rest of the group downstairs at the fire. The inn was busy with the noise of the travellers, and the quick, joyous service of three young women and their portly mother.

"Father is out at the ferry dock," I heard one of the girls answer a northerner. "Tarring the ferry with my brothers. They ought to be finished soon."

"Hello," the beaming innkeeper's wife said as she bustled out of the kitchen with a large pitcher of mulled honey wine. "Is this everyone?"

"Aye," Martel answered.

The woman did a quick headcount and nodded happily. "I did make enough. Very good. The stew is ready. Here, help yourself to some of my home brew. It'll warm you up and bring strength back to your limbs."

Everyone very gratefully accepted a cup of the steaming drink. I sniffed mine suspiciously before taking a sip. A northerner stood after having taken a draught and caught the innkeeper's wife around the waist.

"I taste cloudberries," he said. "I could kiss you!"

"Well don't," the innkeeper said gruffly from the door.

With a dramatic sigh, the northerner released the man's wife and she trundled back into the kitchen, blushing furiously. She returned only a few moments later, her daughters in tow, to deliver large bowls of steaming mutton stew and large rolls of spicy dark bread thickly buttered.

I was certain I had never tasted anything so wonderful in my life, and I ate quickly. I glanced at Martel to see if I could spy him staring at his love interest, hoping that I would be able to identify her from his forlorn gaze. No such luck.

Martel sat on his seat, the cup of warm honey homebrew in his hand, staring blankly into the fire, his expression grim. A northman sitting near Martel noticed my stare and turned to the leader of the rangers. He smacked the man's shoulder with the back of a fist, making Martel jump in his seat.

"Eat," the northerner said firmly.

"Yes, mother," Martel answered back. He put aside the honey brew and took up the bowl that had been placed at his feet by one of the serving girls.

It turned out to be a good night. The northerners told stories of various troll hunts they either participated in or heard about, sending loud laughter up to the rafters as they did so. One or two sang songs, and one, who was more than a little tipsy, stood to give an ode to the cloudberry. It was, I later learned, actually an incredibly old poem composed by a bard in the time long ago when men were new to the north.

Despite laughing himself, Martel quickly tired. After the ode, he stood and excused himself, retiring to bed. Basadia and I were not long behind. I lay on the bed next to Basadia, Martel snoring lightly on the next bed, and fell asleep to the sound of laughter and song from downstairs.

I awoke the following morning feeling refreshed and ready to face the day. I was the last one in our room, Martel and Basadia both probably downstairs at breakfast. With a heavy sigh I slid out of bed and dressed slowly, feeling reluctant to leave the inn for the wilds once again.

Martel greeted me with a nod as I reached the bottom of the stairs. I nodded back and plonked myself heavily on the bench beside him.

"Spiced oats for breakfast," he said, signalling one of the serving girls to bring me a bowl. "It's good."

The girl put the bowl on the table in front of me and wordlessly left. I took up the spoon and ate, burning my tongue on the hot oatmeal.

"Where's Basadia?" I asked, my maille chinking softly as I ate.

"Helping the Innkeeper and his sons bring the horses across the river. Three of the troll hunters are with her and will guard the horses across the river while the rest of us cross. We will be leaving soon, so you best hurry up and eat."

I nodded, taking the time to blow on the spoon of piping hot oatmeal before shoving it in my mouth. The innkeeper trudged back into the inn.

"Most of them are across," he reported to Martel. "The rest will be over the water long before you lot are ready to go."

"Thank you," Martel said, reaching to the purse strapped tightly to his belt. "I suppose it's time to settle the account."

"That would be much appreciated."

I finished breakfast, just as Martel finished paying the innkeeper, and sprinted upstairs to pack. I realised, rather late, that my tack had already been removed from the room and all that remained was my already packed bag and my staff. I gathered my things and met up with everyone outside by the river.

Several of the group were in the process of crossing, leaving only myself, two northerners, Basadia, and Martel. We watched the ferry cross the river, unload and make its way back. It was piloted by the two eldest sons of the innkeeper, one who manned a long pole, and the other who dutifully pulled on a very rusty chain that spanned the river.

The ferry docked and we moved in an orderly fashion towards it. A sudden, sharp stab of nausea hit me and the sound of rushing water filled my ears.

"No!" I barked as I stumbled. Basadia caught me before I fell and suddenly there was chaos.

I heard shouting, and a cow screaming. I lifted my aching eyes to try and make sense of the pandemonium in my swimming vision.

To my horror, a Seeker's Son hovered at the edge of town, absorbing a hapless cow that could not get out of its way fast enough. It took but a moment before the cow vanished into the black mist that swirled around the spectre.

In an instant Martel was at my side, helping Basadia haul me upright.

"Go!" he shouted to the innkeeper as the ghoul resumed its flight towards us. "Take your family and flee! That will not save you!"

I looked and, after a moment of hesitation, the innkeeper slid a small hatchet into his belt. He called his sons over and they abandoned the ferry, joining their father as the innkeeper's wife and daughters fled the inn.

"Run!" Martel roared at them as he and Basadia struggled under my limp weight, trying to haul me to the ferry.

"Go," Basadia snapped at Martel when she realised that the three of us would not make it to the ferry in time.

"No!" I said, but I was prone and helpless, and my body refused to obey my mind's commands. "Basadia!"

"I'm not leaving you behind," Martel barked at her.

"You have no choice. Save the Sky Road Walker. Go!"

Basadia unsheathed her weapon and stood between myself and the Seeker's Son, which stopped short, hovering a mere foot away. Anger and fear lent Martel strength and the aid of a northman who left the ferry ensured that I was on the ferry before the Seeker's Son decided to attack Basadia. Martel did not stay with me. He unsheathed his own sword and sprinted to Basadia's aid. It was hopeless. Everyone in our company knew this. No weapon had ever managed to wound the shade even a little.

Martel did not make it in time. In a rapid strike, the Seeker's Son both unsheathed its spectral sword and swung fast for Basadia's head.

She brought her weapon up to block, but the Seeker's Son's sword merely passed through it. With snake-like reflexes, she ducked from the blade. It swiped nothing but air. She could not, however, dodge the clawed hand that struck down immediately after. The ghostly talons passed through the front of her skull without leaving a mark, but she stiffened and crumpled to the ground, her weapons sliding from her hands.

"No!" Martel barked. He slid on his knees to her, catching her moments before her head struck the ground.

The Seeker's Son reached out a clawed hand to her as if to draw her into itself in its macabre absorption when a high-pitched shriek sounded in the clear air.

I looked up from Basadia's limp form and spied another Seeker's Son as it breeched the forest line. The Seeker's Son hovering before Basadia and Martel issued a deep, reptilian hiss, spun and raced towards the intruding Seeker's Son. Near the edge of the town, the two spectres met, clashing in violent combat.

"Martel!" one of the northerners bellowed, rousing the leader of the rangers.

Martel sheathed his weapon and stood. Grabbing Basadia under her limp arms, he dragged her towards the ferry.

"We have no time!" the northman yelled.

"She's breathing!" Martel yelled back.

Swearing profusely in guttural tones, the other northman abandoned the ferry and helped Martel drag Basadia aboard. They pushed off and pulled the ferry quickly across the water. No one spoke. Once they reached the other side, they helped Martel lay Basadia across his stallion's shoulders and we fled, galloping headlong into the wilderness.

Behind us, a Seeker's Son shrieked in victory.

Chapter Nineteen

We galloped as long as the horses lasted. When the hoof beats lost their rhythm and the horses began to stumble, Martel pulled the group to a halt. Everyone sagged in their saddles, and Martel's proud stallion who had to bear the weight of two, trembled with exhaustion.

"She is slowing us down," a northman growled. "We have to leave her behind."

"We are not leaving her behind," Martel snapped.

The northman growled something I was certain was unpleasant and Martel stiffened. "Cross blades with me, northman," he said in a low, dangerous tone. "And we'll soon see who is right."

I kicked Fas' flanks and walked her in between the two in an attempt to dispel the tension. "Stop," I commanded.

Martel and the northman clamped their mouths shut. I turned to Martel and softly asked, "It's her, isn't it? It's Basadia."

Martel declined to answer and looked away.

I sighed and looked between the two men, each of whom had set their jaws indicating there would be no compromise.

"Is there a settlement on this side of the river," I asked Martel.

"No," he answered.

"Yes," a northern woman said immediately afterwards. Martel looked across at her in surprise. She shrugged.

"There are few enough trees in the north, and we need lumber. It's a milling settlement. We did not think you would notice."

"And they didn't," the northman facing Martel growled.

"We take Basadia there," I said. "They can care for her until we return."

Martel pulled Basadia's limp body closer to him. "We cannot just abandon her."

"We aren't," I replied. "But the northman is right. She is weighing us down, and there is no guarantee that she'll survive travelling with us in the wilds. She needs warmth, a bed, good food and medical care. We cannot give that to her right now."

Grimacing, Martel nodded. He looked at the northwoman. "How far?"

"Three odd weeks north."

I rolled my eyes and cast my gaze up at the sky. "We should have just rebuilt the damned bridge," I muttered. Drawing a deep breath, I nodded at the northwoman. "Lead the way," I said.

The woman nodded and nudged her horse forward, abandoning the tiny track the group had been following to ride through the dense forest in a vaguely northerly direction. Martel remained Basadia's caretaker for the duration of the journey. Not normally talkative, Martel withdrew further, concern for the young Black Blade in his care etching lines across his brow and whitening the hair at his temples.

Basadia herself remained unresponsive, growing paler with each passing day. I was not certain she would even last the three week journey to aid.

Everyone noticed Martel's distress and even the angry northman began to pity him. He elected to ride next to Martel, keeping alert when Martel was unable and helping Martel to get Basadia on and off the horse each day. Neither of them spoke until the middle of the second week.

"She is very pretty," the northman noted in the evening as Martel attempted to feed her broth. Her closed lips did not open at the touch of the warm soup. She would not eat. Martel tossed the ladle he used into the soup pot in frustration.

"I should have sent her back to Saschana," he growled.

The northman reached out and squeezed Martel's shoulder briefly before handing the leader of the rangers a bowl of soup. "Eat," he said.

Martel pressed his lips together and shook his head.

"You will not be able to help her if you faint from starvation," the northman said firmly. "Now eat."

With a sigh, Martel took the bowl from the northman. "Thank

you," he mumbled.

The northman nodded. "You sleep," he said. "I'll take the first watch."

Too exhausted to argue, Martel nodded. He ate his soup quickly then, throwing his blanket over Basadia, lay down and closed his eyes. Moments later, I walked over to the northman.

"How is he doing?"

The northman shrugged. "As well as anyone, given... well... this." He waved his hand vaguely at Basadia.

I nodded, looking at the young woman. She looked almost skeletal in the flickering firelight. Fear of losing her gripped me suddenly. Basadia was too young to wither like this, and she had been a true friend and brave companion. She deserved better. I walked over to her and sat near her head, careful not to disturb Martel, who desperately needed rest.

Pressing a hand on her forehead, I noted that her skin felt cold. I jerked my hand away and stared down at her. Dead?

No. Her chest rose and fell in shallow, steady, albeit laboured breaths. I touched her again. Her skin was definitely cold. I shifted my position so I could examine her more closely. I noticed a slight blue tinge around her lips and along her eyelids, but I could see her pulse beating in the tiny veins near her temple and at her throat. The northman watched me a moment before coming closer.

"What is it?" he asked in a whisper.

"She looks dead," I replied, also whispering. "Her lips and eyes have gone blue and her skin is cold to the touch, but she's still breathing. Look. And I can see she has a pulse."

The northman scowled and shook his head. "I do not like this."

"No," I agreed. "Neither do I."

"Do you know what it means?"

"No. Why? Do you?"

The northman shook his head. "I have never seen symptoms like these, and there is nothing similar in our tales that might identify this. This is magic working; and not good magic."

"Well, great."

"You are a wizard, are you not?"

"What? No!"

"But you walked the Sky Road. Only wizards can do that. You must do something."

I looked helplessly at the northman. "I don't even know my own name."

The northman shrugged and returned to his post. I stared down at Basadia. The hand I had pressed to her forehead was growing numb from the cold, so I switched hands, hoping that my own body heat might help her warm up. It was pointless. Now I had two cold-numbed hands and Basadia was no warmer than before.

Cold and confused, I retired for the night. As I fell asleep, the chant of the aged, dark-skinned woman played in my head.

> *The Seekers Son has taken one,*
> *The Seekers Son takes two,*
> *The Seeker's Son takes another one,*
> *The Seeker's Son seeks you.*

Over and over the chant repeated in my mind, giving me no rest. I woke up exhausted at first light.

I looked around. It was cold. Very cold. My breath frosted in the still pre-dawn air. The campsite was empty; a lonely small clearing covered in drifting wisps of grey mist. There was no one around. The horses were all gone. The campfires had all been gutted, including the one beside which I had fallen asleep. I sat up and stared at it. It looked as though it had not been used in years. Tufts of hardy grasses grew between the cold coals and everything was covered in frost.

I turned again, panicked, feeling a slight resistance and hearing a bizarre crinkling sound as I did. I looked down at myself. Silver silken threads bound me to myself and to the ground. I was covered in cobwebs. I gasped and jumped up, dancing around foolishly as I tried to rid myself of the sticky wisps that clung to me. As I spun and danced, I noticed a figure on the ground, similarly covered in cobwebs.

My dancing ceased and I edged forward to the figure. Though the light was dim and the cobwebs covered everything thickly, I immediately recognised the figure. Or, rather, I recognised who the figure used to be.

"Basadia," I breathed.

But it was not really Basadia lying there. It was Basadia's mummified corpse; paper thin skin clinging to her skeleton, ropy tendon and bleached bone visible through cracks in the flesh. Her once bright red hair had mostly vanished, leaving a few strands that glimmered a deep copper in the dim light.

What happened? Where was I? Or, more pressing, *when*? Basadia was still living when I went to sleep, and, judging from the state of her corpse, she had died... hundreds of years ago. I reeled backwards, confused and upset.

Did Basadia die in her sleep a hundred or so years ago? Did I sleep for a hundred years? Did everyone think me dead as well? Did they all go meet at the rendezvous as planned and leave behind two corpses?

Panic robbed me of breath and the world spun wildly as my brain failed to cope with my heart's frantic pace.

This could not be real. This...

A slow, wheezing noise caught my ear. I looked in the direction of the sound - Basadia's mummified corpse. Again I walked forward to examine the body. It was breathing. Basadia's mummified chest was rising and falling in laboured breath.

I leant in closer and try to reach out to Basadia. The corpse's eyes snapped open, revealing one empty socket and one empty eye, the colour drained completely. I screamed and jumped backwards. Basadia's corpse rose, stiff and unnatural, as if it were a wooden plank heaved upright by unseen hands.

The corpse's jaw dropped open, there being no muscle to keep it shut any more, and it stepped towards me. As it placed its first foot down, it raised an impossibly long sword with a double guard. I recognised it as a boar-hunting sword. But the weapon was barely visible, the edges catching what little light there was and reflecting it blue. I realised with a sudden sinking in my stomach that the weapon appeared to be the same kind of spectral weapon wielded by the Seeker's Sons.

I stepped backwards, and heard a twig snap. I spun around and yelped.

Another Basadia corpse, desiccated and destroyed just as the first, entered the clearing, holding a curved blade that was just as spectral as the boar-hunting sword.

They were both shambling towards me, until they caught sight of one another. Suddenly I was no longer the focus of their malice. I wheeled out of the way, looking desperately between the two animated corpses of my friend and companion. Knowing they were about to clash, I scanned the clearing, but my own weapons were nowhere to be seen.

When they left me and Basadia as dead, did they take my weapons? Even the hunting horn gifted to me was gone.

I turned back to the animated corpses and chewed my lip. Was one good and the other evil? Should I aid one against the other? If so, which one? And how?

Or was this some bizarre dream or alternate reality? And if one of the Basadia's destroyed the other, would that kill the real Basadia who was now sleeping by a fire in the other reality? After all, one cannot be whole with just half of oneself.

What was going on?

These questions gave me a headache. I tried to puzzle through everything in spite of the pounding in my head and the nagging urgency in my stomach telling me I had missed something important. My breath caught as, contrary to their shambling walk just moments before, the animated corpses clashed with whip-like speed, their weapons spewing blue sparks as they struck one another.

I knew I had to do something. But what?

You walked the Sky Road. You must do something.

There was precious little time to puzzle it out. Though it appeared they could not walk very fast, these animated corpses were lightning fast when attacking. They fought in eerie silence, their vocal chords either too dry to function or rotted away.

"Basadia!" I shouted as one corpse raised its weapon high to strike. Both corpses stopped mid movement and turned their heads to me. I swallowed past the tightening in my throat.

"Uh…" I said, not sure what to do now. "Hi."

One of the corpses cocked its head and, as if mutually deciding that I was no threat whatsoever, turned back to the other. They recommenced their battle. Now more annoyed than afraid, I straightened my back and folded my arms across my chest, scowling.

"Children," I chided to no avail. The pair of Basadia corpses continued their battle.

"Stop it the pair of you!" I yelled, sounding like an exasperated mother.

Again I was ignored. The clang of steel echoed in the predawn light and sparks flew as the barely visible spectral weapons connected. I chewed my lip again, trying to come up with a solution. Dawn was slow in coming, I noted, and one of the Basadia corpse things would likely be dead before the golden light touched the clearing.

"Oh for crying out loud!" I grated, stomping my foot. "What am I supposed to do?"

You walked the Sky Road. You must do something.

The battle raged close to me now, and I stumbled backwards several steps to avoid being cleaved in half by the ridiculous weapon that was the boar-hunting sword. My ankle rolled as I stumbled into one of the disused fire-pits. It may just have been my imagination, but I swore that I saw blue sparks spit out from the cold coals as they shifted under my weight. I looked down and rolled one of the coals over with my foot.

There were definitely sparks, striking in their blue hue.

Scowling I reached down and passed my hand over the fire-pit. It was as cold as the ice covering the frosted glade. I picked up a coal. It was cold to touch, and slightly damp as the frost melted in the warmth of my hands. I looked back to the battling Basadias.

The one wielding the curved sabre disarmed her opponent in a swift series of surprisingly lithe moves. As she raised her sword arm to deliver the deathblow, I launched the coal I was holding, noticing the blue sparks stream from it as it whistled through the air. It hit the sabre-wielding Basadia corpse on the arm, exploding into a blue flaming ember as it did so.

With an ear-piercing shriek, the sabre-wielding Basadia dropped her weapon and lurched sideways, clutching her arm. The ember kept its blue flame as it hit the ground. I heard the frost sizzle as the ember continued to burn beside the shimmering, barely visible sabre on the ground.

The other Basadia corpse thing grabbed its weapon. I swiftly bent down and picked up another coal, hurling it hard as the corpse turned to its wounded counterpart, sword raised. The ember hit it on the shoulder, again exploding into blue flames as it struck, and retaining those flames once it hit the ground. The corpse stumbled forward, its swing missing the other Basadia by a substantial margin. Still, it retained the weapon and turned to strike again. Again I bent down, picked up a cold ember and launched it at the corpse. This time, I hit one of its forearms. The ember exploded and fell, still flaming, to the ground.

It worked. The boar-hunting sword fell to the ground with a heavy thud and the corpse clutched its forearm, hissing bitterly at me.

The other one moved forward reaching for its sabre, so I whipped another coal at it, striking it on the back of its hand. It jerked back.

"No," I chastised, as if speaking to a young child whom I had caught trying to steal a cookie from the jar.

Both corpses were now standing still, clutching their burns and staring blankly at me. I assume that was what they were doing, at least. With only one eye between them, I was not sure if they could see at all. I folded my arms in an authoritative manner and stared right back, eyebrows arched.

"You two learn to be nice to one another," I said. "Don't make me get cross."

One of the Basadia corpses cocked its head at me, first one way, then the other. I could hear the bones in its neck creak and crack. It made me grimace. Taking up a few more coals just in case, I took a step forward. The corpses shuffled back a little, still staring at me.

Behind them, I could see the thin line of orange that heralded the cresting of the morning sun.

"Now," I said. "Hug and make up."

The corpses did not move. They stared blankly at me. The one eye they possessed shifted down towards the weapons. I took one of the coals and tested the weight.

"I wouldn't, if I were you," I said casually.

The corpses looked back up at me and I smiled benignly. The sun breached the horizon, spreading golden fingers of light through the trees. The corpses turned around in unison as the light struck them. It was then that I recognised the difference between them.

One spread its arms wide, as if to embrace the light. The other screamed horrifically, turning around and scrambling to escape the golden rays. I moved swiftly, blocking the corpse's path, spreading my arms to make it difficult to get around me. The corpse tried nonetheless, but I moved each time, blocking the way.

Behind me, the corpse who had turned towards the sun burst into flames, turning to ash as quickly as burnt paper. The corpse trying to escape burst into flames shortly after, screeching and stumbling around, as the first one crumbled into cold dust. I watched the screaming corpse until it, too, crumbled into paper ash mid stride.

Silence fell over the clearing and I blinked.

What now?

Did the sun just kill Basadia? Did I?

I blinked again. I was no longer alone in the clearing. As my vision cleared, I found everyone, Martel included, standing around me in a circle, their faces pale and eyes wide. I frowned and, rather suddenly, felt a sharp pain in my hand. I looked down. I clutched a set of smouldering coals.

Yelping, I simultaneously dropped the coals and jumped back away from them. "Ow! Ow! Ow! Ow! Ow!" I screamed as I jumped up and down and shook my hand in an effort to control the pain. I let loose a long string of curses.

"Sky Road Walker," a northman said, his voice thick with awe. He bowed deeply.

In hushed astonishment, everyone else around me also bowed. The pain in my hand was almost forgotten momentarily.

"Wait... what?" I demanded. "Stop that!"

Martel was the first to straighten. I looked at him helplessly. "What the hell is going on?"

Scowling, Martel answered. "How can you not remember? You, and the fighting spectres."

I blinked stupidly. "You saw all that?"

"You stood in the fire, but did not burn," a ranger breathed. "You touched the coals and they did not sear your flesh."

I looked down at the bloody, gaping wound in my palm, the skin there bubbling and crinkling, some of it black. "Yes it bloody did," I growled.

"Just now, yes. But not while the spectres fought."

"How did you make them explode into flames like that? Is there a spell?" another, very young, ranger asked.

"Could you command those spectres at will?" asked another. The clearing exploded into cacophony of questions, thrown so fast and thick at me that I could not pick out one from the other.

"Enough!" Martel roared over the din. The clearing fell into abrupt silence. "If you have not forgotten, we are on a mission. And we have a Seeker's Son stalking us. Come here, Sky Road Walker. Let's get that burn tended to, and we'll be moving on."

Grateful to be out of the press of people, I followed Martel to the fire he shared with his northern friend and Basadia's limp form. I looked across at her, noticing that the blue hue had left her lips.

"Sit," Martel commanded sharply. As if obeying the order of their own volition, my legs buckled and I slumped to the ground. Martel took my hand and examined it quickly.

"Water," a gruff voice in a northern accent said abruptly. I looked up as Martel's northern companion placed a small cooking pot of fresh water on the coals.

Without saying a word, Martel fished out a relatively clean cloth and dipped it in the water. Still cold, it was both extremely relieving and exceptionally painful when it touched my burn. I winced and, despite my best efforts, instinctively jerked my hand away from the pain. Martel's firm grip meant I did not get very far, and he continued to clean the burn. At the other end of the fire, the northman created a paste from several plants he had gathered.

"How did you do it?" Martel asked in a murmur as he accepted the bowl of paste from the silent northman. "Stand in the fire and resist the flames like that?"

"I don't know," I answered, tears sliding down my cheeks from the pain in my hand. "Gods that really hurts!"

Martel took a thick glob of paste and smeared it gently over the burn. It stung on first contact, then immediately the pain dulled and my body relaxed. "Oh," I said. "Thank goodness. What is that?"

"My father was a smith," the northman said. "And clumsy. Mother would make this paste in a cauldron to treat his burns and the medicine would not even last a week. You are lucky that we are far enough north that I can find all the ingredients."

"Thank goodness for your mother," I told him. The northman grinned briefly.

Before long, my hand was firmly bandaged, the paste numbing the pain enough so that, provided I did not move my hand at all, I could barely feel it.

"Did you really see the spectres fighting?" I asked Martel.

"Aye," the ranger replied as he placed a covered pot of last night's soup on the fire. "Though they were almost as fog, barely seen with the forest behind them showing through. We could not see their weapons, but they must have had them, from the way they moved and the sparks that flew."

I nodded. "Two swords, glowing with the same flickering blue haze as the sword of the Seeker's Son."

"Ghost blades, then," the northman said. "Spectral images of the weapons they once carried. It is why we bury our dead with them. They may need it, wherever it is they go after life."

I sat in silence as the soup warmed up. Sometime into the early morning, as the sun stretched further into the clearing, I heard Basadia inhale deeply. Martel started in surprise as I and the northman looked over at her simultaneously. Martel moved to her side and pressed his palm against her forehead. He looked up at me.

"She's warm," he said.

I relaxed. Setting alight the two corpses had not harmed Basadia. At least, not so far.

I watched, hopeful, as Martel took a small spoonful of soup and placed it on Basadia's lips. Her mouth opened and she instinctively drank in the sustenance. Martel looked up at me and offered a shocked, grateful smile. I grinned.

She may just make it after all.

The journey to the illegal northern settlement seemed less oppressive now. Basadia, though still unconscious, was at least eating and her breath was no longer as laboured. Her skin no longer cold and grey-looking, it injected everyone with the hope that she might yet live.

Chapter Twenty

We arrived at the settlement with no further bizarre events, or any sign of the Seeker's Son. We were vaguely surprised to be greeted by Oisín. He grinned sheepishly at Martel, knowing full well the settlement was a direct violation of the agreed borders between the north and the empire. The smile slipped when he spied Basadia. He ran forward to help Martel dismount.

"What happened?" he asked.

"We were attacked at the ferry crossing by a Seeker's Son," Martel replied with a grunt. "I thought for sure we were going to lose her."

Oisín clasped Martel's shoulder and squeezed it briefly.

"Come," he said. "There is a healer's hut where she will be well looked after. We'll get her in and settled and head to the tavern. We'll leave together on the morn."

Martel nodded. "I like this plan."

Before long, we were seated in thickly cushioned chairs by a roaring fire, enjoying warm spiced mead. Martel and Oisín were talking quietly, though I could hear humorous notes in their voices. No doubt they were talking about the incursion into the territory of the empire. The sound of their voices, the warmth of the fire and the softness of my seat lulled me to sleep.

I awoke in the morning exactly where I had fallen asleep, noting that others had done the same. A bowl of spiced oatmeal was shoved under my nose. I looked up to find Oisín grinning at me. He wiggled the bowl until I took it. I ate gratefully.

"Is this why you wanted to come via the northern route?" I asked him. Oisín simply grinned. He leant back on the bench and propped one elbow up on the table.

I chuckled.

"We'll be leaving in a few hours," Oisín noted. "Now that we're across the river, I'm sure there's no need for stealth. We should be at the rendezvous in another week or two, depending."

"How is Basadia, do you know?"

"Her body is growing stronger," Oisín said. "But the healer couldn't tell us about her mind. Martel is in with her. I imagine he has a few things he'd like to get off his chest in private."

I smiled and returned to my breakfast.

Oisín did not lie. Two hours into a leisurely morning, he awakened whoever remained asleep to ensure they were fed and prepared to go. Before long, the now sizeable group moved out together.

We arrived at the rendezvous to find Sylpha and her group already there, along with several other groups.

"You're late," the tall, slender chieftain noted.

"We had some complications," Martel answered gruffly as he swung down from his saddle.

Sylpha narrowed her eyes, scanning the arriving party with a frown. "Where is the young Black Blade?"

"Recovering," Oisín said. "I understand there was an attack by a Seeker's Son."

"Two of them, actually," Martel said when Sylpha raised her eyebrows at him. "Their propensity to attack each other on sight rather ironically saved us."

"The trees had mentioned an evil," Sylpha mused.

I had no time to ask what she could mean. A lone figure appeared at the edge of the clearing, holding up a large stone. The figure's hood was pulled far over its face, so I could not identify the person, but what skin was showing was extremely wrinkled, giving the impression of great age. The cloak must have once been a rich red, but had dulled to a spotted pinkish-brown and the once finely embroidered edges had lost much of their gold thread.

"Looking for this?" the old figure screeched.

With surprising strength for the deceptively crippled frame, the figure launched the stone. It landed just a few steps behind Sylpha. There was no thud. Where the rock landed, the ground opened up in a gaping hole. The caving earth drew Sylpha in. Before she had time to scream, she fell and was swallowed by the darkness. Martel, who had launched forward in an instinctive reflex to save Sylpha, tumbled in after her, closely followed by Oisín, who had grabbed the ranger's pauldron in an effort to keep him from falling.

There was no time to think. I dove in after them. Darkness swallowed me as I tumbled headlong into the gaping hole in the earth. As I fell, I could hear a ranger barking orders to the rest above. Long used to the unpredictability of the world in which they lived, I felt certain that their training and hardiness would ensure that the mission continued on as normal in our absence.

I hoped.

The fall was long. I found myself turning thoughts over in my mind as I tumbled through the black. It was actually not a terrible sensation, once I got over my initial mindless terror.

As I tumbled, I noticed heat rising against me. I looked down and saw nothing. At first. As I fell, I saw a small glowing ball of orange red. It grew larger at an alarming rate as I rushed down to meet it. The heat intensified. I could see the dark silhouettes of Oisín, Martel and Sylpha as they fell.

It looked like I was going to hit the giant round ball of heat and be burnt alive, when another hole opened up and, instead of hitting the undulating surface of the intense ball of magma I was approaching, I fell into cool dark.

The darkness intensified as the second hole swallowed me. So too did the cold. I twisted my body to look up and, against the now faint light provided by the magma rippling along the edges of the hole, I could see my breath frost.

"I'm dead," I whispered to myself. "I'm dead, and this is what happens to someone when they die."

I stared up at the rapidly disappearing ring of red light until it was gone. I twisted again...

And landed face first on iced-over stone. I blinked twice before the pain hit me like an axe striking a tree. My eyes watered and I felt warm wet running down to my lips. Blood. I hauled myself up into a sitting position and gingerly touched my nose. It hurt. A lot. I winced and let the tears stream from my eyes.

I gave myself the luxury of sitting and weeping until the ice on which I sat started to sting my buttocks. After two aching attempts, I struggled to my feet and peered around me. I could see nothing, but a soft ring of dull grey light shining down on me informed me that I was standing on black ice that covered a carefully paved stone... something. Courtyard? A road perhaps? I could not tell, and it was too dark to see in any detail.

Still, I tried anyway, hoping to catch sight of one of my companions. My ears were tuned, actively seeking sound in the dark but all I could hear was my own unsteady breath and the pulsing blood in my own veins.

"Hello?" I called meekly into the murk. "Anyone there? Martel? Oisín? Sylpha?" My voice gained strength as I used it. "Hello? Hell-ooooooooo!"

The last 'hello' I shouted. Distantly, I could hear my own voice echo back at me. That gave me some clues. The area was enclosed, though probably vast, judging by how faint and garbled my echo sounded. It gave me hope that Oisín, Martel and Sylpha had fallen into the same space.

Another sound echoed through the chamber. I tensed and crouched, scanning the dark for more clues. It was a sound I had not made. It could be someone trying to answer me. It could also be something hostile on the hunt for whoever is disturbing the quiet of the chamber.

The sound came again, no louder or softer than before. I creeped forward a little bit, noticing that the soft grey light that illuminated the floor at my feet followed me.

"You're going to give me away," I whispered to the light.

Of course, being light, it did not hear me. Nor did it particularly care. It simply continued doing what it was doing.

I sighed at the futility of my situation.

The sound came again. My pulse raced as I crept around the dark space, always with the faint grey light at my feet. I did not know if creeping around was my best option, but since sitting around and waiting to freeze to death did not seem like a better option, creep around I did.

As I crept, the sound kept echoing through the space to my ears in uneven intervals. I tried to pinpoint it, but it seemed to be coming from a different place each time; not that I had an ear for direction in any case.

Gathering my courage, I stood up and yelled again. "Hello? Hello?"

My voice echoed back, mixed with the sound I had been seeking. A reply. It was a reply. It must have been. I called out again, and the sound replied. My heart leapt in hope. It might be a friend, trying to find me.

"Stay still and call out! I'll come to you!" I shouted. I knew, however, that the message was not going to arrive clearly to the ears of the person, just as I could not hear what they were trying to say.

The sound replied, and I moved towards where I thought it was coming from. When I lost my way a little, I stopped and shouted. A shout replied and I moved towards it. It took more than an hour of searching, but I saw through the gloom a soft green light. I straightened.

"Hey!" I yelled.

"Hey back!" Sylpha yelled. I would have been able recognise her voice anywhere. Grinning from relief I sprinted forward... and tripped over something. I looked back after recovering from my sprawl to find a skeleton, the bones dark brown and covered in a thin film of mummified skin. It wore archaic armour of baked leather and carried a sword of bronze. I stared at it a while before hearing Sylpha's footfalls as she ran to me.

"Are you all right?" she asked breathlessly. She grabbed me under the arms and hauled me to my feet. I turned to her.

"Yes," I replied a little blankly. "I'm all right. I think."

Sylpha looked at me and shook her head. "You broke your nose," she noted, pulling out a cloth from a pocket in her riding breeches. "Here. Clean yourself up as best you can."

I gratefully accepted the cloth and tried to wipe clean the dried and frozen blood from my face.

"I hit the ice face first," I said, wincing as I accidentally brushed my nose.

Sylpha nodded. "I gathered."

"How come you're not hurt?"

"A cat always lands on its feet," Sylpha replied with a quick smile. "But she'll soon freeze to death."

I nodded. "You and I both." I eyed Sylpha a moment. "You're glowing green," I noted.

She shrugged. "And you glow grey. In truth, it will help us find one another in the dark, so I'm not that upset about it yet."

"Speaking of, where is everyone else?"

Sylpha shrugged again, standing tall and craning her neck to see if she could catch any glimmer of light that might identify the other two members of the group.

"Martel!" she yelled. "Oisín!"

After a moment, I heard a familiar voice shout back, "Sylpha! Stranger!" I turned to find Martel running in our direction, glowing a faint gold. "Gods damn it, I wish you would have stayed where you were!" he snapped as he reached us. "It would have been a lot easier to find you!"

"You could tell we were moving?"

"Aye, and in which direction, too. I was shouting myself hoarse trying to get you two to stop."

"I didn't hear you," I admitted.

Martel grunted.

"Have you seen Oisín?" Sylpha asked.

"Aye. He fell on his feet and shattered his left knee. He can't move and is in a fair amount of pain. Come on."

He led the way back in the direction he came. I kept my eyes half on his warm glow and half on the ground illuminated by our combined glows. I did not want to be falling over another body in here. It took a good long time before we approached Oisín. He was lying on the ground, glowing a faint whitish-blue and clutching at his wounded knee, his eyes tightly shut as he tried to focus on his breathing.

Sylpha moved quickly to his side. "Hello chieftain," she said gently.

Oisín's eyes opened and he offered a faint, grey-faced smile. "I'm glad you are well," he whispered. He looked over at me, broken-nosed and bloody, and grinned. "You broke your nose," he noted. He screamed in pain as Sylpha inspected his knee.

"Baby," she chided.

"Die in a fire," Oisín snapped back.

"Happily if it'll give me but a little warmth."

"I'm sorry," Oisín grunted. "Sorry."

"It's all right. You should have heard me cuss when giving birth. My poor husband." Sylpha looked around and pointed. "There is another skeleton there," she said. "Bring me his femurs."

"His what now?" I asked.

"The bones in the upper leg. Bring them both to me."

"Yes, ma'am," I said. I walked over to the skeleton and crouched down. It was the same as the last, with archaic armour, the skin dried and shrunken, stuck to the bones like thin wisps of vellum. "You won't be needing these," I said. "Mind if I take them?"

Apparently the skeleton did not mind. There was not even so much as a twitch as I lifted the brittle bones, mindful of the ice which stuck parts of the skeleton fast to the ground, and carried them back to Sylpha. She took them and created a secure splint for Oisín, who screamed yet more as Sylpha straightened his leg and bandaged the pilfered bones to him.

"The leg must be kept straight," she said. "Even with the best care, it seems unlikely that you'll be able to walk properly again."

Oisín only sobbed in response.

"Will you try to stand?"

"In a moment," Oisín grated through his tears.

It took some time before he felt strong enough to attempt to stand. Once on his feet, he gingerly tested placing his weight on his injured leg and immediately recoiled. He'd have fallen again if Martel had not reached out and steadied him.

"It's all right, chieftain," Martel said gently. "You can lean on me."

"Now what?" Oisín demanded. "Where the hell are we and what are we supposed to do now?"

"We need light and warmth," Sylpha said. "Bone burns well, assuming it hasn't dried out too much, and gives plenty of warmth."

"Smoke as well," Oisín noted, grumbling.

"I'll take the smoke if it means I get to stay warm."

I sighed and returned to the skeleton, collecting yet more bones, stacking them in my arms as if they were bits of firewood. I also brought what scraps of cloth I could tear away from the skeleton. I returned and dumped them in a heap at Sylpha's feet. It was Martel who set about making a pile to light. I raised my brows in surprise when he pulled out two chunks of flint.

"I'm a ranger," he said.

"Always prepared," Sylpha said with an appreciative smile.

Much to my surprise and delight, the cloth caught alight quickly, and the bones soon after.

"Human grease," Sylpha said disdainfully. "Not even centuries can wash it away."

"Look," Oisín whispered, pointing towards a dark form touched now by the flickering firelight.

Martel walked over to investigate it. He ran back quickly, took up a burning bone like a torch and ran back to the shape. He lowered the flaming end of the bone to the form and it sprang to life; a large brazier filled with coal now burning happily in the dark.

It started a chain reaction. Braziers on the floor and torches on the wall sprang to life, bringing much needed light and warmth to the enormous chamber. The light revealed three things. The first being that the chamber was an enormous room, carved from the walls of a great cavern; the floor paved over in neatly fitting stones. The second was that the icy floor of the cavern was littered with bodies, all of them skeletons, all of them wearing archaic armour and carrying weapons of bronze. Third, and perhaps most importantly, the light revealed that we were standing but a few feet away from an enormous dais flanked by two very large doors.

Upon this dais stood a very large throne.

Sitting on that throne was a very large, very muscular, pale-skinned humanoid creature. It was bound to the throne. Thick chains of iron clapped taloned hands to the armrests, its mouth covered over in a cruel-looking iron contraption. At first, the creature did not move. It was not even breathing. But as the fires warmed the air and the ice began to melt the creature took one deep breath in, followed by a long exhalation and another deep breath.

It opened its angular eyes. The eyes were pale gold, I noted, and the pupils contracted as the light hit them - not into a circle, but into deep, dark slits, like the eyes of a cat. Those wide-set eyes of the enormous creature scanned the room and fell upon us.

I saw it tense and slowly frown. Muffled by the iron, I heard the deep rumble of a voice cracked by disuse.

"Help me."

Everyone stared slack-jawed at the thing on the throne. Even sitting, I could tell that the beast must be well over seven feet tall. And it was not a slender seven feet. It was seven feet of bone and tendon and muscle.

"Help me," the croaking voice asked again, sounding much less like a request than a command.

I looked across at the rest of the group, none of whom had moved an inch, and I shrugged. I walked forward.

"What are you doing?" Martel hissed when my movement freed him from his stupor. He would have chased me, but Oisín's weight held him back. Sylpha watched me, but said nothing.

"I'm going to help him. It? Him? That," I replied as I moved forward.

"Are you mad?" Oisín demanded.

I shrugged again. "Maybe it can help us."

The unnerving pale gold eyes watched me as I moved towards the beast. Perhaps I would just release the giant's head, and save the rest for after a questioning. Reaching the throne I saw that the mouth piece was kept in place with a simple pin. It took several attempts and quite a bit of jumping, but I managed to knock the pin loose.

The beast shook its head and the iron plate fell to the side, revealing a long mouth. The beast opened that mouth and moved his jaw around, tilting his head to work the stiffness from the thick muscles of his neck. He turned to look me in the eye. I could not help but notice the two very long, very sharp incisors that peeked through the small opening of his mouth.

"Unbind me," the creature demanded. It yanked on the chains that kept its arms bound to the armrests of the throne.

"You're welcome," I quipped in reply.

The creature raised one eyebrow at me, a smile hovering at the edges of its lips. It was not a particularly mirthful smile, being more akin to condescending amusement.

"Who are you?" the creature demanded.

I opened my mouth to reply, and realised that I had nothing to say. "Never mind," I muttered to myself. The creature heard and cocked its head.

"I can't exactly tell you that," I told it. "Because I don't rightly know myself. I can tell you, though, that we mean you no harm. We were on our way to collect something of immeasurable value and found ourselves here quite by accident. We were hoping you would help us find a way out."

"Treasure hunters, then," the creature said, pursing its lips in distaste.

"Not exactly," Martel said.

The creature turned to him and observed him a moment in silence.

"Unbind my shoulders, nameless one," the creature demanded of me. "So that I might see him better."

I hesitated and looked to Martel. The ranger nodded and I clambered onto the arm rest to yank at the chains wrapped tightly across the creature's impossibly broad shoulders. After a moment of struggle, they came loose and I pulled them off the throne entirely, heaving them to the side. They fell a disappointingly short distance from the throne.

The creature rolled out his shoulders and leant forward. Martel handed Oisín over to Sylpha and stepped boldly up to meet the creature's gaze.

"You seem familiar to me," the creature said in a low voice. "Have we met before?"

"I can say with some certainty that we have not," Martel answered. The creature narrowed its eyes and drew back

"You seek the jewel of the empire," the creature said. "The crowning piece of the imperial sceptre. You will not find it."

"How do you know what we seek?" Martel demanded.

"Look around you, human," the creature snarled. "Do you think you are the first treasure hunters who have hunted that jewel down? Put aside your dreams of fortune and glory. You will perish here."

Martel scowled at the creature. "You are a demon," he stated.

The creature shrugged. "Demons are what you call creatures summoned into a world not of their own," it replied. "By this definition, human, you are the demon."

"This is your realm?"

"It is."

"Tell me, then, how you came to be chained?"

A flicker of annoyance crossed the creature's face. "For this, I blame your kind. Had I not been so distracted with the treasure hunters who last assaulted my domain, my captives would not have so easily overpowered me."

"What captives?" Sylpha asked softly.

The creature straightened as it turned its gaze to her. "You are tuatha," it said softly. "Yet not. One of the purged, perhaps?"

"That is not your concern," Sylpha snapped. "What captives?"

The creature pressed its lips together in a thin line and did not speak. I sighed.

"Though I cannot tell you my name, as I do not know it, I can make better introductions of my companions. The man who seems familiar to you is named Martel. He leads the rangers of the empire, who have been outlawed. Joining him is Oisín, a chieftain of the northern tribes and Sylpha, also of the north. They call me Sky Road Walker, since I am without a name."

Cocking its head once again in my direction, the creature asked, "And what is your quest?"

"That's not your business," Martel snapped angrily.

"To restore the imperial throne," I answered, ignoring Martel's irritated stare. "We do seek the jewel that once sat within the head of the sceptre, but not for vainglorious reasons."

Silence settled over the group as the creature considered my words. "And how can I trust that you speak the truth?" it asked.

"Asks a demon," Martel growled.

The creature turned to him, jerking so suddenly that even Martel jumped back. "Do not dare impugn my honour, human," he snarled. "I have kept my vows exactly as they were spoken."

"What vows?" Sylpha asked, softly.

The creature did not answer. Instead it leant back, his taloned hands gripping the armrests of his throne tightly.

"Go away," he said softly.

"The captives who trapped you here. There were twelve," Sylpha said, her voice never rising. "Weren't there? Twelve disparate pieces of the same soul."

The creature looked at her and nodded - just once.

"You are the Seeker," she said, almost whispering now.

Martel looked back at her, his face lit with an expression of open surprise. "Surely not!" he exclaimed. He looked between Sylpha and the creature in astonishment. "That was thousands of years ago!" he said at length.

"Time moves differently in the realms beyond ours. Perhaps to the Seeker, it was merely yesterday. Or perhaps his kind lives painfully long lives." Sylpha shrugged. "Either way, we are standing before the Seeker, the demon the Mage King summoned to do his bidding; the one who escaped and aided the first empress against his former master."

Sylpha paused just a moment before looking at me. "Unbind him," she commanded.

I hesitated.

"Are you insane?" Martel asked.

Sylpha ignored him. "Unbind him," she commanded again.

I nodded and set to work, wondering if this was indeed the correct course of action. The creature had not uttered any words to confirm or deny Sylpha's statement, so would not be bound to their truth. And even if it was true, it had clearly obliterated previous visitors. There was no guarantee that it would not do the same to us if freed now. Nevertheless, I trusted Sylpha's judgement in this and, after working in tense silence for a good while, I stepped back, having freed the Seeker from its chains.

Very slowly, the creature stood, stopping to wince every so often as disused joints protested the movement. Standing, he was close to eight feet tall, a gargantuan I felt certain could crush my skull in an instant. He stretched and I was acutely aware of the movement of muscle beneath his pale skin.

"I am one of the banished," Sylpha said. "A descendant of the tuatha who fell under your sway in the great battle. I can trace my ancestry back hundreds of generations - straight to you."

The Seeker frowned slightly as he looked at Sylpha. "I bewitched no one," he said.

"That is not what I heard."

"They lied." The creature's frown deepened. "I did not know I had any children."

Sylpha snorted. "How could you not, after all that you got up to?"

A flash of a grin crossed the creature's face. "I often forget the strange taboos your world has placed on certain... acts. I stand before a descendant, and am humbled by her."

"I doubt that," Sylpha replied. The creature laughed.

"If they had children then...." The creature stopped talking and grew slightly melancholy before pulling himself together and facing the four of us. "The rangers were but a fledging corps when I was in your world. How have they come to be outlawed?"

"The Imperial Throne sits empty," Martel replied. "And has for some time. No one knows if there is a descendant of the first empress still alive to take her place. There are rumours, of course. Meanwhile, the empire is failing, and the Mage King seeks to return to power. Only the blood of the empress can stop him, so the story goes. That is why we need the jewel. We must find the heir and stop the Mage King. We seek to restore the throne. This is our mission."

"How long has the throne sat empty?" the creature asked.

"Many generations," Sylpha replied. "Though many an empress has sat on the throne since the first."

"You said it has been thousands of years. Has it truly?"

"Yes," Martel answered.

The creature sat slowly down and folded his hands together, bending his head to rest his lips against the entwined fingers. "She is dead, then," he said.

"Yes," Sylpha answered. "And has been for a very long time."

For a moment, the demon sat in that exact position, staring down at the ground, or more accurately, past the ground into his own thoughts.

"Do you grieve, Seeker?" Sylpha asked quietly. The creature raised his head and smiled sadly.

"Can I grieve?" he asked. "I owe my freedom to your first empress and I find that nothing I have done to date can repay this gift. She was a fearless one, and one of the few who looked me in the eye and treated me as equal. For that, I would have done anything. And yet now on hearing of her death, I find I cannot feel."

"Then help us now," Martel said. "We were to face the sorcerer who has the jewel and—"

"The sorcerer has not that jewel," the creature said softly. He smiled suddenly. "I did not know he yet lived, actually."

"Who?" I asked.

"He called himself Gremblin when he came to me, seeking aid."

"He came to you?"

"Yes. He carried the jewel with him and said naught but that my empress needed my obedience in this one last task - to keep the jewel safe from foes for all eternity. I had no time to answer. The mage delivered the jewel and vanished. I have kept it safe since."

Martel blinked. "The sceptre was broken in three during the Time of Strife, when the last empress was murdered on her throne. That was hundreds of years ago."

"You have the jewel?" I asked.

"I do."

"Will you let us have it?" Martel asked eagerly. The creature narrowed his eyes at him.

"What guarantee have I that all you say is true?"

"Only my word as a ranger," Martel replied. "And since you know nothing of our honour, I fear it will not be enough."

"Your fears are well founded."

Martel threw up his hands in helplessness and turned away, too frustrated to continue.

"Will my word convince you," Sylpha asked. "Since we share blood."

The creature smiled at her. "It is something you have been taught to revile, is it not, this blood we share?"

"And yet I do not."

"And for that I have only your word. Long have I learnt not to trust the word of the people from your realm."

"You trusted the word of the empress," I said.

The creature looked at me and nodded - just once. "But she was unique among you. I have little hope that others share her virtues."

"Will anything we say convince you we speak the truth?" Sylpha asked.

"No."

"Then we are at an impasse. Without that jewel, all hope of finding the heir is lost," Martel said. "And we will not be able to stop the return of the Mage King." The ranger could not hide the bitterness in his voice.

"So, what now?" I asked. "We all just sit here together in this cavernous room, mistrusting one another until starvation or desperation take us?"

The creature looked at me with a crooked smile. "I could kill you now and spare you the trouble."

"You could *try*," Martel growled reaching for his sword.

Chapter Twenty-One

Things grew suddenly tense as the creature observed the ranger and Martel refused to back down. I felt I must do something. But what?

"This is just ridiculous," I muttered to myself. Then, louder, "Martel, take your hand away from your weapon."

Martel looked at me with a raised eyebrow, and did not move.

"Really?" I asked him. "You think we can take him on? Really? Do you have eyes? Oisín is too wounded to move and I don't really know how to fight. That leaves you and Sylpha. Two against him. What do you think, Martel? In the mood for suicide?"

Martel growled, but slowly slid his hand away from the hilt of his sword. I turned to the demon on the throne.

"Where are we exactly?" I asked him.

"In my courtroom."

"A courtroom without courtiers," Sylpha noted. "Interesting."

The beast on the throne shrugged. "We don't get along with one another," he noted, pursing his lips.

"Not at all, I imagine."

The demon narrowed his pale gold eyes at Sylpha. "If you must know," he said. "I was accused of turning native in my time away from this world. I defended the honour of the empress I served, and so was abandoned by my own. They, no doubt, have set up a new court far from here. And I sat obstinately on my throne, king of nothing but memories and regrets. But I had purpose still," the creature whispered this last sentence. "And I remained true to the empress. It became clear that I had but one friend in all the known worlds."

"And the empress was it," Sylpha finished for him.

The creature nodded. He scowled. "And now I have none. You have brought ill tidings with you, strangers."

"The truth is neither good nor ill," Sylpha replied. "It simply is."

"A saying of the tuatha?"

"A saying of the north." Sylpha smiled. "They are a practical people, if a little volatile."

Oisín grunted a laugh, wincing as he shifted his weight. The creature looked him over critically. Oisín shrugged and offered a rueful grin.

"We are, at that," he said.

The creature tilted his head and leant forward to observe Oisín more closely. "There were northmen allied to the empress. The men of the south reviled me, for the most part, but the northmen had shrugged and paid me little heed. They said of me, 'At least he is not a troll.' I have always wondered, are trolls so terrible?"

"They're not especially bright," Oisín noted. "For something that looks so human. And they stink to high heaven. Brutal in battle, though."

The creature pulled away with a soft smile. "I think I like you, northman."

"That's nice," Oisín replied with a shrug. To this, the creature upon the throne rumbled a soft laugh.

"May I ask you a question?" I asked him.

The creature turned to me. "You may."

"I've been asking a lot of questions, because I simply don't know anything about anything. I cannot remember who, but someone mentioned in passing a rumour that the first empress and you were... close."

The creature said nothing.

Thinking that perhaps I did not convey my meaning well enough, I said, "Very close."

"Those rumours were used in an effort to discredit her," Martel agreed. "And still are, sometimes."

Glad that Martel seemed to sense my tactic, I ploughed on. "And mention of children just now, you seemed... regretful. Is it possible that you have children in our world? Children who just happen to be heirs to the imperial throne?"

The Seeker remained silent for a long while, his eyes growing distant as I lost him to thought. I waited patiently.

"It is possible," he said slowly. He frowned. "But what of it?"

"Is your curiosity not piqued? Would you not like to meet them yourself?"

The creature cocked his head. "You will not have the jewel."

"You were a close advisor of the empress," Martel said. "Would you not be so again?"

I could see in the narrowing of his eyes that the Seeker was intrigued.

"You will be able to advise them as you did your empress, and see to it that they do not make the mistakes that her other children did," I said. "You can help write a different legacy for her troubled bloodline."

"And you would be away from this place," Sylpha continued. "In a court with people. Your loneliness would end."

"I would never be accepted."

"If we can defeat the Mage King, you would have the rangers behind you," Martel said. "We will cross blades on your behalf."

"The North, too," Oisín said, looking to Sylpha.

Sylpha nodded. "Yes, the North. And the purged, for whom I speak."

The Seeker leant back on his throne. "The Mage King is stronger than I," he admitted at last.

"You will not be fighting alone," Martel replied. "I swore on my life's blood to see the empire protected. I will not rest, even in death, until the Mage King is vanquished."

"Careful of your vows," the creature snapped. "Or your spirit will know no rest."

"Only if we lose," Martel replied, flashing a quick, vicious grin.

The Seeker leant forward again, thinking hard. "I cannot know you tell the truth," he murmured.

"Then you cannot know we mean to deceive," Sylpha answered.

"Think, my Lord Seeker," I said. "What else could unite a ranger of the empire, one of the purged, and a chieftain of the north but the utmost danger to all peoples. There is no better unifier than a common foe."

"You swore a duty to the first empress," Martel said quietly. "As a ranger of the empire, I call on you to honour your vow."

"The first empress is dead," the creature snarled viciously.

"But her children may yet live," Sylpha answered gently. "Your children. You have a duty to them as well."

"They will rebuke me."

"You do not know that."

"And you do?"

"Yes."

"How can you possibly—"

"Because I stand before you now and call you father," Sylpha said forcefully. "I am one of your children, though many generations from you. Others have shamed me for my blood, it is true. As for myself, I feel no shame, only pride; pride because I see now that you loved the empress who brought peace to the world, that you love her still and that, thousands of years after your vow was fulfilled, you serve her still. There is honour in that few could match."

Silence followed Sylpha's speech. The Seeker's eyes were fixed on her.

I watched the demon on his throne in the empty courtroom as he churned everything over in his mind. I wanted to add to the words that had almost swayed him, but was worried that interrupting his thoughts now would not have the desired effect. Besides, what could I have possibly said that Sylpha had not already so eloquently expressed?

So, I clamped my mouth shut.

And waited.

And waited.

And waited.

And waited.

At length, the Seeker raised his eyes to look squarely at Martel. "Will you enter a pact?" he asked quietly.

Sylpha and Martel stiffened slightly.

"A pact?" I asked no one in particular.

"It is a binding," Martel replied tersely. "A spell of sorts that compels us. Though we may later choose to do differently, if we have entered a pact, our bodies will move independently of our minds."

"And it is more," Sylpha said. "It binds our fates. Should we enter a pact with the Lord Seeker, we are bound to his fate. If he dies at our hands, we die."

"It is my insurance against treachery," the demon said. "If you are true to your word, I will have no reason to invoke that clause of our contract. If I die in battle against my foes, you will be safe. If I die at your hands, or the hands of your allies, all four of you will follow me into death."

"I am bound to another," Sylpha said. "I will not tumble to Helmin with you."

The creature narrowed his eyes and leant forward. Sylpha met his gaze fearlessly. The demon stared directly into her eyes, searching for something. At length, he pulled back.

"The Hunter," he whispered.

Sylpha nodded. "Lord of the wood wights."

The Seeker cocked his head. "And more besides. It is he who rules the Shadow Realm. That is where you will go upon your death."

"Yes."

"I shall alter that clause for you. You will still die should I fall to treason, but I gladly relinquish your soul to the Hunter. The contract remains standard for the rest."

"I'm not keen on selling my soul," Martel growled.

"Then plot no betrayal," the demon replied with a shrug.

"And if you turn traitor and we are forced to fight against you for the cause?"

The demon shrugged. "You do so at great cost."

"That's hardly fair," I noted.

The creature turned to me. "Nothing in life is fair," he said.

"Speak the contract in full," Sylpha demanded. "Before we decide."

"Herein are the words of the pact: In exchange for aid against your foe, you agree to the terms of the Seeker from whom you have requested assistance. These terms are thus:

"Only the Seeker shall carry the jewel, unless slain in service in which case one of those thusly bound by this pact will carry it.

"The holder of this pact will hold in trust the fates of those who seek aid from him. Should any one, or all together, seek to betray the trust of the holder of this pact, and should any such betrayal prove successful, whether by their direct or indirect action, the lives of all signators of this pact are forfeit and souls of all members of the pact are bound to follow the holder of said pact into death; with exception of those whose souls are held in pacts agreed upon before this pact comes into effect."

"I want that last clause changed," Martel growled. "This pact becomes null and void should you turn against us."

"No," the creature said bluntly.

"If you are not planning treason yourself," I pointed out. "How can you take issue with such an amendment?"

"Because I may need to move against you in service to the cause," the creature replied. "My loyalty lies with my empress, not with you. That will never change."

Martel placed his hands on his hips and glared at the creature. The Seeker's impassive expression remained unchanged, which served only to irritate Martel more.

"Will you give us time to discuss this amongst ourselves?" Sylpha asked.

"You have all eternity," the creature said, giving her a vague wave with his hand.

Sylpha cocked her head to the side to indicate that we should follow her. I scrambled down from the dais and followed her to the far side of the nearest brazier. The effort of walking on a shattered knee had Oisín sweating. I looked at his pale face and bit my lip. He was going to need medical attention, and soon. The longer we lingered the more difficulties the chieftain would face.

"I am *not* selling my soul," Martel hissed at Sylpha the moment we all came to a stop.

"Your soul will remain yours if you do not move against the Seeker," Sylpha replied calmly.

"Easy for you to say," Martel growled. "You have pledged your soul to another."

"How could I know that this would come to pass?"

"This gives him free reign to do whatever he wants the moment he is in our world," Martel growled. "And we cannot stop him."

"We can," Oisín said quietly. "If we are willing to die for the cause. And we are. Aren't we?"

"And just how did the Seeker's Sons escape?" Martel asked. "For all we know the demon never left the service of the Mage King and this is some elaborate ruse to speed his victory."

"That makes no sense," Sylpha replied. "Why would the Mage King command his own servant to defect in the first war? What end could that possibly serve? Why defer victory thus? No. I believe that the Seeker speaks true. I also believe that he is cautious and friendless, and is behaving the only way a friendless thing would. He has suffered betrayal before, I think."

"What if the betrayal was the empress'?" Oisín asked suddenly.

We all turned to him. "What if she promised him an empire; a chance to rule at her side, with their children ruling after them? But she changed her mind? What if he is planning treason, for vengeance against that woman and her kind?"

Martel blinked. "It might have happened."

I looked back at the enormous demon sitting on his enormous throne. He leant against the back of the throne, his pale golden eyes closed. I could see his muscles working as he moved them all in turn, testing their readiness.

"Speculation will get us nowhere," Sylpha said. "I can advise only that we accept the pact. The Seeker holds all the cards. If we don't, we may just sit here and rot while the battle rages on without us in the world above. Or we try to attack him in desperation, though I do not like our odds on that score. If we prove to be as honourable as we claim to be, perhaps our actions will convince him that the pact is unnecessary. Or we may be able to convince him to release us from the contract once this war is won."

"Perhaps this is a test," Oisín interjected again.

"A test?" Martel asked in a flat tone.

"It might be," Sylpha said. "A test to see how far we are willing to go for the imperial line. Dare we dedicate ourselves enough to sell our souls and risk eternity in Helmin? Accepting the pact will prove our resolve."

"The fact remains," Oisín said. "He has the jewel, and the way out of this place. We need both. We can accept the pact, or we can attack him."

"I say we fight," Martel growled. "If we die, at least our souls are ours. If we win, we get the jewel."

"And the way out?"

"Can be found."

They all turned to me. "And what of you, Sky Road Walker?" Sylpha asked. "What do you think?"

Knowing this would invoke Martel's ire further, I swallowed loudly and said, "I can see no way around this. We should probably accept the pact."

"And if he turns traitor?"

"We take him down," I replied. "And follow him to Helmin."

Martel opened his mouth to argue, but Oisín chuckled. "He hasn't thought it through, really. Imagine having to spend eternity in the company of the people who bested you."

I grinned at the sudden image of Oisín, Martel, and myself floating in blackness, taunting the Seeker like so many crows protected from the cat by a windowpane. The thought seemed to mollify Martel somewhat. He looked back at the Seeker with a vicious grin.

As if sensing Martel's gaze the demon's almond-shaped eyes snapped open and he turned his head to meet Martel's gaze. Those eyes narrowed as they fixed the leader of the rangers.

Martel turned back. "Let's do this," he grumbled at length. He slipped a strong arm around Oisín's back, helping Sylpha with the chieftain's weight as he hopped back to the demon on the dais.

"All right," Martel said. "We'll sign."

If the Seeker was surprised he did not show it. But he did not react immediately, either. He simply regarded Martel, wearing an expression of deep suspicion that he did not bother to hide. This time it was Martel who returned a hostile gaze with an expression of mild indifference.

At length, the demon gestured. I heard a grating sound and turned to find a wall sliding away, the stones grating against one another to reveal an incredible room. Through the enormous demon-sized door was an expansive library. Thick wooden shelves that reached up out of sight packed with boxes of paper and leather-bound books, stacks of loose leaf wrapped in twine to keep the pages together, and scroll upon scroll. I could not see much through the door, but I could tell that the book cases were several stories tall and they likely covered all four walls. My jaw dropped. Oh, what I would have given to wander those aisles!

I blinked when five tiny little creatures, no taller than the height of my knee, with enormous bulging eyes scurried across the door, chattering excitedly. Two clambered up a shelf out of sight. I could hear them grunting in tiny, high-pitched voices. A scroll dropped into view, deftly caught by the three remaining creatures. There were tiny cheers as all five celebrated the catch and the three tiny creatures carrying the parchment scuttled forward on bandied legs to deliver the parchment to the Seeker.

The creatures looked much like the tiny knife-thief I had caught in the forest so many months ago, but they had no fur, only grey skin, and no tails, either. Could they have been a variation of the same miniature creatures?

They cheered again when they made a successful delivery, then vanished back into the room before reappearing with the other two, all five of them now carrying a wooden box. They panted as they carried the thing to the Seeker and, once the box was safely on the Seeker's lap, they cheered again, dancing and hugging each other as if they had won some monumental victory. I glanced briefly at the Seeker, who was watching the antics of the creatures with a soft smile.

"Rock Imps," the demon said when he caught my eye and noticed my astonished expression. "They have been locked outside of the courtroom for a very long time. Please excuse their jubilation."

"I thought you were alone here," Sylpha said.

"So did I. I had thought them all run off by the idiotic army of treasure hunters whose remains litter my floors."

One of the rock imps turned and chattered excitedly, tears hovering on the rims of its very large eyes.

"They thought I was dead, apparently," the Seeker said. The imp continued its nonsensical chatter, adding animated hand gestures.

The demon continued its translation. "They've been keeping vigil, in case I stirred."

"Why didn't they free you of the chains?" I asked.

"I told you. They had been locked out."

"Who locked them out?"

"I did. I locked down the courtroom every time your idiotic treasure hunters fell through my ceiling."

"Why?" Martel asked.

"Because there are other treasures here besides the jewel, treasures your kind would not recognise and would destroy in your hunt for anything that sparkles."

"Like what?" Martel asked again.

"You can see for yourself," the demon replied, gesturing towards the library.

"Your books," Sylpha said.

"They are precious to me. I have in my library important works from several realms; notable histories; maps of little known places; fragments of pottery and extensive notes I have compiled from my studies of this place, treasures left behind by the people who once lived here, who began the construction of this fortress, and who have since vanished, leaving behind but little hints of their culture. They are as nothing to anyone seeking fortune or fame, but they are invaluable to me. They would all be destroyed in the quest for jewels and precious metals."

"Is this how you spent your time when you were abandoned? In the company of rock imps and digging up the past?" There was no derision in Sylpha's question, only curiosity.

"It is amazing," the Seeker replied, opening up the box so that it became an inclined table, resting on the armrests of the throne. From the box, the demon withdrew an ink pot and a quill. A chattering rock imp clambered nimbly up the dais, climbed the Seeker's leg and made its way to the Seeker's shoulder, where it perched, looking exceptionally pleased with itself. It surveyed my companions and I as the demon carefully wrote the terms of the pact onto the scroll.

"It is amazing how easily time is forgotten when engrossed in the mysteries of the past, how loneliness is forgotten..." The Seeker said no more. Sylpha and I exchanged a glance before the demon put down his quill and motioned to the waiting rock imps. The chattering started again and the imps scurried up the dais, carefully taking the table and lowering it down to the bottom of the dais. Supporting the table on their backs, they turned around so that the table slanted down towards us.

After a brief pause, I walked forward and picked up the quill. I stared blankly at the paper. "Uh... I don't know my name. How can I sign?"

"Make a mark," the Seeker replied. "It matters not the name upon the parchment, only that a mark was made."

Sighing I did the only thing I felt I could. I marked a broad X on the paper. I dropped the quill and stumbled backwards. On the back of the hand that held the quill, a matching mark was cut. It stung as the flesh split. I clutched my hand as blood welled. The unexpected pain brought sharp tears to my eyes.

"It will heal soon," the Seeker murmured.

"It hurts," I muttered.

The demon upon the throne offered only the barest of smiles as an apology. Growling to himself, Martel stepped up next. He did not sign his name either, but scratched the imperial sigil - the long-tailed phoenix - onto the paper. I understood why. He was declaring for the benefit of the Seeker his allegiances and, perhaps, threatening him also. That mark stated in no uncertain terms *I am for the empire*. The Seeker, it seemed, understood perfectly. He cocked his head and regarded Martel with curiosity. There was no hostility that I could detect in that gaze.

Oisín, aided by Sylpha was next, and he scrawled down his mark; a short-handled double-bladed battle-axe. My lips twitched slightly and Oisín, noticing, grinned back. The sheen of pain-induced sweat and his pale skin drawn taught made his grin look more like a grimace. Perhaps it was. Goodness knows how much pain merely moving forward caused him. Sylpha made her mark immediately after. It was a strange, curving runic symbol that I did not recognise.

When everyone had signed, the imps carefully packed the writing implements away, folded up the box, and carried it back into the library. I could hear their tiny, tiny grunts as they put the box back wherever they found it.

"Now we can go," the demon said, standing. He had taken the signed scroll, and I stared as the thing disintegrated before my eyes, disappearing entirely.

I noticed that the demon wore absolutely nothing. He did not seem particularly embarrassed about it though. Nor would I, in all honesty, were I well over seven feet tall and made entire of muscle and sinew.

"You may wish to dress yourself," Sylpha noted casually.

The demon looked down at himself and shrugged. "Humans," he muttered. "I forgot."

He clicked his fingers and the five imps returned, grinning from ear to ear, showing needle sharp teeth. He murmured something to them and the five imps scurried away, returning in several trips with archaic leather armour, and weapons. The weapon of choice for the Seeker was a twin set of short falchions. Well, they were short in proportion to the demon. But the creature also carried a number of daggers of varying length, a stone knife in his boot, and, oddly enough, a sling with a pouch full of rounded steel and stone balls.

With the help of the imps, he dressed himself in his armour. By the time he was done, he looked very formidable indeed, his pale gold almond eyes staring out from an intricately sculpted leather and bronze helm. The impression it gave was of a fierce bird of prey, or perhaps a large wildcat.

The rock imps, meanwhile, danced and cheered once their task was complete... all except one. It stood apart from its celebrating kin and looked up at the demon with large, sad eyes.

"I'll be back," the Seeker told it softly. The imp nodded, but its bottom lip trembled. "Defence of our home will fall to you," the demon said. "Guard my treasures well. I'll be back before you know it."

Again the rock imp nodded, but a large tear trickled down its grey cheek.

The Seeker turned to us. "This way," he said. He walked around the dais and opened the door there. I permitted Oisín, Sylpha and Martel through first. Once I stepped through the door, I looked back. Four of the rock imps were still celebrating, but the fifth stood apart looking at me with enormous eyes, one hand clutching the scrawny elbow of its opposite arm, its lips quivering.

Sighing, I turned and followed the group.

Chapter Twenty-Two

I had not taken more than eight steps, I was certain, but suddenly found myself striding into a sunlit clearing swarming with rangers and northmen. An ancient looking man in faded robes was tied to a stake, sitting quietly on the grass. He was the first to spot us. His eyes widened when he saw the Seeker.

"My Lord!" he croaked, breaking into a bright, toothless smile.

The army of northmen and rangers turned and, with several shouts of surprise, drew their weapons.

"HOLD!" Martel roared, marching forward. More calmly he said, "He's with us."

"That," someone noted, pointing at the Seeker. "Is a demon."

"Very observant," Martel answered blandly. "But he's not just any demon. This is the Seeker, of whom legend tells."

"What legend?" a ranger demanded.

"Wait," a Northern woman said. "*The* Seeker. The Seeker who was the demon-lover of the empress?"

"Alleged," Martel retorted.

Behind him, the Seeker muttered so only those closest could hear, "Not so alleged."

"But yes," Martel continued, ignoring the demon. "The same."

The members of the army all stared incredulously at Martel. "Horse shit," someone piped up.

"That was millennia ago!" someone else shouted.

"Time moves differently in different realms," Sylpha said, sighing. "Now, I need a healer. Oisín has shattered his knee in the fall. And I want some food. I'm famished!"

"My Lord! My Lord!" the dishevelled captive cried out. "It's true!

They said you would walk the earth again! They said it! And they were right! Oh, my Lord!" The man's eyes went wide. "Tell me it is safe? Tell me you haven't lost it?"

The Seeker strode forward, the army parting for him in a long wave. He knelt at the old man's side and untied him from the stake. "I have it still," he said to the old man. "And I will keep it until my task is done and the heir is found."

The man sighed happily. "I have waited hundreds of years to see you again, old friend. How glad it makes my heart. Guard it. Guard it with all you have."

"I swear I will."

The man smiled. "Then I can die happily. My part in this tale is done. The rest is for you now. Goodbye, my friend, and thank you. Your service shall not be forgot."

Still smiling, the man exhaled deeply and breathed no more. The Seeker laid him gently down and stood. Facing Martel, he said, "He was old. Very old."

"My Lord Father," Sylpha asked. "Was this the empress' mage who delivered you the jewel of the imperial sceptre?"

"It was. Though when last we met, he still had teeth."

"Bury him," Sylpha said to the waiting army. "And mark his grave well. He was a brave man."

"Are you sure he is to be trusted?" one ranger demanded, looking not at Martel, but at me.

I glanced briefly at the Seeker before answering.

"I honestly do not know," I said. In my peripheral vision, I could see the demon's lips twist up into a closed-mouth smile, and I wondered what that could mean. "But, he has given his word to help our cause, and we have given our word not to attack him. So for now, until it is proven otherwise, we must assume he is true to his word."

The ranger did not seem convinced. Though he sheathed his weapon, he glared at the Seeker, and kept his hand on the pommel of his sword.

A familiar grunting sound reached my ears and I turned, suddenly terrified.

Three enormous grass dogs, the vicious reptilian creatures of the semi-arid grasslands, stood at the edge of the clearing, their pale eyes shifting constantly as they swept their enormous heads to and fro, casting their soulless gazes across the army.

When the one in the lead caught sight of the Seeker, it immediately straightened. The Seeker, a broad smile stretching across a fanged set of teeth, stood.

He said something in a language I did not understand and the lead grass dog bounded forward, loping towards the Seeker like a giant, hairless wolf. Those in path of the enormous lizard were entirely ignored, and they scattered with shouts of alarm. The Seeker, however, opened his arms wide. The grass dog leapt, clawed limbs extended. It met the Seeker bodily, knocking him to the ground. Martel gave a shout and drew his weapon. He rushed forward, only to have Sylpha catch him by the neckline of his armour and yank him back.

"He's not in danger," she said, nodding at the fallen demon.

I looked. The Seeker was laughing, playing roughly with the grass dog, who snuffed and made bizarre high-pitched chirruping sounds. The creature's powerful tail swung back and forth, knocking people down and injuring some. Those that were not hurt had wisely hit the ground and crawled out of range. Everyone now watched the demon and the grass dog interact.

At length, the Seeker rose to his feet, the grass dog still snuffing and chirping, sometimes standing on its hind legs to place its taloned front paws on the Seeker's shoulders and affectionately rub its face on the Seeker's helm.

"My Lord Father," Sylpha asked. "Do you know this creature?"

"I knew her grandsire," the demon replied. "And she recognises me from his memories."

"Wait," Martel said. "His memories?"

"Well, yes. Being part of the dracaenas family, they are born with genetic memories that stretches back generations. Did you not know this?"

Martel shook his head.

"Dracaenas family? Do you mean that these are dragons?" a northman asked.

"A type, yes."

"Dragons fly," a ranger said.

"Only some," another northman answered. "Lindwyrms cannot fly."

"I am unfamiliar with Lindwyrms," the Seeker said.

"I have never seen one," the northman admitted. "But we have tales of the various wyrms that once infected the north."

The Seeker turned to him and dryly noted, "I dare say dragons have tales of the various men who now infect their lands."

The northman raised his brows and the Seeker shrugged.

"They were here first. Most seem to have fled, but the qilin have managed to do relatively well, I see."

"Qilin?" Martel asked, confused.

"I have heard that word," Sylpha murmured. She looked at the happy grass dog as it wound its way around the Seeker's powerful form to rest its reptilian head on the crown of the Seeker's helm. "It means something like 'forest jewel'."

"In Tuathan?" Martel asked.

"No," Sylpha answered. "The word is foreign to the tuatha, though they use it in reference to a mythical beast. I thought it hand horns or antlers, though."

"The males do," the Seeker said. "Or they used to. That trait may have been bred out."

"How...?" a northman began to ask.

"Hunting," Martel said before the man could finish his sentence. "Those with large ornaments are hunted and so the size of the antlers or horns or whatever it is they are being hunted for diminishes, or sometimes disappears entirely from the animals. It takes generations, but it has been recorded."

"Who the hell hunts grass dogs?" another ranger asked with a shudder.

"Who hunts dragons?" a northman replied, shrugging.

I looked at the Seeker, with the enormous reptile wrapped around his body, its head resting on his. "So this is a qilin?"

"It is. She is the matriarch of her clan." The Seeker nodded at the other two qilin, who remained at the edge of the clearing, testing the air with their tongues.

"And she knows you?"

"She knows of me. Or, at least, of one who looked and smelled like me. Her grandsire was consort of the matriarch of their clan, which had aligned itself with the empress in the battle against the Mage King. It was one of two clans which did so. They were very brave. The rest aligned themselves with the Mage King, or elected to remain neutral."

"You speak of them like they're people," Martel noted.

"Not all people walk on two legs, ranger," the Seeker replied. He reached up and scratched the grass dog beneath her chin. The reptile's eyes half close and she rumbled softly.

"If most of them aligned themselves with the Mage King, then — "

The Seeker put up his hand to silence Martel. "You must understand that a matriarch makes her decision based on the needs of her clan. She does not care for anything else but their continued survival. It is her duty. Human moralities do not apply. Those who fought for the Mage King did so because it was the only option for their survival they could see. It is not a matter of good or evil, ranger."

"My name is Martel," Martel growled. "So what you're telling me is that two clans of grass dogs, uh, qilin, fought alongside the empress and this one here is a descendent of one of those clans?"

"Yes."

"What happened to the other clan?" Sylpha asked.

"They were obliterated," the Seeker responded softly. "I had known that clan well."

"When you say known..." Martel muttered under his breath. The Seeker heard nonetheless and smirked at him.

"Would it shock you?"

Martel said nothing, but his expression turned sour. He raised one eyebrow. The Seeker laughed and the qilin, ruffled by the jumping shoulders upon which her front paws rested, slid back down onto all fours. She raised her muzzle and made a sound that was halfway between a bark and chirp thrice in close succession. Cautiously, the other two qilin slunk into the clearing. They kept their bodies low to the ground and swung their heads from side to side, eyeing the rangers and northmen on either side of them as they approached their matriarch. If one of the army appeared too close, the qilin opened its mouth and hissed from the back of its throat. The offending person stumbled back without fail.

The matriarch greeted her clan with the same snuffing sound as she had used with the Seeker. The two submissive qilin approached the Seeker and offered a very timid greeting. Using his knowledge of qilin custom, the Seeker watched them impassively, and did not reach out to touch them as he did with the matriarch.

"The matriarch and I are equals," the Seeker told me when he noticed my curious gaze. "So we treat each other as equals. I withhold my affection from the submissive members of the clan so that they know that I do not consider them my equal. In this way, they will not consider themselves equal to me, and thus equal to their matriarch and no power struggles will ensue."

"I am impressed by your knowledge of everything," Martel said wryly.

The Seeker shrugged. "I have spent my life in study, ranger. There has been little else to occupy my time. If you doubt the truth of my words, I invite you back to my fortress to look long at my library."

"I take it you do not trust him," a northern woman noted, tilting her troll-horn helmed head towards the Seeker.

"No," Martel replied flatly. "I do not trust him." Sighing, he added, "But the Sky Road Walker is right. We have no choice but to trust that his word is true."

At that moment, Oisín collapsed. Sylpha staggered under his weight, as did the medic who had come to her aid before the qilin arrived. The medic grunted.

"I need space to work," he barked.

The army got to work, clearing a space and raising a canvas pavilion. The Seeker left the qilin clan and walked to Oisín, covering the distance in four impressive, long-limbed strides. He relieved the medic and Sylpha of their unconscious burden, lifting him as if the burly northman weighed little more than an infant.

The medic and Sylpha scurried forward to help the army prepare the medical pavilion. Others went to retrieve their friends injured by the powerful sweeps of the excited qilin matriarch's tail and helped them over to the new hospice.

Yet others returned to their work digging a grave for the ancient mage who had guarded the entrance to the Seeker's realm for so many centuries. Looking around, I realised that the number of injuries accounted for fully a quarter of the force that had met at the clearing. I sighed.

For a while, feeling utterly useless, I watched as the Seeker, having hunched down under the canvas ceiling of the open pavilion, laid Oisín down on the hastily constructed table.

Suddenly, it felt as if the earth gave way. Loudly in my ears rang the sound of rushing water. "No!" I gasped as I stumbled. The sensation of heaving earth knocked my legs from under me.

"Sky Road Walker?" a northern woman asked as she helped steady me.

I lifted my head. "Seeker's Son!" I yelled, though the effort was dizzying.

Heads turned to me, then to my right, where a misty black shape sped through the trees towards the army; towards me. Knowing their weapons were useless, those closest to the Seeker's Son fell back. The small clan of qilin, however, bounded forward.

The matriarch leapt at the spectre as it breeched the clearing.

"No!" I shouted.

Too late. The qilin crashed into the phantom. I stared in utter disbelief as contact was made. The pair rolled across the ground before the qilin kicked the Seeker's Son off. The other two qilin bounded in to join their matriarch. A thin layer of blue light crackled over their skin. The Seeker's Son, faced with the three qilin drew its blade. It slashed out at the matriarch, who ducked. The blade narrowly missed the top of her skull. Sparks flew as the blue light of the blade passed through the blue light surrounding the qilin matriarch and the air filled with a strange, acrid smell.

Immediately following the strike, one of the qilin struck back, its tail whipping through the air with a sharp whistle. It hit the Seeker's Son and the spectre was flung back through the trees with an awful shriek. It vanished from view, but the roaring water still rang in my ears and I was feeling weak and nauseous.

The Seeker's Son reappeared on the western side of the clearing, rushing forward once more. I watched through swimming vision as the Seeker strode out of the pavilion, a stone bullet in his spinning sling. He let loose the rock, casting it straight at the Seeker who, upon seeing its former captor, rushed towards him.

Moments before impact, the stone burst into flame, or what I thought might be flame. The crackling, flickering light around the rock was the same pale gold colour as the Seeker's eyes. When it struck the Seeker's Son, the creature burst into flame. Ignoring the flames, the Seeker's Son propelled itself forward. Stepping back, the Seeker drew his twin falchions. These blades, too, flickered with pale golden flames. The demon braced himself for battle, but the pale gold flames consumed the spectre robes and all. The thing crumbled into a pile of ash.

The Seeker straightened. "It will be back. Soon," he said.

"How soon?" Martel demanded.

"Soon." The Seeker turned. He sheathed his falchions, which were no longer flaming, and walked to me.

Still feeling nauseous, and my vision still swimming, I felt rather than saw the Seeker take my chin in one enormous hand. I saw his eyes, appearing in a multitude before me, narrow as he stared into my own. I had no idea what he was searching for, what secret might be hidden in my eyes, but at length, the demon nodded and let his hand drop.

Turning to Martel, the Seeker said simply, "He must not be allowed to reach the Sky Road Walker. Not ever."

"We've been trying to avoid it," Martel answered, his gaze flickering briefly to me.

The Seeker growled low and turned, marching to the qilin matriarch. She greeted him with a thumping tail and much snuffing. In angry silence the Seeker checked her over for any wounds and breathed a sigh of relief when he found none. He turned back.

"We need to move."

"We have too many wounded," Martel answered. "We cannot move yet."

"Leave them behind," the Seeker snapped.

Martel drew himself up. "We will do no such thing."

"I have a limited supply of those bullets," the Seeker growled. "I cannot keep it away indefinitely. If it returns to its full strength, nothing will be able to stop it. We need to move."

"We head to the city," a ranger suggested. "We have all pieces of the sceptre now. We can find the heir."

"No," a northman countered. "We are an army. It will be seen as an act of war. If we're going to face the city's defences, we need to be at capacity. We head back to the ranger's headquarters. We are protected from the Seeker's Son there and we can heal."

"We should go to the tuatha," Sylpha said. "They were allies of old. They can protect us from the Seeker's Son and we may be able to convince them to add their numbers to ours, as in the days of the first empress."

"You are one of the purged," the Seeker reminded Sylpha. "And they do not like me."

"We can convince them."

"They almost killed Martel last time," a ranger noted.

"We are facing the Mage King again. We need all the allies we can find and or convince!"

Though my head still ached and my stomach still churned, I opened my mouth to speak.

"We need friends," I managed to say through the thick knot in my throat. The words were almost followed by the contents of my stomach, but I managed to swallow that back. "We go to the tuatha. It's our best option."

Martel opened his mouth to argue.

"We take the wounded with us," I said, and Martel shut his mouth again. He turned back to the waiting army of rangers and northmen.

"We stay the night," he said. "And strike south in the morning."

With a collective sigh, the army resumed its work. Firewood was collected and hunters were sent out. Others set up their bedrolls or tended to their horses. Before long, the entire clearing was settled and soldiers were at various fires cooking their dinner.

The northwoman who had caught me when my knees buckled

silently helped me to the fire around which Martel, Sylpha and the Seeker sat and just as silently took her leave, though not before casting a doubting glance at the Seeker. The Seeker was accompanied by the matriarch of the qilin clan, who sat not unlike a lion, her front paws crossed before her and her reptilian head high and proud. Behind her, the two members of her clan rolled around in the bracken, trying to get at various itches across their backs. Their tongues lolled happily as they crushed the vegetation beneath them.

My head was still pounding and my stomach was still upset, so I said nothing to my fellows and rested my head against my knees.

"Why does the Seeker's Son affect the Sky Road Walker so?" Martel asked the Seeker.

I turned my head without lifting it from my knees to look at the demon. He responded with only a shrug. "I assume that it has something to do with his ability to walk the Sky Road. Few of your kind can."

"We never said anything about—"

The Seeker raised one eyebrow at Martel. "One would have to be truly idiotic not to be able to deduce anything from the name Sky Road Walker."

"Can you walk the Sky Road?" I asked the demon.

"Yes."

"And the Mage King can, I suppose." Martel said.

"Yes."

"Anyone else?"

"More tuatha than not, though it is not guaranteed that one can. The purged all should be able to, though there is no guarantee of that either. Very few humans, from what I understand."

"What enables a person to walk the Sky Road?"

The demon shrugged. "The Sky Road was built long before I came to this place. I suspect the builders have long ago perished, or changed and forgotten themselves. I had made a point of studying it when I was here last, but could find no clues as to who built it or why. Perhaps, if the war turns in our favour, I will resume my studies."

I rolled my head back so that my knees pressed lightly into my closed eyes and passed the rest of the evening in that manner. Unable to stomach even the thought of food, I retired to bed early and fell to sleep almost immediately.

The night passed without incident and I awoke in the morning feeling a little better and, more hearteningly, hungry. In anticipation of this fact, the Seeker moved to my side and offered a large platter full of freshly cooked poultry. I did not even stop to wonder where it came from. I just ate it.

"A good sign," the Seeker noted before standing up and stretching.

Chapter Twenty-Three

It was first light, and the camp was already a flurry of activity. The medical pavilion had been emptied and was in the process of being struck. Bedrolls were packed away as camp-mates stoked the fires in order to prepare breakfast.

At our fire, Martel and Sylpha had already awoken and eaten. They were now lounging on the grass, watching the camp at work. The Seeker, having served me my breakfast, had gone to the edge of the clearing to consult with the qilin matriarch.

Before the sun breached the horizon, the entire army was ready to move off. I smiled as Oisín hobbled towards me, one leg wrapped very firmly in a box splint. With each step, the chieftain grimaced.

"How am I supposed to ride like this!" he demanded as he arrived at the fire.

"Uneasily, I'd imagine," Sylpha replied, barely controlling the wicked grin that spread across her face.

Oisín glared at her. "You," he said. "Are not funny."

Martel chuckled. Noticing the signal from one of his lieutenants, stood and fetched the horses. It took Oisín several tries and ample help from Sylpha to get into his saddle, and even then his leg stuck out oddly. I tried very hard not to laugh as I mounted Fas, but the chieftain caught my smirk and narrowed his eyes at me. I could not help it. I chuckled.

"I'll pay you for that," Oisín growled.

"When your leg heals," I answered.

Martel and Sylpha laughed and Oisín, not immune to the ridiculousness of his plight, smiled too.

"All right," Martel barked. "Time to go!"

"Move out!" a lieutenant bellowed and the entire army was on the march. Despite the size of the force moving behind me, the mix of rangers and northmen seemed to know how to move through the forest with little noise. They moved carefully and quietly. I sometimes doubted their presence at all, they moved so well. I turned to look behind me and, excepting the obviously wounded men and women, who could not be quite so careful, I barely even noticed the men and women on horse and foot as they flitted between the trees.

A soft snuffing to my right drew my attention. I turned to find the Seeker resting easily on the withers of the qilin matriarch as she glided between the trees. The demon in full armour atop the dog-like dragon was quite the sight. Slinking along behind the pair were the other two qilin. In spite of their size, they move swiftly and sleekly, possessing a remarkable grace.

We had a hard day's work ahead of us when we reached the ferry crossing. The township on the other side of the river was now empty, the inhabitants having fled when the Seeker's Son attacked. There was no one to help us cross. It took the better part of the day to get the army across the water. The Seeker had no issue. The qilin simply swam across the deep river.

"Of course they do," Martel growled when he saw them cross without effort and slink into an open area to sun themselves.

The Seeker did not rest with the grass dogs. He found a length of sturdy rope to throw across the water to help pull in the ferry, which had lost its chain. Once we had crossed, we all took refuge in the abandoned inn, the sawmill or the various abandoned houses.

It took another month to reach the edge of the tuatha forest. In that time, though I was certain I heard the faint sound of rushing water every now and again, there was no sign of the Seeker's Son. The Seeker was concerned by this, but I was relieved. It kept my head clear and my stomach still.

The army of rangers and northmen had long acclimated to the presence of the demon and the grass dogs. The horses no longer baulked as the creatures moved near them and the rangers no longer talked darkly about the demon who rode in their midst.

On the last day before arriving at the edge of the forest, I turned to the Seeker.

"How is it that the qilin are able to touch the Seeker's Son without being absorbed by it?" I asked.

"They're dragons," the Seeker replied simply, as if that answered anything.

I raised my brows at the Seeker who shrugged. "That is the reason," he said.

"But why?"

The Seeker opened his mouth to answer, but instead jerked to his right as an arrow whizzed past his head. Snarling, he loosened one of his falchions from its scabbard and turned to face the assailant.

A lone tuatha stood in the tall grass on the knoll of a small hill, a powerful recurve bow in his hands. "Go no further!" the tuatha shouted.

I could tell by the waver in his voice that he was terrified, and his hands trembled slightly as he, alone and friendless, prepared to fight an army.

"You are outnumbered," the Seeker snarled.

"Hold!" Martel barked at him.

"Do what you will to me," the brave tuatha youth called back. "My brethren have been warned. You will rue the day you brought an army to tuatha lands."

Growling, the Seeker dismounted and strode towards the tuatha. The trembling youth let loose another arrow at the Seeker, who smartly cut the thing out of the air with his sword and continued forward.

Martel kicked his horse forward. The stallion galloped up, coming to a stop between the Seeker and the tuatha youth. Martel drew his sword and pointed the tip at the Seeker.

"I said hold," he growled.

The Seeker raised his brows. "You do not want to cross blades with me, ranger."

"No," Martel agreed. "But I will if you take but one more step forward. I am Commander of this army. When I say hold, you hold. Do I make myself clear?"

The Seeker cocked his head in mild curiosity, but did not answer.

"Now sheathe your weapon."

The Seeker did not move.

"Sheathe...your...weapon."

Very slowly, the Seeker sheathed his falchion and, turning abruptly, marched back to the qilin matriarch. Martel turned his horse.

"We mean no harm," he said gently to the youth on the knoll.

"No one with an army at their heels means no harm," the youth answered.

"We are an army in need of refuge. And friends. Please. My name is Martel. I have been to your woods before and stayed as a guest."

"Captive," the youth corrected. "You were a captive, if you are who you say you are."

"Captive, guest," Martel replied with a shrug. "It is more or less the same thing."

"Not exactly," a rich, feminine voice answered.

I turned to find Hessa sitting on her stag mount, dressed in full armour and looking something like a very dangerous pile of leaves. Behind her stretched an impressive army of tuatha, each mounted and armed with a plethora of fierce-looking weapons.

Martel turned to face her and smiled. She did not return the smile. Instead, she looked over at the Seeker, then at Sylpha, her lips pursed in distaste.

"You have acquired some very unsavoury friends," Hessa noted, not taking her eyes off Sylpha as she spoke.

Sylpha tensed visibly, but diplomatically kept her mouth shut.

"Necessity makes strange bedfellows," Martel replied.

Hessa turned to him again and looked past him at the Seeker. The demon stood upright next to the qilin matriarch, his muscular arms folded against his chest, his yellow eyes narrowed.

Tension crackled in the air as Hessa and her army took our measure.

"Please, Hessa," Martel said. "We have a lot to discuss, and I'd rather not do it where the Seeker's Son can easily find us."

"These two," Hessa said, pointing at Sylpha and the demon. "Are not welcome. Nor is anyone who calls them friend."

"The chieftain Sylpha is my friend," Martel replied. "And she would be yours as well if you would but set aside ancient and impractical enmities for a moment."

Hessa's mouth twisted up. "You will not vouch for the demon."

"His presence is less a choice and more a necessity."

The demon looked hard at Martel. He shrugged. It was, after all, true.

Hessa shook her head. "No. I am sorry. We have risked too much already. We will not house you, your demon, or *that*." Hessa pointed at Sylpha.

"We share foremothers," Sylpha replied sharply.

"Who were unclean!" Hessa barked. "I will not have your corrupting influence in our home!"

"It is technically my corrupting influence," the Seeker answered before Sylpha had a chance to. "And any who would deny aid to kin for nothing more than an accident of birth are the ones who are truly unclean."

Hessa turned to him and raised her eyebrows.

"The body fades. It dies and it rots," the demon continued. "But the spirit lasts forever. What blackness of soul would cause sisters to turn their backs on one another?"

Sylpha turned to the Seeker and their eyes met briefly. In that brief look, Sylpha offered her deepest gratitude, which the demon acknowledged and accepted with nothing more than a nod.

"I will not be lectured on the state of my soul by a *demon*," Hessa grated.

The Seeker walked forward until he was standing beside Sylpha's horse. "And I will brook no challenge to the state of my childrens' souls. Rage against the choices of your foremothers if you wish, rage against me, who indulged those choices. But save your insults for us. Our children had no choice but to be."

"This is the second time you've referenced the past as if you've lived it."

"Because I have."

"Uh, Hessa. This is the Seeker," Martel said.

"The Seeker. *The* Seeker who fought beside the first empress, who corrupted the weakest of us into wicked deeds? *That* Seeker?"

"Well..."

"If that is true, how could you possibly believe that we would shelter such a creature?"

"I wove no magic," the Seeker said softly. "They came to me of their own free will."

"Silence!" Hessa barked. "You speak only poison!"

I noted the barely perceptible movement of the tuatha force reaching for their weapons, and bit my lip helplessly.

The Seeker sighed. "You are wrong," he said.

"I said, *silence*."

"Lord Seeker," Martel said. "Please. Hold your tongue."

The Seeker looked at him briefly and nodded, just once. In this, at least, he would acquiesce. The tension filled the space between our two armies, one false move or word and there would be a battle fought that minute. I knew I needed a way to get the tuatha to accept Sylpha and the Seeker. The Seeker especially, since we were bound by a pact.

"For the love of all things good," I muttered under my breath. I kicked Fas' flanks and the aged mare trotted forward with a snort.

"Hello Hessa," I greeted mildly when I came to a stop at Martel's side.

"Sky Road Walker," the tuatha replied stiffly.

"Had we known you were intending to come out of your forest to greet us so, we'd have flown our white flag sooner. But as it is, we've only just arrived so you will have to take our word for it."

"Assuming that you have come under a flag of truce," Hessa said finally taking her eyes off the Seeker to look at me. "What terms do you wish to negotiate?"

"We were hoping to speak to your council. There is much we need to discuss. The Seeker's Sons are growing stronger. I cannot be in the presence of one now without becoming ill. The Mage King is set to return, and we fear that it may be soon. Thanks to you, and to Sylpha and the Seeker, we now have all the pieces of the sceptre. We can find the heir, restore the throne and fight the Mage King back. But we need your help to do it."

"Seems to me as if you have it all figured out."

The Seeker growled something in a language I could not

understand; his own presumably. Hessa's gaze shifted again, returning to me. I shook my head.

"Hardly. There are many complications. Which is why we came to you. We came in the hopes that your council would see the wisdom in united action, as they did when the first empress came seeking aid. She would not have succeeded had the tuatha not taken up her cause, and neither will we. Please, Hessa. We need to speak with your council."

"You may speak to them. Out here. I will not permit the demon and his spawn into our woods."

"If the Seeker's Son finds them, our cause will be just as lost."

"Why? They are but two."

"Because," I said with a heavy sigh. "Leaving him out to die would be an act of violence against him, and we have entered a pact."

Hessa eyes widened and she blinked in surprise. Then she roared with laughter. "Oh!" she said. "Oh you poor fools!"

I sat on my horse and deliberately set my face to silently express just how unimpressed I currently felt. Hessa proved unconcerned, and continued to laugh. At length, she calmed enough to say, "You poor, poor fools. He will claim all your souls before your quest is done."

"It was a necessary bargaining," Martel grumbled.

"Only if we move against him," I added.

"You are lost, for he will surely betray you."

"Then we will kill him," Martel answered with a shrug.

Hessa scoffed. "And you will die with him."

"Saving those I love from a fate worse than death at the hands of the Mage King," Martel replied quietly. "Is worth that price."

My mind immediately went to Basadia. The brave young Black Blade recruit who almost died at the hands of a Seeker's Son, with whom Martel had fallen hopelessly in love. I wondered how she was faring in the illegal wood-cutting town in the northern reaches of the empire. Had she recovered? Did she die? Or would she spend the rest of her life trapped in a body that could no longer function? I turned to Martel and, judging by the expression on his face, he was thinking the exact same thing.

Hessa's amusement seemed to subside and she looked at Martel and me thoughtfully. After a moment, she nodded as if confirming something to herself. "Very well," she said. "I can take you into our woods. You are not welcome into our village until I have spoken to our council. When we decide what to do with you, I will let you know."

"Take us prisoner," Martel said. "Again?"

"As a prisoner of ours previously, have you cause to complain of your treatment?" Hessa asked.

Martel shook his head.

"And, consider, that, should you wish to prove your peaceful intent, it would look better if you came willingly."

Martel sighed. "In this I cannot argue. We submit, my Lady."

Smirking, Hessa asked, "My Lady?"

"In the most sincerest terms, I assure you," Martel answered with a small smile of his own.

Hessa laughed and raised one hand above her head, making a circling motion with one finger pointed to the sky. Her army moved immediately, encircling our own to escort us into the tuatha woods. Distantly I heard the soft rush of water.

"You may want to hurry," I told Hessa.

Hessa took one look at my pale face, and nodded. "Move!" she commanded.

Surrounded by tuatha warriors, we approached the forest at a gallop. Poor old Fas tried very hard to keep pace with the younger, faster horses, but I found myself quickly overtaken. The Seeker, sitting astride the qilin matriarch, looked back at me and laughed. The sound of the fast approaching Seeker's Son occupied me too much for me to formulate a pithy response.

It was with a sigh of relief that I crossed the first trees that marked the tuatha forest. The rushing sound ceased abruptly as the power of the tuatha shielded me from the spectre hunting us. I felt, rather than heard, the distant shriek of frustration as our trail went suddenly cold. It painted a smile on my face.

We were led through a set of thick, moss-covered trees on the south side of the village. For two days we marched without rest until we reached an enormous clearing through which ran a joyously chattering brook. The clearing could easily house thrice our number. The army of northmen and rangers flooded into the clearing. No one bothered to set up a fire. Exhausted and relieved, they simply found a place upon which to throw their aching bodies and rest.

The Seeker did not join the circle of leaders, which included Martel, Oisín, Sylpha and myself, but instead took the qilin to the easternmost edge of the clearing to settle down. There he remained.

"I'll go," I said when Sylpha noticed and started off in his direction.

"Hi," I said when I arrived at the Seeker's side.

The Seeker did not respond.

"Any reason you're not with us this evening?"

The Seeker turned to me, his expression impassive but his eyes hard. "I am unwelcome."

"The tuatha—"

"I am not speaking of the tuatha!"

The vehemence in the Seeker's words took me aback. I sighed. "Martel is a little gruff, but he means well. And to be fair to him, there has been no test of your loyalty."

"My service to the empress cost me my people," the Seeker snapped. "I sat upon a throne in a deserted courtroom in a deserted fortress in a deserted kingdom for aeons. I had naught for company but rock imps and the occasional band of fortune seekers hoping to end my life." The demon stroked the hard scaled side of the qilin matriarch. "I had children, but never knew them. And now I learn that the empress I served has been dead for generations beyond count. All I have sacrificed, and still I am met with contempt." Turning his back to the qilin, the Seeker sat on the grass and watched the army settle.

I sighed and sat down next to him. "Martel carries the weight of this entire quest on his shoulders," I said. "Ever since the rangers were outlawed, he has made it his mission to restore the imperial throne. It has been his entire life. And now, now he is so close, and the way has become ever more precarious. If but one thread unravels, the whole thing will fail. And Martel feels that the responsibility of that failure will be his. He does not trust you. But that doesn't mean he will not come to it."

The Seeker looked at me. "In truth I do not know why I desire his trust. I cared little enough when my own people left me. I suppose even demons crave acceptance."

"Will you not join us?" I asked after a long silence.

"Not this evening," the Seeker responded.

I nodded and scrambled to my feet. "Rest well," I said.

The Seeker nodded and I moved back towards Martel's group. Sylpha met me a few feet from where Oisín lay on the ground, snoring.

"Is everything all right?" she asked.

Knowing Martel was listening in, for he was not especially subtle, I simply said, "The Seeker is lonely and friendless in a world that has been taught to despise him."

Sylpha sighed and headed off to join the Seeker, patting my shoulder as she passed. I watched as she arrived at the Seeker's side and sat down. They exchange no words, but I saw an immediate change in the Seeker's posture. The demon's shoulders relaxed, their squared, defensive position lowered and, though light was quickly dimming, I noted the corners of his mouth rise slightly. Turning back to Martel, who was also observing the scene, I settled into the soft grass, lay down and closed my eyes.

"Try to be nicer to him," I advised Martel, unsolicited.

"We do not know that he isn't our enemy," Martel answered.

Without opening my eyes I said, "We don't know that he is."

I did not recall falling asleep, but the distant sounds of the tuatha dawn song woke me. I opened my eyes to the grey haze of first light and listened. Soon the chorus of voices was joined by the delightful addition of birdsong. Feeling fully relaxed for the first time in recent memory, I simply lay and listened and let calm contentedness wash over me.

Two more mornings passed this way. Midday on the third day, Hessa appeared at the edge of the clearing. Martel and I approached.

"Hello," I said.

Hessa offered a brief smile. "The Council is willing to hear you. Bring your representatives. We will leave for the village as soon as you are prepared."

Martel looked across at me. In his silent gaze I knew I was being asked, *who?*

"There will be five of us at the council meeting," I informed Hessa.

Hessa's gaze flickered to Sylpha and the Seeker, who stood together near the three qilin, watching Martel and I speak with Hessa. The tuatha scowled.

"Are you certain about this?" Martel murmured to me.

"Very certain," I replied.

Martel glanced back at the Seeker, looked at me again, and nodded. "There will be five of us," he told Hessa.

"You would bring a *demon* before the council?" Hessa hissed.

"We would be trapped forever in another world were it not for him," I explained gently. "And he has defended us against the Seeker's Son. There is no good reason to leave him behind."

"There are plenty of reasons."

"Spite is not a reason."

Hessa, surprised at my sharp tone, stared incredulously at me a moment. "I warn you now, Sky Road Walker, that his presence will not aid you in gaining the council's favour."

I nodded. "Let us hope they can see reason."

With nothing left to say, Hessa gave a curt nod. I took this as being dismissed, and so I approached the fire that I shared with Martel and Oisín, beckoning to the Seeker and Sylpha. Martel followed behind.

"Right, we're off to meet the council," I told everyone once they had gathered. The Seeker's jaw clamped, the tendon near his back teeth jumping in a silent display of irritation. I turned to him. "All of us."

The Seeker could not hide his surprise. "All of us?" he asked.

"Well, not the whole damned army," I replied with a small smile. "But you, Sylpha, Oisín, Martel and myself."

"Does Hessa not object?" Sylpha asked.

"It doesn't matter," I answered. "We wouldn't have gotten where we are without any of you. We are united in this fight, and if the tuatha are to help us, they're just going to have to accept that fact."

"And if they choose not to help because of it?" Oisín asked.

"We cannot control that."

"You are talking like a leader," Martel said with a smile. "You have changed."

"You keep asking my opinion," I replied. "What else was going to happen?"

Martel chuckled and nodded. "All right," he said. "Let's not keep our patient hostess waiting. Oh, and leave your weapons behind."

Sighing, the Seeker immediately began to disarm himself. The number of hidden blades was simply astounding. By the time he was done removing every knife, short sword and dart, there was a small pile of weapons by the fire.

"What?" he demanded when he looked up to find us all staring at him in astonishment.

Martel snorted in amusement and walked back to Hessa.

"What?" the Seeker demanded again, sounding genuinely confused.

Saying nothing, Oisín, Sylpha, and I followed Martel. With no answer and nothing else to do, the Seeker joined us.

Chapter Twenty-Four

We marched for two days before arriving at the tuatha village. It had not changed. Looking up at the canopy, I could not see any of the structures the tuatha had coaxed from the massive trees. The tables and chairs that grew out of the very branches themselves were hidden from anyone looking upwards. I had not noticed that the first time I was here, and I found myself marvelling at how easily the tuatha could hide.

"This way," Hessa said smartly. It was the first time she had spoken since beginning the march to the village. I could not blame her, really. She was hopelessly outnumbered and in the company of people who made her uncomfortable.

Tired, I dragged my feet as I stumbled behind Hessa to the central tree. This tree was gargantuan. Stairs, woven patiently from aeons of hanging root growth, wrapped its way around the massive trunk, lit by small lanterns at regular intervals.

"There is an unoccupied room which will house all of you together," Hessa said. "Will that suffice?"

"If there are blankets and food, you can stick me in the stables," Martel answered.

The Seeker rumbled a soft laugh from behind him. Hessa could not retain her usual dispassionate expression and a small smile flashed across her face.

"We have both," she replied. "And you will not need to stay in the stables."

"Then I am more than amenable."

"This way." Hessa began to climb the stairs.

I groaned and followed. The stairs spiralled ever upwards; up and up and up high into the air and out of sight. My legs ached from two days of walking, my stomach rumbled for want of food and I felt very much like falling down and sleeping wherever I happened to land.

Sensing my fatigue, the Seeker reached out and grasped my shoulder. "Almost there," he said gently. I nodded, too tired to even raise my head and look at him.

The sun was setting by the time I staggered into a room created from a natural cavity in the centre of the tree. The floor had been worked to provide an even surface, in the centre of which stood a table of polished wood. The table was laden with all kinds of foods, the mere smell of which granted me energy. I straightened.

"You are welcome to eat and drink as much as you like," Hessa said. "We will bring you blankets presently. The meeting will be held tomorrow at midday. I will collect you when it is time."

"Thank you," I said.

Hessa nodded and left. I turned back to the table and, with Oisín and Martel, fell upon the food like a starving dog. Sylpha and the Seeker joined us later, but wisely did not eat nearly so much nor so quickly. I understood their restraint better later in the night, when cramps from an overfull stomach trying to digest a rich meal after so long without kept me awake.

Oisín groaning on the other side of the room, followed by the Seeker's soft, slightly sinister chuckle told me that I was not the only one to regret our rabid feasting.

I slept through the morning meal, having found rest much too late in the night to warrant getting up. In truth, it was a meal I was happy to skip, being still full from the night before. In fact, of the three who ate too much last night, only Martel appeared unfazed by the amount of food he had consumed the night before. He rose early to partake in breakfast.

The sound of soft conversation finally dragged me out of sleep. I opened my eyes to find Martel and the Seeker speaking with one another in soft voices. To my surprise, Martel even smiled at something the demon said. Groaning, I rolled from the blankets just as Hessa arrived.

"We are ready for you now," she said bluntly.

"Thank you," Martel said. He looked over at Oisín, who still snored in defiance of the light, noise and heat.

Rolling her eyes, Sylpha marched from the table and delivered a strong kick into Oisín's side. Oisín sat bolt upright and blinked stupidly as he looked around. Still asleep, it took him a while to see Sylpha standing over him, her arms folded.

"Up," she commanded. "Lazy fool."

Oisín grunted, but clambered to his feet.

Martel laughed.

We followed Hessa along the thick branches that served as roads and paths in the arboreal village. Before long, we stood at the far edge of a large, circular platform. At the other end sat three elderly tuatha, with a fourth chair empty. Hessa moved forward and occupied the seat.

Behind the chairs, stood an audience of high-ranking tuatha. Their eyes were all upon the enormous mass that was the Seeker. The demon straightened under the obviously hostile gazes, filling more space and silently daring any of them to cross him.

"You *dare* bring this demon and his spawn into sacred tuatha lands?" one of the tuatha elders demanded, rising in agitation.

"They are both members of our company," Martel answered before I had a chance to. I looked at him in surprise.

"They have fought at our side and, were it not for the Seeker, we'd have long ago been victims of a Seeker's Son and the world would be without a chance against the returning Mage King."

"We will not treat with friends of this fiend," the elder said.

Martel set his jaw and folded his arms across his chest. I knew him well enough to know this meant he was digging his heels in, and once that happened the leader of the rangers could not be reasoned with.

Trying hard to keep the impatience from my voice, I said, "It is not our intention to upset or offend, but the Seeker and the chieftain Sylpha are members of our company, without whom we would have surely perished long before now. Clinging to old wounds and letting them divide us, in light of the return of the Mage King, is nothing short of idiocy."

The gathered tuatha audience gasped, but I ignored them and carried on.

"They are needed in this fight. We have all the pieces of the sceptre. We can find the heir to the imperial throne. With that achieved, we will still need to confront the returning Mage King. They will be needed in that battle." I pointed at Sylpha and the Seeker who, instinctively, moved closer to one another for mutual defence. "And so shall you."

"The choice is yours," I continued. "You either join this fight, or you don't. I warn you now, history rarely celebrates cowards."

Again the gathered tuatha gasped, and the crowd dissolved into a hushed murmur of outrage. I folded my arms and boldly met the eyes of the four elders, lingering longest on Hessa, who had once defended me bravely. To her, I said, "You almost died so that we might acquire a piece of the sceptre. Will all of that be for naught?"

Hessa did not reply. Instead she turned to the three other elders and watched them as they watched me. For a long time, silence stretched between the elders and myself. Even the birds sensed the tension and stilled their singing.

"You understand," one elder said at last. "That this demon fought on behalf of the Mage King?"

"Yes," I said. "I also understand that he was summoned and bound to that evil man, and rounded on him the moment he broke free."

"Are you certain he broke free?" the elder asked. "And was not turned loose?"

After a short hesitation, I replied, "No. In all honesty, I cannot say this."

"How can you expect us to trust this hulking beast you have brought into our company?"

"Because the empress trusted him," Martel said before I had time to answer. "And because she defeated the Mage King with his help. Because he stood guard over the shattered soul of the Mage King and has kept safe the final piece of the sceptre."

"You will note," Hessa replied rather sardonically. "That the shattered soul of the Mage King has escaped the Seeker's careful attentions, and is currently wreaking havoc once more."

"You can blame treasure hunters for that," the Seeker growled.

"Oh?"

"Rumour of my possession of a jewel of immeasurable worth has been behind repeated attacks on my realm for some time. Idiotic men and women seeking fame and fortune distracted me enough that the evil I guarded was able to escape. I was bound and had to watch as, one by one, the pieces of the shattered soul escaped their bonds and fled."

"If you were bound and helpless as you claim, why did these shades simply not kill you?" Hessa asked.

"I said I was bound," the Seeker growled. "Not helpless. It was far easier for them to simply escape, trusting that I could not chase them, bound as I was. Were it not for my delivery by the others who stand before you, the spectres would have been correct."

"What could you have possibly done being bound as you claim?" another elder scoffed.

"This," the Seeker replied.

Before I could stop him, the Seeker invoked his powers. Yellowish flames licked his body, seemingly feeding on his flesh. Yet despite the heat which I could clearly feel, his skin neither cracked nor withered. The flames lashed out, stopping just shy of the elders, who jumped up out of their chairs in alarm. The wall of flames parted, revealing a channel that led straight back to the Seeker.

Safely behind a channel wall, I stared incredulously at the demon. His eyes had vanished, replaced by flames that licked their sockets in a macabre dance. I sensed that this wall of flame was merely a parlour trick compared to what the Seeker was truly capable of.

I turned to look at the elders, who gaped at the Seeker. "If I wanted you dead," the Seeker growled in a deep, dangerous voice. "Your forest would have been ashes long before this!"

As suddenly as they appeared, the flames and heat vanished, leaving nothing more than a few wisps of acrid smoke. The Seeker stood in proud silence, his eyes once again his own, watching the elders.

"The empress freed me from bondage," the Seeker said, his voice now quiet and sad. "And I loved her for it. That love lost me everything and, it would seem, earned me nothing."

Hessa was the first to recover from her shock. She straightened and adjusted her robes.

"Well," she said, almost breezily. "There is no doubting your power. It is your motives we question. Even if you loved the empress, she is long dead. What possible motivation have you to aid the fight against the Mage King now?"

Wanting to know the answer myself, I turned to look at the Seeker. His eyed flickered to me very briefly before he replied.

"It is my understanding that the imperial bloodline is considered ended."

"Yes," Hessa replied cautiously. "The empress and her Prince-Consort had three children. No known descendants remain, which is why we are sceptical of finding the long lost heir."

"I have no doubt that the children of the empress and her Prince-Consort are no more," the Seeker replied. "But I suspect this legendary heir was never a descendent of the Prince-Consort."

Martel choked, exploding into violent coughing. I stared at him confused a moment before understanding flooded me. Eyes wide, I asked, "You believe the lost heir is a child of yours?"

"Yes," the Seeker replied. "By which I mean, it is possible."

"So it's true," Hessa said. "Even the empress was taken in by you."

"I loved her," the demon snapped. "And I do still. I will know my children by her, with or without your help."

"Well," I said to the council of elders cheerfully. "That adequately explains his motivation, wouldn't you agree?"

The elders, still in a state of shock slowly returned to their seats. They sat in silence once more, but the silence no longer felt distant. It was the silence of confusion; of uncertainty. It was the silence of uncomfortable revelation.

"Assuming we believe you," a hither-unto quiet elder said, her voice cracked with disuse. "What would you have us do?"

"We will not be permitted into the capital," Martel said. "The rangers are outlawed. We have grass dogs in our midst, and a demon. And we are seeking to restore the throne. The Steward is a small, petty man who loves power and little else. The gates will be closed to us. We may need to fight our way in. And there are other enemies we will have to face inside the city. Once there, we will need to establish order while we search for the heir."

"You believe the heir is in your capital?" Hessa asked.

"I believe the heir will be from one of the noble houses," Martel answered. "Fostering was a common practice during the early days of the empire. To foster a royal child was considered a sign of particular favour. If what the Seeker says is true, the child may have been sent to be cared for away from the Prince-Consort. Either way, the child will likely have been treated as one of the house's own, and raised to nobility."

The council fell silent again, seriously reconsidering their position. Whereas before they were openly hostile to us, they were now confused and undecided as to whether or not they should take up arms to restore the imperial throne.

"We cannot possibly in good conscience place demon spawn on the imperial throne," whispered one elder, his voice muffled by the dryness in his mouth.

"Why not?" answered another. "If it will save us all, what right have we to complain what blood flows in their veins?"

"We will be rallying behind a demon!" the first elder replied. "Will you stand with such evil?"

"Whomever knows love cannot be evil," answered the second elder.

The two stared angrily at one another.

I turned to Hessa.

"Hessa, I know you think poorly of the Seeker and I know that, for whatever reason, your kind considers him and his children an abomination. But he is also a father who never knew his children, and he is a man who has lived alone for aeons beyond count. What lengths would you go through for your family? What would you do to finally belong?"

If Hessa was moved by my imploring, she did not show it. Instead, she turned to the Seeker to consider him a moment.

"Tell me, Lord Seeker," she asked. "If she trusted you as much as she claimed, why did she choose another to rule at her side?"

The tuatha hit a nerve. The Seeker straightened and his jaw clamped shut, the tendon on the side of his face jumping in agitation. Silence followed and Hessa raised her brows.

"Well?"

"I cannot tell you," the Seeker replied through gritted teeth. "But it was the beginning of the rift between us. I first retreated to her council, in her presence only when called upon for matters of court. I retreated further, to be master of the archives, summoned only when clarification on points of law or history were required."

"And then?"

"And then I left," the Seeker said. "At her request," he added.

"So perhaps she did not trust you as you claim."

"Perhaps," the Seeker admitted.

"Or perhaps she loved you," Sylpha said quietly. The Seeker turned to her with a questioning expression.

"She had an empire to rule; one that was new and raw. She might not have held so firmly to her territories with you at her side - not without becoming every bit the oppressor the Mage King was, at least. Forgive me Lord Father, but you would not have been accepted by the empire for much the same reason you are not accepted amongst the tuatha. Perhaps she sent you away because it hurt too much to have you so close, and yet be ever removed from you."

"A romantic notion," another tuatha elder snapped, snorting his derision.

"Either way," Sylpha answered firmly. "We cannot know the thoughts of the dead, and to make assumptions in that regard would be nothing short of foolish."

"I had never considered that," the Seeker told Sylpha, seemingly oblivious to the tuatha interjection. "I had assumed she had not..." he stopped himself and looked down at the thick branch beneath his feet momentarily before pulling himself together.

The effort was visible. His shoulders squared and he shuddered as if shaking free of the weight of uncertainty.

"It no longer matters," he said. "What's done is done. I mean only to find my children and aid them in any way I can, as I should have done in ages before."

I noticed Hessa watching the Seeker carefully this entire exchange. For a short time, his golden eyes met her green eyes and some silent understanding jumped between them. Hessa turned to the council.

"I believe him," she said. "That is to say, I sense no deception as regards to the questions we've asked."

"And based on that, you would recommend what?" the least favourable elder demanded.

"What do you think, you dolt?" the other female elder snapped. "He has spoken true. And we have a chance to defeat the Mage King once and for all. We'd be fools indeed if we did not stand with them in this quest."

"And what? Lay siege to the city?"

"We'll cross that bridge, or those walls, as the case may be, when we come to it," Martel said. "In truth, our main concern has been escaping the Seeker's Sons and acquiring your aid. We haven't thought of much beyond that."

"We need an answer," I added. "Will you stand with us, or won't you?"

"There is much in our lore about the Lord Seeker," Hessa said. "We have long been warned against creatures such as he; told that he will cast a spell over us with honeyed words until we have signed our souls over to him, as our sisters had done in days long past. To march with him would be unthinkable. However I find the thought of inaction against the threat of the Mage King yet more repulsive. So it is that I cannot, in good conscience, recommend anything but joining their cause to this council."

"This I second," the other female elder announced, casting an imperious gaze at her argumentative neighbour.

"I cannot," that neighbour declared. "I will not stand with that creature." He stretched out a frail arm to point at the Seeker. "I do not believe his lies, and I feel to the core of me he will do us all wrong before the end."

All eyes fell on the male elder who had sat in ponderous silence beside Hessa most of the meeting, his head bowed. I feared he had fallen asleep. I glanced at Hessa, who stoically ignored me and awaited the elder's response.

At length, the elder raised his bowed head. Rheumy eyes took in the five of us standing at the entrance to the circle.

"The Mage King is a great evil," the old tuatha announced.

I thought that much was painfully obvious, but I wisely kept such thoughts to myself. "I see him, a sooty black mark in our history, and our future. And yet it is not he who troubles me, for I can read his intentions and know them. The demon that stands before us now, however, I cannot read. I cannot grasp his intentions, and this concerns me."

My heart beat savagely against my chest. If this elder voted against us, it would mean another long debate. And another. And another until some conclusion could be reached. I feared that the longer this was drawn out, the less likely our chances of success. Despite the agitation coursing through me, I managed to keep myself still.

"Still," the elder wheezed, observing the Seeker with his watery eyes. "We can only deal with what we know. We know the Mage King seeks dominion over all. We know that he must be stopped. For these reasons, I must move to recommend that the tuatha take up arms against the Mage King."

I did not realise I was holding my breath until I felt it escape my chest in a sudden blast of relief.

"But I also advise caution. Be wary around the demon in your midst. His desires are less certain."

"Or you could just believe me," I heard the Seeker grumble to himself. Knowing this was a victory for us, however, he did not say it very loud.

Hessa heard him all the same, and she tried very hard to conceal a smile as she observed the Seeker. I did not help matters by grinning at her. She nevertheless grinned back. She stood.

"Since it is the will of the council," she said loudly. "It must be done. Warriors, prepare yourselves and your loved ones. We ride in two days." Hessa turned to us. "Come," she commanded as she strode across the circular space to lead us back to our accommodations.

Once inside the large space, Hessa left us, offering nothing more than a short bow.

"Thank the gods," Martel said. "That was tense!" He turned to the Seeker. "What exactly did you do that the tuatha hate you so much for?"

"He gathered a harem of tuatha women," Sylpha answered, moving to the bed she had used the previous night. "And was very unapologetic about it."

The Seeker shrugged. "Should I have been?"

"Do you sleep with anything?" I asked mildly.

The Seeker grinned over at me. "Not *anything*. I have standards."

"Such as they are," Sylpha noted sardonically. She lied down. "That was far more stressful than I had anticipated. I'm exhausted."

"Well, rest," Martel said. "We have two days before the tuatha army will be prepared. You have time."

Rest we did. Also exhausted, I found my bed and collapsed into it.

After a long silence in which I started to fall asleep, I heard Oisín ask, "Sky Road Walker?"

"Yes?"

"What now?"

"No idea."

"Sleep," Martel said groggily. "We'll figure something out in the morning."

But the question pulled me away from rest. What now? What would be our best plan of action? My mind worked through the possibilities. When it came to deciding the plan of action tomorrow, what would I recommend?

I stared up at the ceiling, pondering, until morning.

Martel stared incredulously at me when I explained my idea over breakfast.

"If we sent out riders with a message the sceptre has been found and we're seeking the heir to the throne to all the noble families, and tell them to gather in the palace on a certain date, the Steward would have to let us in to perform the deed, or face the wrath of the entire nobility."

Oisín grinned and the Seeker started laughing.

"I like this one!" the demon said. "A good mind!"

"Yes," Martel agreed. "It's a solid idea. I'm quite disappointed I didn't think of it."

"You aren't very politically minded," Sylpha said. "It is understandable."

"Politics are dull," Martel grumbled.

"Apparently trees are not," Oisín noted.

"No, as it happens. They are not."

The Seeker laughed again. "I suspect none of you know just how true that is."

"Have you slept with them too?" Sylpha asked.

The Seeker grinned. "They go about it a little differently than I do."

Snorting into his breakfast in order to control his laughter, Martel very nearly choked. Oisín started laughing, which made me laugh. Sylpha soon followed, and before long everyone at the table was laughing. I suspected that it was less that something was amusing than the fact that everyone needed to relieve the intense stress of the past few days.

After a while, the laughter died down. At length, Martel said, "It is a good plan. We'll send riders out the moment we get back to the army." The Seeker and I noted the slight darkening of Martel's mood and I immediately guessed as to what caused it.

"We can send a rider north," I said. "For news of Basadia."

"I'm not sure I want to know," Martel replied. "If she died...." He shook his head.

I nodded. "But if she's alive?"

Martel shook his head again. "How can she be?"

"What happened?" the Seeker asked softly.

"A young woman in our company put herself between the Sky Road Walker and a Seeker's Son. It put a claw through her head. There was no blood, but she crumpled like a sheet in the wind."

The Seeker shook his head. "That is not good."

"Oh really?" Martel asked.

Acknowledging the dripping sarcasm, the Seeker tilted his head with a small, sad smile. "I apologise for being so obvious."

Martel sighed. "No. It's all right."

"You were close; you and this woman?"

"Not exactly. It's complicated."

"Ah. You loved her, but don't know how she felt about you."

"That about sums it up," I said when Martel did not answer. "That, and she and Martel are supposed to be on opposite sides of the fight."

"She is aiding the Mage King?" The Seeker looked so confused that I laughed.

"No. She's a member of the Black Blades, with whom the rangers have butted heads."

"They are responsible for the end of the imperial line," Martel growled. "And the disbandment of the rangers."

"Ah. Tricky."

"Wait," Oisín said. "You're in love with the Black Blade?"

"What of it?" Martel demanded.

"Nothing," Oisín said, though his impish smile told me that he found this news hilarious. "It's just an odd choice."

"Choice had very little to do with it," Sylpha said. "Now leave the boy alone."

Martel stared at her with daggers for eyes and she, in return, smiled beatifically at him. Oisín chuckled and I hid my own smile behind a long drink of water. The Seeker, however, had retreated to his own thoughts, and sat still and silent. Where his mind had gone, I could only guess.

"In any case," I said. "We will be sending out riders, and we can spare a rider to go north."

"Lord Seeker," Martel said, drawing the Seeker from his thoughts. "You know the spectres of the Mage King best. Is there any hope for Basadia?"

"I wish I could offer you comfort," the Seeker said. "But I cannot. I do not know if Basadia could survive what happened to her; the thing that wounded her mind but not her body. I have never seen it, nor heard of it happening."

"I figured," Martel sighed.

"It's up to you," I told the ranger.

"Let me think on it."

"Of course."

There was a great deal of waiting around as the tuatha army prepared to march on the capital of the empire. I could not help but feel a little excited at the prospect. We were so close to finding the heir of the empire, if they in fact did exist, and facing off against the Make King in a war for freedom.

Knowing full well I was romanticising the inevitable slaughter, I was nevertheless anxious to reach the conclusion of this fight and, perhaps, if I was very, very lucky, discover at last who I truly was.

I had been far too busy for a long while now to really think on the issue. Now that I had some time to unwind, the question of who I was, and how I ended up on that grassy plain with absolutely no memories now came to the fore. Was I the heir? If I was, that meant the demon in our company was my ancestor. It was a strange idea. If was not the heir, where did I come from? And, perhaps most importantly, why was I here?

I sighed and noted that just as I had come out of my own thoughts, everyone had sunk into theirs. I took the time to enjoy the contemplative silence. Hessa interrupted, drawing everyone's attention simultaneously. She stopped at the door as five pairs of eyes turned to her in silence.

Raising her brows, Hessa paused a moment before stepping in. "We will be ready to go in the evening," she informed us. "The Council still has reservations and so have requested that I stay with and command alongside you. The choice is, of course, up to you, but we would consider it an act of good faith."

I looked to the group. The Seeker and Sylpha exchanged a concerned glance but offered no opinion. Oisín looked at me and shrugged. Martel merely observed Hessa. I could not read anything in his gaze.

"Technically, Martel," I said when I felt the silence had dragged on too long. "You're the leader of this little undertaking. You decide."

Martel's gaze barely flickered to me before he asked Hessa, "May we have a moment?"

"Of course." Hessa nodded and left the hollowed centre of the tree in which we spent the past couple of nights.

Martel turned back to the group. "I am disinclined," he said simply.

"It would not be terrible," I replied. "Hessa is a good fighter, and she is fair."

"But not above petty discrimination," Sylpha noted.

"This may just prove the opportunity that can change her mind. She will be travelling with us, consulting with us and planning with us. We can show her that you and the Lord Seeker are not inherently evil."

"You are not even sure of that yourself," the Seeker said.

I shrugged. "You haven't given me reason to doubt you."

"Yet," Oisín added, grinning impishly at the demon.

The Seeker flashed a grin at this and, not for the first time, I wondered if he was not actually plotting some terrible deception. I pushed the thought out of my mind. Now was not the time for doubts and speculations.

"You are for bringing her in to co-command?" Martel asked me.

"She very nearly died helping me acquire a piece of the sceptre. I feel it is the very least we can do. She's clever, honest and not unreasonable at all. In fact, her worst attribute is being incredibly stubborn, and that is something you yourself are guilty of, Martel. And it's damned handy in a fight."

Martel grunted at this and nodded. "That much is true." He grinned unexpectedly. "All right," he said. "If you vouch for her, I'll permit it. But, since we're both 'incredibly stubborn' I appoint you mediator of any and all disputes between us."

I looked at Martel with a mind to argue. He smirked at me. "Fine," I grated. "But you need to be reasonable."

Shrugging, Martel replied, "I'm always reasonable."

Oisín grunted a short laugh and, rolling my eyes, I rose to beckon Hessa inside.

"We've agreed," Martel said when she stood before the table. "The Sky Road Walker has vouched for you, so we must, I feel, trust you to share the command."

"We are making up a substantial portion of this army," Hessa said bluntly, as if there ought not to have been any other considerations.

"And that may yet prove to be a liability we can ill afford," Martel said.

Hessa's eyebrows rose and her shoulders tensed. Feeling there was going to be a fight, I hastened to add, "What Martel means is that there are potential problems with too many commanders at the helm. That said, I trust that we all can set aside our differences and work together well enough to make this current arrangement beneficial to everyone."

"A consummate politician," I heard the Seeker mumble. Hessa, whose hearing was infinitely sharper than mine, heard it as well. She shifted her catlike gaze to meet his and, for a while, the pair merely stared at one another.

Surprisingly, there was no hostility in Hessa's gaze that I could detect. I was both amused and irritated by the cheeky barely seen smile the Seeker wore as he and Hessa had their silent contest of wills.

"You are disturbing, Lord Seeker," Hessa said after what felt like an eternity of discomfort. "I cannot see you."

"Perhaps you shall have to judge me on the merit of my deeds," he responded smoothly.

Hessa's face split into a smile. "Perhaps," she agreed.

The tension now cut, Martel stood. "Let's get going shall we?"

Chapter Twenty-Five

Another few days of walking through the enormous forest home of the tuatha, with the tuatha army at our back, saw us arriving in our clearing. The qilin hissed and chirped as they bounded happily to the Seeker, their massive reptilian feet causing the ground to shake slightly with every step.

Hessa shuddered. "Grass dogs," she muttered.

Martel looked critically over the army. "All right!" he bellowed. "Get yourselves up, dressed and on your horses! We have a city to take!"

The camp leapt into action. Camp sites were packed away, cleaned and hidden under earth and rangers and northmen were dressed and mounted with surprising speed and efficiency.

"And here I was thinking that the northmen were uncivilised barbarians," Hessa said.

"We are," Oisín replied easily. "How else can we so quickly prepare for combat?

Sylpha laughed.

"We're ready, Sir," a lieutenant called out.

Martel nodded and walked to his horse, who waited patiently beside Fas. The old mare was grazing and ignoring me as much as she could.

"Fas," I said as I approached. She deliberately turned her rump to me. "Come here, please."

At the word 'please', Fas brought up her head and turned to look at me. With a resigned sigh, she walked to my position.

"Thank you," I said with a smile. I gave her a good natured scratch beneath her chin and mounted up. Not ten minutes after Martel bellowed his command, the entire army was making their way through the rest of the tuatha forest towards the capital city.

A week later, Martel called a meeting of the officers and his chosen messengers.

"Right," Martel said once everyone had gathered around his fire. He spoke to his messengers. "This is the plan. We wait at the edge of the forest with the bulk of the army. I need you to ride out to the various castles, manors, and estates of the noblemen and explain to them that we have the sceptre and are prepared to find the heir to the imperial throne. Stress that, giving their close familial connections, it could very well be them or a member of their immediate families. Tell them to converge on the court in three weeks time. When you have all returned with your duty complete, we will ride out together to the city."

"What about the Seeker's Son?" a rider asked.

"I don't think you will be troubled by it," I said. "I have a feeling that it is drawn to me, and since I will remain behind within the tuatha protections, it will have no idea what you're up to or where you are."

The rider nodded. "Very well."

"You ride out at first light tomorrow," Martel said. "Goodnight, and good luck to you all."

With that, the riders dispersed and everyone retired for the night.

I was woken at first light by the sounds of horses shuffling and snorting as their riders prepared the mounts for a hard, swift ride. I sat up to find the Seeker also awake, resting his back against the qilin queen, who snored gently. In the grey light of pre-dawn, I was certain I would not be able to see either the Seeker or the qilin were it not for the long, deep breaths of both, the movement belying their position in the gloom. Rising, I walked over to the demon.

"You're awake early," I noted.

"I sleep very little away from my keep," he replied. He watched as the riders departed, some alone, some together as they spread their secret messages to the noble houses of the empire.

"Does this not exhaust you?"

"I will not feel it until the danger has passed. When the war is over, I will sleep a long while, I think."

I nodded. "Can I ask you a question?"

"You have already."

Ignoring the demon's sarcastic response, I proceeded. "Are you able to tell who might be the heir?"

The demon frowned and shook his head. "I wish I could, if only because it would gladden my heart a little to know a child of mine by her."

He did not elaborate on 'her' but I knew full well he meant the empress.

The Seeker sighed. "This world is still so young. There is so much power here, and so many powerful people. You, this Hessa woman, Sylpha, Martel."

"Wait, Martel?"

"Yes."

"Oh. What kind of power do you mean?"

Smiling, the Seeker turned to me and asked, "What kind of power did you assume I meant."

"Well, magic, really. Since I can walk the Sky Road... for some reason... and Hessa is a tuatha, and they're practically all mages of one level or another. And Sylpha too... But you said Martel, and now I'm confused."

"Magic is such a crude word," the Seeker said. "It is too specific and yet it is all that you have to explain it."

"Let me see if I have this correctly... Martel is magical?"

The Seeker chuckled softly. "Not exactly. But he is powerful. You yourself can sense it, though you might not know it precisely. Everyone can sense it. It is why he was made leader. There are rangers just as skilled as he, just as capable commanders, but none have the power Martel possesses. It is what draws people in, like moths to a flame."

"Martel would argue with you," I said.

"And he would be wrong."

"Hm. What about Oisín?"

"He's a nice enough fellow," the Seeker said, grinning.

I laughed.

"He is not powerful in and of himself, but there is power in his line. I see a child, his son perhaps? There is much power in that boy. It is an ancient power, one that men once knew how to harness but have forgotten long ago. He can do so instinctively."

I stared incredulously at the Seeker. How could he have possibly known about Llei?

"Does the chieftain have a son?"

"Yes," I said at last. "A small red-haired boy who squared off against a Seeker's Son with naught but a staff in defence of his grandfather."

"And the Seeker's Son did not immediately attack?"

"No," I replied. "Now that you mentioned it. It didn't. It just sort of hovered facing him before moving to attack."

The Seeker nodded. "It was gauging its chances. Send a rider north. That boy should be protected at all costs. I feel he will be very important to the survival of the northmen."

"He is defended by his mother, at present."

The Seeker grinned. "Then he is safe. Only a fool would cross blades with an angered northwoman."

"I wouldn't want to," I agreed.

"Shtop talkin' 'bout my wif," Oisín mumbled from his position on the ground.

The Seeker and I exchanged a glance, a smirk, and fell into easy silence. I leant back and closed my eyes.

Birds were singing loudly and the sun was shining merrily down on me when next my eyes opened. I realised that I was asleep against the qilin queen's body and sat upright very quickly. I turned to find the qilin's reptilian snout sniffing me gently.

"Hey, hey! He's awake!" Oisín said from the fire, smirking as he gnawed on a pork chop. The Seeker also sat at the fire, though he was not eating.

"Is that pork?" I demanded, rising to my feet.

"It is," Oisín said. "Martel and Sylpha went for a hunt this morning. They were bored, I think. Come on, then, are you having breakfast or what?"

"It's really more lunch at this point," Martel growled as he walked to the fire. He threw an armload of logs beside his seat and sat down.

"Sorry," I mumbled. "I was tired."

"I don't mind," Martel said. "And I don't think the grass dog did either. She just sat there, the picture of patience, and didn't move."

I turned to the enormous lizard. She watched me a moment before shaking herself, rising slowly to her feet, stretching and sauntering off to find some food. The horses nervously parted as the queen shambled past them.

"While we're here waiting around," Martel said. "We should figure out what we're going to do once we get into the city."

"Uh... aren't we just going to hold court and pass the sceptre around until it tells us who the heir is?" I asked.

"Ideally, yes."

"So...."

"The problem, as I see it, is the Steward. He's likely to hamper us in any way he can."

"Cut his throat," Oisín said with a shrug.

"All the finesse I would expect of a northman," Martel said. "Though I'd be lying if I didn't find it an attractive idea. There are also the Black Blades to consider. They're likely to draw blades against us as well."

This made me sit upright. "Maybe not," I said.

Martel looked at me and frowned. He turned and beckoned Sylpha and Hessa to the fire. I waited until they were seated and settled before I continued.

"Look, the Black Blades saved me," I said. "When I fell off the Sky Road and landed in the market. They were the ones who assigned Basadia to me when they sent me on my way and, as near as I can tell, their ultimate goal is the same as ours. They want the throne restored."

"You're wrong," Martel growled. "They want the throne. End of."

"You don't know that's true."

"You don't know it isn't." Martel shook his head. "Look, I know them better than most, and I am telling you, they are not what they claim to be. They don't give a damn about restoring the throne to the rightful heir. They only want the throne for themselves."

"How do you know them so well?" Hessa asked.

Martel sighed and kicked a dead ember near his boot back into the fire. He refused to answer.

"He had a brief but intense affair with their leader," I provided.

"Really?" Oisín asked me. I nodded. Oisín turned to Martel. "What is with you and falling for Black Blades?"

"Shut up," Martel growled.

The conversation about the Black Blades went on for quite a while. Dinner time approached and no one seemed closer to a plan that adequately dealt with them.

"Look," I said patiently. "We should send an emissary to the Black Blades. Even if they want the throne for themselves, they will still need to get the Steward out of the way. They know the city better than any of us here. They will know how to get to him and restrain him."

"And shut the city to us," Martel growled.

"Not with an army ready to lay siege to it," I countered.

"Not to mention the armies of the nobility that will surely be summoned if the nobles cannot get into the city," Oisín said.

Martel sighed and shook his head. He turned, inviting Hessa to voice her opinion. The tuatha watched on warily, suspicion plainly visible in her expression. Martel smirked at this.

"Behave yourself," I mumbled to him. The ranger's lips split into a grin.

"I do not know the Black Blades as you. We have heard of them, of course, but only that they were the protectors of the Imperial Throne. And that they failed the Imperial Line." Hessa paused to gather her thoughts.

"Failed," Martel growled. "They actively worked against it."

"According to Saschana," I said. "Who is the leader of the Black Blades, it was one of the two commanders of the Black Blades who betrayed the last empress. Farim was his name. He had slain Assa, his co-commander and helped the traitor dispatch the empress."

"What traitor?" Hessa asked.

I shrugged. "I don't know. The one who killed the empress. Saschana has told me that they were looking for the heir as well in order to restore the throne and mend the wounds of the past."

"If the Black Blades were genuinely looking to do that, they wouldn't have had the rangers disbanded," Martel growled.

"They had the rangers disbanded?" Hessa asked.

"Aye," Martel said. He sighed. "Saschana and I, well... We had a brief affair. I was young and starry-eyed and believed all women to be as wonderful as my mother. I did not know how low and conniving they could be."

"Easy now," Sylpha warned.

Martel shook his head. "I thought myself in love. I was an idiot. I was too trusting. Saschana only wanted information from me. When she had it, I could find her no more. Not two days later, when I had returned to my post, the notice of disbandment came through. I knew it was her that made it. She and the Steward... Well, I'll just say that they were close."

I blinked. "Are you telling me that she and the Steward were... um... lovers?"

"I had seen them together. In truth, I had thought him an idiot, looking at her with stars in his eyes the way he was. I was sure she had only eyes for me. Now I know that I was the fool who was played."

"Are you certain it is not a broken heart that clouds the truth?" the Seeker asked. He asked gently, with not one ounce of mockery in his voice.

Martel scowled. "Saschana played me. Of that, I'm certain. I cannot trust her."

"She saved my life," I said. "I owe her my trust. It was she who began me on this quest in the first place. She was also seeking the pieces of the sceptre with the intent to restore the throne."

"No. That's what she wanted you to believe," Martel insisted.

"Why? What possible benefit would there be from acquiring the sceptre?"

"To lend legitimacy to their eventual rule. That sceptre is a symbol of power to them. No more."

"That is not their mandate," I insisted.

"You don't know that."

"I know as much as you."

Martel glared at me.

"Perhaps we might find out the truth," Hessa suggested, breaking the silent battle of wills between Martel and I. Martel turned his angry gaze to her.

"What do you mean?"

"A meeting," she said. "Between this Saschana person and five of her highest ranking Black Blades, and the six of us."

"No," Martel said. "I have no desire to see her again."

"This goes beyond your desire, Martel," the Seeker said, his voice still gentle and kindly. "The fate of the world supersedes that."

Martel looked at him a moment and turned away. "Fine," he grated. "Send your damned emissary."

Before anyone had a chance to respond, Martel rose and stormed away from the fire, looking not unlike an angry bear in his retreat. The Seeker sighed and shook his head.

"At least we know he is genuine in his feeling of betrayal," he noted. He turned back to the fire. "Perhaps it would be wiser to send one of the northmen, instead of a ranger?"

"No," Hessa said. "Without trading papers, the northman chosen will be arrested if discovered. We can send one of the tuatha. Our arrangement with the empire is less limited. We may wander through the empire as we like. And, if what you say of this Saschana is true, the summons of a tuatha will bring her to us without any argument."

"Why is that?" Oisín asked.

Hessa met him with an impatient glare. "Because, northman, it is not nothing that draws the tuatha from their woods."

"And nothing is what brings the men of the North, is that what you're saying?"

"Stop it," I snapped. "Hessa only means that raids aren't really something the tuatha are known for, fun though they may be, and that the presence of a northman in the south may make people think they ought to be preparing for a raid."

Oisín grunted and returned to stripping the bone of his pork chop with his teeth.

"It's decided?" Hessa asked.

I nodded. "Please send an emissary on our behalf."

Hessa bowed slightly and moved to the large contingent of tuatha who had camped in the trees above to relay her orders. Not two minutes later, a tuatha rider breeched the line of the forest and left at a gallop towards the city of Bashan.

The Seeker, after watching the rider leave, stood and began to move away.

"Where are you going?" Sylpha asked.

"To seek Martel," the Seeker replied. When Sylpha raised one eyebrow at him, he smiled sadly and said, "I have felt betrayed as well. Perhaps I will be able to calm him down enough that he can meet this woman without drawing blood."

"Not a bad plan," I said.

The Seeker nodded and continued on his way.

With nothing left to do but wait until all the riders returned, I asked Oisín to help me train. Though he was easy with the jokes, I knew that he was quickly frustrated by my complete ineptitude with weapons of any sort. This set Sylpha laughing, frustrating Oisín yet more. Eventually Oisín gave up and Sylpha took over.

This time it was Oisín's turn to laugh.

It was dusk before Martel and the Seeker returned to the fire. By that time, I was thoroughly bruised and exhausted. I sat in misery by the fire and watched Sylpha roast some wild turkeys she had managed to snare.

Martel sat beside me in sullen silence, quietly accepting a large horn of a bizarre berry wine the northmen carried with them. Its first notes were tart, but it mellowed to a pleasant sweetness after. Though still looking unhappy, Martel seemed to have been placated enough by the Seeker to risk conversing with.

This remained the norm for the week the army awaited the first of the riders to return. Unsurprisingly, it was the tuatha rider who arrived first with word from Saschana.

I watched Martel carefully when the rider relayed her reply.

"The Black Blade agrees to meet," the rider said. "But she would do so only at Scorched Rock. She said she would accept no negotiations about the location. She also said that the army must be left behind. She does not trust the outlaws to keep their word."

"That's rich," Martel snarled. "We are the ones keeping our vows no matter what else may happen."

"Do you know where this Scorched Rock is?" I asked.

Martel nodded. "It's almost precisely the midpoint between here and Bashan on a plain that goes for days. There is nowhere to hide an army. It is a good place for this kind of meeting."

"She also said you must bring the sceptre," the tuatha rider interjected.

Martel's eyebrows shot up. "No," he said bluntly. "Not a chance in Hell."

I sighed. There would be another argument.

"Thank you," Hessa told the rider, dismissing him. Once he was out of earshot, the leaders of the armies gathered together at the fire.

"Absolutely not," Martel said. "It's the sceptre she wants. No doubt she has some scheme planned so that she can take it for herself."

"I can think of many other reasons she would wish to see it," Hessa said.

"Oh, like what?"

"Curiosity for one. Two, as evidence to know that we aren't lying about our intent. Or perhaps to confirm that we do indeed have the correct instrument. Maybe she means it as a symbol of good faith, after all, how can you trust someone who refuses to trust you?"

Martel glared at her. Hessa shrugged. "There are other reasons, is what I'm saying."

"It would be a mistake," Martel insisted.

I sighed, knowing that Martel was not going to like it, I said, "As both an act of good faith and proof that we mean what we say, we should bring the sceptre."

True to my fears, Martel growled low. "This is a huge mistake," he said.

"Be that as it may," I replied. "I can see no alternative that won't produce great insult and thus be antithetical to our desired outcome."

"Big words won't make it right," Martel said. He sat back in a deep sulk. "At least we can reasonably rely on the fact that she also cannot hide an army at Scorched Rock," he mused after a pause.

Everyone nodded in agreement and he muttered, "We hope."

The Seeker sat upright. "We cannot hide an army on the plains around Scorched Rock, but I do know what we can hide!"

I turned to him. He looked at Martel, his pale gold eyes gleaming with mischief. Martel frowned back at him until understanding crossed his features in a comical dawn.

"Grass dogs!" Martel said.

"Aye!"

"No," I said firmly. "Absolutely not. How much insult do you want to deal this woman?"

"As much as possible," Martel replied.

I stared flatly at him.

"They will be hidden," the Seeker said defensively. "If she is not duplicitous, as you claim, she shall never know they were there."

"All these big words are making my head hurt," Oisín grumbled. "It's unnecessary."

"This from a people who use the word Meitha-heitharvegavin-nuverk-frageymslusk-ratidyraly-klakippuh-ringur," the Seeker answered.

Oisín grinned. "Hush, you."

"We take the grass dogs," Martel said bluntly. "This is as far as I am willing to compromise."

"Fine," I said through gritted teeth. "But they stay well back, and very well hidden."

"I can assure you that the second, at least, will be very well adhered to," the Seeker said. Martel grinned at him and he grinned back.

Rolling my eyes, I stood and brushed the dirt from my trousers. "All right," I said. "Let's get started, shall we?"

It took a little under an hour to make the leadership arrangements before, Oisín, Hessa, Sylpha, Martel, the Seeker, and I were riding out towards Scorched Rock. The Seeker opted to walk, easily keeping up with the horses with long strides. The qilin, had slunk ahead of us and were nowhere in sight. Only the occasional movement of grass ahead gave any indication that they were around at all and even so, some two hours into our journey, the last signs of them vanished altogether.

I looked over at the Seeker, who grinned broadly.

"What mischief have you come up with?" I demanded.

He turned to me with wide-eye mock innocence. "Why," he said, sounding hurt. "I am shocked and saddened in your lack of faith."

I narrowed my eyes at him and he laughed. I turned to Martel, who smirked. He deliberately avoided my gaze.

As we left the forest on the horizon behind us, Martel took the lead, expertly navigating to Scorched Rock. It was a little over a week of travel before we arrived.

Chapter Twenty-Six

Scorched Rock, as it happened, was a broad stretch of dark mottled rock on which no vegetation of any kind grew. It sat in the middle of a lush plain of knee-high grass. How the enormous qilin were hiding here I had no idea. I only knew that they were there at all because the Seeker was smirking. A lot.

I spied Saschana standing on the rock, dressed in black with her head wrapped so that only her eyes showed. I knew immediately it was her. There was something about the bold, unafraid stance that told me so. Standing respectfully behind her were five similarly dressed and heavily armed Black Blades. All six stood so still that I could easily have mistaken them for statues carved from the stone upon which they stood. Their horses stood in a nervous circle some way back from the rock, keeping a wary watch on the surrounding grass.

The smirk Martel had shared with the Seeker had faded from the ranger's face, replaced by affected indifference. It was obvious, however, by the slight bunching of his shoulders that he was unsettled. Also, his face was a shade paler than normal.

"Deep breaths," I advised him quietly as we all dismounted. "You cannot change the past."

Martel nodded, but did not look at me.

Leaving behind our horses, who turned to grazing, appearing much less concerned than the horses of the Black Blades; another clue that the qilin, to which our horses were happily acclimated, were slinking around somewhere in the grass.

There was an air of uncertainty as all six of us lined up and observed the unmoving Black Blades. After a brief pause, I walked forward, prompting the others to do the same. Once we arrived at the flat, dark rock, all six of us approached in a line, providing a united front. It was not something Saschana missed. Her hand moved to the hilt of her blade as she watched our approach.

"Hello, Saschana," I said.

"Sky Road Walker," she greeted curtly. Her eyes flickered to Martel. "You find yourself in unfortunate company, I see."

Martel stiffened, but said nothing.

"I owe them a great deal," I said simply. "They have been good companions."

"The horses are nervous," Saschana observed.

I made a show of looking past her to the close circle of uneasy mounts standing behind the Black Blades. I turned my head to the loose collection of horses on which we rode. They remained unfazed.

"Perhaps yours are not so used to being so out in the open?" I suggested.

Saschana narrowed her eyes. "If there is some deception planned," she said. "It will not go well for you."

"There is no deception planned," Martel snapped. "And between the parties present, it is you who has proven duplicitous."

Saschana turned to him, regarding him carefully with a bold gaze. "You look well, Martel," she said, her voice tinged by softness.

Martel only tensed more at the gentleness of her voice. "Don't bother, Saschana. Your charms won't work on me anymore."

"A shame," she said with an easy shrug. She turned back to me. "Have you the sceptre?"

"We do," I answered.

"I would see it," Saschana said.

"Why?" Martel asked, unable to keep the bitterness from his voice.

Saschana turned to face him more squarely. "So that I can be sure that I am not deceived, that it is indeed the imperial sceptre and I shan't be joining some fool's errand."

"You don't need to see the sceptre to decide that."

"You are involved," Saschana said. "Yes, I do."

The words stung Martel. His hands balled up into fists and his shoulders squared. Only the Seeker's reassuring hand on his shoulder kept Martel from flying into a rage.

"There is the question of this demon," Saschana said, her gaze shifting. "What on earth made you take up companionship with such a creature?"

Before the Seeker had a chance to reply, I said, "This isn't just any demon, Saschana. This is the Lord Seeker, who escaped the Mage King and fought for the empress and helped her win the throne."

Saschana turned to me. "That was thousands of years ago."

"Time moves differently for you and I," the Seeker said, his deep voice strained with the effort of control.

"Answer me this, demon," Saschana said. "Were you and the empress ever intimate?"

"Yes," the demon answered easily. "We were, for a time. Even after her marriage to that lecherous moron she called 'husband' there were moments here and there, when we could spend time alone. Fear got the best of her, though, and we were separated. Our times together grew increasingly infrequent and formal. I was dismissed entirely soon after. I returned to my own realm and there I stayed, until these five idiots fell through my ceiling."

I could not help but snicker at the Seeker's description of our meeting.

Saschana stared at the Seeker. "There are few who know this to be fact," she said quietly. "There were rumours, of course, but they were only ever rumours. The Black Blades made sure of it. It was the best kept secret we had."

"We are grateful, I'm sure," the Seeker replied sardonically.

"It was not done for you, demon," Saschana snapped. "But for the empress, who surely would have suffered in the war that would have sparked had anyone known."

"I'm sure the Black Blades had their own motives," Martel growled. "They always do."

Saschana turned to him. "You don't know half as much as you think you do, ranger."

"I know more than you give me credit for, traitor."

"I am no traitor!"

"The hell you aren't! It is because of you the rangers were disbanded!"

"And instead of obeying the order, you turn outlaw. You are the traitor!"

"I swore a vow!" Martel yelled.

"So did I," Saschana answered, her voice cold and distant. "And I intend to see it through. Show me the sceptre."

No one moved for a moment. The grass rippled with a soft hiss in the cool breeze as the two parties of six stood, staring at one another.

"Why did you do it?" Martel whispered.

"I needed the Steward on my side," Saschana answered. "I needed to know what he knew. I needed access to the archives, to the tomes that contained all records of all the bloodlines going back thousands of years. I needed him to believe I was on his side."

"And so you threw me to the wolves."

"If the choice is between you and the empire, the empire wins. Always. Tell me you would have chosen differently, Martel, and I will know you for a liar."

Martel watched Saschana in silence for a brief moment before he said softly, "It would have been you, Saschana. Had you but asked. It would have been you."

"Then you *are* a fool," Saschana snapped. She turned again to me. "Show me the sceptre."

I glanced across at Martel, but whatever hurt Saschana's words had done was hidden behind a stony face. He turned briefly to me and gave a single curt nod. I sighed and pulled a section of the sceptre, wrapped in a dull brown cloth from the inside of my tunic. The Seeker, having spent long hours by the fire examining the device, had figured out how to separate the three segments again and I had distributed the three pieces between myself, Sylpha and Martel. I held the butt of the sceptre for Saschana to see, which I passed to Sylpha.

She retrieved the wrapped middle section of the sceptre from her belt, unwrapped it and pressed it to the butt. There was a small cracking sound and a flash of light. The two sections were held fast once again. Sylpha passed the sceptre to Martel, who affixed the head to it. Everyone watched as the golden phoenix uncurled and stretched out its talons, seeking the final missing piece; the gemstone.

Martel passed the sceptre to the Seeker. Holding the sceptre in one hand, he extended his other, the palm facing the sky. I watched in fascination as a shape slowly took form in the air above his hand. As I watched, a large, slightly jagged crystal began to form, as if the very air itself was hardening. Before long, a fully formed translucent crystal hovered in the air. Unexpectedly, a small cloud of crimson appeared in the centre of the gem, exploding outwards. The colour filled the gem as if it was liquid, sliding thickly all over until the gem was entirely crimson.

The Seeker brought the gem to the phoenix which, in one greedy move, snatched it from the demon, grasping it firmly in its rose gold talons. It moved no more.

For a while, everyone stared at the sceptre, expecting the phoenix to animate again, perhaps. Or perhaps they half-expected the whole thing to crumble into dust.

Saschana stepped forward and stretched out her hand.

"Give it to me," she breathed.

I looked at Saschana and felt uneasy. There was a glint in her eyes that hinted at greed and it did not sit well with me.

"We have acted in good faith coming here alone and with the sceptre. You must do the same. The sceptre stays with us," I said.

A flicker of irritation crossed what I could see of Saschana's face. Frowning, she turned to me. "Has your mind been infected with Martel's stories?" she asked. "Have you no trust for me even now?"

"I trust you, Saschana," I said. "But I am also charged with finding the heir."

"You were charged with finding the sceptre."

"Which finds the heir. It is the same charge."

Saschana shook her head, but dropped her outstretched hand.

"You see we are as we say," Martel said. "We have the sceptre. We intend to restore the Imperial Throne. Will you help us?"

"How do I know you don't just intend to take the throne for yourselves? Perhaps you have all been charmed by the powers of the demon in your midst and are fighting to place him on the throne he feels he is owed?"

"You can keep your damned throne," the Seeker growled. "I come only to find my children."

"From what I hear of your wartime efforts, demon, there should be thousands."

The Seeker grinned. "And one stands with me now," he said. "But she is not also the empress' child."

This took Saschana by surprise. She stepped back and looked at the Seeker with wide eyes. "The empress had no children by you," she breathed.

I looked quickly at the Seeker a moment. He seemed to slump briefly before pulling himself together. "That is not known," he replied.

"There is little about the empress the Black Blades did not and do not know," Saschana answered.

"It is not known," the Seeker snapped before abruptly turning away and marching to the horses.

Sylpha watched him go, sighed and turned to me, silently begging for dismissal. I nodded at her and she followed the Seeker, calling softly, "My Lord Father."

"Must you always be so harsh?" Martel snapped at Saschana.

Saschana frowned at him. "He would find out sooner or later, if that was indeed his mission in this realm."

"It is possible that she conceived a child by him," Oisín said, breaking his sullen silence. "And the Black Blades knew not of it. The empress, by all accounts, was intelligent enough to keep her own secrets."

"That is a big secret to keep."

"You already knew they were intimate. How could you not suspect that she had conceived by him?"

"Suspicions are nothing. She did not conceive by him."

"You don't know that," Martel snarled.

"We do. Is this why he has accompanied you? He believes that the heir would be of his line?"

"He loved the empress," I said quietly. "And his love for her cost him everything. His children are all he has left. Would you not seek the same were you in his place?"

"But it is an impossibility."

"You don't know that," Martel said again, this time through gritted teeth.

Saschana rolled her eyes and shook her head.

"The Imperial Line has ended," Martel said. "All the known descendants of the empress and her husband have left the mortal plane. This is known."

"It is. I have checked the books in the imperial library. The lines have all ended."

"Was the empress intimate with anyone other than her husband?"

"The demon," Saschana said sullenly.

"Anyone else?"

"No."

"And there are rumours of a living heir of the empress, are there not?"

"There are."

"Well then," Martel said. "It stands to reason that if there is an heir, it would be of his blood. And we intend to find that heir and restore the throne. And soon."

"There is no such heir, Martel," Saschana said.

"There better be," I mumbled. "Or we're all dead."

Saschana turned to me and frowned. "What?"

"The Seeker's Son is loose in the world and seeking the shattered pieces of itself," I answered. "The Mage King is set to return. Only the empress' heir has the power to repel him."

"You're lying," Saschana said. "The Mage King has not returned."

"The Mage King has," Oisín said, straightening. "And he killed my father."

"That is impossible."

"It's really not," Martel said. "I have seen it myself. He put a spectral claw through Basadia's skull."

At the mention of the young Black Blade who had been assigned to help me retrieve the sceptre, Saschana blinked.

"She is dead?"

"We don't know," I answered before Martel had a chance to speak. "She was unconscious after her struggle against the Seeker's Son and taken into the care of friends while we complete our mission. She may have died. She may be recovering. We have not had the time to spare to inquire after her."

Saschana's gaze shifted as she turned inwards towards her own thoughts. At length, she looked up at me and asked, "What would you ask of me?"

"My Lady," one of the other Black Blades interjected, a slight urgency in her voice. Saschana silenced her with a sharp turn and sharper glare. Turning back to me, she asked again, "What would you ask of me?"

"We expect resistance from the Steward," I said. "I need help to smuggle our army into the city and the six of us into the court so that the nobles gathered there may all try their hand at the sceptre. We hope one of them may be the heir, but we won't know unless the sceptre gives a sign."

"I had heard it does that," Saschana said. "I assume, then, that word has already been sent to the houses of the empire?"

"It has."

Saschana scoffed, or it may have been a snicker, possibly a grunt? With only access to her eyes, it was difficult to tell what that noise meant. "You have been fairly thorough."

"We try," I said.

"Much has changed about you, Stranger," Saschana noted.

I shrugged. "I'm still useless with weapons"

Saschana laughed. "Very well. I can get you into the city."

"My Lady!" the interjecting Black Blade said again. Again Saschana silenced her with a glare.

Looking past Saschana to the five Black Blades who stood at the edge of the black rock chosen for the gathering, I sighed.

"Perhaps it is time for the Black Blades to stop hiding," I said. "Perhaps, with the restoration of the empress' bloodline, the Black Blades may too be restored."

"What are you saying, Stranger?" Saschana asked.

"I'm saying that when we take the throne room, the Black Blades should be present, and in uniform."

"The Black Blades were disbanded thousands of years ago. Strictly speaking, we do not exist."

"The Black Blades were disbanded by a steward, not an empress. Let the Black Blades face justice when the heir is found. Perhaps their courage in joining our quest will serve in their favour."

"As it shall be for the rangers," Martel said softly.

I looked at him briefly and nodded. "As it shall be for the rangers."

Saschana pondered my proposal for a while. "In truth, I had not expected so serious a search for the heir. The stewards have reigned so long I fear resistance to change coming from more than that family."

"Which is why the presence of the Black Blades is so important. It will lend weight to our goals."

"Or discredit them."

"Only one of the Black Blade commanders was a traitor," I said.

"For now," Martel added. "What will it be Saschana? Honour the vows you spoke and protect the imperial bloodline, or turn traitor yourself and hinder us and the restoration of the throne."

Though she refused to look at him, I could tell Saschana had heeded Martel's words. She stared past me, deep in thought. Her gaze fell on something, and the distance in them recedes as she focussed on that thing. I turned to follow her gaze to find the Lord Seeker and his distant great grandchild standing side by side, watching the long grasses ripple in the breeze.

"There will be fighting if the heir proves to share blood with a demon."

"There will be fighting regardless. There are a lot of nobles whose wishes for imperial power go beyond reason," Martel said.

Saschana nodded at this. "Very well, Stranger. The Black Blades will step from the shadows. There are enough of us to cope with the palace guards, and we shall be aided in this by the element of surprise. When would you like entry into the city?"

"As soon as possible, if we're honest. We have with us a mix of northmen, rangers and tuatha. The meeting is set to take place as soon as all the lords arrive to answer the summons."

"So, soon."

"Very."

Nodding Saschana looked me in the eye. "Do you remember the

way to the tunnel entrance?"

"Vaguely," I admitted.

"Good. We can spirit the army in that way. It would be best if they came to us in small groups over the course of three days. You will have to leave your horses behind."

"Not keen on that idea," Martel said.

"They won't fit in the tunnels," I informed him. "And it is a rocky climb up to the entrance." I turned back to Saschana. "Is there a large clearing nearby where we can house them?"

"There is a large swath of less-dense forest with plenty of grass," Saschana said. "But it is not fenced in."

"If the horses are a concern," Hessa said. "I can assign them a small guard. They will ensure the horses remain where they ought, and keep them safe from any thieves with smart ideas."

"It is settled," I said. "We travel to the wooded grassland first, then to the city in small groups."

"I shall prepare the Black Blades," Saschana said. "We meet at the gate in, say, two weeks time?"

"That sounds agreeable." I extended my hand to Saschana, who grasped it firmly. "Thank you Saschana," I said. "I told them we could trust you."

The edges around Saschana's eyes crinkled and I guessed she had smiled. "I shall see you soon, Stranger."

Giving a signal, Saschana turned and strode to her still-nervous horse. The Black Blades followed. Only the one who had tried to interject before looked back at us as they walked purposefully back to their mounts. I stood and watched as their horses turned and bolted across the plains. I turned back to the group to find that the Lord Seeker and Sylpha had re-joined us. I quickly filled them in on the plans that were made.

"I do not feel I can trust her," the Seeker said, his golden eyes scanning the horizon from which the Black Blades had long disappeared from view. "She may simply return to the city and warn the Steward of our plans."

"I don't think she will," I said as I walked from Scorched Rock to our horses.

"I'm not so sure," Martel noted. "I too trusted her once, and look what happened there."

"On that," I asked Martel. "What secret did she extract from you exactly that was worthy of disbandment?"

"My commander at the time, Lord Gransen, was seeking the sceptre before me in the hopes of restoring the throne. The steward found such loyalty to the empire offensive."

"The steward is your half-brother, is he not?" Sylpha asked.

"Yes," Martel growled.

"Does he look much like you?"

"He looks like our father."

"And do you?"

"Too much for my liking," Martel answered. "Not enough for his."

"I have a proposal," the Seeker said.

"Oh?"

"I like not that the Black Blades are arranging everything on our behalf. Allow me to head to the meeting place. I can observe from there to see if there is any deception planned."

I looked at the Seeker once I had mounted. "What do you fear?"

"I fear that this Saschana will go to the steward with details of our plan. I fear that in going to her in small groups, each group will be vulnerable to swift and unexpected attack. I fear that she will drag us all in to the steward to reap her rewards."

"She's not like that," I insisted.

"I disagree," Martel replied. "I'm with the Lord Seeker in this."

"All right, how about this?" I asked the group. "Martel, you return to the army and relay the plans as told. Ensure they are carried out unless you hear otherwise. The rest of us will accompany the Lord Seeker to keep an eye on things."

"You do not trust me yet, Sky Road Walker?" the Seeker asked with a peculiar twist of his mouth.

"That's not it at all," I replied. "I just don't like the thought of you chancing across trouble without friends to come to your aid."

"Friends? Truly?"

"For my part, at least."

"Why," Martel asked pointedly. "Must I be the one to return to the army?"

"You are technically its leader."

Martel scowled and hunched over in his saddle. "Fine," he grumbled, looking much like a child commanded to their chores. I could not help myself. I chuckled.

With the plans agreed upon, we rode together for two days as a precaution against prying eyes and parted ways. Martel still seemed exceptionally put out to be returning to his army instead of travelling with me, so I lightened his mood some by noting that, since the Seeker's Son was after me, the army will be spared any supernatural visitors and so would be able to assault the city with their full strength should it come to that.

Chapter Twenty-Seven

It took another three days to arrive at the city's walls. The walls were precisely as I remembered them, grey stone rising out of the ground like sombre mourners surrounding the oddly contrasting pink stone of the palace on the hill behind them. I led our small group and circled around to the eastern side of the city.

If one did not know what they were looking for, it would be easy to miss the grated hole above a pile of rocks that marked the secret entrance to the tunnels beneath the city. Indeed I almost missed it myself.

"Intriguing," the Seeker said as he stared through the trees at the greyish smudge in the grey walls of the city. "So since they were banished, they have literally gone underground, and have been building, recruiting and living beneath the city for thousands of years?"

"It would appear so," I replied.

"Why?" Hessa asked.

"Well, what would you do if your entire reason for existing was negated in one fell swoop? If you only knew one way of life, one way to be, and a singular purpose for your life, wouldn't you cling to it as best you can?"

Hessa looked at me. "Who only has one reason for existing?"

Oisín chuckled. "It depends," he said.

"On what?" Hessa demanded.

"On how much one enjoys drinking," Sylpha interjected quickly, shooting Oisín a disapproving look.

"Well, I was going to say—" Oisín started.

"Drinking," Sylpha said firmly.

"Yes," Oisín said, smirking. "Drinking."

"Idiot," Sylpha muttered.

Hessa looked between the pair, obviously not understanding.

"Of course, if 'drinking' becomes your sole purpose, you're in a lot of trouble," the Seeker noted. I heard the amusement in his voice pulling at the words and making them sound tight.

"Only if it's 'drinking' the one person," Oisín answered.

"I do not understand," Hessa said. "How can one drink a person?"

The Seeker and Oisín sniggered and guffawed together. I rolled my eyes, but could not contain my smile. Sylpha looked irritated and Hessa remained looking confused.

"Pair of children," Sylpha said. This served only to increase the mirth of the Seeker and Oisín and they doubled over with the effort of trying to contain their laughter.

A small chirp from right behind me made me yelp and jump simultaneously. As I spun, I saw one of the Seeker's grass dogs behind me. My momentary experience of heart-stopping fear had the Seeker in stitches, and his laughter infected Oisín. Before long the pair of them were on the ground, laughing as silently as they could manage.

Hessa looked at me uncertainly and I chuckled.

"Not you too," Sylpha said with marked exasperation.

I laughed.

It took a surprising amount of time for the laughter to die down. In that time, nothing of significance happened at the secret entrance into the city. After half a day of nothing, our small group grew restless. I turned to them.

"I've had a thought," I said.

"Uh-oh," Oisín said.

"We could use a pair of eyes on the gate, so that we have a better idea of what the mood of the city is."

"Aye," Oisín agreed with a nod. "Sounds reasonable. Who would you send?"

"Well, Hessa and Sylpha have the best eyes. A tuatha advantage, I am told."

"Eyes like a hawk's," Sylpha agreed, though her voice was wry enough that it left me in doubt as to whether or not she was actually agreeing. I stared at her and she offered nothing more than a small smirk.

"Are you willing, Hessa?" I asked.

Hessa regarded Sylpha briefly before answering, "I am."

"Good. Off you go, then."

Hessa and Sylpha exchanged a glance, shrugged at one another, and headed together to keep an eye on the city gate. I watched them go.

"Let's hope they can put aside their old prejudices for the duration of this excursion," the Seeker said. I jumped. The demon had appeared at my side suddenly, making no noise to let me know that he approached.

"Or only one of them will be returning."

I scoffed. My face fell slightly as I thought about it. "I'm sure they can handle themselves," I said.

The Seeker smiled slightly and said nothing. I sighed and returned to keeping an eye on the secret entrance to the city. We waited a week. In that time, either Sylpha or Hessa returned on occasion to report on the gate. Large contingents of nobility were moving into the city, and the city guards were not impressed about it. Apparently Sylpha had slipped behind one of the noble caravans and entered the city to get a feel for the mood of the place. The city guard were caught between the Steward, who was demanding to know why all these nobles were suddenly showing up in the city and the nobility themselves, who used their position of privilege to bully their way in despite the Steward's protests.

The city was tense.

This did not surprise me in the least. Nobles were flooding in from every corner of the empire. While this was a boon for local businesses, it also meant that people could see that something important was happening, and they had no idea as to what it could be. Coupled with the stern, even hostile, rule of the Steward, people were on edge.

Shortly after Sylpha's report, the first of Martel's army arrived. I recognised the broad grins of the accompanying northmen, and I noticed that the tuatha faction stood apart from the rangers and the northmen both. However much the rangers and northmen were able to set aside their differences, the cat-like people of the forest were unable.

I hoped it would not be like this for long. An army uneasy with itself was primed for defeat.

"Sky Road Walker," a tuatha captain greeted. "What news of the city?"

"They are ill at ease, Captain. And for good reason. The rest of the army?"

"Restless. They will be arriving in small groups over the next week. Any movement at our way in?"

"Not yet. We're a week out, however. It should not be long. Make yourselves at home."

The tuatha captain nodded, turned to the waiting group and spoke a few simple commands. The tuatha immediately dismounted and began to set up a camp that would not be seen. The northmen and rangers were slower in their work, apparently still learning the skill of being invisible to watchful eyes. The tuatha very patiently corrected their many mistakes as they worked.

Slowly, in a small trickle, the entire army of tuatha, northmen and rangers filtered through the trees to our location. Last of all came Martel, leading a small group of mostly tuatha. Those tuatha, at least, seemed perfectly at ease with the rangers and northmen in their group. I had no doubt whatsoever that it was due in large part to Martel's easy leadership.

Martel grinned broadly when he saw me. "Well now," he greeted. "You're still here. No trouble, I take it?"

"None," I replied, taking his forearm in greeting. "You need to shave."

Martel laughed softly. "You're right. I should probably not present myself to a palace full of nobles looking like a wild man."

"Though it would be amusing to note their reactions," the Seeker rumbled. "Welcome back, ranger," he added.

"It's good to see you all again," Martel said. "What's happening with the Black Blades?"

"Nothing," I replied. "That we've seen in any case. But we're only just on time. They will open the gate soon."

"I hope you're right," Martel said. "I hope you have not trusted Saschana for nothing."

"I haven't," I said. "She will come through."

I said this for the next two days. In that time, there had been no movement from the secret gate. At length, the leaders of this expedition sat me down.

"Look, we're supposed to be inside already," Martel said. "I don't think Saschana was level with us."

"She was," I insisted.

Oisín sighed. "So now what? We just hang around while the nobles bicker inside, give up and return to their homes?"

"We could storm the city," Martel said, though even he seemed like he did not much care for that option.

"Or we could wait," Hessa said.

"Or we could go investigate," the Seeker replied. "Perhaps Saschana has been honest, and is in some trouble. Perhaps she has not and does not mean to open the city to us. We cannot know unless we seek to know."

I nodded. The Seeker was right. There was no way for us to do anything even remotely considered a good idea if we did not know what was ahead of us.

"Fine," I said. "You're right. Lord Seeker and Oisín, you and I will try for the secret entrance. Hessa, Sylpha and Martel will stay with the army."

"Why do I always have to stay behind?" Martel grumbled. I looked at him and he offered a rueful smile. He knew why. "It's just irritating," he added.

"Why the Seeker?" Hessa asked.

"He is fairly adept at fighting the Seeker's Sons. If one shows up, I'd rather not be dissolved. You and Sylpha both can aid against the Seeker's Sons in case he shows up and attacks the army, and the qilin can help too."

"I am also very good at sneaking," the Seeker said.

"I am less good at sneaking," Oisín interjected. "But I am very good at bashing heads in."

"Let's hope it doesn't come to that," I said.

"I hope it does," Oisín answered. "I am getting bored."

The Seeker chuckled softly. It was a bizarrely sinister sound. I shook my head. "All right, come on, you lot."

"Oh, 'you lot' is it? Well isn't that nice?" Oisín said. I ignored him as I trudged away. He followed, still complaining of his treatment. Once we reached the small meadow between the forest and the pile of rocks that led up to the gate, however, Oisín stopped and became serious once more.

"Let's skirt around this way," I said, pointing to the right. "There is some scrub we can use for cover, and we might be able to stay out of sight from any unfriendly watchers."

"Agreed," Oisín said. Moving swiftly and as silently as we could manage, we skirted around the edge of the lawn as much as possible before making a dash to the pile of rocks. Knowing that we were fairly safe from prying eyes there, we began our ascent.

It was not easy to be quiet and keep our feet. Nor was the instinctive crouching I felt necessary to stealth all that conducive to bouldering, but somehow I managed to scramble over the rocks and reach the gate. I pressed myself against the wall and chanced a peek through the grate.

The passage was empty. I frowned and took a longer look.

The passage was definitely empty.

I tried my hand at the gate. It took some effort, as the iron grate was very heavy. I strained against the weight of the iron until the gate swung free. The release was so sudden that I lost balance. Were it not for the quick reflexes and inhuman strength of the Seeker, I would have toppled backwards down the pile of rocks.

"Thank you," I murmured.

"You're welcome," the Seeker answered in a whisper.

"It looks empty. Let's go in."

My companions nodded. Leading the way, I crouched down and entered the secret underground headquarters of the Black Blades.

I could hear nothing but my own breathing as we moved deeper into the tunnel. Behind me, I heard Oisín's footsteps. Of the Seeker, I could detect nothing. I turned around briefly to find him immediately behind me. I jumped.

The Seeker cocked his head at me with a small frown, giving clue as to his confusion. Why on earth would I be frightened at the sight of him? I knew he was behind me. I offered him a small, sheepish smile, certain I had confused the demon even more, and turned back. I continued on my way.

The click of wood against wood caught my ear. I followed the sound. The slow spread of flickering light as I approached accompanied the growing amount of sound echoing in the corridors of the headquarters. We reached a door on our right through which firelight poured. I peered very quickly around the corner.

We had reached the dining hall. It was largely unpopulated, save for a few of the robed girls I knew to be new recruits to the organisation. They looked miserable as they ate. I noticed also tall men standing guard. They were not wearing the Black Blade uniform. In fact, they were not wearing any uniform that I could see. They were, however, standing menacingly in pairs at each of the exits from the dining room. I could see the bent elbows of the two guards standing at my door.

One of the girls happened to look up as I was taking stock of the situation. Our eyes met.

Cursing vehemently at myself in my mind, I ducked back out of view and urgently motioned for the Seeker and Oisín to go back the way they came. They started and I turned to follow them when I heard a gruff voice demand, "Oi, where are you going?"

I froze. Oh no. I had been discovered.

Wincing, I turned slowly to find that there was no one behind me.

"I want to go talk to Saschana," I heard a girl say, rather loudly.

"What?"

"I want to go to the prison, you know, the oubliette you threw the Black Blades in? It's down the hall, to the left and all the way at the back."

"I know where the oubliette is!" the gruff voice said.

"Good. So you know where I'm going."

"You can't."

"I was told they were permitted visitors," the girl insisted. "And I wish to speak to my leader."

There was a hard smacking sound and a small grunt. I winced, knowing I had just heard the girl getting slapped.

"You mind your tone when speaking to me, girl!" the gruff voice said. "That treacherous bitch isn't your leader no more, and you will go when I says you can. Now get back or I'll hit you again."

I stayed where I was, rooted to the spot as my brain whirled with all the information it has just received. That brave, clever girl. She told me everything I needed to know about what was happening here. And she told me where all the Black Blades were. I could salvage this. But how?

I turned back around slowly to spy Oisín and the Seeker further down the hallway. They remained frozen in place, crouching despite the fact that there was plenty of room for them both to stand fully upright. The absurdity of the sight was overshadowed only by the fact that I was also crouching low.

Smiling to myself, I snuck forward quickly. The Seeker and Oisín parted to let me pass and followed as I rounded the nearest corner.

"All right," I said in a small whisper. "This is what's happened. Someone ratted on Saschana. She and the rest of the Black Blades are locked in the oubliette. All that is left are a few very young recruits. They're in the dining hall right now, and every entrance is guarded by two very mean looking thugs."

Oisín brightened. "Time for some head-bashing!"

"Not yet," I replied. "I need you two to get back to Martel. Let him know what's happened. We could use the army about now. Overwhelming numbers will make fighting back very, very uninviting."

"What are you going to do?" the Seeker asked.

"I'm going to the oubliette to see what I can do for the Black Blades. If we do this right, we can squeeze these thugs between two armies and no one will escape to warn the Steward."

"I like this plan," the Seeker said.

"Can I please provide a distraction? I am feeling a keen need to knock in some heads," Oisín asked.

"No," I replied. "If we move too early we risk having the Steward warned. We need to take the throne room by surprise."

Oisín sighed, but nodded.

"Good," I said. "See you soon."

I peeked around the corner to make sure that the way was still clear and headed off. Running low to the ground. I paused at the line of light that streamed from the dining hall and took a moment to ensure that no one was looking in my direction. Darting across the light, I ran quickly to the nearest corner and ducked around it, pressing myself up against the wall.

Blood pumped hard in my veins. I felt each throb, and my pulse rang loudly in my ears. My breathing came raggedly in response to my racing heart. It all sounded too loud. I was certain that the guards at the door could hear my breath and the pounding of my heart that rattled my chest like a drum.

"I could have sworn..." I heard a deep voice say from the hall.

Biting my bottom lip in an effort to control the instinct to run, I waited.

"Oi," another voice said. "There's nothing there. Now come back. The girls are going to riot, I swear."

"There was something that ran across here. Dog sized, it was."

"You probably saw a rat."

"Rats are not that big."

"Aye, but your imagination might be. T'was nothing but a rat and shadows. Now get back inside."

I heard the first man mutter, and was fairly certain he was swearing. It made me smile. The sounds died off and I waited some time before risking my neck, sticking my head back around the corner to make sure the coast was clear. Seeing nothing, I crept out from the side hall and continued to make my stealthy way down the hall until I came to the first left.

Fairly certain this was the turn the girl intended for me to take, I pinned my body against the wall, took a quick look and, finding it dark and deserted, rounded the corner and recommenced my sneaking. The hall down which I was travelling was long and dark. My legs ached from the crouch I had thus far maintained, but for some reason, the thought of standing upright scared me.

Wondering if the army had entered the headquarters yet, I pushed on. I reached the oubliette after what felt like an eternity. It was too dark to see, so I only noticed I had arrived when I tripped on the trapdoor to the gaol and hit my face against the far wall. I muttered a curse and heard shuffling down below.

"Hello?" I whispered down into the dark.

A moment later, the wan light of a single candle threw the barred grill that served as the trapdoor into sharp relief.

"Saschana?" I whispered hoarsely.

"Who's there?" a harsh female voice I did not recognise echoed up from the dark.

"Uh... It's me. The Sky Road Walker."

"Sky Road Walker?" Saschana's voice echoed up. It sounded weary. "Impossible."

"Impossible? Why?"

"They said you were killed in a skirmish with the city's watch."

"We've had no encounters with the city watch," I whispered back. "We've been waiting for you in the woods beyond the walls."

"How can I trust it is you?"

"Why else would I be up here whispering?" I demanded. "For fun? I'm here to get you out. Martel is leading the army into the headquarters. We're going to sandwich the thugs that are running the place between his army and yours. But I don't know how to open this door."

"There are three keys hanging on the left wall," Saschana said after a pause. It might have been my imagination, but it sounded like she was struggling to hold back hope. "One of them unlocks the trap door. The other two, when used in the same lock, will unlock a mechanism that springs a trap. The first trap will flood the oubliette, drowning us. The second will fire javelins above the trapdoor, impaling you."

"Fantastic," I muttered. "Which is the correct key?"

"I don't know," Saschana admitted. "They had a locksmith with them. They changed which key unlocks which mechanism."

"That's just great," I growled.

"That's all I know," Saschana said.

"Any chance I can get that candle of yours up here? It's black as pitch and I can't see any keys whatsoever."

I paused as I heard scraping and a young Black Blade climbed up the rickety ladder towards the grate. In the thin light, I could see that she was bloodied, a gash in her forehead still leaking a little. She smiled wanly at me and lifted the stubby candle, pushing it through the grate until there was enough of it for me to grasp. Hot wax spilled on my hand as I lifted it up and I cursed quietly.

"Good luck," the Black Blade whispered, her large eyes staring up at me. I turned away from her hopeful gaze and spied the three keys on the far wall. They gave no clue as to which key might be used for what.

Chapter Twenty-Eight

"Gods above and below," I muttered. "This is ridiculous. How am I supposed to know which key does what?"

I briefly looked for clues as to which key might unlock the oubliette trapdoor and which might spring either one of the horrid traps.

Unable to come to any conclusion about any of them, I reached out and grabbed a silver key with an ornamental bow.

With a trembling hand, I slid it into the lock and twisted. I heard the lock click and then, from somewhere deep below me, issued three ringing clunks and a thud. I heard the sound of water gushing.

"Not that key!" Saschana shouted up at me.

"Damn everything!" I hollered back. There was no point in trying to keep quiet now. The sprung trap had almost certainly alerted the thugs to my presence and, to make things worse, the oubliette was quickly filling with water. I needed to choose another key, and fast, or the Black Blades would be drowned, and I would be surrounded by angry mercenaries.

Knowing I had no time, I blindly reached out and snatched the next key, a brass one with an open bowl.

I thrust it into the trapdoor lock. I turned it. Half expecting to be skewered by javelins, I squeezed my eyes shut and tensed my body, preparing for impact. It took me a moment to realise that no such impaling had occurred. I turned the key further and hauled the trapdoor open.

"Quick!" I called down, having to shout over the sound of rushing water. "I got it open!"

The first person out of the hole was the young woman who handed me the candle. She scrambled out and turned around to help lift out the rest of the Black Blades. They were all, without exception, wet and bedraggled. Last out was Saschana. Blood caked the side of her head and a large bruise had begun to turn green on her cheek. She winced as she stood upright and several joints popped.

"Gods, but that was close," Saschana said, looking down at the trapdoor that opened into the oubliette.

I followed her gaze. The hole was now completely filled with water. "Yes," I said. "Very close."

No thugs had come running down the hall to engage us though I was certain I made more than enough noise to be noticed. I scowled as I peered into the gloom that was the hall. Everything was quiet. And dark.

Taking up the candle stub, which now threatened to burn through its base, I walked cautiously forward. The Black Blades moved with me as I crept down the hall. They were surprisingly silent as they moved. I kept the pace slow, worried about what we would find at the end of the long hall.

I slowed to a crawl as we approached the end of the hall. Peering down the corner, I saw nothing. Screwing up my courage, I rounded the corner and we continued on our way. Still only darkness and silence answered my searching senses.

"This isn't creepy at all," I murmured to myself.

Unthinkingly, I rounded the corner.

A large, serpentine eye stopped me in my tracks. I jumped at the reflection the paltry light of my candle made in that glassy surface. Unable to contain my surprise and terror, I screamed. The great lizard before me snuffed; a strange grunting sound repeated in a pattern. It was laughing at me. *Laughing.* I stared up at it wearing a stupid expression before realising I was staring at the qilin queen.

"You scared the ghost out of me!" I whispered harshly to her. Her snuffing, grunting noises increased in speed and volume.

"It's not funny!" I snapped.

"What's not funny?" a deep voice asked from the gloom. I recognised that voice.

"Your lizard friend scared me senseless," I said to the Seeker.

"That scream was you?" he asked, striding from the shadows. His pale skin and pale gold eyes gave him the appearance of something truly demonic in the dim light of the halls. The fact that his incisors were incredibly long, and incredibly sharp, and incredibly noticeable as he grinned did not help his image any. "I thought a rodent had its tail stepped upon."

"It would have had to have been an enormous rodent," I retorted.

The Seeker shrugged. "Or perhaps a little girl who had her pigtails pulled."

I narrowed my eyes at the Seeker, which only made him grin more. He looked now like a slightly deranged demon.

"You found the Black Blades?" he asked.

"I did. Where is Martel?"

"Martel, Oisín, Sylpha and Hessa are all in the dining hall, making jests about our new captives. I was sent to search for you."

"And the qilin?"

"They were bored, so they accompanied the army into the tunnels. Not a single drop of blood was shed. The enemy dropped their weapons the moment the qilin made their appearance. Oisín was very disappointed."

"I can imagine," I said, finally able to relax. "We should join them."

"If it's at all convenient," Saschana said in my left ear. "Since you have things under control here, I would like to dismiss my Black Blades to find food and rest and tend to their various injuries."

"That is more than fair," I said. "You better seek medical aid also. You do not look well at all."

"I do not feel well, either," Saschana said with a rueful smile. "I will seek aid."

"Good."

The Black Blades and I parted ways here for the moment. Their army dispersed, each one tired and limping. Shaking my head, I turned back to the Seeker. He wordlessly led me to the dining hall. What I saw when I walked in made me smile.

A group of about thirty thugs sat at a long table, their hands tied firmly behind their backs. They looked exceptionally unhappy. Standing guard over them with a crude spiked club was Oisín. He stared at the men, swinging the club ominously. With his back to the door through which I strode, he did not see me enter.

"The answer is still no, Oisín," Martel said firmly.

"The answer to what?" I asked, smiling at Martel as I entered.

Oisín turned and brightened at seeing me. "Finally!" he said. "Someone with sense. Martel won't let me bash any heads in. Perhaps you can convince him to let me hit at least one of them."

"There was a disappointing lack of resistance," Martel noted sourly.

"So the Lord Seeker informed me," I answered. "Gentlemen," I greeted the captives. Behind me, the Seeker chuckled his deep, slightly sinister laugh.

"Just one," Oisín said, hopefully. "All I want is to hit one."

I laughed. "I have a feeling there'll be plenty of time for bashing heads later."

Oisín shook his head. "Fine," he said, sighing dramatically. "Fine." He turned back to the group of surly men and pointed his crude club at them. "But one of you puts so much as a toe out of line, and I'll have the rest of you lot clean that poor bastard's brains off the walls. Am I understood?"

"It's a good thing I wasn't hungry," Hessa muttered under her breath.

"Our northern neighbours are a little battle-mad," Martel replied.

"I lost my father for the sake of this quest," Oisín growled, suddenly serious. "Someone must pay."

"And they will," the Seeker said softly.

"Right now we need to figure out our next move. If my count is right, we have a few days before the nobles gather in the throne room to find out what my mysterious invitation was all about," Martel said. "And we haven't the Black Blades to ease our way."

"They are resting for now, but we should have them," I said.

"But they will not have replaced the palace guard as planned. It will be a battle the entire way into the throne room."

"A ruse?" the Seeker asked.

"Like?" Martel demanded.

"You are an outlaw, yes? Have some of your fellow rangers drag the six of us in as prisoners. We were caught trying to get into the palace through a window or something."

"That doesn't solve the problem of the palace guard."

"That's where the Black Blades come in. Once the door to the throne room is closed, no one may enter or leave, unless that has changed since last I stepped foot in the palace."

"To the best of my knowledge, that tradition holds."

"Good. With the doors closed, the Steward will not be able to see what is happening outside and will not be able to stop it."

"Perhaps we could have you as part of a retinue," Sylpha offered. "Oisín MacFergus of the north has come to discuss a new treaty with the empire?"

"That would get you and Oisín in," the Seeker replied. "And no one else."

"Be part of my retinue," Hessa said. "The tuatha may have whomever they please as attendants and none of you would be any the wiser."

I pondered a moment. "Martel, the Steward is your brother, is he not?"

"Half-brother," Martel growled.

"I take it you've never gotten along?"

"No. Never."

"Hmm."

"What does the Steward know of the tuatha, Hessa?" I asked the tuatha elder. "Would he not find the mixed company of your retinue suspicious?"

"I assume he is well read enough to know that the tuatha are not to be trifled with," Hessa replied. "But as to the workings of our political systems and just to whom we are allied is unlikely to be in any books of any imperial library."

"Hmm. Would there be any reason for the men of the North to seek counsel with the Steward of the empire?" I asked Oisín.

"Honestly, no. But we don't have to be honest, do we? Perhaps I have gotten tired of the constant raiding from my neighbours and am seeking protection from the empire."

"That seems unlikely," Sylpha said with a soft smile. "Tired of raids? You?"

"Yes," Oisín said with exasperation. "But the Steward doesn't know that, does he?"

"Hmm," I said again.

"I think the best way in is to be part of Hessa's retinue," I said. "If we are to pretend arrest, chances are we'll be thrown in the dungeon without ever getting an audience with the Steward. And, well, no offence Oisín, but it seems really unlikely that you would come seeking the empire's protection."

Oisín shrugged. "True," he admitted with a lopsided grin, turning his fierce features boyish.

"That's what we'll do. In the meantime, we need to stow these thugs somewhere," Martel said, tilting his head at the group of men sitting not far from me.

"The oubliette?" Sylpha offered helpfully.

"Uh..." I said. "I may have accidentally flooded the oubliette. I mean, you can stick 'em in if you want to, but they'll drown."

Oisín brightened. He turned imploring eyes on Martel who, despite himself, laughed. "No," he said bluntly, though the authority of the word was somewhat lessened by his mirth.

"You take all the fun out of this quest, you know that?" Oisín muttered darkly.

"If the Steward acts up," Martel said. "I'll let you bash his head in."

"Deal!"

Sylpha rolled her eyes and shook her head. Hessa stood, her head cocked, looking between Martel and Oisín with an expression that was unreadable. Behind me, I sensed the Seeker's mirth.

"So what are we going to do with them?" Sylpha asked. "We can't just leave them here. They may escape."

"The oubliette can't be the only place capable of holding them," I said.

"I say we throw them in anyway," Oisín said.

"They will stand trial," Martel said. "When the Imperial Throne is once again occupied."

"Or we could drown them now and save the time and expense."

"Would you stop it with the drowning?"

Oisín sighed. "Fine. But we should just drown them."

"I will try and find suitable ... accommodations," the Seeker said. "Perhaps they have some gibbets or something similar."

Martel nodded. "In the meantime, I would love some food. We can work out the finer details of the plan over dinner."

"I can get that for you," a young female voice said from behind me. I turned to find the brave young woman who had faced the guards to tell me everything I needed to know about the fate of the Black Blades. A large bruise had formed on the left side of her face. It was yet to darken, and was now a red, swollen lump with, I noted, a cut at its centre.

"All right," Oisín demanded, turning to the group of thugs at the table. "Which one of you struck her?"

The men shifted and looked away. No one spoke. Oisín turned back to the girl. "Which one was it?" he asked her kindly. "I can take his hand. You can keep it, if you like. My people keep the heads of our enemies in a case of pine oil. My great grandfather had a collection of some three hundred or so."

The girl blinked in surprise. She looked at me and asked, "Is he kidding?"

"Likely not," I answered.

The girl turned back to Oisín. "It's all right. He can keep his hand." She looked across at the men bound at the table. "For now."

"I like her," the Seeker said. He offered the girl a small smile before excusing himself to search for a makeshift prison for our captives.

"As soon as I saw the Black Blades freed, I sent some of our sisters on a hunt. They should soon have enough food to feed your army and then some," the girl said.

"Thank you," Martel answered. "What is your name, acolyte?"

"Meredei," the girl said.

Martel blinked. He smiled. "My mother's name is Meredei," he said. "It is a noble name, with a long history."

Meredei smiled. "I am no noble, sir. I was born in an alley behind the lower market."

"I am no noble, either," Martel said. "So enough with the 'sir's. My name is Martel. How fares Saschana and her Black Blades?"

"They are exhausted and dismayed. It was one of our own who warned the Steward of Saschana's plans. No doubt he is gathering his palace guard to seek you out."

"If he expects to find us beyond the walls, he will be sorely disappointed."

"Though probably aware that we made it inside the city's walls," Hessa noted. "We'll have to move fast."

"The meeting is in two days," Martel replied. "We can take that time. If I know my half-brother, he will try to use that meeting to discredit us before using the noble's annoyance to help fill out his army's numbers. We are three armies combined. His palace guard would not have a chance otherwise."

"Sound reasoning," Hessa said. She yawned. "Pardon me."

"The food should be here soon," Meredei said. "But they are out looking to take down a couple of elk. I will fetch you bread and cheese in the meantime."

"Thank you, Meredei," Martel said quietly.

Meredei, stopping short of a full curtsy, bobbed her head towards Martel and scurried out of the room.

"Gods, but I'm hungry," Martel said.

It was not long after that Meredei returned with a large platter of warm bread. Behind her, a string of girls and a few mute boys, marched into the room. Some carried platters filled with cheese and butter, and others carried in jugs of mead and water.

"Saschana and the others are also eating," Meredei informed Martel. "They will probably be asleep when dinner is ready, and so Saschana wishes you to know that she likely will not join you for the meal."

"They've been through an ordeal," Martel said. "They are more than entitled to sleep."

"I assured her of as much. Enjoy your pre-meal. I will be back once the meat is cooked."

"Thank you."

Again almost bowing, Meredei left the room, trailed by her helpers, and we were left to ourselves. The bread was fresh and warm and exceptionally delicious. The butter, also fresh, melted into the hot bread. I ate almost three full slices before I remembered that there was also cheese to be had. I felt quite sated by the time the food was gone.

The Seeker returned moments later, grinning. "It's not a gibbet, but it's just as good," he announced. "There is a room entirely filled with manacles. Shall we bring them over?"

Martel nodded, standing wearily. Deciding that he and the Seeker should not be left to deal with the captives alone, I also stood. Oisín jumped to his feet, swinging his club in ominous slow movements. "Let's go," he said.

Looking utterly defeated, the party of hired thugs stood slowly and marched from the room. The Seeker led. Martel, Oisín, and I followed the pack. No one made a fuss as they entered the room filled with manacles. The Seeker ensured they were properly secured before we left the room.

"The best part?" the Seeker said. He slid a heavy iron bar across the door. "You don't even need to lock it." The bar clicked into the specially designed latch and the Seeker turned to me. "There is a room similar to this in the palace," he said. "Behind the library. Only the bar is on the inside. Handy for keeping irritations out while you're trying to study."

I smiled at the Seeker and, exhausted, wordlessly led the group back to the dining hall. When we arrived, the first of the platters of meat had already been delivered, and Meredei waited patiently for our return.

"Not elk," she said. "But they did get five deer and three boar piglets, so there is plenty of food regardless."

"Oh thank the gods!" Oisín said. He descended on the platters of meat as if he had not just finished eating large amounts of bread and cheese.

"Good grief, Oisín," Sylpha said. Oisín pointedly ignored her.

I ate and, full and fatigued, slept. None of us bothered to find a bed. The benches in the dining hall worked well enough.

Not long after dawn, though I could only guess at the time - there was no sunlight in the underground headquarters of the Black Blades – I was shaken awake by Martel. He grinned.

"Last night," he said when everyone was awake and had been

served with bowls of steaming oats with fruit and honey. "Saschana and most of the Black Blades stole into the palace. They have very quietly replaced almost the entirety of the palace guards, taking over their duties. Only a few officers have not been replaced, though those men are expected in the throne room for the meeting, Saschana tells me. We will have no problem getting into the palace today."

"She must have been out of her mind," Sylpha said with a yawn. "Does she not sleep?"

"From what her messenger says, she was feeling a little salty over the betrayal and wanted some satisfaction as soon as possible."

"What time is this meeting supposed to take place?"

"The third hour after dawn. So hurry up. We want our envoy ready to arrive in time to interrupt the proceedings before the Steward has a chance to get going."

It was not long before we were prepared. Hessa dressed in her armour, its polished surface gleaming even in the dim light. Martel elected to dress in his ranger's uniform. It would irk the Steward most, and Martel was not above some pettiness. Oisín and Sylpha both chose to wear the armour of the north and the Seeker decided that only trousers would be necessary. Trousers and the enormous chest and shoulder contraption required to keep a massive sword strapped to his back. He grinned at me when he caught me staring.

"No armour, Lord Seeker?" Martel asked.

The Seeker flexed his admittedly powerful muscles. "Arrogance is sometimes better armour than armour," he replied. "Ultimate confidence will make an enemy think twice."

"It's true," Oisín agreed. "I have heard that we used to battle naked, hoping our physiques and obvious lack of fear would terrify our enemies. It worked, until the first empress, damn her."

Martel straightened.

"Lovingly, of course," Oisín added.

Once armed and armoured, we were led out of the secret headquarters and found ourselves in the market. We formed up, the Seeker in the lead, acting as Hessa's champion. His pale skin and pale golden eyes, not to mention his extreme height and mass ensured that people scrambled out of the way. The street guard, who were supposed to stop strangers in the city when they looked like trouble, shrank back and slunk away, pretending they were not at the scene and thus having a good excuse for not intervening.

Our group walked boldly to the palace and were stopped by a woman in the uniform of the palace guard.

"What is your business?" the woman demanded. Martel stepped forward.

"We are here to see the Steward to renegotiate the terms of the treaty between the empire and the tuatha people."

The woman shrugged. "Off you go, then," she said, offering the barest of smiles. "I can't get fired for this. Technically, I don't actually work here."

Our procession through the palace was joined a moment later by a small contingent of women dressed as palace guards. I recognised Saschana as their leader, and tried hard not to smile at her. With the aid of our escort, we had no issues making our way to stand before the doors to the throne room. Saschana raised a gauntleted fist and pounded at the door. The noise beyond the door fell silent. Saschana pounded again.

The door opened but a crack. "What?" a palace guard demanded. "You know we cannot open the door when there is a session in the throne room."

"You can and you will," Saschana said. "Tell the Steward there is an envoy here from the tuatha people, demanding an audience."

"Hold on," the guard said. The door closed again. Moments later, it reopened a crack.

"He apologises but maintains that the protocol cannot be broken. He'd like to offer the envoy refreshments while they wait."

Saschana turned to me and smirked. It made me smirk. I turned and saw the Seeker looking intently at me. I could tell by the set of his shoulders that he was itching to get inside. I cleared my throat, stepped aside and tilted my head towards the door, giving the Seeker permission to do what his silent regard told me he wanted to do.

The Seeker smiled. It was a vicious smile, made more so by those exceptionally long and sharp incisors. Sensing his purpose, the entire group stood aside. In two strides, the Seeker moved from the rear of the group to the front. The guard, who was still peeking through the door and waiting for an answer realised a little too late. Though he managed to get the door closed, there was no time to slide the bolt or place a bar across the doors.

The Seeker lifted his foot and kicked the door hard. The doors flew open with a crash, flinging the poor palace guard down the short hall that led into the throne room. The doors were flung open with such force, the left door splintered, and the right one came off the top hinge.

Oisín peered down the hall and blinked. "Remind me to never get you angry," he noted to the Seeker.

Palace guards flooded the hall. I counted ten.

The Seeker growled. He moved forward with his long, powerful stride to meet the first of the guards. The guard swung his sword, but the Seeker caught the man by the arm, stopping the strike. He twisted. The guard screamed as his joints snapped out of place. Picking the guard up with his free hand, the Seeker threw him at the other guards. With nowhere but backwards to go, most of the guards were instantly neutralised. The two who remained standing pedalled backwards quickly, their eyes wide and their hands trembling.

"I really don't want to make you angry," Oisín said as he followed the Seeker into the small hall.

"Go on," Saschana said, looking at the downed palace guards with pity. "We can handle this lot."

I nodded and followed Oisín into the hall. Martel joined us, and Sylpha and Hessa made up the rear. The uproar in the large circular space that was the throne room created by the ruckus at the door fell silent as the Seeker entered the room with the rest of us in tow. The Seeker's gaze locked onto the Steward who was sitting, not on the carved ebony seat at the base of the dais, but on the tall, plain pink marble throne.

Knowing what was about to happen, I tried to grab for the Seeker's wrist, but I was too late. With a guttural snarl, the Seeker strode forward. Before I could even open my mouth to call him back, the Seeker ascended the stairs to the dais and grabbed the Steward by the throat.

"He's fond of that," Oisín noted quietly by my side.

Everyone in the room stared as the demon lifted the Steward in one hand. "This is not your place," he growled at the terrified man in stately red and gold robes.

"My Lord," Martel said gently. "Please put him down. As much fun as it would be to see his head pop off his shoulders, the empire is founded on the rule of law."

"And what charge would you lay at the feet of a Steward who presumes to sit upon the throne he is supposed to guard?" the Seeker demanded.

"Treason."

"And what is the penalty for treason?"

"Death," Martel answered.

Seemingly satisfied, the Seeker slowly lowered the Steward. He let go of the man's throat, pushing him backwards as he did so, his golden eyes blazing in a manner I had never before seen.

"I really, really don't want to make you angry," Oisín said, his voice oddly cheerful in the fearful hush that had enveloped the room.

"You bastards!" the Steward shrieked, clutching his throat and fighting his own coughing reflex to speak.

"Mind your tongue!" Sylpha snapped.

"To be fair," Martel said, folding his arms across his chest. "I am."

"What is going on here?" a nobleman demanded, finally finding his voice.

Martel turned to him and smiled. "I apologise," he said. "We really should get under way. First, I would like to thank you all for coming today. I honestly didn't expect absolutely everyone I invited to arrive on time."

"That was you?" the Steward demanded, rasping harshly. "You're the fool who sent everyone the letter saying the heir to the imperial throne has been found?"

Martel turned to his half-brother and regarded him coldly. "No, I said we have the means to identify the heir, and I asked everyone to gather to do just that."

"You idiot!" the Steward said. "You've always been an idiot. There is no such device and there is no heir!"

"There is an heir," the Seeker snapped. Quietly he added, "There must be."

Martel watched his brother a moment.

"What do you mean?" the noble asked.

"We have the Imperial Sceptre."

Chapter Twenty-Nine

A whisper ran through the crowd of noblemen gathered in the Throne Room.

"Impossible!" the Steward rasped.

Martel ignored his half-brother and reached for the fabric-wrapped piece of the sceptre he had tucked into his belt.

"There is no such thing!" the Steward shrieked as Martel unwrapped his section of the sceptre. The butt end of the golden sceptre gleamed in the sunlight streaming through the windows above the dais. Martel held it up so everyone in the room could see. I snuck a glance at the crowd. The theatrics were working. Those nobles who had previously looked like they were ready for a fight now settled in their seats. Many whispered to one another.

Martel tossed the sceptre to Sylpha, who unwrapped a similar parcel.

"The Imperial Sceptre was destroyed years ago!" the Steward said, his voice rising in pitch.

"It was broken in three," Martel answered. "And my companions and I have been searching the length and breadth of the land seeking the pieces."

Sylpha placed the two pieces near one another. As before, they snapped together with a loud crack. The join vanished, revealing a complete, unblemished two thirds of the sceptre. Following Martel's example, Sylpha held up the sceptre for everyone in the room to see, before tossing it to me.

I caught it, though I fumbled. My heart stopped. Luckily, I did not drop it. I took the head of the sceptre from my belt and unwrapped it. Half expecting the phoenix to move on its own without cause, I brought the pieces of the sceptre together. One louder crack, and the sceptre was almost whole.

"Now what?" the nobles' spokesman demanded.

"Wait," Martel said. He nodded at the Seeker, who stretched out his hand. In the centre of his large palm, the crystal piece began to form. It fell gently into his hand once it finished reconstituting. The Seeker walked to me. I held out the sceptre and, very slowly so that all in the room could see, the Seeker brought the crystal towards the phoenix. Once it was close enough, the phoenix unfurled its wings and stretched out its eager talons, snatching the stone from the Seeker's hand.

I stared down at the completed sceptre in silence, feeling slightly disappointed. I was half hoping that the sceptre would reveal me to be the lost heir. What else would explain my sudden appearance in this land, with no memory and no other purpose but to restore the Imperial Throne?

"Now what?" the nobleman asked again.

"Now we pass the sceptre around the room," Martel said, looking at me oddly. "It will reveal the heir."

Sighing, I took the sceptre to one side of the round room and handed it off to the first person. The sceptre remained still, the crystal dark as it changed hands. Disappointed faces watched the sceptre as it moved on into the hands of eager noblemen and women. Martel moved over to me.

"I honestly thought it would be you," he said.

I shrugged. "I'd be lying if I said the thought hadn't occurred to me also. At least I would know why I'm here."

The sceptre made its way all the way through the crowd, giving no sign.

"See?" the Steward snapped as I took the sceptre from the last noble. "There is no heir. You have wasted everyone's time with this foolishness, and I'll note, you wear a ranger's uniform. They were disbanded. You are an outlaw! Guards! Arrest him!"

The two remaining palace guards looked at the Steward, they looked at Martel, then at the Seeker, who pointedly examined his nails. They looked at one another and took a collective step backwards, away from Martel.

"It only means the heir was not amongst this crowd," I retorted sharply. I was as disappointed as the waiting crowd looked. Was all of this for naught? "And I hardly think one accused of high treason..."

The words fell away as I was hit with the sudden sensation of nausea, a screech and the sounds of rushing water assaulting my ears at the same time. I stumbled and dropped to my knees, clutching the sceptre tightly.

"Seeker's Son!" I managed to bark. Screams from the hall told me that I was too late.

Saschana ran into the room, bleeding. "Martel!" she barked before the Seeker's Son made its appearance immediately behind her. It reached out one spectral hand and clutched her shoulder. Saschana stiffened.

"No!" Martel barked as she was quickly absorbed into the Seeker's Son. Oisín's strong grasp kept him from running forward to engage the Seeker's son.

"Behind me!" the Lord Seeker bellowed over the chaos that ensued. He, Sylpha and Hessa formed a line facing the Seeker's Son and the nobles scrambled to get behind them.

A shadow passed over the windows behind the throne and I turned. Another Seeker's Son entered the room, passing through the glass as if the barrier did not even exist.

"Go!" the Seeker yelled to his tuatha companions. Hessa and Sylpha broke from the line and circled around the terrified nobles to face the other Seeker. I saw a bluish light flicker between them. The light stretched, joining the yellowish light of the Lord Seeker as the demon formed his own magical barrier. The barely visible shield of light encircled the group in the middle, leaving Oisín, Martel and I outside of their protection.

Everything slowed down and the sounds dimmed as a cold realisation swept through me. It was me the Seeker's Sons were after this entire time. I knew it. It was me that must save these people. I looked up to see Oisín trying to drag Martel into the protective field. Martel's face was twisted by rage and grief, but he was beginning to accept Oisín's wisdom. I looked down at the sceptre. The heir needed to be found, and I could buy them time to do that. I had to lead the Seeker's Sons away. The people of the empire would need the sceptre.

Screwing up my courage, I turned.

"Martel!" I bellowed.

Martel looked to me and I tossed the sceptre in the air towards him. Not sparing the time to see if he caught it, I turned and started running. The Seeker's Son by the hall moved towards me so swiftly that, though I was prepared for its spectral sprint, it very nearly got a hold of me. I twisted to the side, spinning around the back of the shade and sprinted across the room. It was my intention to draw the Seeker's Sons close enough that they would be forced to fight one another, buying us all some time to escape.

Red light flooded the room. I stopped dead, thinking for a moment that I had been caught by one of the spectres, and what I saw was the pain that would hit at any moment. I was wrong. High-pitched screeching sounded in my ear and I turned to find that both Seeker's Sons were aflame, their spectral forms licked by the garnet tongues of magical fire. They had forgotten all about me, all about one another, and all about the gathered nobles as they writhed and flailed in their blankets of flame.

Standing, frozen in a crouched running position, I could do nothing but stare as the Seeker's Sons imploded, vanishing from the room. I sought out the source of the light and found it in the stone in the phoenix's grasp at the head of the sceptre. Drawing my gaze back, I found the sceptre in Martel's grasp. He stared at it, wide-eyed with shock. Everyone stared at Martel.

Oisín stepped back and away from Martel, giving him room. The flood of red light diminished, softening to a small glow that pulsed in time to Martel's heartbeat. Martel blinked.

"What does that mean?" someone whispered.

Startled into action, Martel dropped the sceptre. It hit the floor with a metallic thunk and the light of the stone ceased. For a long time, everyone stared at either Martel or the sceptre or alternated between the two. No one spoke.

Breaking the oppressive stillness, Hessa walked forward. She picked up the sceptre. The stone remained dead. She handed the sceptre to Sylpha. Sylpha passed it to Oisín, who passed it to the Seeker. The Seeker took the sceptre, but did not bother to look at it. Instead, his pale golden eyes were fixed on Martel.

"No," Martel said, his eyes meeting the Lord Seeker's. "No. It's not what you think. That is not possible."

"You are the heir," the Lord Seeker replied quietly.

"No," Martel said again, stepping backwards in response to the step forward the Seeker took. The Seeker extended his arm with the sceptre towards Martel.

"No," Martel said again.

"Take it," the Seeker said, his soft voice never altering.

"I don't want it," Martel whispered.

"Take it."

Everyone remained silent as they watched the exchange. Martel stared up at the Seeker helplessly. Very slowly, he extended his hand and took the sceptre. The stone immediately jumped to life, its pulsing glow synchronising with Martel's heart once more.

Martel's face turned ashen as he stared down at the stone.

"Impossible!" the Steward squawked. He marched forward and snatched the sceptre from Martel's grasp. The stone fell dead once more.

"It is impossible!" the Steward raged waving the sceptre in the air. "We have the same father, and the stone does not glow for me!"

"It is your mother," the Seeker said to Martel, his voice still soft, almost reverent.

"Impossible!" the Steward shrieked.

"Clearly not," Sylpha told him, the tone of her voice informing the Steward of the derision with which she obviously regarded him.

"No," Martel said. "My mother was a maid in a nobleman's house, not a noble herself. My family has no noble connections at all. It never has. We certainly do not trace our ancestry to the empress!"

"If the empress was trying to hide the identity of her child," Sylpha reasoned. "Hiding the child's nobility would be the first order of business."

"Why would she try to hide a child?" the Steward snapped. "That makes no sense whatsoever!"

The Lord Seeker looked to me. In turn, I looked to Martel. The ranger turned slightly green, but he nodded to me. In turn, I nodded to the Seeker.

"Because," the massive, pale demon said. "That child was mine."

The hall fell into shocked silence before it exploded into frenzied activity. There were gasps and several outcries. Nobles muttered to their neighbours while some simply nodded, grimacing.

"Not possible!" the Steward yelled. "That would make you thousands of years old!"

"Yes," the Seeker answered, as if that fact was somehow irrelevant.

"Nothing lives for thousands of years!"

The Seeker raised one hairless eyebrow. "And yet, here I am, the Lord Seeker, who was once advisor to the empress, standing before you."

"Not the same Lord Seeker, obviously."

Grinning, the Lord Seeker leant forward. "No? Ask me any question about the empress you please. I will have the answer."

"When you sought her out to free you from the Mage King—"

"That is your first mistake," the Lord Seeker said. "She sought me out to make the bargain."

The crowd buzzed with knowing affirmations of the Seeker's assertion.

The Steward scowled. "Anyone who can read would know that. It is not proof."

"Stop trying to trip me up on known details. Ask me something only one who knew the empress would know."

"This is foolish," Sylpha butted in. "Nothing except what is written of the empress would be verifiable. However, if it makes you all feel better, I can vouch for the Lord Seeker."

"Oh can you?" the Steward snarled.

"Yes," Sylpha answered. "Not that you would know or care, but a number of the tuatha were exiled after the war that founded the empire for having, in the tuatha council's words, sullied themselves by association with a demon."

"I'm not sure I follow."

"My ancestors were driven to exile by the tuatha council. I am one of the purged. The Lord Seeker and I are also kin."

The room erupted into chaos again. While the nobles expended their sudden energy, the Seeker took a single stride to the Steward and snatched the sceptre out of his hands. He walked to Martel, and again offered the sceptre to him.

Again, Martel refused the symbol of imperial power. He took a step back and shook his head, holding his hands out before him as if to ward away his newly found power.

"Martel," the Seeker said. "You must."

"No," Martel snapped.

His sudden loud syllable attracted the attention of the chattering nobles. The hall again fell silent as they watched.

"I came to see the throne restored," Martel said, reining in his panic and trying to sound reasonable. "Not to sit on it."

"That choice is no longer yours to make," the Seeker replied. He held the sceptre out steadily.

"I don't want the damned thing!" Martel shouted. "I am a ranger! My place is out in the wilds, not cooped up in some... some... stone chamber!" His temper expended, Martel stared at the Seeker, his expression imploring the demon for help. "I am just a ranger; the bastard son of an unfaithful nobleman and a housemaid. I wouldn't know the first thing about ruling a kingdom. Do you know how many lives could be ruined by my ineptitude?"

"I know how many lives will be lost if we cannot defeat the returning Mage King," the Seeker answered. "And for that, we need you."

Martel shook his head. He turned away and wandered, as if thoroughly lost, to the dais. He sat on the first stair and hung his head. "I can't do it," he said.

"You must," the Seeker said again, his voice still soft. "There is no other choice."

"We are ever beside you," Sylpha said. "And will guide and council you to the best of our ability."

"As we always have done," I added.

Martel looked between us. I could still see the panic in his eyes, but his shoulders straightened. "Promise me you will stay by my side."

"We swear," I said.

Sylpha nodded and answered, "We swear."

Martel nodded. Clenching and unclenching his teeth rapidly in an effort to dispel his ill ease, he stood. He took a long, unsteady breath as he stepped forward to accept the sceptre from the patiently waiting Lord Seeker. The moment his fingers wrapped firmly around the shaft, the stone began its pulsing light, the visible heartbeat of the emperor; the pulse of the empire.

The Lord Seeker stepped back and fell to one knee, bowing his head. Oisín, Sylpha, Hessa, and I followed immediately. The rustle of fabric behind me informed me that the noblemen had also bent their knees.

"Stop it," Martel growled. "Stand up. Get up. Now."

I grinned as I rose. Martel glared at each of us in turn. "Don't ever do that again."

"What?" Oisín asked innocently. "Bow?"

"Yes that. It makes my skin crawl."

Oisín laughed.

The nobility stood, facing Martel expectantly. They waited for a grand speech, perhaps. Martel looked at me in a panic.

"What do I do?" he mouthed to me.

I smiled slightly at Martel and tried to mouth the word 'appointments.' Martel stared blankly at me. I mouthed the word again. Martel frowned, shaking his head slightly in a signal that he clearly did not understand. Rolling my eyes, I said a little too loudly, "Appointments."

"Oh!" Martel replied. "Yes. We should. I should. What am I supposed to appoint?"

The Seeker chuckled to himself, drawing everyone's attention. "Perhaps, your Grace," he said. "You should first restore the Black Blades and the rangers as legally recognised orders? And dismiss those who you appoint to be their leaders so that they may gather their soldiers and start the necessary rebuilding of their own bureaucracies."

Martel nodded. "That. Yes. We'll do exactly that." He stopped as his eyes fell to the palace guard armour which once protected the body of Saschana. The pile of fabric, steel and leather sat on the floor as a melancholic testament to the bravery of the leader of the Black Blades.

Martel's expression changed from nervous and unsure to resolved.

"I need a messenger to be sent to Meredei. She is an acolyte of the Black Blades." The leadership Martel had consistently displayed throughout this quest returned. He scanned the crowd, looking for volunteers.

"I'll go," Oisín said. "I know the way into their headquarters now, and Meredei knows me."

"Thank you, Oisín. Tell her that we were successful. The heir has been found. The Black Blades are no longer outlawed, and may return to their traditional posts. I will expect a guard of five in this room by tomorrow. Also, please let her know of Saschana's brave sacrifice, and that new leaders will need to be selected in whichever way the Black Blades settle these matters."

Oisín bowed slightly, then left the throne room to do as he was bid.

"I would have a statue of Saschana commissioned," Martel said. "Someone find me an artist who can do her justice."

"Your Grace," a young noblewoman piped up from the back of the group of gathered nobles, her voice trembling slightly. She bowed awkwardly when the group parted, giving Martel a direct line of sight to her.

"My cousin is a sculptress. I can send word to her if you wish?"

"Yes," Martel replied. "Please. Sorry, your name is?"

"Melissa, your Grace."

"Thank you, Melissa. And if it isn't too much to ask for, my name is Martel. Please use it. Titles make me uncomfortable."

"Of course, your... I mean... Martel."

"Thank you."

Melissa bowed again and scurried out of the room to send a message to her cousin. Martel rubbed his brow. "Will someone please fetch me paper and a quill? I have to compose a missive and I will need a courier."

"One of the palace guard should do," the Lord Seeker noted. "They are yours to command as you will."

"The palace guard," Martel growled. "Is there a master at arms at the palace?"

Silence answered his question.

"Is there a similar position?"

More silence.

"For crying out loud, who is responsible for training the palace guard?"

"That would be the commander of the guard," a nobleman supplied. "But the position has been largely ceremonial for centuries."

"So what you're telling me is that the palace guard don't actually know how to fight," Martel asked slowly.

"They know... in theory."

Disbelief crossed the new emperor's face briefly before he set his jaw. "Hessa, may I ask a favour of you?"

"You want me to teach your guard how to fight?" Hessa asked, her head cocking in a bird-like manner.

"Only until I can find a suitable instructor. I wouldn't presume to keep you on staff forever."

Hessa smiled slightly. "I am not a patient woman, your Grace."

"Don't call me that. And good. I suspect we don't have that much time before the Mage King returns, and I would like to have a functioning army before then. Beat them if you have to. Our lives depend on this."

"I accept," Hessa said. "I can begin tomorrow if you like."

"The day after," Martel said. "We are going to use tomorrow to give them time to get used to the new way things are going to be run from now on. Further to that, I would like all of you to submit a nomination for the new position of Master-At-Arms. The Master-At-Arms will be responsible for training the palace guard, and will answer directly to me. The Master-At-Arms may also be called upon to speak before the council of advisors at my request, but this will not be the same position as War Advisor. I will have those nominations tomorrow, so think closely on it."

The group of noblemen and women murmured to themselves and their neighbours.

"I would also like nominations for War Advisor and Master of Laws. For now, my council consists of the Lord Seeker and the Sky Road Walker. Hessa, I welcome you as formal ambassador for the tuatha people. Sylpha, you and Oisín I welcome as formal ambassadors for the northmen. You have been good friends and I am grateful for your alliance in this time of crisis for the empire."

"Spoken like an Emperor," Hessa noted with a small smile. She bowed. "I am pleased to call you an ally, as the empire was in times of old."

Martel rolled his eyes, but offered Hessa a smile. "To the rest, call your armies. The Mage King has returned and, as you can see, the threat to us all is very real. I intend to put him to rest once and for all. When all arrangements have been made, we will reconvene here to discuss our next move. Until then, you are all dismissed."

After a pause, the room slowly emptied. Martel watched them go until the last person was out of sight. He sank slowly to the ground, his eyes straying to the pile of steel and leather that used to be Saschana's disguise.

"What now?" Martel asked, his voice distant. "I don't know what I'm doing. I don't know what to do next. I don't know where to go."

"Hessa," the Lord Seeker asked the tuatha leader. "Would you please find someone to clean up the vestibule and pick up the armour. I am going to take his Grace to his new quarters."

Hessa nodded, and immediately left the room.

"Don't call me that!" Martel snapped. He buried his head in his hands. "I hate this. I hate this so much."

Immediately, the Lord Seeker was at his side. "You will find your feet," he assured his descendent. "But for now, you must eat and rest. We have a war to prepare for, and you must be ready."

Ever pragmatic, Martel nodded. He stood, but he trembled with fatigue and uncertainty.

"Your quarters are this way," the Lord Seeker said. He looked to me. "Come, Sky Road Walker. I will find a place for you."

"You know the way?" Martel asked.

The Seeker looked down at him and smirked. "I have made my way to the empress' quarters many a time. I would know the way blindfolded."

"That was a little too much sharing," Martel grumbled.

The Lord Seeker laughed and led the way. Martel and I followed, passing by servants who were scrubbing the puddles of blood from the carpet in the vestibule. The Lord Seeker delivered Martel to the imperial bed chambers.

Chapter Thirty

The furniture in the dark room was covered in sheets of dusty canvas. The large windows were covered in thick, heavy drapes, blocking out all light, and the fireplace was dusty and empty. Martel stared around the expansive room, looking utterly lost.

"We will have this fixed in no time," the Seeker said gently.

It was as if Martel did not hear. He simply stared around the room.

I looked to the Seeker wondering what it was I should do.

Giving Martel the space he clearly needed, I began to remove the cloth that covered the furniture. Puffs of dust filled the air, making me cough. Shaking his head, the Seeker walked to the windows, threw apart the curtains and opened them. An easy breeze moved the air in the room. I paused a moment to watch as the dust danced in the streaming sunlight.

The light drew Martel's attention. He turned to the window and slowly walked over. The view stretched over the wealthier quadrant of the city, with the marketplace providing a patch of pale grey against the sea of red-tiled roofs of the merchant houses and lordly manors. Beyond the marketplace rose the wall, an imposing barrier of thick grey stone. Even from this distance, Martel could see that it had been sorely neglected.

And why should it have been maintained? There had been no serious threat to the empire in an age or more. The tuatha kept to their woods and the northmen had kept to the north... more or less. Martel shook his head. Repairs to the wall would be one of his first priorities. If it came to a siege, he'd rather the wall not crumble on the first strike.

The sounds of the city filled the room. The buzz of people going about their daily business; the talk and the laughter, the tears and the rages all coalesced into a vibrating murmur, punctuated every so often with the distant bray of a donkey or the irritated squeal of a horse.

"The city is on edge," Martel said.

"And they would be," the Seeker answered. "Lords and ladies from all over the empire have descended upon it, not to mention the motley crew that served as the delegation from the tuatha that marched through the city this morning. No doubt several hundred saw the two spectres that attacked the palace."

Martel sighed. He rubbed the side of his face with his palm. "And I have no good news to offer them," he said. "Only that a battle approaches and they must all prepare. What news to come from a leader they do not know and have no reason to trust."

"They will come to trust you, Martel," the Seeker said. "How could they not? Remain true to yourself, and they will come to love you as well."

I continued to free the furniture of their dusty shrouds, listening intently to the conversation between the Lord Seeker and his progeny, sparing a moment to glance their way every so often. I tried to find the similarities in their appearance, but could not manage it. The demon was simply too unusual, too exotic and Martel, though handsome, was plain in comparison.

"I will speak with them," Martel said. "After the business is concluded. I will address them myself."

"That can be arranged. I will send word to the city herald and he will announce your succession when he delivers the morning news. Since we do not know how long it will take, we can give him the time of your address to announce once the business is complete."

Martel nodded. "That sounds agreeable." He added, "You are quite good at this."

The Seeker shrugged. "I spent much time in the court whilst I lived here, and the empress was an extremely efficient ruler. That and, before my own people abandoned me, I ruled my own court."

"You had said they abandoned you because of the empress. I don't understand why that would be."

Smiling, the Lord Seeker answered, "Humans do not have a monopoly on prejudice."

Martel scoffed. He turned away from the window. "Come on,

then," he said. "This room will not clean itself." He helped remove the cloths from the furniture.

Before the Seeker joined us, he tugged hard on a bell pull near the fireplace. Three maids scurried into the room, their eyes cast down. They curtsied so deeply their knees touched the ground, and there they stayed.

"Your Grace," one girl said.

"Don't," Martel said moving to them. He took each one gently by the shoulders and helped them to their feet. "Don't do that. On your feet."

The girls obeyed, but did not look Martel in the eye. I could see one of them, however, sneak a peek at the new Emperor. The girl smiled, blushed and darted her eyes back to the ground.

"We require help getting the room fit for habitation," the Seeker said. "We will also need the next bedroom made ready for the Sky Road Walker. My old chambers behind the library will require attention as well. We also need a meal for his Grace, the Sky Road Walker and myself. It does not need to be grand. His Grace was a ranger and is used to chewing leather straps."

"Not quite," Martel said, though he smiled.

"Will that be all, your Grace?" one of the maids, who still refused to look at Martel, asked.

"Yes, thank you," Martel said. "What is your name?"

The maid did look up at this. She blinked at him in surprise. "Your Grace?"

"Your name. Surely you have one?"

"Aife, your Grace."

"Thank you Aife, that will do for now."

The girl curtsied and left to relay the orders back to the palace staff. The other two set to work immediately. With the five of us, the work went quickly. Soon everything was uncovered. A team of servants arrived and Martel, the Lord Seeker, and I were all pushed to the side.

Martel protested at first, trying to help as much as possible, only to find that he was getting in the way and being a general nuisance. At length, he joined us to watch as the efficient staff replaced the bedclothes, took the rugs for a good beating, swept and mopped the floor, cleared the chimney, lit a fire and replaced the drapes. The tables and chairs in the room all received a thorough cleaning as the three of us sat at the newly cleaned table in front of the fireplace.

Food arrived just as the cleaning was completed. The servants laid the food on the table, bowed or curtsied and left in silence. The cleaners did the same, the last one to leave closing the massive doors to the chamber and curtseying at the same time.

Martel sighed and, prompted by the Lord Seeker, began to eat.

My hunger surprised me and I found myself unable to do much of anything but eat for a while. The silent meal was interrupted by the arrival of a servant carrying paper, quill and an ink pot. The young lad placed the materials on the newly cleaned bedside table, bowed and left. Not once did he look at Martel.

"Why do they not look up?" Martel asked no one in particular. The Seeker answered all the same.

"Perhaps they fear to look in case you are not real?"

"That," Martel said flatly. "Is ridiculous."

"Great pains were made to hide the empress' indiscretion," the Seeker said. I detected a slight bitterness in the Seeker's voice. "You are not supposed to exist."

Martel sighed. He sat back, taking up a cup of wine. For a while, he stared down at the table. He looked up at the Seeker.

"I have regarded you with suspicion in the past, Lord Seeker," he admitted. "And I find it difficult to reconcile that with this new knowledge that you are, in fact, my grand sire."

"If it makes you feel any better, I have regarded all of you with suspicion," the Lord Seeker said with a shrug.

"Why did you accompany us, then?" I asked him.

The Seeker shrugged. "At first I saw a chance to escape my bonds. Upon hearing your quest, I saw a chance to find the family I had been denied; my children, most important of which would be the child born to the only woman I have loved."

"The way you say that makes me think that you have loved before," Martel said. "Just not women."

The Seeker smiled at him. "Does that upset you?"

"No," Martel answered after some time thinking. "You have not been shy about admitting your many... um... interests. I have had time to get used to the idea. I cannot fathom falling in love with a man, or something other than human myself, but I do not feel I can judge you for it."

"Then you are wiser than most of your kind. Even the empress had difficulty accepting that about me. It took some... convincing."

Martel smirked and shook his head. "Too much sharing."

"Sorry."

"Are all your kind as you?" I asked, suddenly curious.

"Most, actually," the Lord Seeker said. "It is considered normal to find both the sexes attractive and I find it difficult to fathom why one would deny themselves the full breadth of pleasure one can derive from engaging with them both."

"Such denial is considered virtuous," Martel noted.

"That's the stupidest thing I have ever heard."

I laughed, noting Martel's yawn. "We should leave you to rest," I said. "You've had a trying day."

"It's the middle of the afternoon," Martel complained through another yawn.

"Shut the drapes, then," the Seeker said as he stood and drained his cup. "We will see you in the morning."

Martel nodded, too tired to argue. I followed the Seeker from the room.

"I'm headed to the library. I'll show you to your room, if you like," the Seeker asked.

Deciding that I was not quite as ready for bed as Martel, and though I did not wish to hover annoyingly around the Seeker, I opted to join him briefly before exploring the palace myself. The Seeker showed me my room, which was quite literally right beside Martel's chambers.

"It used to belong to the Vizier," he told me, when I noticed the table with a silver bowl set into it near the corner of the room. "The man was obsessed with alchemy. Idiot."

I snorted. "Why is there no Vizier now?" I wondered aloud.

"I would imagine that much of the Imperial Court has been retired, since there was no ruler. The Steward's only task was to guard the throne. Without the power to enact new laws, there would be little cause for a council of advisors."

I accompanied the Lord Seeker to the library, and walked with him through the tall cases of books and scrolls. Dust laid thickly over everything and the Seeker's mood turned sour. "That is no way to treat books," he growled. He stopped walking at the far end of the large hall that was overcrowded with books and tomes, scrolls and boxes of loose papers, and half-bound stacks of vellum.

The Seeker growled low, like a large cat issuing a warning. I stopped and turned to him in surprise. "That does not go there," he hissed. He took a thick book from the shelf and put it in the crook of his arm. He looked back at the shelf. "Neither does this!" He selected another book. "Who was responsible for this mess?!" he snapped. He was lost to me, completely absorbed in the task of correcting the apparent mess that had been made of the library shelving system.

Smiling to myself, I went to the door we had been walking toward and peeked inside. The room itself was surprisingly Spartan, but had the saving feature of large doors that opened into a wide balcony overlooking the forested hills near the city. Otherwise, there was only a bed, a wardrobe, a table large enough to seat two, a fireplace and a large bathtub in the corner.

Shrugging to myself, I turned around and wandered back out of the library. The Seeker did not notice me leave as he hissed and muttered curses under his breath in a language I did not understand. It put a silly grin on my face, though. Once out of the library, I weighed my options and decided to go left.

The palace seemed incredibly vast to me, with more rooms than I could possibly conceive a function for. Most of the rooms were bare, or dark with canvas cloths thrown over the furniture. The more I explored, the more depressed I became. The palace must once have been grand and filled with life. Now it was old, with cracks in the tiled floors, frescos faded beyond recognition and cobwebs in most corners. It was in decay.

Perhaps it stood as a visual testament to the state of the empire; once proud and full of life, now dying and crumbling to dust. My thoughts put me in a sombre mood, and I ceased to pay attention to where I was going. When next I looked up, I was in the dungeon.

"Well, well," said a vaguely familiar voice. I looked around and met the sunken eyes of the Steward. "Look what the cat dragged in."

Sighing, I turned around in preparation to leave.

"I have heard about you, Sky Road Walker. They say you fell out of the sky into the market place. It is a pity you did not see me. I would have steered you clear of the foolish path you now tread."

"The Mage King is coming," I said to him. "There will be no paths at all if he has his way. Whether you want to believe it or not, Martel is the only hope we have of stopping him."

"You would put demon-spawn on the throne?"

"I would put the heir on the throne," I answered. "And we are fortunate indeed that he also happens to be a good man."

"No son of a whore is good," the Steward spat.

"You're an idiot," I decided aloud. With nothing left to say, I walked out of the dungeon.

Having had enough of exploring and finding nothing but depression for my trouble, I headed to bed.

The following morning was chaos. I accompanied Martel to the throne room, which was already full of noblemen. They were currently engaged in a shouting match which, judging by the number of beet red faces, had become heated. At the end of the small hall, waiting for Martel stood Sylpha, Oisín and Hessa. Oisín rolled his eyes at Martel as the Emperor approached, tilting his head towards to roaring crowd inside the room.

"Any idea what they're fighting about?" Martel asked him.

"At the moment? Whose 'real estate' is larger, if you catch my meaning."

"Please tell me you're joking."

Oisín grinned and shook his head.

Martel closed his eyes and sighed before bracing himself and marching forward. It took a long time for most to notice he was in the room. The delegation from the Black Blades noticed immediately. A man and a woman stood side by side, both in black armour with twin blades strapped to their backs. Unlike the men in the Black Blades I had seen previously, this man's head was not entirely covered with only his eyes revealed. He stood tall beside his counterpart, dark brown skin shining in the early morning light. He wore an expression of fierce pride. Meredei, the brave young acolyte who helped me rescue the Black Blades, stood quietly in her grey robes before the two.

I also noticed an older man, his hair almost completely grey. He stood apart from both the crowd and the Black Blades and wore the armour of the rangers. He looked utterly exhausted. His armour was well kept and highly polished, but his face unshaven. He had prepared to meet the Emperor, I assumed, but did not have time to clean himself up before today's meet. He must have travelled hard to get here on time.

Ignoring the yelling match in the room, Martel marched to the dais, his face set like hard stone. He caught the grey eyes of the ranger and gave him a weak smile and a curt nod. The ranger responded with an equally curt nod. Behind Martel strode the Lord Seeker and I, being the only two permanent advisors on Martel's make-shift council. Behind me walked Hessa, who was now in charge of training the palace guard and so had a position of honour. Sylpha and Oisín, who were now official ambassadors of the North, followed.

Martel did not sit on the throne, but stood before it, waiting with an inexorable look on his face for the nobles to notice he was waiting on them. Nothing about him indicated he was the new emperor. He refused point blank the Lord Seeker's choice of wardrobe, opting for far more simple and practical tunic, trousers and high boots. He threatened a fight when the Seeker insisted he at least wear the imperial cape. That disagreement had been hilarious to observe.

At length, apparently as tired and cranky as he looked, the new ranger stepped forward and bellowed, "Shut up, you pack of inbred field mice!"

Silence fell over the hall immediately. All eyes turned to him, then to Martel, who now had his strong arms folded over his chest.

"Thank you, Tris," Martel murmured.

"Aye, well," Tris answered. "I'm tired and hungry and I have to meet with the heir before I can eat and sleep. No man is keeping me from food over long for any reason that isn't important."

"You haven't changed."

"So, when's he arriving?"

"Who?"

"The heir?"

Martel smiled slightly.

"You are looking at him," the Lord Seeker informed the ranger. It took a moment for Tris to realise just what the demon meant. His eyes widened with comic understanding. He looked to Martel for confirmation, who shrugged.

"Who would have known?" Martel said, smiling ruefully.

Tris opened his mouth to speak, thought better of it, stepped back and waited for the court to be in session.

"Thank you all for coming," Martel said. "And for being so clearly lively this morning. First order of business, I see the Black Blades have sent a delegation?"

Meredei stepped forward and curtsied before Martel. "Your Grace," she said in a clear voice. "In a moot that lasted the night, the Black Blades have selected their leaders. As in the days before the end of the imperial line, there are two; a matched pair of leaders whose strengths are best used in compliment of one another. It is therefore with great pride, I present to you Commander Asime and Commander Mhu.

The woman and the man stepped forward as their names were spoken. They bowed in unison and said, "Your Grace."

"Welcome, Commanders," Martel said. He smiled at Commander Mhu. "I am relieved to see that you have your voice back."

The tall dark-skinned man smiled. "As are we. Never again will our vows be broken."

"Never say never," Sylpha muttered under her breath.

Martel ignored her. "I trust you have a guard selected?"

"Yes, five of us will guard your person as we always have done, one commander and four guards of their choice in alternating shifts. If it pleases your Grace, I would be honoured to take the first post."

"Nothing could please me more."

Commander Mhu smiled. He bowed and signalled. Materialising from the crowd, five Black Blades stepped forward, each wearing their black armour and expressions of fierce pride that matched their commander's. There were three women, each with twin short-handled battle axes strapped to their backs and two young men, now also without their head scarves, bearing long swords. In silence they took their positions around the throne room, Commander Mhu coming to stand beside Martel.

Commander Asime bowed and took her leave, returning to the Black Blade headquarters to continue their preparations.

"Next, Commander Tris, please step forward."

Tris did so, looking at Martel with open suspicion.

"I have a favour to ask of you."

"Aye, well then, out with it, whelp."

Oisín grunted a short laugh, and looked uncertainly at Martel. Martel merely smiled, looking at the grumpy old man with genuine affection.

"I need you to take up your old post as commander of the rangers."

"I'm retired."

"I know. It is only temporary. We need to get word out to them and let them know that their disbandment is henceforth retracted, and they are to report immediately to the palace and prepare for battle. They need to hear this from someone they trust. You trained most of us, old man. They know you. They trust you."

Tris rubbed the underside of his chin with his thumb in thought. "Aye, they do."

"I will also need you to help bring them back up to standard. Not too many of them have kept up with their weapons training I'll wager."

"No doubt."

"I'm asking you because you're the only person I know who can still strike the fear of the gods into me with nothing more than a glance. You'll get them into shape quickly."

Tris sighed. "Fine. All right. I'll do it. But I want a nice retirement package for all this trouble, and the promise that even though you're emperor now, you'll find the time to visit me at least once a year. I miss my star pupil, truth be told. Was never prouder than when you were voted in as commander, legal or no."

Martel's smile broadened. "I will visit you twice a year."

"Aye, then. Good. May I be dismissed to find some breakfast and some rest? I'm dead on my feet."

"Of course."

Tris did not bother to bow. He turned his broad back and ambled like a bear out of the room. "Find me food and a bed," I heard him bark at one of the servants just before the door to the throne room closed. Martel suppressed a laugh, and turned his attention back to the waiting nobles.

"I will hear your nominations for Master-At-Arms, War Advisor and Master-Of-Laws now," he told the nobles.

They merely stared at him.

"We don't have time for any games or any kind of standoff," Martel snapped impatiently. "You may not be fully aware of the danger we are all currently in, so let me make it as plain as I possibly can: The Mage King has returned. You saw him yourself yesterday. I embarked upon a quest to stop him by finding the heir. Imperial blood stopped him before. It was my genuine hope that it would stop him now. Things took an unexpected twist recently, but I am still determined to stop him. Now, you can help me or you can do nothing and wait to be absorbed by the Mage King like Saschana was. Which is it? Hurry. I haven't time or patience to wait more than a minute."

An old noble cleared his throat. "I might have been of some use when I was a lad, but I am old now. I can't lift my sword any more, let alone swing it. But I do know my battle strategy, and there's nothing wrong with my mind. I nominate myself for War Advisor."

"I second that nomination," a sharply featured woman said. "I have known Hugh a long while. He knows his battles."

"I would also like to nominate my daughter," Hugh added. "For the position of Master-At-Arms."

A young woman stepped forward. She had a round face that might have looked sweet, were it not for the jagged scar that stretched from the bridge of her nose to her lower right jaw.

"I second that also," the sharp woman said. "I've seen the lass fight. She knows her way around a weapon."

"That's preposterous!" a young man called. "A woman for Master-At-Arms? I nominate myself!"

The young woman rolled her eyes and shrugged.

"Aye, and I nominate myself too," another young man said, stepping forward.

"I have one nomination for War Advisors, three nominations for Master-At-Arms. Are there none for Master-of-Laws?" Martel asked.

No one said anything. At length, Oisín cleared his throat. "I nominate the Lord Seeker."

Martel looked at him in surprise. Oisín grinned at him as a murmur raced through the crowd.

"A demon?" someone demanded. "Preposterous!"

"Are there any other contenders?" Martel countered. The hall fell silent again.

"None of you are familiar with the laws of your own damned empire?" Martel rolled his eyes. "Fine."

"Hugh, Lord Seeker, welcome to my council. The matter is now the question of the Master-At-Arms." Martel rubbed the side of his face as he looked at the three youths before him. I leant over and whispered some helpful advice in Martel's ear.

"May I suggest a contest?" I asked Martel. "It will help find the better fighter, and probably go a long way towards establishing a solid respect for the winner. The last thing we need is an army that does not respect their leader."

Martel sighed. He whispered back. "And yet more time we must throw away. Still, you're probably right." Turning his attention to the three contenders for Master-At-Arms he said, "If I had been raised in this palace, surrounded by you all, I would know who would best fit the position. Alas, I was raised a ranger. And so I suggest we hold a contest. The winner of that contest will be made Master-At-Arms. We are short on time. I want the contest over by this evening."

Rolling his shoulders, Martel scanned the crowd of nobles. Many of the older men were nodding. Martel's blunt manner sat well with them, it seemed. The younger men, however, looked as if they were preparing to challenge Martel's right to rule. Martel took a deep breath and sighed it out loudly, a physical sign of his shortening temper.

"I don't care what objections you have to my rule," he said. Many of the younger nobles looked surprised and chagrined at having been called out before they could speak or act. "We can fight about it after the coming battle, if any of us make it through. Until then, the immediate threat has precedence over any of your petty objections. I have very little patience for games and politics, and I'm not in the mood for any challenges at the moment. Do I make myself clear?"

The tone Martel employed for his speech was, I noted, precise and perfect, compelling obedience in the way only a true commander could. The young nobles, though unhappy, clamped their mouths shut. Their silence was aided by the smiles Oisín, the Lord Seeker, Sylpha and Hessa all wore.

"Aye," Hugh said almost to himself. "You'll do."

"For now at least," Martel answered. "I expect that you have all sent word to your banner men by now. Your armies are required for the coming storm. If, for some idiotic reason, you have not yet sent word home, you will do so today. In the meantime, I will address the city. You are dismissed, though I will expect your presence for the contest this afternoon."

No one moved. Martel stared at them expectantly. "I said," he said. "You are dismissed."

The Lord Seeker, barely containing his mirth, informed the emperor, "They are not used to being spoken to as common soldiers, your Grace."

"Don't call me that," Martel growled. "And that is hardly my problem. All men bleed, be they soldiers or noblemen. They need to toughen up. I need fighters, not an army of flowers."

Hugh rumbled a soft laugh. He turned to the nobles and says, "You heard him. Court is adjourned."

"Is that what I have to say?" Martel asked him as the noblemen and women slowly file out of the room.

"Usually, though I quite enjoyed the bulging eyes caused by your preferred method," Hugh replied. "It's good to remind the youngins of their place every so often."

Martel tilted his head from side to side, stretching the tension out of his neck. "All right," he said. "I need the sceptre for this speech. I'll make it in the market place."

"I'll arrange for the herald to announce it," the Lord Seeker said. He bowed slightly before leaving Martel's company.

"Stop that!" Martel snapped. The Seeker chuckled as he left the throne room.

Martel shook his head. "Anyone else hungry?"

"Starving!" Oisín said.

"Let's get food."

Chapter Thirty-One

We found ourselves in Martel's enormous chamber, eating a large meal. Martel was in his element here, amongst his peers. He relaxed a little, and was able to laugh some.

The Lord Seeker arrived part way through the meal to announce the herald had departed for the centre of the city, and all would be prepared for both Martel's address and the contest to be held later in the afternoon. Not long after, I was in Martel's company as he rode out to the market place, still refusing to dress in anything more regal than chainmaille, and even that only at Commander Mhu's insistence. The sceptre was wrapped in velvet and strapped to Martel's back as he rode. Commander Mhu led the parade, followed by Martel, who was flanked by two more Black Blades. Another Black Blade rode behind him, followed by myself, the Lord Seeker and the newly appointed War Advisor, Hugh, riding abreast. Behind him rode Hessa, Sylpha and Oisín.

Martel muttered to himself about the ridiculousness of the parade as the horses moved through the streets, which were lined with people. I could not help but smile at Martel's worsening mood.

The herald awaited us on the platform that had been erected specifically for Martel's address. Waiting with him was a young lad with a ridiculously long trumpet. Immediately on seeing the party approach, the Herald signalled, and the lad raised the trumpet. It surprised me how musical the announcing blast was.

"His Grace, the Emperor Martel!" the herald bellowed.

Martel sighed, dismounted and climbed the stairs onto the platform, wearily following Commander Mhu. The gathered crowd bowed as Commander Mhu moved aside and Martel stepped forward.

"Don't," Martel sighed in exasperation. He scowled. "Up," he said loudly. "Everyone stand up. I will look at the people I address."

Unsure, only one or two people rose from their bows. "Up!" Martel barked the command as if addressing rangers in training. "On your feet. Now!"

The crowd bolted upright.

"That's better." Martel looked down at the paper the Lord Seeker had given him with the key points he ought to touch upon when addressing the lay people. He looked down at the paper a long while before, much to the Seeker's annoyance, scrunching it up and tossing it away.

"My name is Martel," Martel said loudly. "And as you can see, I don't much look the part of emperor. The truth be told, I don't feel I'm much the part either."

"That is not inspiring confidence in your rule, Martel," the Lord Seeker growled under his breath. I tried hard not to smile, twisting my face into what must have been an odd expression. Oisín caught sight of my contorted features and tried unsuccessfully to stifle a guffaw. The Seeker threw him an irritated glance, which only served to make Oisín laugh harder.

"Will you behave yourself?" Sylpha snapped at him, making Oisín laugh harder yet.

Martel, no doubt hearing it all, did very well to ignore the shenanigans behind him. "The truth is, I am the son of a serving girl and an unfaithful nobleman, sent to the rangers as a lad in an effort to hide my father's indiscretion. I am not an emperor. I am a ranger. I am a soldier. I am a commander. As it turns out, that's precisely what is needed at present."

Scanning the crowd, I noted with satisfaction that Martel had their undivided attention. Proving himself the emperor was not what Martel was trying to do. He was trying to prove himself capable and honourable. It seemed, from the expressions of the people in the crowd, to be working.

"There should be revelling," Martel said. "Some sort of celebration to announce that the heir has been found. But I find myself incapable of celebrating at present. My succession came at a heavy price, and accompanies heavier news. Many of you have heard rumours of evil stirring. I can confirm these rumours. The Mage King has returned, and is once again plotting to take the empire for himself."

The crowd stirred, gasping and murmuring amongst themselves.

"And so I can offer nothing to celebrate, and ask only for your cooperation in defence of everything you love. The walls need repairing. We must build an army. We will need weapons, engineers and war machines. We will need help to feed the army, to clothe them and to arm them. If anyone is willing, you may volunteer for the army I am building. You will be clothed and fed. I need this from you."

The crowd fell silent again. Martel paused, not sure what to say next.

"The day the rangers were disbanded, I began a quest to restore the imperial throne. But it has become so much bigger than that. Everything I love is at risk, and I cannot sit by and watch the empire be swallowed by an ancient enemy."

Reaching to the sceptre tied to his back, Martel unhooked it and brought it forward, slowly unwrapping the cloth that surrounded it as he spoke.

"Darkness is coming," Martel said. "But within each of us is a candle. Stand together against the oncoming night, and we will burn brighter than the sun." He placed one hand on the rose gold handle of the sceptre and the blood red crystal in the talons of the phoenix glowed bright red.

"The approaching evil can be defeated."

"Very prettily put," Hugh noted in a soft murmur.

I nodded having found myself swept away by Martel's blunt and honest speech. Martel re-wrapped the sceptre.

"We all have work to do," he said. "Let's get on with it."

With nothing else to say, Martel eschewed the stairs and leapt from the platform, walking back to his horse. Commander Mhu joined him quickly.

"Some warning when you're going to do something like that, please," he said curtly. "Your Grace," he added.

"Sorry," Martel muttered.

"You might as well stay," the Lord Seeker said. "They're setting up for the contest."

I looked over at the market place to find palace guards on scene rapidly constructing a barrier that would mark the fighting ring. The three contestants had also arrived, each watching the soldiers build and shoo the crowd as the Herald announced the next order of business for the market place.

Oisín leant over to me and asked, "Want to wager?"

"No gambling," Martel said before I could answer.

"Fine," Oisín said. He grinned at me behind Martel's back. "So," he said in a conversational manner. "Who do you think shall win today's match?" He flashed up both hands five times while mouthing the words, *fifty gold*.

Grinning, I shrugged and said, "Never underestimate a pretty face. A rose conceals many thorns. Hugh's daughter will win."

Oisín considered. "I don't suppose it's much of a bet if I place my money on the same person," he mused. "She was my choice, too."

"There will be no gambling," Martel said again, turning to Oisín.

"Of course not," Oisín replied glibly. If he was in any way chagrined at having let the bet slip, he did not show it. "I'm merely saying that if we were to place bets, it wouldn't work if both of us bet on the same person. Since we're not placing bets, the point is rather moot. That said, I like the look of that broad lad in his plain armour. He knows well enough the scratches armour will get in battle. So, not that I would, but if it were an option, I would place my money on him."

Martel glared at Oisín, who merely grinned in return.

"What are the odds?" Commander Mhu asked. "I mean," he corrected when Martel turned to him. "What would be the odds?"

"Two to one, at the moment," Oisín replied. "Unless money is put on that enamelled lad. In which case it would become three to one. Not that anyone here is placing bets. Hypothetically speaking, which would you bet on?"

Commander Mhu pondered briefly before answering, "Hypothetically?"

"For the love of..." Martel growled under his breath. Oisín's grin widened.

"I would go for the enamelled lad," Mhu said. "He may prove a surprisingly competent fighter. Money can buy the best teachers, after all. What is the hypothetical buy-in?"

"A hypothetical fifty gold."

Commander Mhu whistled. "I'm in," he said. "Hypothetically speaking, of course."

Oisín roared a laugh. "Commander Mhu, I do believe I rather like you."

"My esteem, however," Martel noted sourly. "Has fallen dramatically."

"It will rise again the first bolt I spare you from," Mhu remarked.

This time, I could not refrain from joining in Oisín's laughter.

"Shut up," Martel growled, though he sounded utterly defeated.

The herald took to the cleared area in the market place and announced the terms of and reason for the contest. The crowd cheered and a few enterprising young bakers, hunters and brewers moved through the crowds selling their wares. The three contestants entered the hastily erected ring. Memories of my arrival here, when three men fought over me in this very spot, flashed through my mind. How might have this adventure gone differently had someone else won? Would I now be working for the Steward, hunting down the outlaws that had defied his order? Hunting down Martel?

I looked at the new emperor's broad back and thought back to the times when I very nearly lost him. He would have died had I not successfully intervened with the tuatha, and where would that have left the empire? There would be no heir at all; the bloodline would have truly ended and the empire would have been defenceless against the coming Mage King. The very thought that I had held the life of the entire empire in my care for even a moment filled me with a much delayed sense of dread. My body broke into a cold sweat.

"Don't worry," Oisín said. "I will do good things with your gold."

I turned to him, eyes uncomprehending, before pulling myself out of my thoughts enough to offer a shaky smile.

"Are you unwell?" Oisín asked.

"No," I replied. "I was just thinking."

"Ah. That was your mistake."

I nodded. "It really was."

Oisín's next utterance of concern was hindered by the sound of clashing weapons, drawing both our attentions back to the contestants in the fighting ring. The movements were surprisingly fast, considering the size of the blades each contestant carried. Hugh's daughter had eschewed a shield and had opted instead for a second blade; a long knife, or perhaps it was a very short sword. I could not decide. The other two both had shields and long swords.

I watched with surprise as Oisín's champion was eliminated almost instantly, smacked upside the head with the flat of Mhu's champion's blade. The man staggered and dropped to his knees. He struggled up again and stumbled. The young man's second ran in to help him out of the ring. He slurred his protests as he weakly struggled to get back in the fight.

"Well, we must give him points for spirit," Mhu noted mildly.

Oisín stared at him incredulously, struggling to come to terms with his loss. "Damn everything," he muttered.

"That should teach you," Martel answered.

I chuckled and, now with a good chance at earning one hundred and fifty gold, watched the fight keenly.

Hugh's daughter and Sir Enamel, as Oisín just declared him, squared off in the centre of the ring. That was when I noticed something peculiar about Hugh's daughter. She fought with the shortest weapon forward, something I might have thought inadvisable. I understood why, however, when she moved.

Knowing she was at a physical disadvantage against most opponents, Hugh's daughter had obviously been spending a great deal of time training her speed and her accuracy. Her feet did the majority of the work as she moved. If she found herself unable to strike with her weapons, she used her feet to trap her opponent, sending him sprawling.

I watched on with a half-smile as the young woman threw her opponent twice merely by placing her legs so that he tripped over her feet as he tried to manoeuvre himself to match her.

"Oh," Hessa noted. "I like her style. Very fluid; almost tuatha."

"She has drawn much inspiration from your people," Sir Hugh noted with pride. "She has spent the last three years in self-study, learning of your techniques from an obscure book she has borrowed from the library. Of course, she is not tuatha, and far more comfortable in heavy armour. She had to make adjustments, but she has done very well, I think."

"Self-study, you say?"

"Yes. She insisted after her teacher admitted he had taught her everything he knew. She has ever been curious about fighting and battles."

"A curious occupation for a girl," one of the gathered nobles who happened to be eavesdropping noted.

"It is evident that you do not know girls very well," Mhu replied.

"My girls prefer more refined activities," the nobleman snorted defensively.

"Aye," Oisín scoffed. "And we all know that women are all so very alike." He pondered a moment. "I should introduce you to my wife and let you try and convince her to take up these 'refined activities.'"

"You don't want that to happen," Sylpha told the nobleman. "Any man who tries to tell her what her place should be ends up with their head in her collection."

The nobleman looked between Oisín and Sylpha, unsure if they were joking. They both looked back at him, their expressions sombre.

"It's true," I advised the nobleman. "She's a fierce woman."

"Aye," Oisín said, straightening with pride. "Aye, she is. Gods I miss her."

"If you're very lucky, you'll see her again soon," Martel said.

The crowd issued a collective 'Ooooh!' as Hugh's daughter narrowly missed a beheading. I turned my attention back to the fight and noted that 'Sir Enamel' had been pressing hard, forcing Hugh's daughter back a fair way. I bit back my anxiety about the outcome of the fight and willed her to recover quickly.

Sir Enamel struck fast three times, the third blow glancing off her pauldron as she barely managed to dance to the side. It took the dimming of my vision for me to realise that I had been holding my breath. I let it out slowly and steadily and watched on.

Hugh's daughter remained on the defensive, ducking and dodging, facing many narrow misses until an opportunity arose. Sir Enamel struck low, hoping to chop into her knee through the joint in the armour. Risking everything, Hugh's daughter plunged her longsword into a crack in the cobbles, both protecting her knee and using the sword as a crutch for something truly spectacular.

Despite the weight of her armour, she jumped over Sir Enamel's swinging arm, landing in a crouch. Driving with her legs, she slammed the pommel of her short sword under his chin, the momentum lifting him off his feet. Using that same momentum, she bent and drove Sir Enamel's back hard onto the ground, knocking the wind from him. She pinned him down with on knee on his chest, the pommel of the short sword still pinned against his chin.

"Well," Sir Hugh said. "That's new."

The crowd sat in shocked silence a moment before erupting into thunderous applause and cheering. The winner had been announced. Sir Hugh's daughter, quite clearly the better fighter, had earned her place as Master-At-Arms in spectacular fashion.

And I had earned one hundred and fifty gold.

"Pay up," I said to Oisín.

Grumbling, the chieftain lifted his purse from his belt and grudgingly handed it over. I turned to Commander Mhu.

"Don't be ridiculous," Commander Mhu snorted. "It was hypothetical."

I blinked, then laughed.

"But..." Oisín said. He shrugged. "I, at least, am a man of my word."

"As am I," Commander Mhu replied. "And the word was hypothetical."

I laughed harder, until I heard someone at the back of the crowd scream. The silence that fell on the crowd was by far more deafening than their applause ever was. I turned towards the sound to find the crowd nearest the gate parting. A young man was running. He could not have been more than ten, and his body was covered in old blood and festering wounds. His skinny, underfed legs moved despite his blank expression.

Martel moved immediately, storming to the boy and catching him moments before he collapsed.

"Help," the boy whispered, his glassy eyes fixing on Martel. "Help."

"What happened?" Martel asked, his voice gentle and fatherly.

"An army... black... they came... mother... help."

"Where?" Martel whispered. "Where did the black army come to?"

"Westwick Village," the boy wheezed. His breath ceased, escaping his lungs in a short, sharp gasp, his eyes staring up at Martel from a now blank face.

"Westwick Village," Commander Mhu mused.

"That's the westernmost edge of the empire," Sir Hugh said. "It would take a rider two months to get there. An army would take longer."

"Then we have less than a month to prepare," Martel said. He stood, lifting the boy's body easily. "Preparations start today. I want riders sent out to warn the western villages. They are to flee immediately. There is not time to get them inside the city, so tell them to take to the hills. We will call for them when the fighting is done if we still stand." He took a deep breath. "I need riders to the north and east. Tell them we need fighters, and we need them now. Get them back here as quickly as possible."

"The enemy will already be at the city gates by the time most of them get word," Sir Hugh said.

Martel grimaced. Sir Hugh was right. "I need my advisors in the throne room. Now! You!" he shouted at Sir Hugh's daughter. "Your name?"

"Providence," the young woman replied.

"I need you to gather as many people as you can. We need a functioning army in a week. Have them training by this evening if you can manage it."

"Yes, your Grace." Providence bowed and moved off, sprinting in her armour.

"Strong legs," Commander Mhu noted appreciatively.

"And someone find me an undertaker for this poor lad. We should give him a proper funeral."

"I can take him, your Grace," a tall, slender man said as he nervously played with the hem of his black and white robe. "I am a priest of Maha."

Nodding, Martel handed the boy over to the man. "Thank you."

He turned and addressed the crowd once more. "Hold fast!" he barked at them as they verged on all-out panic. "Now is the time to light your candles. Keep the flame steady. I need you all to do your part. We will come through this. If any of you have services you can offer the army, you must attend to our new Master-Of-Arms. Heads up. We will overcome."

The short speech proved effective. Panic was replaced with a resolve so steely I could feel it like an invisible shield created by and surrounding the crowd.

"Advisors," Martel barked, storming back to his horse. We followed. The crowd parted reverently as Martel led us back to the throne room at a gallop. We gathered in the small chamber adjacent to the throne room, sitting at a large table to discuss possible plans of action.

Sir Hugh spoke first. "I will leave the decision to you, your Grace, but we would have more time to train our army if we dig in for a siege."

"I do not like that idea," the Lord Seeker noted. "There are too many secret entrances into this city. It is indefensible. More to the point, the qilin would be more effective in the open. We should march out and find a suitable field and await the black army. We will be rested, ready and in terrain of our choosing."

"Qilin?" Sir Hugh asked.

"You call them grass dogs."

"Oh." Then, "Ooh." Sir Hugh shuddered. "The city, incidentally is not indefensible. We will have to pull back to the inner wall, but that will help concentrate our forces."

"We could take to the forest," Hessa said. "The tuatha are skilled in that terrain. There are many places to hide, and trees make for good defence against missiles."

"The tuatha are the only ones skilled in that terrain," Sir Hugh countered. "Well, and the rangers. We don't have time to train the regulars to use it to their advantage."

Martel sighed. He stared down at the knots in the table, thinking.

"I do not know battle all that well," I admitted. "But the Lord Seeker's advice seems the most sensible. If we can enter a fight well rested and in favourable terrain, without civilians to trip over, we would be doing fine."

Martel grunted. He rolled his shoulders in an effort to dislodge the tension that had settled there. "I like the idea of drawing the battle away from the city," he agreed. "The fewer civilian casualties, the better, I think." He nodded as if confirming something to himself. "Good. We travel out in a week. Someone have the herald announce our departure so that the craftsmen know how much time they have to supply the army. Hessa, can you have the palace guard trained in a week? I would leave some behind to defend the city and keep the law while we're away fighting."

"For keeping the law, I need only a few days. I would need months to prepare these people to defend the city," Hessa answered.

"There would be no point to defending the city," the Lord Seeker growled. "If we fail this fight. The Mage King will overcome all."

"Let's not fail," Martel answered. He stood. "Sir Hugh, will you aid me in organising the supplies? Sylpha, please assist Providence in arranging supplies for the army."

"Yes, your Grace," both Sylpha and Sir Hugh answered in unison. They turned and hurried to do as they were bid.

"Commander Mhu, please send word to the Black Blades. We ride out in a week."

Commander Mhu bowed, turned and, with a flick of his fingers, sent a young Black Blade scurrying from the throne room.

"Is there anything I can do, your Grace?" the Lord Seeker asked.

"You can stop calling me that, for starters," Martel snapped back. He rolled his shoulders again and looked sidelong at the demon. "Where did the empress battle the Mage King the first time?" he asked.

"If you recall where you met Saschana to strike the deal to enter the city," the Lord Seeker said. "The last stage of the battle was fought there. That scorched rock upon which we stood was the place where she struck down the Mage King, and I rent his soul into twelve."

"Where was the first stage fought?"

"At the fords of the River Morrush, a week's ride from there."

"Is that a good place to battle, in your opinion?"

The Lord Seeker rubbed the side of his face. "It may be. We will have a nearby supply of fresh water, in any case. Of all the things an army needs, fresh, clean water is a must. The terrain is broad as well, with forests in the north east. There will probably be game for hunting, so if the battle lasts long we will be able to feed ourselves. More or less."

"But the empress was pushed back," Martel said.

"Yes," the Lord Seeker said. "Though her fortunes were turned around when she freed me from slavery."

"Are you claiming credit for the victory?" Martel asked with a smirk.

"Not at all. My freedom was unexpected, the possibility of which the Mage King had not even considered. In this, the empress had the benefit of surprise. It is an advantage you will not have, alas."

"We might have an advantage yet," Martel mused, turning his thoughtful eyes to me.

I blinked stupidly as everyone else turned to me.

"Why are you looking at me?" I demanded. "I don't even remember my own name! There is no possible way I can be an advantage to you!"

"You are something of a mystery," Martel replied. "I think now might be the time to find out how and why you turned up."

"Um..." I answered.

"It is highly convenient," the Lord Seeker noted, thoughtfully. "A Sky Road Walker. Only those with magical ability can see and walk upon the Sky Road. And to show up at the beginning - to be here in time to fight the Mage King... There is something about you we're not seeing."

"If you're looking for heroics, you won't find it in me," I said. "I can barely walk a mile without falling down and smashing my own face."

The Lord Seeker's lips twitched with the threat of a smile. "By your leave, your Grace," he asked Martel. "I would like to spend the week we have before riding out in the library. Perhaps I can muster up some information about our mysterious friend, here."

"You have it," Martel said. "And if you find anything, you will tell me first."

"That's hardly fair!" I protested.

"Neither is life," Martel answered with a shrug.

The Lord Seeker bowed and left the throne room. Martel dismissed the rest of us, and I found myself wandering around, feeling utterly useless. Not knowing what else to do throughout the week, I lent my energy to whomever asked. With my aid, Providence was able to outfit the new conscripts in two days, in which time they were already in training; the weapon supplies were organised, catalogued and packed to travel; the supply train was organised and ready to ferry supplies to and from the planned battleground; and the nobles' vassals and soldiers were housed, fed and ready to march.

Chapter Thirty-Two

The flurry of activity left me feeling breathless. Before long, the week was done and I stood in the throne room for what might be the last time.

"We march out today," Martel said, staring out over the city, silent in the pre-dawn gloom. "And I have a concern."

"Oh?" Sir Hugh asked.

"My half-brother, the former Steward." Martel shrugged. "I don't want to leave him here."

"Worried someone will set him loose again?" Hessa asked.

"And that we'd have to assail the city if our fight against the Mage King proves successful," Martel said, nodding.

"Who would free him?" I asked. "He's an idiot."

"He's an idiot with riches to promise," Martel answered. "And the palace guard were free to do what they wished under his rule. He will likely have friends amongst them still. But dragging him with us will prove a drain on our supplies, and on my patience."

"We can feed him to the Mage King," the Lord Seeker offered helpfully.

Martel smirked. "I'm tempted."

"Can we send him to the tuatha?" I asked. "I mean, their prisons seemed pretty effective."

Hessa looked at me with a raised brow. "We do not have prisoners. We have guests."

"That you poison."

Hessa's lips twitched in an effort not to smile at me. Her stern expression did not change. Keeping that bizarre expression, Hessa turned to Martel. "If you would ask it of us, your allies will of course take on this Steward of yours for the duration of the battle. But no longer than that. We don't want the human stink in our forest any longer than absolutely necessary."

Martel tried unsuccessfully to contain his smile, drawing Hessa's smile out at last. "We will try and spare your delicate noses," he replied.

"I will dispatch a guard to escort him as we leave the city."

"Good. It is settled. Breakfast should be ready. We'll leave as soon as we've finished eating."

With that, the meeting was over. I followed Martel to his chambers where he ordered a spread for himself, the Lord Seeker, and I. Everyone else, save Commander Mhu and his Black Blades, who stood guard while we ate, retired to manage their own affairs.

After the meal, we were all fully armed, armoured, and on horseback. I rode at the head of the enormous army with Martel. The army itself was multi coloured, the tuatha riding together in their green armour. They rode beside the marching infantry, led by Providence, who, in solidarity with her soldiers, walked beside her horse. They were a motley crew, made up largely of street urchins and vagabonds, former thieves and the children of struggling honest families all of whom had signed up more out of need for food and shelter than any true patriotism. Yet Providence had worked wonders with this ragtag mix of men and women. They wore grim expressions of determination as they marched, looking cohesive in their matching red uniforms with dark brown leather armour. Some of the starving youths who had signed up stood taller, their difficult lives now given purpose. A full three meals a day certainly helped.

The army had a mounted division, made up mostly of the children of farmers who were already familiar with the beasts they rode. Providence had assigned three infantrymen with a rider, who would teach the infantry the proper care of horses as they marched. Her plan was to create a flexible fighting force, where infantry could become cavalry and vice versa when and where needed.

Providence had proven an efficient and exacting general, and her army was as well trained as it was possible to be given the time constraints. It was clear that her army respected her a great deal.

Flanking the army, opposite the infantry of the empire, were the Black Blades, each man and woman dressed entirely in black. As has become their custom, they marched in silence, their officers riding at their rear, save the two commanders, who flanked the emperor. Their number was staggering, making their presence felt in the great swath of shadow they cut through the ranks.

Encircling the entire army were the rangers, wearing their brown and green leather armour. They also served as the scouts. The fighters from the north were the least uniform group; their armour mostly self-made concoctions of hide and fur. As such, each piece of armour was as individual as the warrior who wore it. The confusion was exacerbated by the nobles' own armies, forming blocks of colour in the madness as they marched behind their respective lords.

Every so often, one of the qilin would show themselves, slinking past the army in a bizarre walk that was at once awkward and sinuous. The qilin queen walked beside the Lord Seeker, who seemed to find a great deal of comfort in her presence. It was easy to see by the set of the massive demon's shoulders that he was tense.

"A coin for you thoughts?" I murmured to him.

"I do not fancy being made a slave again," he replied bluntly. "The Mage King may be powerful enough to draw me in, most certainly if he is whole and marching now."

"You are powerful in your own right. And you know he might try, and so can defend against it." I paused. "Can't you?"

"If I see it coming, yes. The Mage King is smarter than to try anything obvious, however."

Not able to give comfort, I simply nodded. "We have a better shot of taking him than any other army, though. So there's that."

The Seeker laughed. "There is that."

"Let's talk of something lighter. A farce, perhaps?"

"What farce would that be?"

"Me, of course."

The Lord Seeker did not laugh at this, but smiled at me. It was a knowing smile. "There is more power to you than you can possibly know."

"Do you know?" I asked. "Did your expansive knowledge of history and week-long sojourn in the library reveal anything to you?"

"Did you know that the Mage King and the first empress share a common ancestor?" the Lord Seeker asked, apparently ignoring my question.

"No," I replied sullenly. "Stupid question, my Lord. I know nothing. But you know that already."

"A very long time ago, long before either the Mage King or the empress, there lived a powerful sorceress. She ruled the kingdom of Noth."

"I have never heard of such a kingdom," Martel interjected, finally breaking his silence.

"No indeed. It was one of the four great kingdoms of the continent. The kingdom of Noth was the largest and most powerful, as one can imagine. It had a sorceress as its regent. She had two daughters. They were to co-rule after her passing. But the youngest was greedy and cruel. They fought. The eldest had the people of Noth behind her and so the youngest was defeated. She should have been struck down, but the reason the eldest was so beloved - her goodness - prevented her from killing her own sister. So instead, the younger princess of Noth was exiled. She vanished from the records, though I came across the half-mad scribblings of a scribe who had located her in the realm of shadow.

"His visions saw her with child, bearing all manner of evil monstrous children. One of those children was the Mage King. He returned to this realm to reclaim a birth right he felt was his. By that time, many generations on, the four great kingdoms had risen and fallen in their turn and were lost to living memory. In their place were many kingdoms, each smaller and less powerful than any of the four had been. They were ripe for the plucking."

The Lord Seeker rolled his shoulders and shook his head. "The irony is, had the Mage King never sought to take back the lands that once belonged to Noth, the empire would never had risen. The empress would never have won the support and loyalty of the many kingdoms on the continent. She would never have mustered her armies, never have rode into battle, and would never have been crowned empress following her impressive victory. In his effort to reclaim the glory of the four kingdoms under his cruel banner, he set against himself the foe that would eventually defeat him."

"And she was related to him?" Martel asked.

"Yes, for she is the direct descendent of the queen of Noth; the elder sister who struck down her younger, but could not bring herself to slay her."

"So, what you're saying is that I am related to the Mage King?" Martel stared incredulously at the Lord Seeker.

"Yes, which is why the bloodline is so important."

"I don't understand," I said.

"Think of it in absolutes. The younger sister was evil, the elder was good. One can only be resisted by the other if they are equal in strength. Thus the bloodlines."

"If they are equal in strength, what advantage do we have?" Martel asked.

The Lord Seeker nodded at me. "The Sky Road Walker," he said.

"I really don't understand," I said.

Smiling, the Lord Seeker said, "Now try and think that nothing is absolute. It is entirely possible that evil was once good, but twisted by hatred or jealousy or some other force. Deep in the shadows of that evil would lie a kernel of goodness still."

"I'm so confused," I admitted.

"That makes two of us," Martel muttered.

"Never mind," the Seeker said. "It will all be made clear soon enough. Just take my word for it that the Sky Road Walker is our advantage."

"Or you could be clear about it," Martel said.

"I can be no clearer. I fear to speak more of it at present, lest I inadvertently turn us away from victory."

Martel opened his mouth to protest, shut it again and sighed. He resumed his silence.

After a week on the march, we came to the scorched rock where the Lord Seeker cleaved the Mage King's soul in twelve. There we camped. The armies were swift in their settling for the night. Fire pits were dug and lit, food was cooked and bedrolls were laid out in record time. Soon groups were sitting around fires, eating and talking in low voices. I sat with the rest of the commanders, staring down at my pack.

I carried with me a sword and fighting staff for weapons, as well as a knife that would serve in a pinch. I was not comfortable with any of the weapons, honestly, but I knew enough to serve. I also still carried the hunting horn given to me by the king of the wood wights. I stared at it a moment. I was warned never to blow it but in greatest need or suffer the wrath of the wood wight king. But when would such a moment come, and would I be too late in calling for aid for fear of his shadowy retribution? With thoughts of the oncoming battle, I laid down in my bedroll and attempted to sleep.

I awoke, staring up at a dark sky. It took me a moment to remember where I was and why. Frowning, as I could not hear any stirring of the army around me, I sat upright in my bedroll and looked around. A few fire pits still had glowing embers and one or two of them had soldiers sitting around them, huddled and ponderous. For the most part, however, the camp was silent.

Upon closer inspection, I noticed that the glow from the embers was steady, not the slow flicker it ought to have been, and the men huddled around the fire pits were not moving at all; not even to breathe. I scowled. Throwing aside my blanket, I was acutely aware that I ought to be cold, but I did not feel anything; not the cold, not the heat, not even so much as the soft breath of a breeze. There was nothing.

I moved to stand but a movement in the corner of my eye made me freeze. I looked to find the Mage King, wearing a tattered black robe and thick ancient armour, striding across the scene. He did not see me, apparently, and I realised that the lack of my normal reaction to the Mage King meant that he was not actually within the encampment.

Opposite him strode a woman. I recognised her by her thick waves of auburn hair immediately. The Empress Moua. She wore armour of an unusual design. Around her shoulders, trimmed in grey fur, sat a pale blue cloak. On her brow, she wore a simple circlet of leather with a large pearl at its centre. She walked forward to meet the Mage King boldly, looking every inch the general that led her army to victory.

"What are you doing here?" the Mage King demanded, his voice a thin rasp, as if his throat had been crushed.

"To offer one last chance. Turn aside. You will find no victory here."

I realised that I had been holding my breath. I let it out slowly. Had I come across a spectre of the past, some remembrance of the land upon which I slept as to what happened here so many thousands of years ago.

The Mage King laughed, an eerie reptilian sound. "There will be no victory for you and your ilk. Your line is destroyed, made weak by long years of forgetfulness."

My heart dropped. Not a scene from the past, then.

"You underestimate my blood," the empress said, a soft, sure smile on her face. How could she be so confident? Her empire was crumbling, and had been in decay for many years. Its leader did not want to be emperor, and its army was nothing more than a mob of the desperate.

Again the Mage King laughed his sickly laugh. "There is nothing left. The empire will be mine."

The empress turned her head away from the Mage King's vehemence. Our eyes meet and I tensed. She saw me, and upon seeing me, she relaxed, her soft confident smile returning. Keeping her eyes on mine, she replied, "You forget yourself, Mage." She turned to face him again and offered him a mocking half bow.

Laughing, the Mage King slowly vanished, his laugh echoing long after his form disappeared. When at last the scene was once again silent, the empress turned to leave. She paused briefly to smile at me, her eyes locking with mine once more. There was knowing in those eyes, a silent message, as if her words were spoken not for the benefit of the Mage King, but mine.

I struggled with the knowledge that I had witnessed something profound this night, but I could not fathom what that might be. Seemingly satisfied that she had impressed upon me the importance of what I had just witnessed, she turned and strode away, vanishing into a mist that travelled a few paces more before dissipating.

A sudden earthquake jolted me. I sat up with a gasp, surrounded by concerned faces.

"I told you they weren't dead," a soldier said. "Idiots."

"You were cold as ice," Martel said to me, pressing a hand against my cheek. It was still night as far as I could tell. I blinked stupidly as I tried to orient myself. A dream. It had all been a dream. I scowled at Martel.

"Miaohavedrempt," I said. Martel raised his eyebrows at me.

"Pardon?"

"The Sky Road Walker was dreaming," the Seeker helpfully translated.

I pointed at the Seeker and nodded, my tongue feeling too heavy to function properly.

"Good thing you speak 'not quite awake'," Sylpha noted sardonically. She shook her head. "Let me in, Martel."

Knowing he was not the person to try and make me feel better, Martel stood aside and Sylpha came to me, offering a steaming cup of murky green water. "It's tea," Sylpha said. "Made from lichens. It will help you relax and warm you up."

My hand trembled violently as I reached for the cup. I frowned at it. My teeth chattered in my skull. I felt suddenly very cold. Grunting, I took the tea and sipped. It burned my tongue, but I did not care. The moment the tea hit my stomach, I started to feel better. It spread pleasant warmth through me.

"What was it about?" Martel asked.

"Pardon?" I replied. The tea had apparently loosened my tongue.

"Your dream. What happened?"

"It must have been some nightmare," another soldier remarked. "Look at the state of you."

I shook my head. "Not a nightmare. A conversation."

"A conversation?" Martel asked.

Nodding, I continued. "Between the Mage King and the empress. I don't think I was supposed to be there, but I happened to awaken in the camp. Everything was still, as if time had stopped. The Mage King and the empress came from opposite sides of the camp and met in the middle. I don't think the Mage King knew I was there, but the empress saw me. I think she was glad I had heard their exchange. I think it was supposed to mean something. I can't imagine what though."

"What was said?" Martel asked.

"Well," I replied, trying to recall. "The empress gave warning to the Mage King, telling him to turn aside. He laughed at her and said..." I looked at Martel, who folded his arms across his chest and looked back at me expectantly. "Well, he said that her bloodline had become weak."

"Did he now?" Martel mused softly.

"But she seemed so confident. She just smiled at him. And at me. That's the thing that I remember the best. She smiled at me, and her eyes seemed to tell me that there was something important in that exchange." I looked up at Martel and shrugged. "I don't know what, though."

Martel sighed. "Well, we must give her credit for her bravado."

"It wasn't bravado," I said. "She seemed really confident that the Mage King would be defeated."

"Your Grace," a soldier said. "First light."

Martel nodded. "Wake the camp. We ride out come dawn."

No more was said of my dream as the camp jumped to life, restarting the fires, eating, packing and marching. It was another week and a half before the army reached the river. The scenery was stunning. The mountains in the distant west were purple, their snowy peaks the source of the cool clear river that cut the grasslands in half. In the north east, a thick forest stretched back all the way to the horizon and beyond. The banks of the river were marked not by sand, but a few rocks and the flowering plants that bloom above the water, but take root below it. The air was crisp and clean.

The army camped in the hillocks at the southern edge of the grassland.

"These are not hillocks," the Seeker noted as he touched the steep side of the small mound behind which Martel had chosen to camp. "They are graves. Those who fell in the first war against the Mage King rest here."

Martel lifted a single eyebrow. "Perhaps we should camp elsewhere," he said.

"No," the Seeker whispered. "We are not unwelcome here."

"You can tell how the dead feel?" a soldier asked.

"So can you. You would know if these mounds were unfriendly."

The soldier turned pale.

"Ignore him," I advised the young lad. "He has his moods."

The soldier nodded, though did not look any less pale, and scurried off to find work.

"You should stop scaring people like that," Martel said.

"The dead are not frightening," the Seeker protested.

"The Mage King is pretty frightening," I noted.

"Ah, but he is not dead," the Seeker answered. "Not quite."

I shuddered and helped build the fire.

"Not there," the Seeker said. "Or you will be burning the bones of the buried."

"Where, then?" I demanded.

"Behind you. There are no bones there."

As I built the fire, I turned my mind to my part in the war. The Mage King affected me terribly, and I feared that the nausea would claim me, making me next to useless in battle. But I was important, or so I had been told, and so I must have some part to play in the battle. What was I to do? Would I hide from the battle until my purpose was made clear? Would I engage and hope I had somehow overcome the sickness the Mage King inspired? The question plagued me as I mindlessly munched on dinner while the sun slipped behind the horizon.

I posed my problem to Martel during dusk at the end of the first week of camp. He looked at me mildly, a small smile on his face.

"What?" I demanded. "Why are you smiling?"

"You are trying to ask me for my opinion," Martel replied with a shrug. "But you seem to have already made up your mind."

I stared down at my bowl, and sighed. "I just... I would like to know if you think it is a good idea."

"I think that what I think matters little," Martel answered. "We all must do what we feel is right in the end."

"You are particularly unhelpful," I grumbled.

Martel chuckled, and the conversation was over. Sighing again, I decided that I would stand with the army and face the Mage King. The making of the decision eased my mind somewhat, but I was still concerned as to whether or not it was a good idea. I went to bed with my mind still a-whirl.

A distant rumble awakened me before dawn. I sat up and looked to the west. Martel had done the same, his face etched in concern. The Seeker was on his feet before anyone else, standing and looking in the direction of the sound. I strained, trying to see if the rumble was getting louder as all around the camp awakened.

The Seeker turned back to Martel. They locked eyes and the Seeker nodded; a short, curt sort of nod. A quiet confirmation.

He was here.

Chapter Thirty-Three

Martel threw aside his blankets and stood. The camp burst into a flurry of activity. Soldiers awakened, donned their armour and packed away their things. They formed up, standing across the river, staring into the gloom as the rumbling increased in volume. The ground beneath my feet began to tremble as the sound formed into something I recognised - marching, the perfectly synchronised steps of a very large army.

I stood with the officers of our own army, dressed in armour with my staff in hand as the hills on the horizon began to move, their dark slopes convulsing as if they were puddles into which pebbles had been dropped. It took me a moment to realise that the hills were not, in fact, moving, but that the enemy was swarming over them, looking like an army of black bodied ants over a carcass. I swallowed.

"Hold fast!" Martel barked as some of the soldiers took an involuntary step backwards.

The sound of rushing water hit my ears and the world spun. I stumbled in an effort to keep myself upright before collapsing to my knees. I wrapped one arm around my torso, as if the action might help quell the painful heaving of my stomach.

"Easy now," I heard someone say. "On your feet."

Strong arms grasped my middle and hauled me upright. My vision spun and I shut my eyes tightly.

"Stand," the voice commanded. I forced my knees to lock, my thighs screaming at the effort. I wobbled a little as the supporting arms were removed, but I found my balance and managed to stay on my feet.

"Better," the voice said. I turned towards the sound to find that it was the Seeker who had helped me to my feet.

"I'm going to vomit," I told him.

"No," the Seeker answered. "You won't."

I scowled at him.

"You and only you are lord of yourself. Do not yield to the grasping dark of the Mage King."

The words were effective. Somehow, they set my resolve and I fought back the nausea and dizziness that the Mage King inspired until they were under control. They never faded, but at least now I had control of them instead of them controlling me.

The enemy surged forward, coming to a stop at the far end of the field across the river. I noticed in the increasing light that they were all without exception corpses. Slack-jawed and sallow-skinned, the marching dead stared out at us with rotting eyes. I scanned their ranks and gasped as my eyes fell upon a familiar face.

"Basadia," I breathed, feeling nauseous all over again.

Martel had seen her too. His eyes fell to her and were immediately stung with tears. I knew what thoughts he had at present, because mine were undoubtedly the same. Could we have saved her? If we had gone back for her, would she now be standing against the Mage King, instead of with him? Might she have lived if we had brought her back with us? I looked at Martel. Would she have been queen?

I felt myself harden, slow anger flushing heat into my veins and easing the pain of the Mage King's presence. My resolve strengthened. If only for Basadia, I would fight this spectre to the death. Damn him. Damn him and all the dark arts that brought him here.

Even as the hot flush rocked through my body, I saw the Mage King approach. He rode the remains of a horse, its dark pelt rotted to reveal the skeleton. There was no meat left on the frame of the horse, save for a few dried strips clinging between the ribs and the beast's rump. The horse had no eyes, having rotted out of the head or else been plucked out by crows long ago.

Martel rode forward, his eyes now dry and his face set in grim determination. He was prepared to die today. The Seeker mounted the qilin queen and followed, with the rest of the party that had travelled for so long together.

More than a year ago, I set out to discover who I was, and found myself with a company of friends on a quest to save the world. We would end this together. Gathering up my courage, I mounted and pressed Fas forward, riding beside the Seeker. Oisín nodded at me as he rode to my side. Sylpha rode on the other side of the Seeker, Hessa beside her. Providence elected to ride beside Oisín, with the leader of the rangers riding easily beside Hessa. The leaders of the Black Blades rode half a step behind Martel.

Our company met the Mage King in the middle of the fjord cutting the field in half. For a time, the Mage King sat in silence, observing us. I used that time to do the same. It took all of my concentration not to keel over in my saddle being this close to the spectre. However, I noticed that despite the solid skin and bone of his undead mount, the Mage King himself was less than complete. Every so often I caught a glimpse of his army behind him through him, as if he was not yet quite solid. I was unsure as to whether this was an advantage or not. If he was not yet fully complete, he was not at his full strength. However, how could we kill a spectre? A sword would not harm it in the slightest.

"Turn aside," Martel said, breaking the silence. I could hear his voice echo across the field, resonating as if possessing a strange power. The hills and trees, the water and the sky heard these words and chose to remember them. Had they done the same with the empress when she first encountered the Mage King on the battlefield? I suspected so. I felt a strange stirring behind me. I glanced over my shoulder and saw nothing but the army and the burial mounds behind them. When I turned back, I noticed the Seeker observing me. He smiled.

Frowning, I nodded at him. Why was he smiling? Did he also feel that strange stirring behind us, as if a sympathetic power had answered Martel? Were the two of us the only ones to feel it? I looked to the Mage King and imagined the spectre offering a gruesome grin beneath his tattered black hood.

"You have not the power to turn me aside," the spectre hissed. "Lay down your arms and kneel before me. You will find I can be most... merciful."

Martel smirked, exuding a confidence I knew for a fact he did not feel. "I will not ask again, vile puppet. Turn aside."

The Mage King laughed, a hissing sort of chuckle that made every hair on my body stand on end. The hooded figure turned to me, locking me in place with its unseen gaze.

"You are mine," the spectre hissed.

"I am my own," I answered, my voice strong in its defiance. "And you will learn it well 'ere this battle is over."

"As you will," the Mage King hissed. "You will know differently when I feast upon your soul."

Unable to control the surge of anger that ripped through me, I pressed my heels to my horse's flanks. Fas snorted, but trotted forward. Taking up my staff, I brought it across my body and lashed out; a back strike that cracked hard across the spectre's cheek. There was a flash of greenish light and a crack like thunder when the staff connected. I felt the impact of the hit all the way up my arm. My staff struck not a spectre, but a solid thing. Yet my eyes told a different story. The Mage King shrieked and flickered like a disturbed black candle flame, as if momentarily losing himself.

"Back!" I heard Martel shout.

I did not need to be told twice. I turned Fas around and galloped as fast as the aged mare could go, heading back to the army. Behind me, the Mage King shrieked once more, and the Seeker rumbled his deep laugh.

"What the hell was that?" Martel demanded as he pulled up beside me. I pulled Fas to a halt, having reached the front of the army.

"I don't know," I answered, turning Fas around to face the corpse army behind us. "I just got mad."

"Give me a look at that staff."

Shrugging I handed it over to Martel. "It's just a staff, just a bit of wood," I said. "It's never done anything special before."

"It's not the staff," the Seeker said. The demon's golden eyes shone brightly as he regarded me.

I blinked. "It has to be."

The Seeker laughed again. "Still don't get it, do you Sky Road Walker?"

"No," I snapped. "I don't. So why don't you tell me instead of being so damned cryptic!"

"You are a mage," the Seeker said with a shrug.

"What?" Martel and I demanded in unison.

"Impossible," I added.

"And not only a mage," the Seeker continued. "*The* mage."

I stared blankly at the Seeker, who laughed again.

"The Seeker's Son has taken one. The Seeker's Son takes two. The Seeker's Son takes another one. The Seeker's Son seeks you."

The Seeker grinned as he finished reciting the poem I heard first from the strange elder woman who had gifted me with the Wood Wight's knife. I stared at him, chills running through me.

"I'm not..."

"Twelve pieces I shattered his soul into," the Seeker said. "And he has them all. He has them all save one." He looked pointedly at me and my jaw fell slack.

"I am not part of that," I hissed, pointing at the Mage King, who had now collected itself.

The Seeker merely smiled at me.

"That's not even possible!" I shouted.

"We can argue about it later," Martel snapped. "Riders on the flanks!" he bellowed. The army behind us moved, the horsemen splitting in the middle and moving to the side.

I faced forward. The black army had begun to move forward, shuffling towards us with their weapons drawn.

"Iron tortoise!" Providence shouted.

The infantry moved forward, the soldiers in front brandishing oversized hexagonal shields before them. Their fighting partners walked half a step behind, carrying stout lances and pikes made for piercing armoured horseflesh. They hit the edge of the river and the shield bearers planted their shields in an overlapping scale wall, with others raising theirs to create a shell that curved up and over the army, protecting the heads of the shield bearers at the front. In the minute gaps in the shell, lances and pike men slid their weapons, planting the butts of the long arms into the ground and holding firm.

The cavalry of the enemy, skeletons riding skeletons, thundered forward, easily outstripping the shuffling dead infantry. They splashed across the fjord easily, crashing against the iron tortoise in a tidal wave of bones. I watched as the skeletons shattered, falling into many pieces. Martel smiled grimly. The smile vanished as the bones reformed, the skeletons unharmed by the impact against the shield shell.

"Archers!" Providence called. The archers standing near the rear of the army let loose a volley of arrows. Many found their mark, and the skeletons stumbled backwards, recovered and came forward again. Behind the ranks of his army of the dead, the Mage King laughed, the sinister chuckle reaching my ears even over the din of the battle.

"How do you kill the dead?" Providence muttered to herself. The sentence was laced with a profuse number of cusses.

Martel shook his head, lost.

"Fire," I said suddenly. "Fire! We need fire."

"Conjure some up then, mage!" Providence snapped.

I glared at her a moment before turning to the Seeker. "Can you? Can I?"

"I am not sure what you are capable of yet, Sky Road Walker," the Seeker said. "But fire would be a good idea."

Martel turned to a small group of rangers. They nodded and vanished from the ranks, seeking hot coals from the camps to start fires with.

"The best way to fight the dead," the Lord Seeker said. "Is with the dead. You felt them answer, Sky Road Walker. Call them forth."

I stared at the Seeker. "You have gone mad," I said.

"They answered the emperor. Call them forward."

"How?"

"How the hell do I know?"

Shaking my head at the Seeker, I wore an expression of bewilderment. He merely looked expectantly at me. Martel, I noted, was also looking expectantly at me.

Not knowing what to do, I raised my staff high and, feeling incredibly foolish, I bellowed, "Rise! Rise defenders of the empire! Rise and ride again!"

For a long moment nothing happened. I slumped in my saddle. Then, as if the earth itself heard me, the ground began to tremble, rumbling like a waking bear. I turned around with wide eyes and my breath caught as the burial mounds heaved, crumbling. Skeletons and mummified warriors, stained reddish brown by the soil in which they were interred, pulled themselves from their graves, wearing their armour still and clutching their archaic weapons.

Their reactions were those I would have expected from the bravest of the living. They spied the enemy, pushing hard on a beleaguered infantry and bolted forward, their weapons held high. Some whose faces had not rotted away wore fierce expressions as they sprinted into the battle. I watched on as the red brown dead clashed with the black and stark white.

"That will hold them for but a little while," Providence said. "They far outnumber us, your Grace."

"Decapitate them!" a northman shouted from somewhere in the broken mess of what remained of the iron tortoise. "Take their heads!"

"How so very northern," Providence mused.

"No," Martel replied. "I think he means it will stop them."

"It will!" I said. "Look!" I pointed to a northman as he took the head of a skeletal cavalryman who had lost his horse. The skeleton stopped, shuddered, and collapsed into a pile of unmoving bleached bone.

The discovery came too late, alas. The enemy broke through the defenders, moving mindlessly forward.

"Cavalry!" Martel yelled. The horsemen moved instantly, riding from the flanks crosswise through the enemy. Heads went flying, but the number of the dead never seemed to wane.

"He's animating our own!" Hessa yelled.

It was true. Members of our own army who had been slain and still had their heads rose again, turning against their own in slack-jawed obedience to the might of the Mage King.

"We're losing ground," Providence said. "We must fall back!"

"No!" Martel barked. "This ends here."

With that, Martel kicked his fiery stallion and galloped headlong into the fray.

"My Lord!" Providence yelled. Swearing, she rode after him.

"It's been nice knowing you all," Oisín said. He put on his helm and followed.

I dismounted. "It's not fair that this should be your end as well as mine," I told my horse. "Go home. You deserve broad fields of fresh grass, not death and damnation."

Fas snorted. I turned and, bracing myself, sprinted into the fight. As I ran, I raised the ancient hunting horn that hung at my side and blew three strong blasts. In the distance I heard a returning horn; a single long howl echoing through the trees.

"Wood wights!" Hessa's voice screamed above the tumult of battle. "The wood wights have been summoned. Fight on! Help is coming!"

The news lifted the spirits of the defenders some and despite the overwhelming swarms of the enemy, they pushed back.

From the forest line poured the wights; the shadow spirits who called the woods their home. Leading them was their king, riding a great stag, the creature's eyes unnaturally fiery. He himself wore a stag-skull helm, the antlers large and proud. Shadow battled shadow as the wights joined the fight.

I fought alongside my companions. Hessa, Sylpha, Oisín and I stood with Martel, the Seeker at his other side, using the majority of his considerable power to shield the new emperor from harm. The qilin queen lay unmoving on the battlefield, prickled all over with javelins. The Black Blades struggled to protect their charge, and were cut down in alarming numbers.

Half a day of fighting passed. Everything hurt and my breath came in ragged pants. We were surrounded. The Wight King and his mount stood at my side, protecting me as he had promised he would. Of the hundreds of his spirit army, he alone remained. The Lord Seeker stood with Martel, looking wan. His power had been spent, and though great swaths of the enemy army had fallen to his magic, yet more shuffled forward to take their place. One qilin, heavily wounded, but still fighting remained by the demon's side. Hessa stood protectively over Sylpha, who lay in the mud, unmoving. Oisín's head, despite his helm, bled heavily. Providence stood with the last remaining Black Blade commander, their forces now combined into one small, utterly ragged army. The northmen and rangers fared little better. Of the some thousand their combined forces were at the beginning of the battle, there remain but ninety.

The enemy surrounded us on all sides, many of our own now staring blankly at us, having died just moments ago and compelled now to fight against us by the terrible art of the Mage King.

"Lay down your arms," the Mage King hissed.

"No!" Martel growled. He escaped the protection of the small army that had gathered around him in a last attempt at saving the last of the imperial bloodline. The dead army parted to make way for him as he strode forward, his sword and the imperial sceptre in either hand. The Mage King dismounted and walked through the army to Martel.

"You have no claim here!" he bellowed at the Mage King. "Not now, not ever!"

And with that he launched himself forward at the Mage King. The two engaged. It was a fierce battle, with Martel's long years of swordplay serving him well. He lasted long, fighting fiercely against the Mage King, who came to the fight well rested and untested.

The Black Blades struggled to reach their emperor, their oath being to protect him at all costs, but they were repelled by the surrounding army of the dead. I watched in mounting horror as Martel, already tired and bleeding began to slow.

"No!" I shouted as the Mage King landed a heavy swipe across Martel's chest, lifting the emperor into the air and throwing him backwards. I ran to him, dodging through the enemy army, none of which moved to strike me. I slid on my knees beside Martel. He struggled to open his eyes, giving a thick cough. Blood flew from his mouth as it was expelled from his lungs. He had lost his sword, but gripped the imperial sceptre tightly, though it was slick with his own blood.

"Your Grace," I said, my eyes stinging with tears.

"Bastard," Martel muttered through the blood. "Help me to my feet," he choked. "I will finish this fight."

I turned as the shadow of the Mage King loomed over us. His tattered robes swirled, moved by the earthly breeze that whispered over the battlefield. Time slowed as the Mage King reached out, not for me, but for Martel. Behind the spectre I spied something shiny. I peered through him. Standing on the field in her brilliant armour and pale blue cloak, was the first empress. She looked me in the eye, her expression so serene and calm it filled me with peace. My mind whirled with a thousand voices.

You underestimate my blood.

Only Imperial blood will stop him.

He has all of them. All of them save one.

There is more power in you than you possibly know.

One was good, the other evil. But nothing is absolute... what was once good may have been turned evil, and hold some grain of goodness in them yet.

He has all of them. All of them save one.

You underestimate my blood.

The Seeker's Son has taken one.
The Seeker's Son takes two.
The Seeker's Son takes another one.
The Seeker's Son seeks you.

"No," I whispered. "My apologies, your Grace, but this monster is mine."

I took up the sceptre - Martel had not the strength to wrest it back from me - and, seeing that the bright light of the gem had not faded now that it was out of Martel's grasp, I dove forward, intending to tackle the Mage King to the ground.

I hit nothing but earth, rolling several times before coming to a stop. I scrambled to my feet to find myself standing on the battlefield, only it was not quite the battlefield. I recognised the shape of the hills in the distance, and there was a broad ugly gash in the earth where the river ought to be. But the land was parched, the earth cracked and dry. Where the woods once stood there was nothing.

Everything was a strange deep bluish-grey, an eternal dusk. The skies were devoid of stars, the ambient blue light coming from nowhere and everywhere. The red light given by the sceptre competed with the blue light, but did nothing to ease the strain on my eyes.

Confused, I spun around. Looming several tens of feet in the air stood two statues, both of them women. One woman stood in flowing robes, her eyes turned upwards and her lips turned down. Water dripped from her eyes down her carved stone face and onto her feet. The other statue snarled down, grasping hands extended out as if she was about to grab something to thrash the living spirit out of it.

I stared up at the statues. They played out a tragedy, a story of two sisters torn apart by power. Though in the tale, good won over evil, and evil was banished forever, I realised now, looking up at the weeping statue, that there was no joy in such a victory. The cost was dear, and though good won, its heart was still broken.

Doing good, fighting the fight, even for the right reasons was difficult, it had a cost, it broke hearts and destroyed bonds. Doing good, I realised, was the province of the courageous and of the strong. Far easier was it to avoid the trouble, the strain and the heartache. Far easier was it to march mindlessly in the flood of injustice than to stand resolute against it, far easier to manacle oneself to evil and chafe under its bonds than fight for good and be cut deep, far easier to hide and weep than fight and weep.

Too many had done so. Too many had chosen the easy path, the path of meek acceptance and silence. The easy path had led to the crumbling empire, the corrupt rule of the line of Stewards and the banishment of both the Black Blades and the rangers. That is how the spectre of the Mage King had grown, that is how the shadows had engorged and now threatened civilisation. In fact, were it not for Martel's refusal to take the easy path, for his staunch belief in his sworn oath that caused him to resist the tide of corruption that had disbanded the rangers, evil would have won long ago. The spectre of the Mage King would have been made real, and all the empire would have succumbed.

How much harder for the Mage King would it have been if all had been as courageous as Martel?

I stared up at the weeping statue as these thoughts flew through my mind. Behind me, the dim sound of rushing water approached and I turned again. There stood the Mage King, looking as real now as he ever did.

"Mine," the Mage King hissed. "You are mine."

"No," I replied. "I am my own. You no longer have power over me."

The Mage King laughed his sinister chuckle. "I am you."

It was not far from the truth. Standing here in the centre of the Mage King, facing him as he was in his own mind, I recalled the splitting of the souls. I remembered the profound relief of finally throwing off the oppression of the millennia of evil that had attached itself to me. Though it meant imprisonment, I was, in fact, finally freed.

I was the kernel of good.

But in my other life I had taken the easy path, the path of silent acceptance, and because I had proved such a coward, evil had won, and I was lost. That would not be the case any longer. No. I had found my courage at last. I would resist.

Raising the sceptre, still glowing with the strength of the blood Martel had spilt defending the empire, I replied, "No, you are nothing more than the result of my inaction. In choosing to remain silent in the face of evil, I created you. I will unmake you."

The Mage King chuckled his sinister laugh once more, but the sceptre glowed a little brighter.

"I stand against you," I said, my voice gaining strength. "I stand against all evil that would tear the world apart. And I call on all to stand with me."

"Stand with you we will," someone said from behind me. I turned to find Martel, not a mark on him, walking from the gloom to my side.

"All of us," Oisín said as he strode from the shadows. He grinned over at me as one by one my companions came to my side, called to my aid by the light of the sceptre and the strength of Martel's blood. Hessa stepped forward, her slender, curved blade gleaming. Sylpha was next, looking radiant, youth restored to her. The qilin queen chirped as she lumbered forward, glowing a faint blue. Next strode the Lord Seeker, his hands flickering with golden flame, his powers restored.

"Please tell me that you're not all dead," I whispered to Martel, knowing the qilin queen had definitely been slain.

"Not all," Martel answered.

"One last time," Sylpha said with a smile. "One last fight before I walk into the unknown."

My heart sank. "Not you," I whispered.

Sylpha smiled again, looking more radiant than ever. "There is no need for grief," she said. "I am ready and my heart is eager to see my family again."

I swallowed back the grief that threatened despite Sylpha's serene countenance, and turned to face the Mage King. Shadows had gathered behind him, each one shuffling, eager for the fight ahead.

"I warned you," a velvety feminine voice said.

I turn to find the empress, her pale blue cloak hanging from one shoulder, her armour glistening despite the gloom.

"You underestimate the strength of my blood." She smiled at Martel, the last of her direct descendants.

"One last fight?" I asked her.

She nodded. "One last fight."

The Mage King shrieked and ran forward.

"Take my sword," the empress told Martel. "And trust in the strength of your heart."

Martel nodded, taking the ancient weapon. He walked forward into battle. He fought the shadows that followed the Mage King into the fight, giving me the room I needed to grapple with the sinister side of myself; the greed, the anger and envy, the unhealthy desire for power, all of the terrible things that twisted the Mage I once was into the spectre I had become before the cleaving of the souls.

Using the sceptre and the power of the bloodline now infused in it, I fought the Mage King. Blow after blow was deflected by the light of the sceptre. I danced between strikes as the Mage King sought to subdue me once more. But memories were returning, the deaths my inaction had caused, the fear of reprisal that pushed me into denial and my refusal to take responsibility for my inaction all colluded to make me weak. In that life, I convinced myself that I was not to blame. How could I be? I did nothing. And slowly evil took hold, without my even noticing. More people died, suffering in astounding numbers. And still I convinced myself that it was not my fault. Until it was.

By then I was so far into my delusions that I could not see my deeds for the evil they were, and I felt justified in my greedy quest for power and in all the terrible deeds I performed in order to achieve it; even hating those who grieved for all I had done. The fools. How could they not see the grandness of my intentions?

Now I was free, and I could see every misstep, every delusion, every act of cowardice, and it gave me fuel. I would right my wrongs.

Three rapid strikes very nearly cut me open, but I managed to step aside each time. An idea struck me. Instead of striking out with the sceptre, I reached out with my hand and clasped the icy wrist of the spectre. Time froze.

"It's all right," I told the spectre. "I forgive myself. I was a fool and a coward, but I have learned. And I forgive it all."

The Mage King shrieked, twisting in an effort to escape my warm grasp.

"I did these things," I said aloud. "And they were terrible things, but I have learned. And I will make it right. There is still good in the world, and in me. It is not too late, and I forgive you."

The Mage King shrieked again and I felt it weaken. Something strange happened. Instead of it absorbing me, as it might have done had we met under any other circumstance, I absorbed it. All the power the Mage King had accumulated, I inherited. All the memories, all of the self-loathing, the delusions, I received it all. In the mere act of facing each squarely, with an open and courageous heart, each lost its power, the evil that used them finding itself without tools until it had nothing to grasp at all. With one last shriek, the evil vanished.

The Mage King stumbled, the black tattered robes gone. In place of the terrifying spectre stood a young man, a youth of no more than sixteen with large grey eyes. They peered out at me as if seeing for the first time. The youth smiled, leant back and let himself fall, disappearing before he hit the ground as if no more than a mist on the breeze.

The gloom lifted and, from the horizon rode the Wood Wight King on his great stag. He looked solid here, not a shadow or a memory of the trees. With every step the great stag took, grasses and flowers sprung from the ground, the tears of the weeping statue finally finding purchase in the parched earth to feed the plants.

"I have my home again," the stag-helmed spirit said. "And my brothers and sisters will find peace at last. Thank you."

I blinked. "But I thought the woods were your home."

"The woods were our shelter in exile," the Wood Wight said. He smiled. "We were the Wild Hunt once, and we rode out in the dusk to hunt down evil things and take them away, and to bring brave souls to pleasant rest. But we were assaulted and overwhelmed and our realm was poisoned. It is purged, and we will ride again. Do not fear if you hear the horn of the Wild Hunt, nor the bay of our hounds. It is evil we seek, and you are safe from our arrows, for you have repented."

I nodded. "You knew. You knew who I was when you met me."

"I suspected, but your deeds were good and kind, and you spoke with courage. And I saw in you what I rarely saw when I was a-hunting."

"And what is that?" I asked.

"The strength to redeem yourself. I am glad I was not mistaken. Now, you have something of mine I would like returned."

The Wood Wight King, the once and now leader of the Wild Hunt stretched out one gloved hand. Nodding, I took the hunting horn from my belt and handed it to him. "Thank you," I said. "For all you have done."

The leader of the Wild Hunt nodded at me once, turned his great stag mount and galloped away, heading into the forest that was growing rapidly in the east. I heard him blow a long blast when he was out of sight and the call was answered by the bay of the hounds of the shadow realm.

"Balance has been restored here," the empress said. She stood at the feet of the weeping statue, looking up at the face.

"She knew," I said, coming to the empress' side. "She knew what heartbreak would come of her choice."

"Yes," the empress said. "And still she chose it. She was brave."

"A trait all her children have shared," I replied.

The empress smiled. Turning to Sylpha, she offered a hand. "Come," she told the banished tuatha. "It is time."

Smiling, Sylpha walked forward and took the empress' hand. She turned and beckoned the qilin queen, who happily bounded forward.

"It was an honour to know you, Sky Road Walker," Sylpha said simply. "Look for me in the passing of the Wild Hunt. I will be riding with the King, and I shall be smiling."

Before I had a chance to answer, she, the empress, and the qilin queen vanished, their serene smiles the last thing I saw. Before the Empress Moua disappeared from view entirely, her gaze shifted to the Lord Seeker. What exchanged in their gaze brought the Lord Seeker to tears, as he offered his love a final farewell with a small smile.

"I feel dizzy," Oisín muttered. I turned to him to find blood rushing down his face, from under his helm. Martel coughed up blood and collapsed. I stared down at him, blinking.

It took me some time to realise that we were no longer in the shadow realm, but on the battlefield. A small army of eyes stared at me, each one wide with awe. I looked around. The sun shone brightly, birds sang gaily in the forest in the west. Piles of bleached bone lay scattered around the army, joined by the now inanimate bodies of the slain.

From his position on the ground, Martel coughed thickly. I knelt beside him.

"A dream," he muttered. "A strange dream."

"Not a dream," I answered. "Not a dream. The Mage King is defeated. You won."

Martel frowned up at me, then fell unconscious.

"Get the emperor a healer!" I barked. The army jumped into action.

Epilogue

I closed the tome one last time. In the vellum pages of the leather bound book were the words of my life, beginning from the moment I awoke in the grasslands, the last sliver of goodness the Mage King possessed finding refuge in the body of a recently dead traveller so that it might thwart the evil that escaped the captivity of the Lord Seeker.

Looking out the window I smiled. Martel's two daughters played in the courtyard with sticks, testing their swordplay against one another, laughing.

"It's finished?" the Lord Seeker asked from the entrance to the study. He had lost none of his youthful strength, though I was now old and grey.

"It is," I replied. "Took me long enough."

The Lord Seeker smiled and placed a hand on my thin shoulder. He looked out at the two girls. An imp chattered noisily on his shoulder, the bug-eyed creature waving its hands animatedly.

"Hush," the Lord Seeker chided gently. The imp shut its mouth and crossed its arms across its chest with a tiny "Hmph."

"Martel has summoned us all to lunch on the green. Will you come?"

"I suppose I must."

"Good. The court mage needs to make an appearance every so often."

I grunted. Taking up the cane that leant against my chair I struggled to my feet. Smiling, I looked back at the book I had just finished.

"It was quite an adventure, wasn't it," I said fondly.

"An adventure, was it?" the Lord Seeker answered. "Age has made you sentimental. It was hellish."

I laughed and, old age aching in my bones, shuffled to the green on the grounds of the palace to dine with my emperor.

Books By S.M. Carrière

The Dying God & Other Stories
Ethan Cadfael: The Battle Prince
The Summer Bird (The Seraphimé Saga: Volume 1)
The Winter Wolf (The Seraphimé Saga: Volume 2)
Human (A Shadow Empires Book)

Read more at:
http://www.smcarriere.com/

www.ingramcontent.com/pod-product-compliance
Lightning Source LLC
Chambersburg PA
CBHW030352030726
47497CB00002B/303